Woes of Destiny

A NIghtstone Renaissance Novel

Book 1

Allie Dars

Book Cover by Joe Tricomi (@jtricomi)

Map by Cassandra Lynn (@oakleaf.arrow.studios)

❀ Created with Vellum

Introduction

Below is a note provided by Zevlor Nov, Scribe Keeper of Nocturnal Manor, at the request of the Nightstone family:

This scripture tells the story of a human woman wandering through a world unlike her own. From the technologically advanced, war-driven world of 2042 Earth, to the medieval, colorful yet dying world of Dorthos, Rosella Smith must survive at all costs. Because of the events that take place in both of her worlds, readers and listeners alike must take heed and consider continuing if the list below is disturbing:

i. Apocalyptic events (bombs, fallout effects shown on page)
ii. Death (shown on page, mentioned, heard)
iii. Aftermath of death (viscera)
iv. Loss of control over mind and body
v. Post traumatic stress disorder
vi. Intense and graphic use of weapons

vii. Mild clastophobia

If the events experienced by those in this story are not disturbing to you, then continue on.

Welcome to the world of Dorthos, and may the gods guide your path.

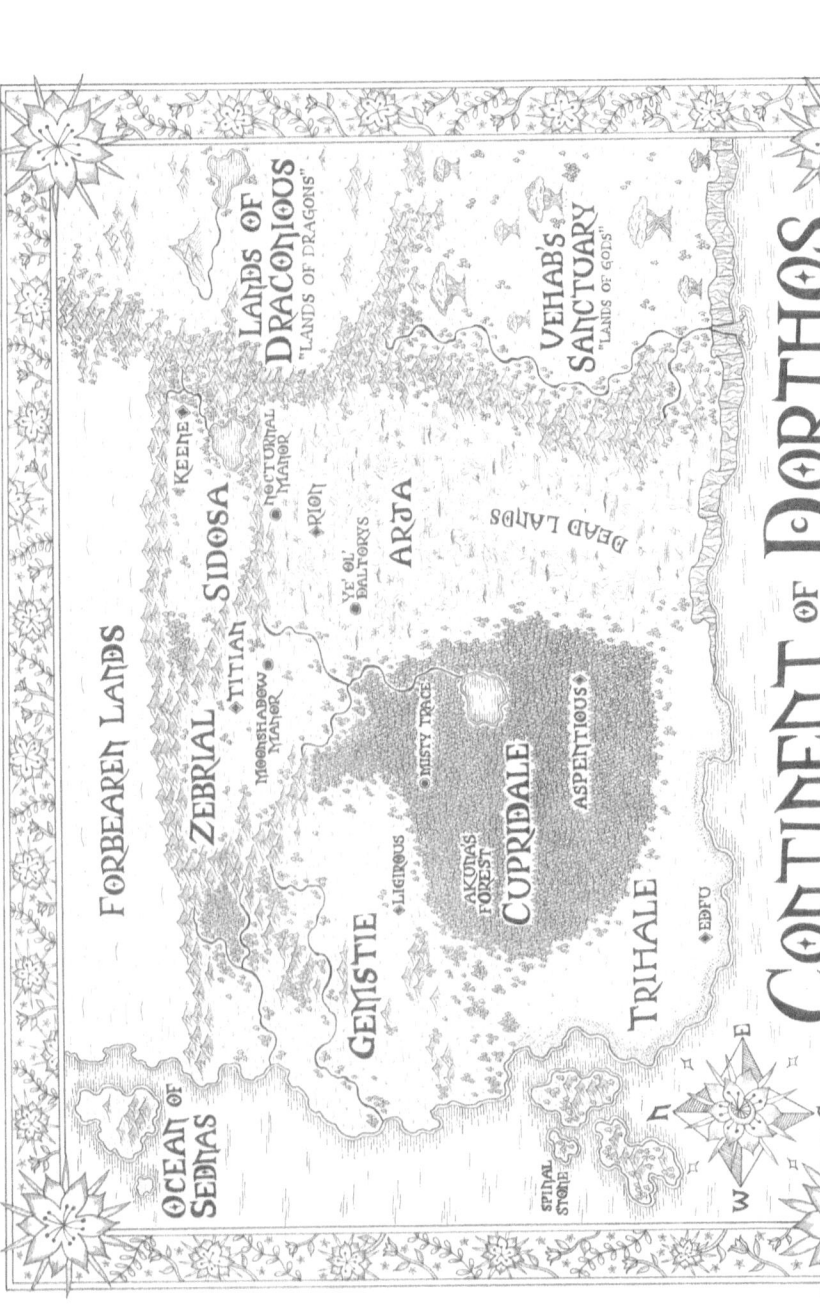

CONTINENT OF DORTHOS

FORBEAREN LANDS

ZEBRIAL

SIDOSA

TITIAN

KEENE

LANDS OF DRACONIOUS
"LANDS OF DRAGONS"

NECTORNAL MANOR

RION

VEHAB'S SANCTUARY
"LANDS OF GODS"

MOONSHADOW MANOR

YE' OL' BALTORYS

ARJA

DEAD LANDS

GEMSTIE

LIGIROUS

MISTY TRACE

AKUTAS FOREST

CUPRIDALE

ASPENTIOUS

TRIHALE

EDFU

OCEAN OF SEBYAS

SPINAL STONE

N E S W

For my parents.
Thank you for always being supportive and
for teaching me the ways of life (even if I don't listen sometimes).

Also to Ezra, our cat.
Thank you for letting us love you, and for loving us in return.

Rest in peace, Dad and Ezra.
May the gods have kindness and patience over your souls.

"Don't get too lost in what people say, watch what they do. Base your decisions on whether or not to trust them off of what they do, not what they say."

— Noshir Dalal, in reference of Bode Akuna (Star Wars: Survivor) and Kotallo (Horizon: Forbidden West)

Part 1

1

Mother Nature's Purification

A loud disturbance shook the once gentle air of the corporate office. Everyone's cellphones were simultaneously blaring sirens that could not be quieted, and Rosella Smith quickly pulled out her own to try and stop her own. On the screen, in large unmistakable letters, a message from the United Nations read: *ALL CITIZENS SEEK SHELTER IMMEDIATELY. BOMBING IMMINENT. THIS IS NOT A TEST.*

Panic, ever so quickly, started to drench the air every-one breathed. The sirens began to cease but were replaced with scrambling feet and terrified voices. Calls were being made, texts being sent, curses shouted, items dropped, and desks dismantled from the chaos of hurried bodies.

"Rose, where are you?" screamed Wren O'Leary from across the office.

Rosella glanced back and found her best friend Wren at her desk, red-curly hair bouncing as she frantically looked around. Brushing past her co-workers and having to readjust herself after being knocked off balance, Rosella made it to Wren's desk.

"Come on, we have to go!" Rosella urged as she pulled her long wavy black hair with poliosis in a ponytail.

"I can't find my phone! I need my phone!" Wren cried out as she tore through her drawers.

Rosella scanned around and under the desk and chair. When Wren bumped into the chair, a flash of reflective glass and metal hit Rosella's eyes, and she bent down and picked up the over-large cellphone.

"Here! Now get your shit and let's go!" Rosella said while shoving Wren's phone into her hands. As Wren gathered her things, Rosella grabbed Wren's gallon water jug that she always had without fail. "I got your water! Quickly now!"

Wren let out a loud squeal and finished tightening her go-bag onto her back. They ran the length of the office and made it to the doors that led to the parking lot. The air hit their faces as they noticed that in the time it took to find Wren's phone, everyone else in the office had made it outside. Many were trying to get to their cars while a few others were pulling out of the lot and speeding down the road.

Fear had been trickling down Rosella's neck since the alert was sent out, but now it was pouring into her entire body like a waterfall. Rosella had packed her bag to the brim weeks before, but she had not gotten around to finding a bunker. The day of the bombs dropping was a fever dream to her, thinking that the countries around the world would never destroy each other in that manner. The world was already dying from resources running low and plastic killing everything, so why would humans accelerate the process?

"Rosella!" came Wren's voice, breaking her panicked thoughts. "I cannot be the calm one in this situation! Which way are you heading because I cannot drive like this!"

Rosella shook her head to clear it before answering. "I'm going near Shire Oak. You?"

"Grimoire. I'm on the way to your bunker. Drop me off!" Wren said and darted toward Rosella's car.

Why didn't she say she didn't have a bunker to go to? Why did she say a random street? Letting out a strained breath, she got into her car after Wren. As Rosella struggled to get them out of the parking lot, she grabbed her obsidian snowflake necklace and tightly palmed her mother's final gift.

Mama, I'm so glad you're not here right now. You're not here for what is to come.

"Praying to your mom?" Wren asked, her voice strained with each syllable.

"Yeah, something like that," Rosella replied, squeezing the pendant once more before grabbing the steering wheel.

"Cancer is better than this. She got lucky. Three years ago, right?"

"Yep. Just before this stupid 'Golden War' started."

"Good, good. An opening! *Go, Rose, go!*" Wren screeched, frantically waving her hand.

Rosella placed herself in the small gap and turned, avoiding racing cars on the main road. Air-raid sirens began to sound as she quickened her speed.

"Tell me about those dreams again, Rose," Wren squeaked.

Rosella, taken aback by the odd request, furrowed her eyebrows and inhaled sharply. "The dragon with glowing red eyes and purple smoke growling, calling my name. The purple snickering shadowy man. And yesterday—" Rosella froze, unsure if this was the time for new information. She heard Wren whimper next to her as she braked for a group of people running into the street. "A short man dressed in silver."

"A man in silver? Wh-what did he say, if anything?"

"'Save them.' That's all he said. My tattoo glowed, like it always does, but this time when I woke up, it ached," Rosella said while placing her hand over her chest where her tattoo of a crescent moon and three stars resided. Her hand flew to the steering wheel to take a sharp turn, whispering to herself, "It's never ached before."

"What the fuck? This guy has never shown up in the three years you've been having these dreams. Why now?" Wren questioned, the warble in her voice ebbing.

"I'm not sure. He had a peaceful air to him, though, unlike the other two," Rosella responded. Her own anxiety was peaking as she had to drive around a dead dog on the road. Silence fell between the two for a moment, though Rosella's pumping blood was muffling her ears.

"We were supposed to grab coffee today," Wren whimpered. Rosella chanced a glance, and she saw Wren's eyes were watching cars pass, her chest heaving.

"I know. We're going to be okay, Wren."

"We were supposed to grab coffee after going to your archery practice. We were going to meet Olympians!"

"I know."

"I just wanted to see your badass archery skills, go get coffee, and hang out with my best friend! I didn't want the world to end!"

"I know, Wr—"

"*Stop saying, 'I know'!*" Wren shrieked.

Rosella swerved to avoid an oncoming truck, and Wren screamed. Her fingers ached as she gripped the wheel tighter.

"I'm sorry," Rosella pushed out, driving around a crashed van. A family was scrambling to gather their belongings, the father's face covered in blood as he grabbed his daughter's hand. "We're almost to your bunker. We'll be safe."

Instead of saying anything, Wren placed her shaky hand on

Rosella's elbow and squeezed gently. When she pulled away, Rosella grabbed her hand and squeezed back, trying to convey everything she couldn't say into that one touch.

After a strenuous and chaotic ten minutes, they made it to Grimoire Road. Wren pointed out the house, and Rosella pulled over. Wren got out of the car, and Rosella made the quick decision to get out as well and grabbed her purse, bag, and Wren's water jug, leaving behind her archery equipment and her gym bag

"What are you doing?" Wren asked, when she noticed Rosella get out of the car.

"I—I don't know. I don't have a bunker. I need to find one and Shire Oak is too far. Here, I'll help you with your stuff first though," Rosella said quickly as she walked to Wren's side and grabbed her bag. She knew she was not thinking normally and that adrenaline was taking over her decision-making. "I'm not going to ask to join yours. I just need to walk around and find one close by, I think. Maybe someone didn't make it to theirs."

Wren's eyebrows shot up and her mouth fell agape, then her skin paled as her eyes drifted toward the sky. Rosella turned, and her eyes fixated on an object miles away with a white stream following it that was growing larger by the second, hurling toward the ground.

The time it took for the object to seemingly hit the ground and the shockwave to hit Rosella and Wren was less than a few breaths.

The two were knocked off balance as the wave hit them, dragging leaves and tree branches with it that scratched their faces and exposed arms. Wren had fallen over, so Rosella did her best to pull her back up before the next wave hit.

"You're my best friend, Rose. Of course you can come into my bunker!" Wren yelled out, the cut on her lip spilling blood down her chin.

Relief trickled inside her as she and Wren ran through an open gate to the back of the house. When another shockwave hit them, one that was closer this time. The two were flung forward. Wren landed right next to the bunker door, with Rosella not far behind and thankfully not thrown too far due to the bags.

Rosella got to her feet, grabbing the water jug and Wren's bag as she struggled to stand. Running to Wren was difficult with the weight she was carrying and because the air around them began to thicken and turn crimson. Her breathing felt like she was sucking in water and not able to cough it up.

When she approached Wren, she saw a large cut on her forehead where she had landed on the sharp corner of the concrete bunker structure. Wren lay motionless, and there were no audible exhales coming from her mouth or nose.

Rosella turned her friend's body over and saw there was a deep indent in her head where the cut was, and she realized the bunker foundation had caved Wren's skull in. Curls of red hair were plastered to her face as sticky blood continued to flow out of the cut.

Her best friend couldn't die, not like this. They were right there at the door. Someone inside had to let them in.

"Wren? Please wake up!" Rosella shouted and coughed while reaching her leg over to stomp on the bunker door, and she noticed she couldn't hear herself or the pounding of her foot. Realizing the blasts must have blown her eardrums, she stomped harder on the bunker doors in quicker succession. "Help us! Let us in please! Please! *Please!*"

Rosella's body was full of pure terror as the reality set in completely when another bomb fell much further away and the wave hit her moments later. Thankfully she was only pushed aside and not shoved to the ground. She readjusted herself and grabbed onto the bunker door and pulled as hard as she could. The doors would not budge, as if they were locked from the inside.

Rosella fell to her knees and elbows. She screamed and cried harder than she ever had before. Harder than when her mother gave her the family heirloom and died moments later. Harder than when her cat died last year.

She shut her eyes because of the heat, and the crimson sky and blood on her friend's head was pure agony to look at. Her closest friend, her confidant at work, the person that made her laugh with the silliest of jokes. Wren's always-cheerful demeanor brought light to Rosella's lonely world. Rosella had no one when she met Wren. The same Wren who lay on the ground like a red rock. Emotionless, lifeless, soulless.

The air around her grew hotter than a volcano, and Rosella knew this was the end of her life, her story. The more she screamed, the more her throat dried and seared. Her eyes heated and any moisture from her tears evaporated as quickly as her heart beat against her sternum. Her skin blistered and split, the blood instantly drying from the hot air around her. Her lungs felt like they were shriveling up the more she yelled and choked. Immeasurable pain coursed through her entire body as she felt the end of the world, and there was nothing she could do.

Everything was burning. Everything was dying. Everything Rosella ever knew was about to be wiped away in a burning red haze.

The world shifted underneath her, and as she opened her eyes, she saw through blurry vision that everything around her vanished quicker than Rosella could blink. Instead of burning trees, blackened grass, and red skies above, she was spinning and flying through air that was filled with warm purple smoke.

Rosella's now audible screams drowned out her mind as her body twisted and shook violently within the smoky air.

In a matter of moments, she landed hard on a grassy surface, and she tumbled to her knees and elbows. The scream she was releasing became too loud for her own ears, and her eyes were shut so tight that she could visibly see glitter against her eyelids. Her now emptied hands flew to her temples as she let out one more scream.

When she finally took in a breath, she was expecting the thick red air she had inhaled moments ago. However, she noticed that the air was different again and cleaner. She took in another breath and noticed that the air itself *tasted* different. Her other senses began to shock her system as she felt soft warmth on her head, heard a gentle wind in her ears, and the smell of flowers in her nose. Slowly, she relaxed her eyes before opening them, and saw a bed of odd yet beautiful flowers in front of her face that tickled her nose. With her still on her knees and elbows, she let her eyes take in the details of the flowers as she began to loosen her muscles.

Were these flowers here before? she thought to herself as she lifted her head.

Wren was no longer in front of her, along with the bunker. Rosella stood up and noticed she stood on a large circular patch of purple and white flowers, and there were trees with leaves colored like Skittles surrounding her where houses and a fence should be. Both go-bags, her purse, and the water jug lay against a tree outside the bed of flowers. She looked down to see her arms as they were hours ago before the bombings; normal and blister-less.

"What the actual fuck?" she said out loud, scanning her skin for abnormalities.

"I suspect that is the most appropriate response to this situation," a deep voice from behind Rosella said.

She spun around and right at eye level were a pair of red eyes on a head of white scales and a long snout. Rosella hurried backward with a start and let out a frightened yelp.

Before her stood an iridescent white dragon with red frills, hair tufts, and claws that stood at the same height as Rosella. Steam puffed out of his nostrils as his red eyes bore into Rosella's blue ones. These were the same red eyes as those that had been haunting her dreams for the last three years. The same eyes and voice, his voice, that spoke were both terrifying and intriguing at times, were now as real as the breeze that blew through the trees.

With shock written all over her face, he said, "By the way, you're welcome for saving you."

2
Isn't It Lovely Being Alone

Rosella stared at the dragon as it slowly sat down, not breaking eye contact with her as the red eyes froze her where she stood.

"Don't forget to blink, human," the dragon said, and Rosella noticed that the dragon's mouth didn't move when it spoke.

"Uh. You're the dragon from my dreams," she squeaked out. Those words were all she could muster as she tried to loosen her limbs and take in a deep breath before speaking more. "But you're a dragon, and you don't exist in my world. So where the fuck am I? Am—am I dead?"

"Astute observation," the dragon said curtly as it stood up and walked around the patch of flowers which Rosella still stood in the middle of. "My name is Vikshae Akuna Daltorys, and your name is Rosella Nightstone. You are of Earth, and the residents of this world call this one Dorthos. I transported you here for reasons that will be revealed in due time, but now you shall remain here on Dorthos, never to return to Earth. Do you have any questions?"

Rosella took in the words the dragon was saying and had to take a moment before responding, only just realizing he was now circling her around the flower patch. She looked up to the sky and saw a rainbow of colors with an absence of smoke, fire, and burning red skies.

"Did you heal me?"

"Yes. You were seconds from death had I not healed you. I did my best, as it is difficult for me to heal what I cannot see."

"Internally, you mean?"

"Obviously."

"Oh, well, thank you. You did fine enough, I think," Rosella said, rubbing her skin and taking a deep breath through her anxiety-tightened throat and aching lungs. Her eyes drifted down to the bags and her mind sent a shockwave of nerves through her body. "Wren, my friend. Is she truly dead?"

The gentle footsteps circling her stopped, and a huff sounded before Vikshae's words hit her. "Yes, she is dead, and I am sorry for the loss of your friend."

Stinging tears welled up in her eyes, but she placed her palms against them. Her closest friend was dead, truly dead, and there was nothing Rosella could have done to save her. Crippling pain overwhelmed her at the realization that everything she knew was gone, but she also knew she needed to push it down for now and gather her wits, as her mother would say.

"You called me Nightstone? Nightstone isn't my last name," she said cautiously. Vikshae probably had to know at least her name to bring her here, right? He was giving the impression that he knew more than he was letting on.

"That is your ancestral name. That stone you wear is of the Nightstone family, therefore you are a Nightstone. Besides, Smith is quite mediocre in comparison."

"My stone? No, it was given to me by my mom on her deathbed. She told me this necklace was passed down from woman to woman in our family."

"Your *night stone* may have been given to you by your mother, but here that stone is significant. I recommend you never take your necklace off."

"I never do," Rosella reassured, grabbing her pendant gingerly.

"Good. Any other questions?" Vikshae asked as he stopped in front of Rosella and sat down, still on the edge of the flowers.

As he did this, Rosella noticed that while his scales shone and the red parts of them were bright, there were deep scars riddling his face and body. His red frills that lined the sides of his head were riddled with holes that resembled Swiss cheese. Four white horns tipped in red sat on top of his head and curved back then poked up into the air, with the two horns on top being larger than the others. His folded white wings were so massive, the bones stretched from his head to halfway down the tail. The long tail was now wrapped around and elegantly placed on his front feet like a cat. The tip of his tail was red, arrowhead-shaped, and flicking side to side, cutting the grass as it moved back and forth. Sharp and jagged spine spikes were also red and stretched from his head to the tip of his tail, meeting the arrowhead.

"Do I call you Vikshae, or do I say your full name every time?" she asked curiously, hoping that a simple name would do instead of one that was a mouthful.

"Akuna will do for your human tongue, and not many know of that name. I'm a male dragon if that information is necessary. Now will you get out of my flowers?" he asked while dipping his head in a slightly menacing way.

Rosella stepped carefully to avoid the flowers and stood next to Akuna. Standing next to him made her fully realize her situation, and panic set in once more like it had throughout the last hour.

"My world, Earth... It's..." she said while looking into Akuna's eyes, hoping for answers.

"Gone. Your world succumbed to the destruction of the bombs you felt before coming here. As far as I am aware, the only civilization alive are those in the Salus Dome. Others may have lived in other countries, but I was unable to determine that. Either way, you cannot ever go back," he said in a smooth, calming tone.

"Is this another planet, or is this a multiverse situation?" Rosella blurted out.

"I'm afraid I cannot answer something that complex at this time. That will be revealed in due time."

"Seriously?"

"Yes, seriously. I'm afraid your human brain will combust if I give you significantly more information. I know not of human limitations, so frankly you need to be handled with extreme care as far as I'm aware. Now, we must organize your things and move on. I suggest putting necessities in one bag and non-essentials in another."

Rosella's head was spinning as she processed and dissected the information Akuna just told her. She moved to her bags that were propped against nearby trees and sat down, but she did not move as she stared at the grass. Her heart pounded so heavily that the muscles in her chest began to ache, accompanying the pain from her lungs.

Before any thought could cross her mind, she felt Akuna's presence next to her as he moved and lay on all fours. He did not speak as she mindlessly touched the soft grass with her fingers and felt the wind on her skin, the smell of flowers and earth gently filling her nose.

"So, this is my life now? I have to make my way through this world, alone? Without my friends or remaining family?" she asked softly, not facing or looking at Akuna.

He let out a deep sigh before saying, "I'm sorry for what you have lost, though I know you will be able to find a new life here. A new family, new friends. I will not leave your side, so you will never be alone."

Her eyebrows furrowed to his response. "You won't leave my side? Really? Why would you stay with me?"

"Because without me, you would certainly die."

"Quite confident of yourself, aren't you?"

"I'm a two-thousand-year-old dragon; of course I'm confident. Now, we need to get to Arja, so you need to organize and prioritize your items. This will make travel easier for the both of us," he said simply with a hint of a chuckle, and Rosella grunted in response.

"Arja?"

"The land where the Nightstones reside."

"Why are we going there? To go see the rest of the Nightstones?"

"In due time."

"I—that—never mind. Answer me this then, please: are there other dragons in this world? Elves, dwarves, red caps, griffons? Like, how fantasy-like is this place?" she asked, trying to get her own hopes up. Tugging the bags toward her, she removed everything from them and her purse. In a way, she was thankful she had held onto the water jug that Wren had filled before the sirens went off.

"Yes to all of those things, along with knights, castles, and magic. You'll discover how 'fantasy-like' this place is soon enough," he said as he watched her empty the bags and organize the various items in front of them.

"Okay, what about mermaids?"

"Mermaids? Is that an animal from your world?"

"People that are fish."

"Preposterous," Akuna snorted.

Rosella gave a small smile as he snorted, her nerves relaxing.

After some time, the items Akuna and Rosella deemed useful —food, medical supplies, feminine and hygiene products—were put into Rosella's bag and the things that were "a waste of space" by Akuna were put into Wren's bag. Rosella stood up to put the bag on. If this place was anything like the countless things she had read or watched on TV, she would stand out like an elephant in a supermarket. Her attire was nothing close to medieval and she would probably be called a witch and burned at the stake.

"Akuna, I can't go out like...this!" she exclaimed while gesturing to her blue blouse, black jeans, and her blue and white sneakers. "What am I supposed to do, rob a cottage so I can fit in? I need to look like one of those adventurers in a fantasy book!"

Akuna stood up, and his eyes traveled over her attire. He let out a small huff. Then, he reared his head back slightly and released a stream of purple smoke that encircled her. Her muscles clenched as she was frozen in the spot.

When the smoke dissipated, fabric dragged across her arms, something tight wrapping around her torso. Looking down, she saw that her attire was now all black except for the royal blue breathable long-sleeved dress. The leather mid-cut cuirass that was tightened with leather strings held the dress to her body comfortably. Knee-high boots appeared as she raised the ankle-length dress up to examine her new footwear, a little saddened that her favorite shoes were gone. There were bracers on her forearms with an intricate design of the crescent moon and three stars embossed on them that looked remarkably like her tattoo.

Her hair was still pulled up, but instead of a ponytail it was now in two Dutch braids, and her necklace lay on top of the dress she wore. She felt the weight on her back dip as the bag itself transformed to a leather backpack with a cinch to close the top.

"Holy fuck!" she exclaimed as her hands flew all over to feel the new clothing and materials. "How'd you do that?"

"Magic," Akuna said simply, as if the answer was in front of her but she chose to ignore the obvious.

"This is so cool! Wait, could I get a belt, please?" she asked hopefully while looking at Akuna's unimpressed scaly face.

He reared his head again and let out a smaller stream of smoke that encircled her waist, leaving behind a leather belt with a pouch and a metal clasp to loosen or tighten.

As she touched the leather with her fingers, she said, "Thanks! Wow. This is real, then. What do we do next?"

"Well, we go into town and start your new life. However, I believe we need to do something with the water and the spare bags first," Akuna said as he walked over to the three items left on the ground and blew the same purple smoke onto them. When the smoke vanished, a leather canteen with a long strap appeared next to a medium-sized leather pouch. "That canteen will always have clean water, and the pouch has infinite room in it, so if you did in fact want to take your friend's items and your Earthly purse with you, you could."

She gingerly picked up the pouch and examined it, and when she opened it, the only thing she saw was a bottomless void. "How am I supposed to find anything in this when there is no bottom?" she asked as she leaned in closer to the hole.

"Stick your hand in the hole, name or picture the item in your mind, and it'll appear in your hand. You can attach the pouch to your belt just like the other. Do not stick any living being in there, monstrous things will happen to the creature. Oh, word of advice. Do not stick any other body part than your hand or arm in there, otherwise you'll be sucked in and die."

"Wicked," she exclaimed softly as she worked to shove the contents of Wren's bag and the bag itself separately into the pouch, then attach the pouch to her belt. She slung her water canteen around her and adjusted the backpack. A tidal wave of emotions crested within her, but she stifled it as best as possible. Her world was destroyed, and yet she stood in front of a dragon that had pulled her to safety. Shaking her head slightly to clear the thought, she looked back up to Akuna. "How do I look?"

"Like a human playing dress-up, but it'll do for now. You won't be able to fit in fully as you are the only human on this planet, so just say you're a cross-breed of a dwarf and an elf if asked," he said as he looked back at the flower patch. He let out a small puff of steam before turning away and walking through the trees. She puffed out her aching chest before taking her first few steps away from the flowers. As she followed him, his words finally hit her square in the chest.

"*Wait*, okay, hold on. So I'm *officially* the only human on Dorthos. Like, can't you make my ears pointy or something?" Rosella rambled as she followed Akuna. "Obviously, you healed a lot of me like my eardrums, so you can do something about the shape of my ears, right? Make it so I don't stand out so much? I don't want to be studied like a lab rat because I'm the only human here. A new species, or race. Something."

She gingerly touched her face to see if there was dried blood or any open cuts and found neither. Her skin no longer burned, and while her chest still twinged her lungs filled gratefully with clean air without coughing. Impressed, she trotted up and walked alongside Akuna, waiting eagerly for a response.

"I cannot add bodily things to you, only fix. You are stuck that way, unfortunately. Now, we shall travel to the next town, and when we get there I need you to only communicate with me through your head," he said as he periodically looked over to her while walking.

"What, like telepathically?"

"Yes. I am speaking in a way that your ears hear my voice, but when we speak telepathically, you will hear me in your head. Clear your mind, then picture me in your head and speak."

Rosella tried her best to clear her mind despite the day she just had, thinking only of the dragon that walked next to her. She thought of how his iridescent scales reflected and gleamed in the light that poured through the rainbow trees. Unblinking red eyes that glowed each time he performed magic swelled in her mind like the dreams she'd had ever since her mother died. When she saw his red and white face flood her mind completely, she said, *"Your frills look like Swiss cheese, by the way."*

She felt a rumble of deep laughter in her head, and she blinked wildly, startled by the sudden intrusion of another voice. *"Hard-earned battle scars, I'm afraid. Keep talking so I know you can talk to me this way."*

There were thousands of questions running through her head, so after a moment she asked, *"So, there are other dragons? What is the dragon population of Dorthos like?"*

"You can find us all over if you look hard enough, various shapes and sizes and all wild. We are not to be kept as pets. We can be eaten, and our body parts can be repurposed like your animals on Earth, but we are difficult to kill. There are those that hunt dragons, Slayers, for money and glory. Most don't survive hunting us, and the few that do are held as heroes. So, you will see small dragons and many large ones during your lifetime here. Also, be aware that if we do meet another dragon, do not assume it can use magic."

In an odd way, hearing his deep calm voice speaking to her in her head settled some of her tingling nerves. Wren had told her she was open-minded and cool-headed many times, but right now the only thing keeping her actively grounded was Akuna. She needed him to keep talking so that she could feel normal and not panic-driven.

"*Are you one of the few that can use magic? Is it rare?*"

"*Yes, quite rare among dragons. Though, every dragon does have its own ability, like fire-breathing or air-manipulation, that we are born with. So if you please, do not mention to anyone that I can use magic or that I am even with you. The consequences would not be pleasant.*"

"*For you, me, or the people asking?*"

"*For those outside of you and I that think our business is their own and keep poking around.*"

"*Wonderful. Okay, so you're just gonna walk around with me everywhere I go? How will this work?*"

"*Ah, no need to worry about that just now.*"

"*Alright, Cheese-Ears. One more thing for now then,*" Rosella said, side-eyeing Akuna. "*How are you able to speak English? Is that the language of Dorthos, somehow?*"

"*English is your tongue. Ours is known as Dorthish, though both languages use the same phonetics and alphabet. The underworld uses a different language, same with the Forbearen Lands,*" Akuna said, gentle steam trailing behind him as he huffed.

"*I don't have enough energy to get into that and how it would make sense.*"

Stiff laughter tickled her head in response, and they walked side by side for some time without speaking. Despite the need for his voice to help settle her nerves, Rosella also needed the time to ingest everything that had happened so far, and she believed Akuna knew that as well as he did not disturb her thoughts again.

She had a sneaking suspicion that he could read her thoughts and emotions.

After some time, the large trees seemed to shrink in size, and more sunlight poured from the treetops. After walking further, the only trees that were around were saplings planted distant from each other. At the edge of a row of saplings on the edge of a hilltop, Rosella let out a soft gasp of shock.

Before her and Akuna was a vast land that was so colorful that there were shades she didn't know existed until seeing this sight. The green and purple grass was vibrant and uniform, and the singing wind made the grass sway majestically as if the blades were dancing. The blue and yellow sky was vivid and almost blinding as the orange Dorthos Sun shone brightly, warming Rosella's face as the rays touched her cheeks. The clouds were fluffy white and pink puffs, and Rosella understood at that moment now why people on Earth called clouds cotton candy.

The land itself rose and fell in gentle then sharp slopes, and in the furthest distance that Rosella could see was a snowcapped mountain range that stretched to each side of the horizon. Small animals could be seen frolicking in the distance, and colorful birds flew above. Further in the distant sky she could see two dragons flying next to each other, their wings cutting the pink clouds. Trees with leaves of all colors littered the land and in some places made it more difficult to see the grass below.

"This is the land of Cupridale, and they are responsible for the wood production of Dorthos. There is a village nearby called Misty Trace. We shall go there and find a room for the night as you need your rest," Akuna said, breaking the silence between them, and started moving down the hilltop.

"That sounds nice. Today has been too long, and I can't wait for a long, hot shower," she responded, stretching her limbs and following him.

What sounded like a soft chuckle flowed through her mind as Akuna said, *"There are no showers in this world."*

"Wait, really? Can't you just use magic to make a shower or something, please?" Rosella asked telepathically and stopped in her tracks.

Akuna, however, did not stop walking, so she had to jog to keep up. *"I use my magic for myself and for what I choose, and I do not need to shower. Perhaps you can ask a magic user when we get to town, but then you would have to explain to them what a shower is. In fact, the next magic user you meet, you should ask, because it would be entertaining to watch you squirm while trying to figure out what to say."*

"Wow, you save my life then wish for me to embarrass myself? I feel right at home in this human-less world."

"You're stuck with me. Get used to it."

"I want a different dragon buddy."

"No, you don't. I'm the best you're ever going to get, human."

"Yeah, okay, but I can't even ride you because you're so small."

Akuna laughed so hard that smoke came out of his mouth. *"Oh, darling, I have never been ridden by anyone or anything before. Dragons are not ridden. That is a thing of fable."*

She smiled and adjusted her bag. The faint hint of pain from her shoulder muscles were starting to hit her nerves as the straps moved. *"Why are dragons not ridden? That is the opposite of fables or stories in my world. People want to be dragon riders to rule a kingdom, or to shorten the amount of time traveled. There are lots of shows, movies, and books just about riding dragons."*

"Well, the dragons here will vaporize you for even going near their horde, and before you ask, no, I do not have a horde. Besides, how many of those dragons want to be ridden in your

fables, as it sounds like it was the rider's choice to ride a dragon? So no, there are no dragon riders on Dorthos unless I decide so"

"If you decide so? What, are you the ruler of dragons or something?"

"In a way."

"But you'll explain more 'in due time'?" Rosella questioned dryly.

"Look at you, you're learning. You're now the smartest human in Dorthos."

"Not by choice, lizard. Is there anything else you can actually tell me now? An answer I don't have to wait for?"

Akuna stopped in his tracks but did not look at Rosella. Her eyes fell to the heavily scarred wings at his sides and saw that, even though they were closed tightly against his sides, his wingspan must be massive due to the amount of space the wing membrane took up. She always envisioned dragons to be gigantic, and yet Akuna stood at her height. Was he actually a young dragon, or was he just a smaller breed?

"I chose this size because it would be less intimidating for you to comprehend. Should I have picked something else, like a cat?" came a chortling voice from her head.

She whipped her head to find his eyes looking at her. He had turned his head, and there was an unmistakable smile, his teeth bared, but the corners of his mouth were upturned.

"Bruh, *seriously*? You can read my fucking thoughts?" she exclaimed, speaking aloud and not afraid to hide her shock.

In response, he reared his head back and closed his eyes, laughter ringing out in both her ears and her mind. The laughter continued as he started walking again, Rosella having to jog to keep up.

"Have you always been able to read my thoughts? Since I've gotten here, at least."

"Oh, yes, it's a gift and a curse for both of us. Don't worry, I can tune you out whenever I want, and I will teach you how to do the same. For now as we are getting closer to the village, you need to find the inn and rest," he responded telepathically as his laughter subsided.

"Are you going into town with me?" she asked, letting slight nerves show through her voice.

"Yes, I will. Again, I will always be with you. We are tied together for the rest of your lifetime."

"Is that a normal thing, dragons being tied to other beings?"

"No. This is a first, to my understanding."

"Why us?"

"In due time."

"In due time!" she mocked audibly, and after a moment of silence, she heard him chuckle to himself.

3
Once Upon a Dream, I Knew You

Before long, Rosella and Akuna reached the top of a small slope that overlooked Misty Trace in its entirety. The wooden buildings were painted in a rainbow of colors, and the surrounding fields added to the aesthetic of the cozy town. There were packed gravel roads, people walking around with full baskets and children running with sticks and pot lids in hand. Horses of all colors could be seen attached to carts or in fields with the farmers at work. The village of Misty Trace itself was not large, with Rosella counting around twenty buildings in total including houses. The fields around the town were strewn with either lively crops or browned with dead plants.

"So, this is Misty Trace? Why do only half of the crops look alive?" Rosella asked as she adjusted her bag once more.

"Cupridale is not responsible for crops. Arja is. As Arja is, well...not healthy right now, the other regions are suffering. We will discuss that more later. We cannot worry about that right now," Akuna said sternly.

She looked up to the sky and noticed that the sun had sunk

closer to the horizon, and a moon much larger than hers on Earth started to peek over the mountain range.

"Despite the crops failing, Misty Trace, Cupridale, and Dorthos are pleasant so far."

"Do not let the pleasantries fool you. Remember this: don't get too lost in what speaking kinds say; watch what they do," Akuna advised sagely while taking a few steps back.

"Where are you going?" she asked when she noticed him backing away from the hill's edge.

"I cannot be seen."

"So how are you going to go into town with me?"

He stared directly at her, then exhaled a puff of the same purple smoke that he had used on her earlier in the day. Instead of the smoke surrounding her though, the smoke wrapped itself around his body, and in the blink of an eye, he disappeared.

"Akuna?" she called out telepathically at the lingering smoke where he once stood.

"If you step on me, I'll make your foot my next meal."

She looked down, and below her was a guinea-pig-sized dragon standing next to her foot. The turquoise dragon beheld her with narrowed amber eyes and huffed out a puff of steam. Kneeling, she saw the same Swiss-cheese scars were present on his frills and knew this was still Akuna. A rush of joyous glee filled her chest as she gazed down at the tiny dragon, smiling so broadly that her cheeks hurt.

"Why so tiny, and why blue?" she asked as she got on all fours to try and be eye level with him.

"So I can fit in your pouch, and because I want to be blue. Now pick me up and put me in the empty pouch on your belt," he said calmly and defiantly.

She giggled and placed a flat hand in front of him to climb on. While his paws were small, she could feel the razor-sharp talons on his fingers as he sat in the middle of her palm. Slowly, she stood up while balancing the surprisingly light Akuna in her palm. When she stood to her full height, she held her hand in front of her face so she could look at Akuna when she spoke.

"So, you're just gonna live in my pouch? How will you see? Also, something I didn't think about, what do you eat? Also also, will I have to clean the pouch if you...do your business in there?" she asked, smiling hard at the adorable little Akuna, despite him looking more annoyed after each question. *"Also also also, do you just get to change to whatever size or color you want? Because that's awesome."*

"You're asking a lot of questions when you should be walking."

"You're grumpy when you're tiny. I'm just trying to be logical here," she said while finding the pouch and opening the flap.

A deep sigh for a creature with tiny lungs escaped Akuna's chest as he stepped into the pouch. *"I will be in your pouch when we're around other speaking kinds. I can see just fine. I eat lots of things. I can use magic to whisk away my droppings. And I can be whatever size or color I want, but my true colors are the white and red you know me to have."*

"Seeeee, that wasn't so hard, now was it? And 'speaking kinds,' like humanoids or people? I guess 'speaking kinds' make more sense since there are no humans here so why would you call them humanoids, and 'people' is too generalized, I guess." Rosella shrugged as she flipped the flap over Akuna's head, who let out another puff of steam, and she started walking down the hill toward Misty Trace.

"You can call them people if that is easier for your tiny human brain."

"And you say that I'm the one that needs rest, grumpy lizard."

As the buildings grew closer, she noticed that there were intricate designs on the walls depicting various flora and fauna.

One building had a large tree and what looked like a few small birds on the branches while another building had something resembling a beetle with zebra stripes. She wanted a closer look at the designs, but she knew she needed to find the inn first. The rest of her life was going to be spent in this world, so she had time to explore later. She made her way further into the village, and she noticed a few people watching her as she walked by.

"You weren't kidding about me being the only human," she said to Akuna, examining the people around her. Dwarves with long, braided hair and various skin colors, green and blue-skinned elves with long pointed ears, even a large person with a missing eye passed by carrying a large crate. She wanted to look at all of these different races of people longer, but she realized she might come off as creepy, and being noticed was something she was trying not to do. Instead, she peered ahead and saw the inn's sign that was swinging gently above the door.

Once inside the inn, the noise was abundantly merry, and the sound hit her ears with a soft *whoosh*. Every table except for one in the far left of the room was filled, so she headed directly for it, passing tables swiftly so as to not draw attention. Once she sat down, she took in everything around her with wandering eyes and extreme curiosity.

The light wooden interior with lit iron chandeliers were scattered all over the ceiling to brighten up the inside of the inn, and the dark wooden furniture made the room feel cozy. A large hearth was on the other end of the bar but was not lit, and there was a massive taxidermized wolf head above the fireplace. The bar on her left, which was covered in paintings, was full of patrons and staff of various races of people.

"Welcome to the Foggy Snog. Can I get you anything, love?" asked a kind feminine voice from the right side of Rosella by the window. A person that resembled a lizard with yellow scales stood patiently while holding a notepad and a piece of wood that resembled a rudimentary pencil.

"Uh, could I get an ale, food, and a room for the night, please?" Rosella asked nervously, taking out her pendant and fiddling with the stone.

"Sure, dear. Just the house special for food?" the waitress asked while writing down the order.

"Yes, that should be alright."

"Alright, love, that'll be twelve gold chips for the ale, food, and bed," she said as she pocketed the notepad in her flowery apron and stood expectantly.

"Akuna? Money? What should I do?" she asked telepathically to Akuna, who had failed to mention that Rosella would have to still pay for things.

"Magic pouch. Imagine in your mind how much you need."

"Something the matter?" the waitress asked as Rosella was talking to Akuna.

"Oh, no! Sorry, I spaced out. Let me get those twelve gold chips for you," Rosella said, scrambling with the clasp of the pouch.

Once she put her hand in the opening, small pieces of cold metal the size of her fingernail appeared in her hand. Astonished, she lifted her hand and gave the waitress the gold chips. The waitress dipped her head in thanks and walked in the direction of the bar.

"Did you really not count the gold chips before handing them to her?" came Akuna's voice, grumpier than before.

"If someone had maybe told me about the currency of this world, then maybe I would have! It's not my fault I panicked. What are these races—sorry, speaking kinds anyway, as you prefer to call them?"

Before Rosella could figure out what was going on, her vision tunneled, and an opaque lavender film washed over her sight. Her eyes started moving of their own accord as they shifted from one patron to the other. If she tried to move her own eyes, she simply felt blocked or held in place. No pain shot through her body, so she released her muscles and let what must be Akuna take control.

"These are mountain elves. They have blue or gray skin. These over here are plains dwarves sitting with cave dwarves. You will learn what region the elves and dwarves are from by their skin color. Adaptation and evolution, of course. Of all the speaking kinds, elves and dwarves make up most of the population. These are miniature ogres. They are usually green or brown. Yes, they are actually called miniature ogres—don't ask me why. These are devlairs, or in your world, tieflings, or horned devils. They are usually red, yellow, or orange. The waitress and bar staff are lizgons. They can be all sorts of colors like dragons, or lizards in your world. There are many other species like felinettes, hobdrigs, and shiftlings."

"Shiftlings?"

"Shapeshifters. They're extremely rare, and only other shiftlings can see one's true identity."

Once he was done describing the patrons, the lavender film and tunnel vision subsided, and she had full control of her eyes again. She rubbed them with her hands and blinked a few times.

"Uh, what was that?" she asked, trying not to let her nerves control her voice.

"Magic."

"That can't be your go-to answer for things."

"Try me."

Rosella let out a sigh as the waitress walked over with an ale and a plate of food.

"Everything alright, love?" she asked politely as she set down the food and drink.

"Oh, yes, I guess I'm more tired than I thought."

"Well, I have your key here, and whenever you're done, you can go up those stairs behind you and find your room. The room number is on the key. Let me know if you need anything else!" the waitress said as she placed down an iron key next to Rosella's plate and left.

Rosella looked down at the overloaded wooden plate with a massive piece of grilled meat that resembled poultry, various seasoned rainbow-colored vegetables, a buttered roll and a buttered potato, and a large wooden tankard of ale. The silverware was also wooden but were polished so much that they could pass for brown metal utensils.

"Yeah, you definitely gave her more than twelve gold chips."

Rosella rolled her eyes and cut the piece of poultry in half. *"Here, because you're obviously hangry,"* she said, exasperated, and opened the pouch where Akuna was curled up in a ball. He looked up and saw the poultry be placed next to him, sniffed it, and tore a large chunk and began to chew. Satisfied, she turned back toward her plate and gave him half the potato and a few vegetables.

"Did you say I was hangry?" came Akuna's voice, and despite his chewing, his voice sounded normal.

"Yep. A state of being or a mood you get into when you are hungry and angry at the same time. Eating is the only way to cure being hangry. So obviously, you needed to eat because you were being grumpier than a human toddler," she said as she filled herself up with the delicious food. The fuller she got, the more she realized just how tired she was from the day.

"Interesting. Well, I used a lot of energy to bring you here, and I was going to hunt for rats after you fell asleep."

"Gross."

"They're more plentiful than sheep, and rats are not missed. So it works in my favor, whether it's gross for your human tongue or not."

Rosella chuckled a little and shrugged as she took a sip of ale. When she lowered the tankard, a hooded male was sitting at her table across from her. The man, possibly an elf, had dark royal blue, almost black hair and piercing gray eyes. His half smile presented white teeth that shone brightly against the black leathers and upturned hooded cloak. He propped his elbows on the table and rested his chin on his clasped hands, tilting his head to the side.

"Can I fucking help you?" she questioned sternly, refusing to break eye contact with the elf. As she stared, she noticed three scars cutting through his icy purple skin: a small scar on his left eyebrow, another which stretched ear to ear over his nose and the last on the right side of his lips. She grew curious what this elf did to get those scars.

"That is no way to speak to a stranger," said the elf in a rumbling low tone that oozed with oil. He leaned back in his chair, now giving a full sneering smile. She saw that his black leather armor had dark red trimming throughout the intricately designed chest piece. Over the chest piece was a pendant necklace with a stone bearing white swirls.

With a shock that made her spine shiver, she realized that this man looked and sounded a lot like the shadowed man from the numerous dreams she'd had. Questions entangled with thoughts flooded her mind, and she felt an odd rumble vibrate her head. The man held her gaze with a cocky smile, and her mind quieted long enough for her to get annoyed with his arrival and lingering presence.

"And that," she said, pointing at him with her fork, "is not how you enter someone's personal space. So leave me alone."

"And if I don't?"

"Listen. I've had the literal worst day of my life that I can guarantee will beat your worst month, and I just want to eat in peace. If you want to talk to me, talk to me tomorrow or never. I don't care. For now, fuck off."

"Hmm, alright then. The name is Elaras Moonshadow, by the way," he said as he held out a hand for her to shake.

She glanced down at the hand then back up at him. Her heart fluttered softly when she met his eyes, her muscles trembling lightly at the smile he gave her. Pushing past her fluster over this strange man, she took her fork and speared a piece of purple carrot, ignoring his outstretched hand. As she fed herself the carrot and started chewing, she took her middle finger and flipped it to him. By the slight rise in his eyebrow, she knew immediately that this gesture would not have the same effect as it would on Earth.

"Tell this one your first name only," Akuna said suddenly in her mind.

Rosella narrowed her eyes at Elaras as she contemplated Akuna's words. "The name is Rosella, and this," she said, gesturing to her still uplifted finger, "means fuck off, Elaras Moonshadow."

The confusion was replaced with a wide smile as he pushed his chair back. "I'll see you around then, Rosella," he said as he shoved his chair back in.

As he left, she heard a clatter on the floor under the table. When Elaras walked through the front door, she peeked below and saw what seemed like a sheathed knife. Picking it up and taking a closer look, she confirmed that it was, in fact, an ornate knife that was the length of her forearm. She took the blade out of the sheath and noticed that the metal work was a deep black along with the hilt and the leather-wrapped grip, a quarter-sized ruby embedded in the pommel. When she ran a finger along the edge, the blade sliced through the first layer of skin like butter. The matching sheath bore an embossment of a full moon on the side, and the back had loops big enough to go through a belt.

"*What the fuck?*" she exclaimed as she examined the ornate knife a little longer.

"*Whoever he was, he thought you were attractive,*" Akuna responded with a slight chuckle to his tone.

"*Excuse me? He just showed up out of nowhere and gave me this knife. Or was that an accident? Do you think he meant to give me this?*"

"*Dagger, not knife. And yes, isn't that what creatures do to show affection or show that they are attracted to them so they can mate? Except in this case he possibly gave you a magically imbued weapon to show his interest.*"

"*I don't need your lizard brain logic right now about the romance, but keep going about the magic part.*"

"*I'll take a better look at the dagger tomorrow. For now, you have to think of a witty response to him giving you a mating gift.*" Akuna laughed heartily as Rosella put the dagger in her magic pouch to put on her belt later.

She shook her head and finished her food and ale, smiling to herself. Without another word said between them, she ventured upstairs and found the room she was given. She took off her bag, canteen, belt, and boots, and after using the restroom, she lay flat on the bed. Once she closed her eyes, she fell into a hard, dreamless sleep.

When she awoke the next morning, she saw that Akuna was still in his guinea-pig-sized form and was fast asleep on one of the pillows, curled up like a slumbering cat.

4
May the Shadows Bless the Stars

"What am I supposed to do when I run out of toothpaste?"
Rosella asked telepathically when she walked out from the
restroom with her hygiene bag. Admittedly for her, seeing Earthly
items like a toothbrush and bottled lotion in this magical fantasy
world was strange. The culture shock had not fully set in, and she
was waiting for the inevitable, so she moved her pendant to the
outside of her dress so she could use it to ground herself when
that time came.

"Speaking kinds use a paste made of salt and sage, and
sometimes mint. Well, most of the speaking kinds do. I can't
speak for the ogres," replied Akuna in a groggy voice. Rosella
looked over to him and saw he was stretching on top of the pillow.
"What? Did you really think this world had Crest toothpaste?"

"There are flushing toilets!"

"So? Plumbing and dental hygiene are quite different, as they
pertain to different orifices."

"Good point, but you're no help."

"You'll be fine. Now, let me look at that dagger."

Rosella groaned and packed away her hygiene bag. She went to the belt with the magic pouch attached to it, thinking of the dagger she received from Elaras yesterday. As she pictured the dagger in her mind, stiff cold leather and metal landed in her hand the second she reached inside and grasped the handle. The ruby on the hilt glinted brightly in the sunlight from the window, and the metal work and leather band of the handle was darker than she remembered. She scrutinized it a moment longer, then placed it in front of Akuna to examine as she started to put on her boots and belt.

"This is underworld metal on the handle, and the ruby seems to be imbued with magic. Take the blade out of the sheath so I can see it," Akuna said, his head lowered as he walking around the dagger that was currently triple the length of him.

She reached over and pulled the blade completely out of the sheath and rested it next to Akuna on the bed.

He sniffed the metal, nose scrunching up in response. "The blade is also underworld metal. This is not necessarily a bad thing, but we will also not know its true power until you wield it."

"I guess you are unfamiliar with underworld magic?"

"I'm not familiar with many things related to the underworld."

"So you expect me to use this thing? I'm only good at cutting food for meals and even that needs more work."

"How else do you expect to protect yourself?" Akuna said as he looked up, eyes narrowing at her.

"Not with that! I did archery in my spare time, but I've never killed a living creature with archery," she said as she placed her hands on her hips, astonished that her dragon companion expected her to fight or hunt anything or anyone.

"How else do you expect to eat? There are no inns every few hundred feet, human."

"Why can't you use your fancy magic to give us food, dragon?"

"Because I don't want to, purely out of spite."

Rosella raised her arms in the air in exasperation and turned to grab her bag and canteen. *"Fine. I'll need to get a bow and arrows, then. Unless you can use your magic to create some for me, if you're not feeling too spiteful yet?"*

She heard a huff of annoyance from Akuna before purple smoke appeared in the corner of her eye. Turning, she saw a beautifully crafted black oak Penobscot bow with blue engravings of moons and stars along the sides. The grip was wrapped black leather, and despite the polished wood of the bow itself, the grip looked worn in. A leather quiver with what must have been thirty arrows sat next to the massive black bow.

Picking up the bow, she noticed just how light it was given its size, and the quiver housed a pouch with various tips. The arrows were long but light, the feathers on the end perfectly cut. She held the bow in her grip, and she was correct in thinking the leather was worn, as the edges of the wrap were soft under her fingers and palm. While she missed her equipment at home, these were admittedly a great upgrade.

"This is beautiful. I'm just curious though," Rosella said as she squeezed the grip of the bow, *"did someone else own this before?"*

"Consider it a Nightstone family heirloom."

"Thank you, Vikshae," she audibly whispered as she traced the wood of the bow with her fingers.

There was a soft rumble in her chest that did not come from her own lungs, and she knew that somehow that was Akuna responding to her gratitude. She put the bow around her body and set the quiver along the back of her belt like Link in the *Zelda* games. The black dagger was situated onto her belt as well and sat next to the magic pouch. Once she had everything on her person, she went and held Akuna's pouch open for him to climb inside.

"*May I ask something of you?*" came Akuna's voice as Rosella left the room with him in tow. "*We already spoke of not letting others know of my existence, though I need to press it further. Do not speak my name in front of others. You may refer to me as something else in case the need arises, but to others I must not exist.*"

Rosella considered this and nodded. "*Because of the whole 'dragons do not do anything with speaking kinds' thing?*"

"*Precisely.*"

"*Cheese Ears it is then. Or maybe just Cheese. Or Gouda? Cheddar? Swiss? I'll figure out a good name.*"

"*Stop it.*"

"*Mozzarella?*"

"*May the Great Golden Dragon take me in my sleep so I do not have to suffer more of this human.*"

Rosella laughed as she made her way downstairs to have breakfast.

―――――――

"*I may die sooner than expected. There is no coffee in this world.*"

"*Don't be so dramatic. If coffee is a caffeinated beverage like black tea, you'll be fine, human.*"

"*Coffee tastes better. Figure out how to make coffee, and I'll be less annoying.*"

"*That'll be a marvel,*" Akuna said as he let out a large sigh, and Rosella saw some steam escape the sides of the pouch he resided in.

She smiled to herself as she walked down the road toward the market, opposite where they came into town. As she approached the stands of the market, she saw colorful food and various trinkets. There was fruit that was similar to apples but were blue, strawberries that were orange and even asparagus' that were pink. As she was picking up a bundle of yellow grapes, she felt a presence on her right.

"Rosella, how lovely to see you again. Did you get my gift?" came the unique, smooth voice of Elaras.

She looked up at him and saw that his hood was down and that his blackish blue hair fell down past his shoulders. He had the classic elf ears she always pictured elves to have and black spiked hoops as earrings in his lobes. He glanced down to her belt where the blade sat, and a large grin appeared on his face. "Ah, you did indeed get the gift I left. What do you think of Shadow Breaker? Beautiful, isn't it?"

"So it was a gift. The elf must find something pleasing about you, then," Akuna snickered.

Giving the most exaggerated side-eye she could muster, she found a basket and placed the grapes inside. She moved in a way that forced Elaras to move out of her way so she could look at the blue apples. "Did you name it yourself? Because I'm sure a child could come up with a better name for it."

He laughed and moved to her left side, picking up a particularly large apple and examining it before placing it in her basket. "I did not name it, but I'm sure you'll find the name appropriate."

"Why did you give it to me, anyways?" she asked, taking the apple he had picked and putting it back on the counter with the rest.

"Hm. Want the truth or a pretty lie?" he asked while depositing another large apple in her basket.

"What do you think?" she snapped back as she took the same apple and returned it to the counter just like before.

"Well, I gave you Shadow Breaker because you looked helpless. I can't let someone interesting be defenseless, though now I do see you have quite an impeccable bow. That, my dear, makes you even more interesting." He smiled and stared at her, grabbing a third apple blindly then reaching into her basket once more.

"Helpless *and* interesting?" she said, slapping his hand with the apple in it and letting the apple roll away. "I wasn't aware backhanded compliments were something that could come so easily from someone so egocentric and *annoying*. You're as loud and irritating as a cricket, you know that?"

The smile that spread across Elaras' face and the laugh that escaped his throat made Rosella's heart skip a beat, as it was one that seemed genuine and softened his face.

"No wonder you didn't have a significant other on Earth." Akuna's chuckling voice chimed in, and Rosella could not help but show a surprised expression on her face.

Elaras' eyebrows shot up, and he leaned in toward her. "Are you surprised by your own words, or is there something going on in your pretty little head? I'd very much like to know more," he teased.

Rosella caught a whiff of pine and leather as he leaned in, and the scent made her nerves tingle, but she sneered at him before responding.

"Wouldn't you like to know, *Cricket?*" she replied and turned away to finally pick an apple of her choosing. After she found a suitable one, she saw there were two more already in the basket. She looked up to where Elaras had been standing before and saw that he was gone. He was nowhere to be seen. Even the apple she had slapped from his hand was gone.

She turned back and continued shopping, grabbing various fruits and jerky. Paying the merchant for the food, including the apple that had disappeared, she made her way out of town into the vast green and purple fields. Further away from town were neat rows of colorful trees of varying ages. She had wanted to look at the paintings on the buildings she saw yesterday, but she started to feel claustrophobic and anxious. Was she feeling this way because of Elaras finding her again? Was it because the last twenty-four hours were a whirlwind, or a combination of both? She wasn't sure and just wanted to, quite literally, move forward and see more of this land before her emotions came crashing down on her.

"You know, that comment was unnecessary while I was talking to Elaras," she said, letting annoyance lace her tone.

"I only speak the truth, dear. Maybe you shouldn't be so hostile to someone that just wants to tell you that your head is pretty," Akuna said, chuckling to himself. Rosella couldn't help but smile as they walked further from town.

"So, are there gods in this world?" she asked curiously, hoping that he would actually give her an answer this time so his voice could calm her nerves. *"You mentioned a Great Golden Dragon earlier."*

"Oh, yes. There is no singular god that this world worships or becomes zealots over. I have the Great Golden, the speaking kinds that are one with nature have their god, the royalty in the grand city have their god, so on and so forth. The gods are not there to be used for control, and the gods do not take kindly to those that use their name for evil. Even the evil-natured gods do not like their names used for harm. Those gods prefer to keep to themselves and to do what they desire, while holding the title and power of a god," he responded as he emerged from the bag and

climbed up her arm and onto her shoulder. *"The gods of this world are not like the ones you had on Earth, Rosella. The gods here can intervene and talk to those that seek them out. Their hands can touch our ground to shift the mountains and make the crops grow. They are all powerful here, the gods, but only they and their closest speaking kind followers are allowed to use that power, as long as said power is not abused."*

"So, did the gods create magic in this world?" she asked, feeling the talons on his feet piercing the bag strap and her dress. The feeling reminded her of her cat, and she felt a touch of sadness in her throat that passed when Akuna spoke again.

"The gods created this world, and so the gods created magic. Remember, not every dragon nor every speaking kind can use magic. Do not assume either one can wield it. For speaking kinds, it's rare to see one wield magic that is extremely powerful. For dragons, we usually only use magic for ourselves or our young. Again, we dragons do not interact with the speaking kind except for our current situation."

"Okay, so how does magic work in this world?"

"There are three types of magic users in this world: magic by birth, magic by gods, and magic by stone. Many magic users are born with abilities, and their powers range from minimal to world-altering. Those that are close followers of gods, Clerics, can be more powerful depending on the relationship with their gods. However, there are not many Clerics in this world, especially High Clerics. Those that rely on stones for their magic can only do what the stones allow you to do.

"You have your necklace and Shadow Breaker, so right now you can use magic, but it is only limited to those stones' abilities. No matter what, magic will appear as smoke of various colors, and stone users and Clerics will reflect the color of those they

pull the power from. Born magic users' smoke will display magic that reflects their soul or power. One user may be red because they are angry, another may display as blue as they are sad or lost. Dragons will display their magic reflective of their scales."

"If your magic is purple but your scales are white, what does that mean?"

"I like purple," Akuna said as he let out a rumble of laughter that reverberated into Rosella's chest.

"Isn't that a bit of a contradiction to what you just said, then?"

"Your existence here is a contradiction, darling."

She huffed an annoyed breath, then gazed up at the sky, her hand thumbing the cool ruby on Shadow Breaker's pommel. "So, what if magic is performed against me? How can I defend myself?"

"Sometimes, you can't. That is why you have me."

"Comforting," Rosella quipped, processing the information as she continued walking. Questions were floating around in her mind, but she kept them to herself for the time being despite knowing Akuna could read her mind.

After a few hours and Misty Trace was out of sight, they came across a dense patch of trees with vibrant autumn-colored leaves. When they got closer, Akuna jumped off Rosella's shoulder and flew toward the close-knit trees.

"We can rest here for now," he said as he flew further into the packed trees.

Rosella followed him inside and found a large patch of wild resembling orange blackberries. As she drew closer, however, she saw Akuna fly upward into the treetops and disappear. Confused, she was about to call out and search for him when she heard a shuffle behind her.

"What have we here? Twice in one day, what a coincidence!" Elaras' oily deep voice said, and she heard him approach her.

She let her head hang back slightly and let out an audible sigh before turning to face him. "I don't have enough energy for your shit again today, Cricket. Once a day is too much."

"I think once a day isn't enough for me, and I think you actually enjoy my company," he said as he stepped closer to her, eating a few berries as he spoke.

"I doubt that, and hearing your obnoxious voice once a day is enough for me. I'll be on my way now, and I hope you don't follow me. You really are like a cricket—you're everywhere, and your existence is *exhausting*," she said and started to turn away from him.

Elaras chuckled as he asked, "Do you even know how to defend yourself? I'm curious, Rosella, if you truly know how to use your bow along with Shadow Breaker, or if you're wearing both to look tougher than the average non-magical person."

She narrowed her eyes at the trees in front of her as she grabbed her bow and an arrow. She turned her body and saw that Elaras was holding up a berry in the air above his head, his pompous sneer on his face.

Without second-guessing, she nocked the arrow, raised her bow, and after a few calculated moments of adjusting to the new bow and its draw weight, released the arrow. The berry exploded from the impact, and the arrow itself flew into a tree trunk a few meters behind him.

A flash of surprise fell on Elaras' face but was quickly replaced with ice as Rosella nocked another arrow. In the blink of an eye, Elaras was gone. A warm and steady hand clasped over her bow hand, and fingers wrapped under her chin.

"Color me impressed," Elaras whispered in her ear from behind, making her shiver. "Now that I'm confident that you can use a bow, give me the truth. Do you know how to use a dagger?"

"No," she said sternly, trying to wiggle out of his grasp. Each time she tried to raise her bow arm, his hand pushed back effortlessly. Deep fury that was not her own filled her chest. Rosella knew Akuna was watching but was still out of sight.

"Shame. Call for me when you're ready for me to teach you, as you may need all the help you can get, Rosella *Nightstone*. Just use your second gift I gave you and whisper my name into the stone. Ta-ta," he said as his voice drifted away.

Before she could understand what was happening, she felt the hand disappear from her throat and a whoosh of air on her back. When she whipped around to face him, he had once again vanished without even a footprint left behind.

An unfamiliar weight hung from her neck, and she looked down to see the same pendant he wore before around her neck. His necklace hung lower than her night stone, and while the brown and white stone's chain felt warm against her neck, she only felt pure hatred.

"Fucker!" she yelled out, and she saw a flash of blue fly towards her and hover in front of her. "How did he know my name, and how the fuck was he able to move like that?"

"He saw the night stone around your neck and knew it belonged to the Nightstone family," Akuna said calmly. "Only the Nightstone family wore a night stone, acting as a family crest. As for Elaras' movements, that was magic that is rare. He must be a displacer, one that can freeze time. To him, he moves at a regular speed, but for us he moves in a blink."

"Great. A magic user is now stalking me and knows *exactly* who I am *and* he can use some magic to magically show up somewhere. Fantastic!" she yelled before stopping and taking a deep breath. She picked up Elaras' pendant and examined it closely. "What kind of stone is this anyway?"

Akuna hovered close to her extended hand, his eyes tracing

every swirl of the stone. "That is a moonstone, but more of a darker coloration than I have seen."

"Why would I even need his help?" she asked abruptly, staring into Akuna's amber eyes.

Akuna, stoic and annoyed since Rosella had met him, lowered his eyes for a moment, and his body drooped slightly before he looked back into Rosella's eyes. "Because you are the only Nightstone on Dorthos, and you need to claim the throne to heal the land of Arja."

Rosella's heart painfully skipped a beat. The pendant fell from her hand as her eyes tunneled onto Akuna, the world growing silent around her.

"Excuse me?" she said stiffly, feeling the air in her lungs get sucked out as she spoke.

"The entirety of the Nightstone family was killed off thirty years ago," Akuna said, and when Rosella did not respond, he continued. "They were a family of forest elves that ruled a great portion of land in Dorthos called Arja. The land is mostly farmland, ranches, and a few small villages, and the Nightstone family was vastly popular throughout Dorthos and well loved by most. They were so loved because of the charity they would contribute to the citizens, and the kindness was widely known to be outmatched by the rest of the nobles in the land. They put the people first instead of themselves, and the citizens felt that wholeheartedly."

Akuna spoke, as if reading articulately from a history book. His body lifted into the air back into her eyeline. "The land is, or was, rich with minerals that makes farming easy, so the land provides most of Dorthos its crops and agriculture. Arja itself holds monstrous power, therefore the Nightstones themselves were powerful. Despite keeping to themselves and being peaceful, a rebel family of devlairs killed the entire family line to usurp the land and rule in their place. Those devlairs have since been taken care of, but now the land is without a true ruler. So, as far as this world and its gods know, you are the only Nightstone."

Rosella clenched the bow so tightly that the leather shifted under her fingers as the information embedded itself in her mind. All sounds became muffled, all movements frozen. The wind did not blow the fabric of her dress or make the leaves in the trees dance. Deafness from the bombs was preferable to the explosive emotions in her chest. She had to clear her throat and blink many times before the courage to speak made its appearance.

"Is that why I was brought here? To continue some family line that I didn't even know existed? To be the new 'well-loved' Nightstone and rule some land that only belongs to me because of some stone my mother gave me on her deathbed?" she asked, feeling rage and confusion fuel her veins. She started to pace back and forth, Akuna watching her closely as Rosella made a path in the grass. "And what did you mean, 'was rich with minerals'?"

"That is part of it, yes. The land of Arja is slowly faltering and diminishing, and the rest of Dorthos can see the damage this is causing the world. Put simply, the land is dying, and only the power of a Nightstone leader can heal it. You have a night stone, and you are of Nightstone lineage, so you are the rightful heir."

"So what, now I'm going to be a queen? I should have asked sooner why I was brought here, and you should have told me sooner. I am only *human*, Akuna! I do not have *power* nor was I born to be a leader! How do we really expect me to rule a land that I am not qualified to rule in any way, shape, or form? I was *not* born here and I'm, what, a multiverse version of this Nightstone family? I can't be a fucking *queen*, Akuna."

"As for not being qualified, you will find that just because you do not have magic does not mean you are not powerful. Many nobles of this land do not have powers, or do not hold the same respect as the Nightstones did. Your name alone will help you along your path," Akuna reassured. From the few glances she made toward him, she could see he was fluttering his wings faster but remained in one spot. "I did not tell you sooner because you were overwhelmed as it was, and you did not ask because you yourself recognized that you were overwhelmed and did as I told you to do. Do not fault yourself for not asking questions when your mind was unstable."

"My world gets blown up, and I become a queen and save a land I don't even know. Make that make sense, *Akuna,*" Rosella spat out. Disdain toward Akuna became palpable, despite his only offensive action being not disclosing information to her. She took in a deep breath before slowing her pacing. "Wait—save the land. In my dreams on Earth, you were in them as well as Elaras, but you had glowing eyes, and he was shrouded in shadow. Someone in silver kept saying, 'Save us.' Is that what's happening now? Were my dreams, what, projected into me or something?"

Akuna tilted his head in thought, then said, "It seems like it, but that was not my doing, so I cannot give an accurate answer. Someone or something was trying to tell you something. Did you have the same dream last night?"

"No. In these dreams, I never got details of faces either, or understood what anyone said besides the one in silver. My tattoo glowed as well, glowed silver," she said and pointed to her sternum where the tattoo resided.

"Is your tattoo of a moon and stars?" he asked, and when Rosella's face expressed shock, Akuna simply nodded. "Yes, my guess now is that a god was trying to communicate to you, probably Elyphr, the goddess of night. The Nightstones worshiped her and worked closely with her, so it is possible that she knew of you and communicated to you, and I without her knowledge brought you here."

"Can you talk to the gods?"

"No, only Clerics can choose to talk to the gods and be answered, but I know the Clerics that served with the Nightstones, and I believe the High Cleric still resides in the manor."

"Manor? Nightstone Manor? Clerics, gods, responsibilities, and destinies. I'm starting to really get stressed out, Akuna," Rosella said, chewing her inner lip with growing anxiety.

"If it means anything, you'll get unlimited food, and there is an archery range on site of Nocturnal Manor. Oh, and the manor is more of a castle, but the two terms are interchangeable in regard to your home," he said, as if any of this information would reassure her.

"That's all fine, but I have to get there, and what, am I expected to show up with open arms when I myself want to curl up and scream? So you realize the pressure that is now put onto me?" Rosella stammered as she fiddled with her necklace. The very necklace whose stone held much more significance than she could ever possibly imagine. "Also, side question, how the fuck am I going to continue the line? And do I just live out my days after claiming the land as my own? Be the queen of some land I've never heard of or seen? Should I even expect the people of that land to accept my rule?"

"I have high hopes that they will accept your rule, one way or another. As for continuing the line, I can think of one speaking kind that would gladly help you," Akuna said, his voice slowly turning into a mischievous snicker.

Rosella stopped in her tracks, and she saw that he was baring his teeth in a wide grin, and the look on her face made him chuckle both audibly and telepathically.

"I hate you so much," she said, shaking her head, then went to retrieve the arrow she shot earlier.

As she stalked away, she couldn't help but grin at the thought of Elaras' face when she perfectly shot the arrow at the berry and wouldn't mind seeing that look again.

5
El Cielo Rojo Ardiente

After resting and having lunch by the berry bush, Rosella and Akuna made their way out of the dense trees and continued on their way. Rosella had asked Akuna where the Nightstone land was, and he directed her toward the mountain peaks far in the horizon.

"Arja will be just before those, and the estate is on the foothills. The land itself stretches all the way to the Ocean of Sednas. It will take us time to get to Arja," Akuna had said as Rosella gathered her things to leave. That reminded her of a fantasy book from back home where a group of adventurers had to travel to a volcano, but at least in her own story she didn't have a cursed ring.

As they traveled, the land rose and fell, and the grass sang along with the wind, the never-ending trees dancing with the grass. She kept herself entertained by counting the animals she saw and noted the colors of their fur or feathers. After some time, she noticed that she had not seen a single dragon aside from the pair she saw the day before, flying or even resting their wings in the distance. Her own dragon companion was noticeably quiet, so she looked down and opened the flap where he resided. Akuna, in his adorable tiny form, was curled up in a deep, peaceful sleep. Smiling, she closed the flap and continued on with her path, admiring everything she saw.

I have to say, this world is a lot more beautiful than Earth, she thought to herself, then realized her words probably invaded Akuna's mind and would wake him up. When she did not feel a stir or see steam bellow out of the bag, she remembered that he said he could tune her out if needed. In a way she was thankful, but now she realized that she was alone. Not just alone—she was now a solitary person. There were likely thousands, millions of people in Dorthos, and yet she was the only human. The only person from Earth in Dorthos.

She was *truly* alone.

She grew more thankful for Akuna for being by her side and not leaving her absolutely alone, but he could not fully understand her thoughts or emotions for her situation. No one in this new world, her new home, could.

Wren, her true best friend, died in front of her eyes. Her mother did not have to suffer Earth's destruction, same with her beloved cat. What about everyone else on Earth? Those people in the dome must be really happy, but how were they feeling? Knowing the world outside the dome was completely destroyed, and how long would that dome survive? As for Rosella, she was in a whole new world, and everything had changed for her. Was there a single person on Earth living a completely normal life?

Slowly, the solitude and weight of her situation started to bear down on Rosella the further she walked. She had lived for twenty-eight years in a world that seemed simple, and now whatever was simple was gone. No more work, no more video games, no more driving. No more having conversations about average things like the taste of the work coffee or what new TV show was on Netflix or CrunchyRoll. No more picking up a cell phone and seeing what the weather would be like that day or seeing why some celebrity Rosella didn't care about was on the news. As she was thinking this, part of her brain clicked, and she stopped in her tracks. Quickly, she opened the magic pouch and stuck her hand into the black void.

"My cell phone!" she exclaimed out loud. Less than a second later, she felt something flat and cold appear in her hand. Lifting the object, she saw her cell phone with the glittery case on it, feeling a sudden rush of anticipation and excitement. She tapped the lock button and saw it illuminate instantly, the service bars empty but the battery at a hundred percent. "Holy shit! How is it fully charged?" she whispered to herself as she unlocked the screen.

There were no messages or calls, but that was expected, and the clock showed zeroes. She opened her camera and held up the phone to get the distant mountains and the rainbow saplings in one shot. After taking a moment to let the screen focus, she took a picture and immediately looked at the photo library. Surprised, there the photo was. She smiled, held the phone to her chest, then looked at the photo on the screen again.

She swiped through the photos and felt her eyes get hot and her chest tighten. The nostalgia was stronger than any other emotion she had felt the last two days, but she knew she needed to keep walking and pay attention. Sighing, she locked the screen and put the phone back into the magic pouch, feeling a kernel of peace flow through her chest.

"Human."

"Dragon."

"How long have we been walking?"

"Long enough for my legs to fall off my body."

"That'd be a hilarious sight."

"No, because then I would have to ride you, and you'd hate that."

"...I take back what I said."

"Mhm."

Rosella smiled and shook her head as she entered a small cave she had spotted along their path. There was a log near the entrance so she went to it and sat down, immediately stretching her legs. They had been walking for so long that the sun had mostly set behind the mountains with dregs of light piercing the sky.

Akuna emerged from the pouch and perched next to her on the log. Looking around the small cave, he spread his wings and hovered in front of her.

"Shall we rest here for the night?" he asked simply, and when she nodded yes, he flew to the entrance. Without effort, he blew out purple smoke, and before her, a curtain of thorns and ivy covered the mouth of the cave. "This will do for now since we will only be here for the night," he said as he flew back to her.

She nodded in response and took off the backpack and belt. As she was doing this, more purple smoke appeared, and she glanced over to see Akuna transforming to the form she had originally met in him, the white and red version of him that stood at her height. Something else she noticed were his wings, which were currently blowing up rocks and sand into the air. Instead of the stereotypical two massive wings she always imagined Western-styled dragons to have, she saw he had two sets of wings on each side of his body.

"Four wings?" she yelled, trying her best to keep her eyes

open from the dust flying around. She felt a rumble in her chest as he lowered himself to the ground and folded his wings to his body.

"Yes, and no, it is not normal. I am what you would call 'unique' among the dragon kind."

"Fucking obviously! What else is unique about you?" she asked excitedly, wiping the dust off her face.

Akuna chuckled and walked over to the log. "Many things, but I will not reveal all of my secrets. For now, let's worry about eating and sleeping."

Slightly disappointed but still fascinated, Rosella opened her bag and grabbed the food from the go-bags and the market from earlier. They ate in silence and as they finished, Rosella grew extremely tired. Akuna must have noticed because he blew up purple smoke and conjured a sleeping pad, a pillow, and a blanket. Thankful, Rosella lay down on the pad and fell asleep almost instantly. Her dreams turned into nightmares the instant she shut her eyes.

Bombs were blowing up in front of her face, her friend almost at the bunker but never making it inside, the sky turning red as the air around her thickened and burned. Her throat closed up as hot tears incinerated her face like acid, her screams silent as the bombs blew out her eardrums. Fires starting around her and the ash in the air scorched her skin with fourth-degree burns, the smell of smoke and death around her filling her nose. Begging to be saved by whoever was in the bunker but never making it inside as another bomb dropped on top of her and Wren.

In a flash, she saw a vast land of trees, mountains, lakes, and rivers in the colors of the rainbow. She stood on her balcony in her massive manor, her tiny dragon companion on the balcony railing sitting next to her hand. Years had passed since she became queen, and she was watching as the fields flourished and the sky glittered with gold. She wore a large gown and a black crown with detail she could not make out, but she felt royal and important. People of this land relied on her, and she felt the true weight of the crown that took her many years to accept.

As she looked at the cotton candy clouds, she saw that they were burning. The gold flecks had turned into black spots that were falling to the ground, the sky slowly turning to a vicious blood-red. The fields exploded, and the trees were blown out of their roots. People, her people, ran toward the castle, and Rosella screamed for them to turn around, that they were not safe. A black tube grew closer and closer to her, and the scream she released was guttural and surreal. Akuna grabbed onto her hand and grasped so tight that his claws sliced into her skin.

When the final bomb dropped on her, Rosella woke up, and though she was screaming in the nightmare, she was silent when she jolted awake. Her eyes flash around the cave and only saw darkness and whatever little moonlight the thorns and ivy let in through the cracks.

Taking in a deep breath, she tried to get up, but realized there was a massive weight on her torso and along her right side. As her eyes began to adjust to the low light, she saw that Akuna was resting his head on her and his body was between her and the entrance. Grateful for his presence, she laid her head back down and stared at the ceiling. The tears that were building up earlier and the ones she felt in her nightmare came to the surface, and she welcomed them wholeheartedly.

After countless minutes of crying deeply, her chest loosened, and she felt herself getting tired again. She wiped the tears away and sniffled hard, knowing she would have a massive headache in the morning. Before she fell asleep, she rested her hand on Akuna's nose and stroked the tip with her thumb. In her own way, this was the only way of thanking him for being there for her the entire time she'd been in this world.

Before she closed her eyes, she thought she saw a small gleam of a red eye being opened, then closing again. As she shifted herself to be more comfortable, she felt her hand pushed slightly to adjust it more fully onto Akuna's nose, and she knew that this was him welcoming her gesture.

6
Sulfur on Your Breath

Grand mahogany double doors with iron bars over the windows stood proud and tall in front of Elaras Moonshadow. A mansion stood even taller than the doors and was as long as a tiny village. The land the mansion resided on was a few miles outside Arja and north of the border, residing in Zebrial. The outside was bricked in black stone from the underworld and was crafted to mimic a castle.

Distant tapping could be heard while a soft *tsk tsk tsk* like a whisper caressed his ear. Images of a smiling woman with braided black hair crossed his mind, and he shook his head. He turned and saw that he was alone and that he himself was making the tapping noises with his foot. Why was his mind so distant, and why was it not recognizing simple things like his own foot tapping? Was it really Rosella taking up his mind already, the woman he met days ago but had dreamed of for three years?

Before he could even ponder an answer, the locks clicked and groaned, and the massive doors swung open away from him. In the entrance stood an elf man with deep purple skin and bright yellow eyes, his long dark violet hair slicked back into a low ponytail. His clothes were obnoxiously elaborate with gold trimmings on purple and black flowing fabric. He stood a few inches shorter than Elaras, and his face was clean and scarless, and it showed disdain but cleared when his eyes met Elaras'.

"Brother!" yelled the elf man as he rushed forward to hug Elaras.

Taken aback by surprise, Elaras wrapped a single arm around his brother and only held there for a few seconds before pushing him away gently. Elaras cleared his throat and straightened his cloak before walking inside.

"Alryo, no new scars, I see. Making the Clerics work harder than ever to hide them? What are you doing here, anyways? Shouldn't you be hunting the western lands? You know, doing Slayer duties and making lots of gold?" Elaras asked in a tone that was quick and light, confused why his brother would be here and not tracking a dragon. As they talked, they meandered toward the far end of the left wing of the mansion.

Alryo laughed loudly and clapped his older brother on the shoulder. "Did you not hear, Elaras? I'm going to be wed in three months!"

"Wed? To whom? Is this why Mother sent a sparrow for me?" Elaras stopped in the middle of a hallway, shocked and confused even more as to whom his younger brother could marry, and why he was to be wed at all.

"Lycilla Rockshire!" Alryo said excitedly while raising his arms in the air in joy. "Oh, brother, do you know what this means?"

"Rockshire? No, explain it to me clearly, Alryo," Elaras said, his body getting more tense with each breath he took.

"Elaras, it means that I will own the Arja land and bring it back to livable conditions! Isn't that amazing?" Alryo said as he grabbed his brother's shoulders and shook him.

Elaras stared at his brother as he stepped away from him. "The entire Rockshire family was killed after they all murdered the Nightstones. How is there a Rockshire left thirty years later?" Elaras said, crossing his arms, closely watching his brother.

"She told me she was away at a friend's home when the family was killed. She saw all of her family dead when she came back the next morning and ran away. Lycilla returned once things settled down but realized she would not be able to rule with her own name, given the history." Alryo grimaced. His eyebrows furrowed as he shook his head mournfully. Perking up in an instant, his eyes fell on Elaras once more, a grin spreading on his face. "So, when she found me patrolling the border of Arja for dragons, we got to know each other and after a few weeks, she begged me to marry her! Mother and Father already approved of the marriage, and me and Lycilla will both rule the grand and beautiful land of Arja! Aw, come on, brother, this is the best news! Why aren't you excited for me?" Alryo finished with a flourish.

While Elaras felt ice pierce his leathers and tasted bitterness on his tongue, he could see his brother was joyful. Alyro's entire body was bouncing, and his eyes were wide with glee. His smiling mouth bared teeth that reflected the lit wall-sconces. Elaras felt he was staring at a live portrait of a jester, begging for approval.

"How do you not see this as problematic? Again, the Rockshires *murdered* the Nightstones to usurp them. They were killed off for a reason. They killed a widely beloved and historic family, and now you want to help continue that hateful and vengeful legacy? Of course she won't end up ruling or being accepted. What makes you believe she was not involved? She could be lying to save face," Elaras said, trying his best to contain his anger towards his brother. The more his brother spoke, however, the more furious he was growing.

"Because we don't live in Arja, and she was hiding for the last thirty years? Duh? It's fine, and since she's marrying me, her rule should be more accepted because of Father's position! She wouldn't lie to me!"

"Why would they accept your rule more than hers? Father is still not well known up here on the surface, brother. Because to my knowledge, the people don't know you, and we aren't native to this land. What makes you so confident they will immediately accept your rule when they are waiting on a Nightstone? Yes, the land is dying, and crops are failing there, but even in their desperation, Arja will not accept a Rockshire. And *of course* she would lie to you if it meant changing the perception of her family!" Elaras said as he stepped closer to his brother. Rosella crossed his mind once again as he stared intently at his brother and knew at this moment that telling Alryo or his family that another Nightstone did exist was not smart. He needed to keep that information to himself. He needed to make sure she stayed safe.

"So you don't support my marriage or have faith we will rule Arja?" Alryo asked, not moving away from Elaras and having the gall to downturn his smile and let his shoulders droop dramatically.

"Fuck no! To be honest, your Rockshire girl will probably be killed before she can truly take power!" Elaras yelled, waving his hands in the air in frustration. He pinched the bridge of his nose and took in a strained breath. "You're better off marrying the princess of Gemstie, Alryo."

"*Her*? She looks like an ogre mixed with a dwarf!" Alryo exclaimed, scrunching his nose. He looked up to the dark walls, Elaras following his eyes for a moment. These halls were dark, and misery filled Elaras' veins as his eyes traveled the length of the hall. Alryo's voice brought him back from a shadowy-filled depth. "Besides, what about you, Mr. Lonely and Grumpy? When are you going to meet someone and marry off? Why haven't the parents arranged something for you by now?"

"Because I'm never home long enough for them to arrange anything for me, and it'll stay that way. Where are they?"

"In the sitting room. Come on," Alryo said as he gestured to the closed sitting room doors just to their right.

Elaras did not hesitate to take the double doors and push them open dramatically. He entered and saw his mother, Evanora, with her lavender skin with gray eyes like his and her deep blue hair that was in a neat bun. She was wearing similar lavish clothes as Alryo, as well as his father Kaine, who was sitting next to his mother on the loveseat drinking from petite teacups. His father had deep midnight-blue skin and graying violet hair cut short, so his piercing yellow eyes were the main focus of his face. As the doors banged against the walls, they both looked up, and pure excitement spread across Evanora's face.

"Ah, Elaras, my sweet boy! You came!" exclaimed Evanora as she sat down her tea and walked over to him. She wrapped her arms around him and held him tightly, her fingers digging into his leather armor.

Feeling the annoyance he felt of coming back home, he didn't hesitate to embrace her in a loving hug after giving her a peck on the cheek.

After a moment, she released him but held him at arm's length, looking at him up and down. "Darling, where have you been? I've missed you."

"Just been patrolling and making inquiries about things, you know. What about you, Mother? Approving doomed marriages?" Elaras smiled, noticing that he was still speaking quick and light, but he held a smile as he was genuinely happy to see his mother.

She playfully smacked his shoulder and drifted back to the

loveseat. Kaine, Elaras noticed unsurprised, had not gotten up to greet Elaras.

"Well, you see, darling, there aren't many positions left to take power in this realm," Evanora said as she picked up her tea again but remained standing. "Your father agreed that if the Moonshadow family is to make an imprint on Dorthos after leaving the underworld, one of our sons needs to wed into a powerful family. The most available and most attractive, and frankly the easiest, was the Rockshire girl because her family did successfully take over the Arja province."

Elaras took a few steps toward his mother and crossed his arms. "The Rockshire girl is not the true ruler of Arja. You know that. No one but a Nightstone could rule Arja. So why approve of this? She will get killed before she takes power, along with Alryo simply for marrying her. And now that I think about it, she doesn't even have a night stone to her name, and the true family has those stones and can wear them and sit on the throne. She will be unsuccessful one way or another."

In that instant, Kaine stood up so quickly that his legs bumped into the table that was in front of the loveseat, causing the table and its contents to fly and shatter. "What would you know about royal politics, *boy*? All you do is walk around this filthy land and fight anything that even looks at you. At least your brother is a Slayer and does something productive with his time. We will help *make* the people of Arja approve of Lycilla, and we will gain more power in turn. If they do not listen, then the *emperor* will make them listen," Kaine snapped as he stormed closer to Elaras. "All you do now is be a pest to those around you. What good have you done for this world and for us since we have come to the surface?"

Elaras scoffed and stood firm in his place, maintaining eye contact. "I feel like I'm the only one thinking logically about this.

As I see it, you're letting your younger son marry into the very family that destroyed one family to gain their seat, just to get their own line destroyed by a still-unknown force. And all for what, power that doesn't exist for others outside of the Nightstone family? I know the emperor is smarter than that, so I doubt he will ever back you. If another Rockshire rises, I believe that the same unknown force will come back and kill off your new daughter-in-law and your son, and perhaps even you, Father. This will not work, and besides, the people of Arja will not accept her. I will not take part in this re-usurpation of land that does not—"

"*Enough!* You know *nothing* of politics. You *will* accept Alryo's marriage, and you *will* take part because this world will die if Arja goes any longer without a proper ruler! Do you understand me?" Kaine yelled, using his magic to amplify his voice. Shallow orange smoke seeped from his fingers and the corner of his mouth when he spoke, dissipating when he was finished speaking.

Elaras' ears rang, and he had to readjust his vision, but he still stood in front of his father, angry that he would still use his magic against him. Kaine stared at his son with a furious blaze in his eyes, breathing so heavily that each exhale caused Elaras' hair to move.

After a minute of this, Elaras hesitated to nod with a smirk as he uncrossed his arms, a hand near a concealed dagger. He risked taking a step back, and when he saw his father did not move after him, he walked toward the door. Notably, his mother and brother were frozen where they stood and did not speak.

"Lovely chat, Father, but I must be on my way. Nothing productive will be done if I am here. Mother, I love you. Be safe, please," he said as he opened the door and looked back at his mother.

Evanora was still panting but was standing tall and defiant.

She nodded subtly with a small smile, then looked back to Kaine and walked over to place a hand on his back.

Elaras turned and left through the double doors and entered the hallway that led back to the main entrance. As he walked away, he heard the desperate voice of his brother call for him. Alryo was running to him, the lavish fabrics flowing behind him as he got closer.

"What, brother?" Elaras asked, annoyed he couldn't make his grand escape.

Alryo stopped short and took a ragged breath before asking, "Are you really not excited for me to get married?"

Elaras took an annoyed deep breath and placed a hand on his brother's shoulder. "If you were marrying someone else, yes. Instead, you're marrying someone I cannot stand behind and may be your ruin. Do you even like her, or is this all *politics*?"

Alryo shrugged and looked down the hallway toward the sitting room. "I do like her, brother, and I'd do anything for her. No, I don't understand everything that will happen, but I have to trust our parents, right? After all, they scraped their way to the surface on their own, and the Moonshadow name isn't completely unknown. I'll remember what you said, since you have seen more of the world than I have."

"Well, you've killed more dragons than I have, so that is something," Elaras joked as he placed his hand on top of another dagger, one that wasn't concealed.

"That's because you've killed *zero* dragons! What do you even do on your own?" Alryo asked curiously. "And don't give the same answer you gave Mother."

"Simple: I explore. I meet people, annoy people, fight those that annoy me, lots of stuff. Anything to stay away from home. By simply talking to the people of Dorthos, I have learned so much, and I don't need to kill dragons to feel fulfilled," Elaras said in a manner that was meant to romanticize, but Alryo looked unimpressed.

"So with all of your traveling, you haven't met one person you could marry? How boring. At least you're some sort of rogue. That's interesting, I guess."

"Meeting someone isn't my focus. Eventually it may be, but I have things to do until then. Now, if we're done chatting, I'll be off. Send a sparrow whenever you both make the invites for the wedding," Elaras said as he sauntered away from Alryo and headed to the door, his cloak billowing behind him. The last thing he wanted was to spend another minute in this house and with his controlling father and idiotic brother.

Mystrias Nightstone, the kind and loving princess and daughter of the stoic and strong King Raynne Nightstone, had been Elaras' teacher when he was young. Elaras learned at the age of six that he could use magic, and Mystrias was the teacher at a primary school for magic-wielding children. She taught him for ten years, and she was still one of the most powerful and humble magic teachers he had ever had. When he was sixteen, he learned of the devlairs that killed the Nightstones, and he along with many others in Arja vowed that they would avenge her and her family's death. However, someone completed the task first.

Now, if he ever found the one responsible, he would have to tell them that a Rockshire was still alive and planned on taking over the land again. There were no clues as to who killed the Rockshires, just that there were traces of magic and fire at the scene. He had been following leads throughout the land for the last thirty years that led to theories, learning more about magic and about the people and the land along the way.

The last time he was in Arja, an interim leader had been appointed in the capital, Rion, until a rightful ruler would come along. The leader was doing their best, but he knew they were there purely for delegation and control management reasons. He knew they were waiting for another Nightstone to appear because of how loved the family was, but after thirty years, the search seemed doomed. Admittedly, Elaras thought the idea of waiting around for a new Nightstone was laughable until he started having dreams of a black-haired woman with a white streak in her hair. The night stone necklace dangled from her neck, and she was smiling at him, her voice cooing at him, but he was unable to understand her words.

The last three years he had been searching for this woman all across Dorthos, never stopping and exhausting every resource. He took a chance in Misty Trace, his gut telling him something would happen while he was there. Something about the inn drew him in, and when he turned to see Rosella, he knew instantly she was the woman from his dreams. The night stone pendant around Rosella's neck was not to be mistaken for any other stone, and her hair was exactly as it was in the dreams. Her voice—however curt—sang to him like it did in countless dreams as she spoke to him in that dingy inn. Rosella had been tired and had seen better days, he knew, but he felt like his life was beginning anew.

A sudden pang of anxiety filled his chest as he thought of Rosella and came to the realization that she was in fact a true Nightstone, a historic noble and of pure royalty. She was meant to be the ruler of Arja, and they were waiting for her. Did she even know there were people needing her? She looked young, so perhaps she had no idea what even awaited her, but how could she not know? What was odd was that it seemed that Rosella didn't seem too worried about, well, anything. Why, then, was she in Cupridale and not in Arja? Why was she so far from her home and from her throne? Was she a distant cousin or someone that was hidden away early on and managed to escape, and had no idea what happened to the family?

Elaras needed answers. He needed to understand why she was in his dreams. The overwhelming weight of desperation to help filled his chest that sat next to the anxiety as he peered down the path in the direction of where he last met Rosella. Rosella needed to know that someone was after her throne, and to be warned of what his father was capable of. Arja needed her, only her, and he felt deep in his soul that he needed to help her however he could.

Tingling nerves and quickened breaths made Elaras stop on the path and look up. The night sky with the light of the full moon cast dark and long shadows through the leaves and onto the path in front of him.

"Who are you, Rosella Nightstone?" he whispered to himself before taking a deep breath.

When he inhaled, the world around him darkened and froze the air around him, causing his purple skin to prickle, and his dark blue hair stood on end. When he exhaled, he saw his breath appear slowly as white fog in front of his face and float up at a snail's pace. The fireflies that flew above stilled in midair, acting as stationary lanterns along the path in front of him. For some reason, fireflies always shone brightly while he was in his haven, and he had grown to cherish their presence while he was in this silent space.

Smiling, he continued forward at a normal pace, watching the world around him stay still and silent. He increased his speed to a run and headed in the direction that he guessed Rosella would take, towards the border of Arja.

"I'll find you, Rosella," he vowed, "I have to."

7

The Giant's Mournful Croon

"*Ow!* Akuna?" yelled Rosella as she tried to peer out of the hanging wall of thorns and ivy the next morning. As she placed her hand on the flora, the thorns had poked her finger, and it was now oozing a green liquid. Her vision started to blur. "Oh my god, what is happening?"

"Did you touch the thorns?" came a bored voice from behind her. Akuna stepped forward and looked down at her finger. "You did. You should have asked first. Those are bronka thorns, and the acid inside them can cause dizziness, hallucinations, nausea, dysentery, or death."

"You sound like a medicine commercial!" she screeched and looked frantically between all five Akunas that stood before her. She held out her hand to the closest one and said, "One of you, heal me please!"

Laughter rang through her ears as she saw purple fly through the air and toward her finger and her face. A moment later, her vision cleared, and the throbbing in her finger subsided.

"Why didn't you tell me those were acidic thorns?"

"Do you not have those on Earth?"

"No!"

"You should, they're quite useful, really."

"Sure, let me go tell some botanists to mutate some thorns. *Oh, wait*, they're probably dead."

"Maybe one remains in that dome? Shall I send you there to discuss this with them?" Akuna chortled.

"Oh my god, no." Rosella exasperated while pinching the bridge of her nose.

"Which one?"

"One what?"

"Gods. Which god are you referring to?"

"*Any of them!*"

Akuna laughed as he let his purple smoke float out of his mouth and onto the thorns and ivy. Seconds later, they disappeared, and the early morning sun poured into the small cave opening. "Had enough to eat?"

Rosella was gathering her things and met him at the entrance of the cave. "Yes, and the canteen is full again. I do have a request though, if you don't mind?"

"What is it, human?" Akuna asked quizzically, regarding her with his bright red eyes.

"Could you make me a cloak, please? I've always wanted one, and I think it'd help hide my appearance," she asked while fidgeting with her night stone. She wasn't sure why asking him for this made her nervous, but was happy to see a stream of that purple smoke surround her.

When the smoke was gone, a long, black, light-weighted cloak hung onto her body with the clasp being of a night sky with a crescent moon. The hood was large, and the edges of it stretched from one shoulder to the other, and despite its size it was comfortable to keep the hood up. Excitement took over, and she spun around in circles to see the cloak float and twist, then she lifted the edges and swished up and down like they were wings in her hands. As she felt the soft fabric of the cloak with her fingers, she realized that the cloak covered her backpack and made the cloak lift up significantly in the back.

"Do I look like a hunchback?" she asked, turning her body so Akuna could take a look.

"Oh, yes. Let's just put all your items in the magic pouch, except for the bow and quiver," Akuna said with a chuckle.

Rosella giggled a little at the thought and slipped the backpack off and somehow, with a little bit of effort, stuffed the entire thing in the pouch.

"This pouch reminds me of Mary Poppins' bag!" she said when she saw her backpack disappear.

"Who?"

"An icon, simply put."

"Hmm, I guess that makes you Mary Poppins then, since you have a bag similar to hers."

"Fuck yeah!" she said excitedly as she put on her bow and attached the quiver to her belt. The arrows dragged against the cloak slightly, but it did not bother her. "Ready to go?"

"A moment, please," Akuna said, and he blew purple smoke once more.

This time he blew it on himself, and before her eyes she saw him turn into a small emerald-green dragon with vibrant purple eyes. He still had four wings, but they were flapping more rapidly than in his bigger form. She smiled at him as she held a hand out flat for him to climb on. He flew the short distance and landed swiftly on her hand.

"Thank you for the cloak, Vikshae. It's wonderful," she said softly and smiled at him. The same deep rumble she had felt before shook her chest, and it made her smile even more. "How do you do that anyways?"

The look of surprise and confusion on his face was unexpected for Rosella, and her smile faltered.

"What do you mean, exactly?" he asked her while tilting his head.

"There is a weird, shaky feeling I get whenever something makes you happy, I guess? I've felt it a few times now. Do you not realize you do that?"

"No. I guess I'm pouring more magic into you than I thought, or that we are more connected than expected. It seems you can feel my high-level emotions, as I can feel yours."

"Last night, you felt them?"

"Yes."

"That makes sense. Thank you for being there for me then, too. I- It's been a long few days," Rosella said sheepishly. She looked down at her boots and tried her best to make the prickling feeling in her eyes disappear by blinking rapidly.

Akuna stood up in her hand and gently rubbed his face on her thumb, and the feeling of tiny scales rubbing up against her skin was odd but also comforting. A small lump got stuck in her throat, and her face heated more, so without saying much more, she smiled back up at him and started to move him toward his pouch.

"Let me rest on your shoulder inside your hood. I made the hood big enough so I could hide inside with the hood up or down," Akuna said, gazing up at her.

She nodded and lifted him up to her shoulder inside the hood. Once he was settled, she walked out of the cave and into the sunlight, toward Arja.

Three full days of traveling later, Rosella was cresting a sapling-covered hill that led to a small valley when a noise came from her left. As she looked to see, Akuna's voice turn harsh and quick.

"Duck!"

She flattened herself onto the ground, covering her head.

An instant later, a large gust of wind rushed past her, and a huge shadow crossed over them. When the shadow passed, she lifted her head and felt Akuna's head rub against hers to move past the cloak. In the air above the bottom of the valley was a shimmering, beautiful pink dragon with white horns and spine spikes, bigger than Akuna's normal size. The feather-like tuft at the end was a blur as the dragon flew around. The dragon dipped into the valley and was now making circles around a flock of sheep, as if corralling them and picking which one to take. As they flew, they opened their mouth and song notes came out in a calming and mesmerizing rhythm.

"Another dragon! And they're singing?"

"Salista Dila Brentious. She has a kind soul if you don't get in the way of her food. She uses her throat to sing prey into submission for easier consumption."

"Got it. Should we wait till she goes away, then?"

"Probably best, though I've known her long enough that if she spots you, I can talk her out of incinerating you."

Below, Salista picked up two sheep from the flock with her jaws and swallowed them whole while still flying in circles. Rosella was enchanted by her movements and her effortless ways of getting the sheep to be calm despite a dragon flying overhead. The sight was nothing like Rosella had ever experienced, and she knew she could watch Salista all day if she was able.

However, when Salista made the motion to grab a third, a large arrow bolt the size of a tree flew through the air above her head. The song Salista sang stopped abruptly, and the air from her wings blew up grass and rocks as Salista recentered herself.

Rosella whirled in the direction where the bolt came from, and in the distance saw someone setting up a second bolt into a massive ballista. Salista saw this too and flew toward the scrambling elf Slayer, letting out a monstrous roar that echoed through the valley.

"*Should we do something, Akuna?*" Rosella asked in a panicked tone, watching the Slayer carefully as they scrambled to finish setting up the ballista.

"*No, we must watch this play out. We cannot intervene. If the bolt hits Salista, that is just the way of life here. If she kills the Slayer, then that is one less killer we have to worry about,*" Akuna said in a dark tone, and Rosella felt helplessness surge through her veins.

As Salista drew closer, the Slayer got behind the ballista, aimed, and fired. The bolt shot out at a surprising speed, and it struck Salista in the neck.

A loud cry of pain erupted from her as she flew straight into the ballista and crashed on top of it. Her body covered the entirety of it, but it still seemed to stay intact. As Salista released one last cry of pain, loud cheers could be heard from a pair of people. The purple-skinned elf Slayer, who was dressed in black and purple robes, and a young woman with dark orange skin and large black horns protruding from her forehead then arched over her head and poked upward at the back of her head. The devlair that wore green and black robes cheered with the Slayer as Salista's wound bled out and her wings drooped over the ballista.

A deep and guttural sigh took over Rosella's mind and chest, and she felt a tremor next to her head. She dipped her head down as she herself felt anger and sadness trying to erupt through her throat, but knew she needed to stay where she was and not make herself or Akuna known. When she lifted her head again, she saw that the Slayer had ripped the bolt out of Salista's neck and was setting it to the side of the ballista.

"How the fuck is this okay? They just killed a beautiful dragon! Any dragon in general!" she snapped, not taking her eyes off the Slayer and the devlair. A feeling of sorrow filled her body as she felt Akuna dip further into her hood to lay on her upper back near her neck. She had the feeling that he could not bear the sight of one of his kind being killed, and she was happy that he decided to not look any longer.

"Honestly, I could not tell you. What I am thankful for is that not many dragons get killed throughout the year, but the loss is still felt," Akuna said, sadness lacing every word he spoke.

"Well, I fucking hate it. You are not leaving my sight, ever. If a Slayer wants to kill you, they have to kill me first," Rosella said, hoping that even though she was a human and Akuna was a dragon, that the sentiment of the words rang true to Akuna.

In response, she felt the same rumble as before but softer and gentler. Along with the rumble, a balmy warmth filled her chest, and she took in a deep breath to try and relax her nerves.

They lay there on the hill for what felt like an hour as the Slayer and the devlair loaded Salista onto a flat cart pulled by a few draft horses. When her lifeless body was tied down and the ballista was hooked onto another set of draft horses, the two set off in the opposite direction of where Rosella and Akuna were.

Rosella let her head lie flat into the soft green and purple grass to breathe a sigh of relief. *"Ready to go, Akuna?"*

"Yes. Arja is another day's travel, but there is a village nearby we can rest at."

"Sounds good. A warm bowl of soup sounds good right about now," she said as she stood up and stretched her sore limbs. Tiny

claws stuck into her skin as he climbed off her back and onto her shoulder.

"*Soup?*" he asked as he appeared on her shoulder, his purple eyes looking up at her. He had not changed his shape since the cave a few nights before, and she did not expect him to in the next coming days since there were now people nearby.

"*Yeah, it's meat and veggies put in broth. You drink the broth and eat the soggy food. It warms the soul, really, if made correctly. How do you not know what soup is?*"

"*That sounds disgusting, and because dragons do not drink soup.*" Akuna huffed and turned forward, judgement resting on his face.

"*You eat rats!*" she said, appalled as she walked down the hill and away from where the Slayer and devlair went.

"*We discussed this, and you will lose this discussion again, human.*"

"*Try some soup, and you'll change your mind.*"

"*Eat a rat, and you'll change your mind.*"

"*Ugh, no thanks.*"

"*Mhm.*" Akuna chuckled, and they made their way until they came across a small village and found the inn.

After eating and having some ale, Rosella brought a bowl of soup up to their room for Akuna to try. When she was done bathing and changing before bed, she came back to an empty bowl and a sleeping and noticeably rounder Akuna.

"Ha, told you," she said quietly to herself as she continued to get ready for bed.

8
Lunar Invasion

The next morning, she made her way to a nearby market that resembled Misty Trace's. She bought some fruit, dried meats, and surprisingly some soap that one vendor was selling. The soap smelled of wildflowers, so she bought two bars and stowed them away in the magic pouch.

"Akuna, how much money do I have anyways?" Rosella asked curiously as she walked out of the market and into a nearby forest that led to Arja.

"You don't have to worry about that," he said in a cool tone, and she felt him poke his head out beside her neck to see the path ahead. By now the village could not be seen through the trees behind them, so he must have felt safe enough to make an appearance.

"What? Why shouldn't I worry about money? Won't I run out?"

"Let's just say the Nightstones were very wealthy, and now their entire fortune is yours."

"Wait," Rosella said, and she stopped in her tracks as what he

said hit her like a brick. *"Did their wealth not go anywhere? What do you mean, exactly, that their fortune is mine?"*

Akuna appeared in front of her as he hovered, staring at her with a weird mixed look of annoyance and perplexity. *"Some of their wealth was used to keep Arja afloat until those in Arja could maintain their finances, but the rest is now in your possession as you are the only Nightstone in this world."*

"So, I'm rich now? Was the money given to me when I came to Dorthos via this pouch?" she asked while tapping the top of the magical pouch where she had always pulled the gold chips from. When he nodded in response, she let out a sigh and let her eyes drift into the trees. "Holy fuck," she let out audibly as she felt her chest pound with her own anxiety. "This is another thing to remind me that this is real, not a dream."

"In a way, yes. Remember, you are the rightful queen of Arja. I know this is still a lot to take in, but once you get into the manor, I think the nerves will settle, and the transition will be easy."

Rosella took a deep breath and looked forward onto the shadowed path, and for a reason she wasn't sure of, she placed her hand on the grip of the dagger that rested on her belt. As she strode forward, she noticed a faint red glow come from where her hand rested on the dagger. Looking down, she saw that the ruby that was in the pommel was glowing so brightly the grass around them reflected the red light.

"What the fuck?" she said quietly but audibly as she let go of the grip. She stopped walking as the ruby dimmed quickly upon release. Surprised, she placed her hand on the hilt again, and the glow returned. "Is this part of the magic Shadow Breaker holds? Do I have to have my hand on it to activate it or something?"

"Something like that, Rosella," said a smooth and cool voice, and there was a shuffling of feet behind her.

Taken by surprise, she whirled around with her right hand

latching on the dagger again and her left outstretched to hit or defend from whoever was behind her. When her left hand made contact with whoever was behind her, a loud *boom* sounded, and a red light with sparks exploded from her left hand.

The person that she hit flew through the trees and landed with a thud into a tree trunk out of sight. Below her feet was a small crater where dirt, rocks, and dust got pushed outward, and a ring of the debris surrounded her.

"Holy shit!" Rosella screamed as she lifted both hands to her mouth and gaped in the direction the person flew. At this moment she realized that her hood had fallen back from the shockwave but did not move to turn it up again.

"Holy shit *is appropriate. That dagger, Shadow Breaker, must give you explosive strength when you hold it,*" Akuna said in a curious tone as he carefully peered from behind Rosella's neck to look down at the dagger.

"Hello?" Rosella called out, taking a few steps forward. She hadn't intended to hurt the person; she was just caught off guard.

"Ouch," came a soft but familiar voice. When Rosella heard the voice a second time, she immediately dropped her hands and rolled her eyes, putting her hood back up in the process.

"Elaras, you're an idiot for not telling me what this thing could do," she called out, not moving forward anymore as she grew annoyed that Elaras would sneak up on her.

"I figured it would be fun if—ow—you figured out the magical properties for yourself," came his voice from behind the trees, and slowly he reappeared. His hand was rubbing his jaw liberally, but there was an unmistakable look of being impressed on his face. When she saw him, she felt tingles run though her body, but chose to ignore the feeling.

"I figured out it was magical when you gave it to me, but I still don't know what it does or even how to use any dagger. Also, I am not sorry for hitting you," she said, crossing her arms. Turning down onto the path again, she took a few steps away. "Anyways, since I didn't call for you, have a good day. I need to get somewhere before the end of the day." As she walked on, she heard quick footsteps coming up behind her.

"I just want to talk, Rosella," Elaras said as he met Rosella's stride and strolled alongside her. When she rolled her eyes and kept walking forward, he laughed and stepped closer to her. "Are you playing hard to get?" he asked in a cheeky tone.

"There is nothing to get, Cricket. I'm just making my way to a place and preferably without you. I need to be alone," she said in a snarky tone, taking a step away from Elaras. She knew that he might be valuable to have as an ally if she ever needed one, and he really was not bad company, but she wanted to just be with Akuna. Akuna was the only thing that she trusted in this world, and she wanted to learn as much as possible from him before anyone else joined them.

"Is it Arja that you are going to? Given that you are a Nightstone, of course. Where else would you be going?" he asked, and at his question, she side-eyed him.

"Yes, and I'm guessing you put that together and figured out my name from my necklace?"

"Of course. Only the Nightstone family can wear those."

"Duh, otherwise whoever would have the nerve to steal it would be stupid, and mine was given to me by my mother," Rosella said, a small tang of nervousness filling her chest.

"Ah, so your mother gave it to you. What was her name?" he asked as he turned around and walked backward. He held a mischievous gaze that was also lined with curiosity.

"Yeah, not gonna tell you. Anyways, what did you want to talk about? Since it seems I can't get rid of you," she said, rolling her eyes and immediately finding the connection with Akuna. "*I feel like I have to be really careful with what I say now. Am I doing alright?"*

"You're doing well. I will take over if the need arises," Akuna said, and she could feel him move around in her hood. She pulled her braids to sit on top of her cuirass rather than inside her hood so he could hide easier behind her hair. He was still in her hood but resting at the base of her neck on her upper back.

Rosella was so focused on Akuna's words and movements that she did not immediately see that Elaras had stepped in front of her and stopped dead in his tracks. She collided with him, and it felt like she ran into an obnoxious wall that was covered in leather and daggers. Her eyes shot up in annoyance and saw he was staring back at her, but his eyes were full of apprehension and seriousness.

"Rosella, I know you won't believe me because we don't know each other very well. All I have done is tease you and frustrate you, but would you please trust me at this moment?" he asked her warily, and she noticed that his smooth voice lost its oily texture. His tone was now sharper and more careful rather than loose and rebellious.

"Okay? What is it?" she asked, not breaking eye contact.

He nodded and placed his hands on her shoulders, making her skin prickle in a pleasant way but making Akuna shrink back into the hood. Before Elaras spoke, he took in a deep breath as if he had to brace himself. "How much do you know about what happened to your family?"

"Assume I know enough. If I don't know something, fill me in later. I've been...away, so I may not know everything," she said, ending what she said quietly because as she spoke she realized it was probably the wrong thing. Thankfully, Elaras pushed on rather than questioned her.

"Well, one of the Rockshires, the devlair rebels that killed the

Nightstones, is still alive. I'm not sure how or if she was even involved, but she is set to marry my brother, Alryo, despite my protests, to have more power behind her for when she tries to take over Arja," he said with the same look of apprehension, but was calm and patient. "I think we need to get there as quickly and quietly as possible to make sure they don't take over."

Rosella knew instantly that what he just said affected Akuna deeply because her vision blurred with a purple hue and emotions that were not her own filled every millimeter of her body. Fury and anger dropped in her stomach so hard that her knees became twigs instead of bone and muscle, and her skin prickled and her face burned with malice. A blood-curdling scream became lodged in her throat, but she pushed it down before every muscle in her body tensed up.

Akuna's tiny claws dug deep into her back, and Rosella tried her best to not flinch in pain and keep eye contact with Elaras. Through his magic, her eyebrows furrowed, and she bared her teeth as he took in a heated intake of air as if about to breathe fire. As he did this, her vision turned a deeper purple once more, and Akuna spoke with Rosella's voice.

"A Rockshire is alive?" Akuna said, each word biting into the other and her own throat straining with each syllable. "They will be the end of Arja as we know it if we do not stop her."

Elaras nodded and gripped her shoulders tighter, and Rosella curiously wondered if he could feel that her skin was overheating. "Yes. Lycilla Rockshire. I think she's lying to my brother about being in hiding and not being involved. I think she's saying that for a better perception. The last thing I want is for her to take over, and not just because I believe my brother will die in the crossfire too. Honestly, I will not be saddened by his loss."

Akuna's anger was growing, and Rosella thought that her body was about to explode with how hot her skin was getting and how intense her insides were shaking. Before she could try and ask Akuna if she would be okay, he spoke again to Elaras with her strained voice. "We need to find out how she is alive, and we need to end her. I need to save Arja, and that usurper will *not* succeed."

"I agree! And I do believe we need to find out as much information as we can! I just wish we could find and tell the thing that killed the Rockshires in the first place what is going on too, then they'd be able to help. I've been trying to find them for years with no luck," Elaras said excitedly while letting go of her shoulders to gesture with his hands, the stress his face held slowly seeping away. "So, could I travel with you? It'll be better to have an ally rather than go alone to face her and my family. You may be a Nightstone, but one person cannot take on my father. The necklace should be enough, but I'll help solidify your position. I know the people of Arja, and I know they will side with you. Let me help you stop her."

While Akuna was still very angry that she could feel his anger in the core of her body and her skin, his control faded, and her vision returned to normal.

"We shall travel with him. I do not see him turning on you, and if he does, he will be dealt with," came Akuna's voice, his voice still clipped and straining with anger, and she could feel hot steam on the back of her neck where he sat. She looked up to Elaras and laid her hands on his outstretched arms.

"Alright, on two conditions," she said in a serious tone, hoping he would not mistake her words for anything else. When he nodded in response, she continued, "First, whatever I tell you about myself, no matter how crazy it is, you must keep to yourself only. Do *not* tell anyone, or I will shoot your eyes out. Second, whatever question I have, answer it with no judgment. Don't dance around the subject and tell me I need to figure it out for myself. If I'm to take back the Arja throne for the Nightstones, I need to be as prepared as possible. Deal?"

Elaras leaned in so close to her to the point that she could see the details in his gray eyes. Her heart quickened as her fingertips dug deeper into his arms, her body begging to touch more of him.

"Deal," he said simply before pulling out of her grasp. He turned toward the path and extended an arm to lead her forward.

9
Dive In, Take a Breath

They hiked through the forest toward Arja for most of the day, surprisingly not saying too much to each other. Elaras walked in silence, taking out a dagger every now and then to polish it or to thumb the edge of a blade. Rosella, on the other hand, was having a few conversations with Akuna. Towards the end of the day, the trees thinning out, Rosella started another conversation with him.

"Okay, so what do we do if he sees you? Wouldn't that be bad?"

"Obviously, but if he does see me, there are two options: I kill him, or I rip his tongue out."

"That is a bit much, isn't it? Maybe we could make him swear to not say a word, threaten him with it like I did earlier?"

"It would be fun to intimidate him, maybe make him pee a little. That would be an enjoyable sight, to see a speaking kind embarrass themselves."

"Akuna! Well, you're not wrong though, that would be entertaining," Rosella said, accidentally letting out a small giggle.

Elaras immediately looked over at her with a smirk on his face, his sixth dagger in hand. "What's so funny, Nightstone?" he asked, stowing his dagger and putting his hands behind his back, straightening his spine.

"The way you smell," she quipped and failed to hold in a chuckle when she saw his astonished face.

"I do not! I smell of pine and leather! Pine from the soap and leather from all this gods-damned leather!" he said while gesturing to the leather he was wearing. "Honestly, woman, if you're going to lie, at least be good at it."

She looked up and down at him and scoffed. "Yeah, and you're probably sweating a ton underneath all that leather. Unless, what, it's filled to the brim with magic?" she asked, not thinking that magic could help with things like body odor. When he laughed, she couldn't help but smile at the sound of his genuine happiness.

"Yes, it does, actually! This armor does not have many other magical properties besides odor controller, so it is more armor than magical. My magic comes from myself and myself only," he said as he danced his fingers in front of her face. A puff of deep blue smoke that was similar to the color of his midnight blue hair appeared from his fingertips. The smoke curled into a ball and sprang upward, then within a second, a black rose appeared fully bloomed. She glanced at the now smokeless rose, then looked back up at his gray eyes.

"Cute, but I hate roses," she said while taking the rose from his hand and smelling it. "How do you do that weird disappear-then-reappear again thing you did by the berry bush, though?"

His smirk grew wider than ever before he disappeared from sight. Slowly, she looked around and found him right behind her with purple baby's breath flowers held in his fingers.

She took the baby's breath and eyed him suspiciously before saying, "That didn't answer my question."

"That's for me to know and for you to figure out, Rosella," he said in a cheeky way, examining his nails as if this was a casual conversation.

"Hmm, well, it's really cool," she admitted, not being able to hold back her own astonishment. She had only seen Akuna's magic, and even his magic still surprised her whenever he used it.

Elaras walked up to her and grabbed the flowers from her hands. "What is a flower you love, then?"

"I don't have one. I don't really care for flowers," she said while shrugging.

"And why is that, *Rose?*" Elaras sneered playfully.

Rosella's eyes heated, and her fists clenched.

"Careful," Akuna's level voice came through, but Rosella grew more furious.

"Do *not* call me that, Elaras."

"And why is that, exactly?" the jovial purple elf said, leaning back, the flowers dancing in his hand.

"Only two people got to call me that, and they're dead—*that's* why," Rosella spat.

"Duly noted. Again, just say the word, and he'll no longer have a tongue," Akuna said while gently vibrating Rosella's chest.

Elaras' smile faltered, and his eyebrows shot up, then his expression relaxed. His blue smoke erupted from his fingers once again, and the rose and baby's breath disappeared in a deep black flame. He twisted his fingers again, and in front of her was a hand-sized snow-white flower she had never seen before. The flower had a ring of petals surrounding the pollen stems in the middle, and more petals descended outward from the center that increased in size. The fragrance of the flower burst through the air, and the aroma was intoxicating, the petals themselves dancing gently in the wind.

Rosella smiled so hard despite her anger at the sight of the flower that she felt her facial muscles stretch and crease. Grabbing the outstretched flower, she studied it closely, feeling the soft petals in her fingertips. While the flower itself had filled the air with its fragrance when it appeared, the aroma became more subtle. With each petal she stroked, the more relaxed she became. "This is beautiful. What is this?"

"The night queen, or the queen of the night," Elaras said softly with his usual smooth tone gently lacing his words. "It's the flower of your house, actually, but you probably already knew that. Naturally grown night queens bloom once a year for a week on the anniversary of the coronation of the current queen in power, but I can conjure them in a bloomed form whenever you want one. The ones at the castle have not bloomed in thirty years due to there being no queen. However, I suspect that will change when you take the throne."

She glanced up, and Elaras had an expression on his face that she had only seen infatuated men have in romance movies and TV shows. However, almost as soon as she made eye contact with him, the look disappeared, and he put on a shy smile while averting his gaze.

In a way, she was thankful because what he had said about the natural night queens struck her hard, and the look on his face made her a little overwhelmed. When she became queen, these flowers would bloom for years after. How many years would they come back? Would they symbolize something for the citizens? Would they celebrate? Choosing to focus on the smile on his face, she smiled and tried to ease the increasing anxiety in her chest.

"Thank you, Elaras. Unfortunately, this is my new favorite flower. Thanks for actually making me like flowers now. Well, this one at least," she said in a playful manner, stepping closer to him in hopes that he would face her. Despite her being rude and standoffish to him in almost every interaction, she wanted him to know that she was being genuine. She also needed that smile to face her. She needed to be distracted; she did not want to think of anything else.

He looked down and met her eyes. Their faces were less than a foot apart, and the way he was gazing down at her made her heart flutter even more and her breath shudder. Thoughts of the throne and of Arja disappeared, and all she thought of and saw was his gray eyes.

His shy smile became sweet and soft as he said, "I'm glad to hear that, Rosella. I'm guessing you don't like roses because of your name?"

"Yep. People think I love them, but it's the opposite. This," she said as she held up the night queen, "is a trillion times better than any rose."

He nodded and grinned, then a moment later he took a small step back. "Good, because it's *your* flower. That would be awkward if you didn't like your own flower. Now, let's get a move on. We're almost at the border. There's a cave I know of that is right on the edge and out of sight. We can rest there for the night. How does that sound?"

"That's fine. Arja is still quite large given its state, correct?" she said, carefully choosing which words to use to not stumble and embarrass herself.

"Of course. The land size has not changed. If anything, cities and villages have grown due to needing to house people, and that is based on when I was last there years ago. I'm worried the land has gotten worse since I was there last," he said, turning and leading the way to the edge of the forest.

She nodded and followed him, twirling the flower in her fingers, mesmerized by the dancing petals.

"And you scoffed at the thought of continuing the Nightstone line with him," Akuna said while laughing in her head, and she

gave such a big eye roll that she hoped he could feel it in his own eyes.

After another thirty minutes of walking in silence, there was a small cave opening to the left behind a small clump of trees that, without Elaras pointing it out, Rosella would not have seen.

"Are we going to be able to put up that wall of thorns again? Or do we just have to trust Elaras?" Rosella asked nervously as they made their way to the cave opening and inside.

"This will be the first test of trust. All creatures are at their weakest when they slumber," he said in a stoic manner.

Rosella and Elaras spent some time eating and drinking, making small chitchat before going to bed. She noticed that he positioned himself closest to the cave entrance but still out of sight from the outside, and she was thankful that he would take the measure. Within moments of setting her head on the pillow with her flower next to her head, she was asleep.

10
Bloodied Bloom

Whimsical music swelled so loudly that the notes of strings and
horns overwhelmed Elaras' ears, but the sight of Rosella
spinning in his arms in a blue and white dress made him feel
like he was floating. The ballroom was adorned with a rainbow
of colors, people of all races were dancing happily with one
another, and laughter of fellow members of high society filled
the room with positivity. He felt hair brush against his face as
he spun Rosella in place, her smile and her gentle touch
making him swoon deeper and further than he'd ever been
before.

"Don't drop me!" she yelped as he picked her up and spun her
in a circle, her arms wrapped around his shoulders.

"I can't drop you. We're levitating!" He laughed and looked
down to see that there were pink clouds holding them off the
ground. He stared back at her and smiled widely, her crystal blue
eyes sparkling in the silver and gold glitter that hung in the air
like stars. Placing her back on the cloud, he leaned in for a kiss
but stopped right before his lips brushed against hers.

"Are you happy to be queen?" he asked, his tone light with an edge of seriousness.

She smiled at him, her hand moving to hold his cheek. "Yes, and you helped me become queen. You saved me, and I'm forever grateful to you."

"Are you happy I'm here with you, to be your king?" he asked, nervous about the answer.

"Wake up!" said a soft voice from behind him, but it was harsh and quick.

Rosella didn't react to the voice, so Elaras ignored it.

Her eyes sparkled more than ever, and her face was full of happiness as she said, "I'm happy you're with me at all, Cricket. You aren't here for power. You just want to be with me, and because of that I—"

"Wake up!" interrupted the harsh voice again but louder.

Elaras turned around to see where the voice came from but saw no one. They had levitated so high on the cloud that the only person in his eye line was Rosella, with the others on the floor of the ballroom still dancing to the swell of the music.

He turned back and gripped her face gently in his hands. "I'm sorry, what were you going to say?" he asked desperately, hoping that whatever kept talking would stay quiet long enough for her to speak.

She laughed heartily, and she gripped his head tightly with her hands, her nails digging into his skin around his ears. "Darling, I was going to say, *wake up!*"

As she said the final two words, her face quickly transformed into a massive white and red dragon with menacing bright red eyes. The eyes glowed so vividly that the light blinded him, and the voice was loud and boisterous. The music had stopped, and the room fell into an unfamiliar shadow, the dragon being the only thing he could see or hear.

The dragon head roared and yelled once more, *"Elaras, wake up or she will die!"* Elaras fell backward off the cloud, and instead of hitting the ballroom floor, he woke up on a cave floor. Before him stood a devlair man, a dagger in his hand that was placed against Rosella's throat and his foot on top of where Rosella's night queen flower sat.

As blood spill from her cut skin, Elaras surged to his feet and tackled the devlair. He grabbed for the dagger, but the devlair flung his free fist to hit Elaras hard in the ear.

As his ear rang loudly and bled, the devlair man struggled to get up to run out of the cave. Elaras grabbed a hidden dagger along his thigh and threw it, striking the devlair in his retreating back. The devlair's dagger fell out of his hand, but he spun around and held out his hands in defense, begging for mercy.

"Why are you here?" demanded Elaras, fisting a dagger in each hand as he got up and stalked toward the devlair man.

The devlair, who was confident not even moments ago, was faltering under Elaras' gaze. "How are you alive?" the devlair cried out, shrinking in place as Elaras stepped closer to him.

"Answer my question first!" Elaras yelled, now holding up a dagger to the devlair's neck.

"I was hired! I'm a Slayer, but I was told to go after an elf with your description and whoever was with you! I wasn't given details past that. That's all I know!" he cried, his words coming out clipped and shaky.

"Who hired you?" Elaras spat, not caring if he woke up the whole forest outside the cave.

"Please don't kill me!" came the devlair once more before letting tears shed from his eyes.

"Elaras?" came a soft voice, and Elaras felt his heart skip a beat at the sound of her calling for him. Without looking at her,

Elaras sheathed the dagger and grabbed one of the devlair's horns.

"I'll be right back, Rosella. Don't go anywhere," he said coldly. Without another word or waiting for a response, he took two deep breaths and stepped forward.

The world around him and the devlair turned completely dark and icy, the shadows frozen on the ground. Elaras stared down at the devlair who was not frozen but scrambling to get out of Elaras' grip, his eyes flashing around the frozen cave. "You are not worthy of keeping alive, Slayer."

The devlair shot his fearful eyes to Elaras, and without a second thought, Elaras started to run, lifting the devlair in the air as he did so, feeling weightless in this state. He ran as fast as he could, and when he skid to a harsh stop, he dropped the haven at the same time he threw the devlair in the direction of a nearby boulder.

The devlair's body, meeting unfrozen time once more, flew so far and fast before he landed against the large rock with a loud crack and a splatter. Not waiting to confirm if the devlair was still alive, Elaras brought his haven back and ran to Rosella through the dark and icy air.

When he approached the cave mouth, he slipped out of the dark and welcomed the warmth from the campfire. He walked up to Rosella, who was propped up on her pad, looking around the small cave. When she saw Elaras approach her, he saw her face relax, and she lay back down on her pad.

"Why are you making so much noise, Cricket, and why are you up? I'm trying to sleep and so should you," she said, annoyed, but not taking her eyes off of him.

He leaned down and grabbed her chin, lifting her head upward to see the cut the devlair assassin left on her skin. Instead of sticky red blood splattered on her skin or clothes, he found a bare neck with no cut or bruising.

"What the Hells?" Elaras exclaimed as he shifted her head to the other side. He knew the assassin cut her. He saw the blade go into her skin and blood seep out. Elaras grabbed her wrist and pressed two fingers against her pulse.

Rosella, annoyed by his touching, tried to pull away from him, but he tightened his grip on her wrist and placed his other hand on her shoulder. Strong rhythmic pulsations made his nerves tingle pleasantly as he felt her heartbeat, and his own started to match her smooth rhythm. The hand on her shoulder squeezed deeply, and he felt the heat of her skin under his hand. Her warmth brought him out of his worry and panic, and he knew that despite what he saw, she was alive and unhurt.

"You alright, Elaras?" Rosella asked while staring at him with her tired eyes.

He let his gaze fall into hers, and he smiled, not letting go of her wrist or shoulder. "I'm sorry, I just thought..." he started, but realized that he would not know how she would react if he told her everything he just witnessed.

As he searched for words to say, her eyes began to droop, and her breathing slowed. Was she tired, or was she weak?

"I was going to heal you. I thought you got hurt. Did you heal yourself?" Elaras asked abruptly.

In the faint light of the campfire, he saw her face go into the same look of deep concentration he had seen her wear a few times since they had met, accompanied by a lengthened pause. He did not question her, seemingly wanting to be careful with her answers.

"I'm too tired to answer that. Are you okay, though? I'll be okay if you're okay."

"If *I'm* okay?" Elaras asked slyly, and Rosella's face grew annoyed, but a shy smile appeared as she turned away from him.

"Yes, if you're okay. Obviously, you are, so I'm going back to bed. Maybe put some protective shielding up or something in front of the cave entrance? Goodnight, Cricket," she said as she adjusted herself on her pad and turned away from him.

A pang of anxiety flooded his chest. He wanted to make her turn back around, to answer more questions that were flooding his mind, to ensure that she truly was okay. Nonetheless, he stood up and walked to the mouth of the cave, trying to steady his rapid breathing.

If she was injured and healed herself that quickly, that would mean she was an extremely powerful magic user. She didn't even seem aware of her wound. Did she subconsciously heal herself? He had heard rumors of people performing magic subconsciously, and it was possible she was one of them since she came from a powerful family. Was he wrong about her being a regular person? What else was he wrong about when it came to Rosella?

As questions flowed through his head, he whispered an incantation and watched as his blue smoke shot from his hands. A thick wall of black and blue ivy and roots covered the mouth of the cave and blocked out the early light of dawn. While he did so, something the devlair said while Elaras interrogated him was still stuck in his head, and the words took over every other thought.

"How are you alive?" the devlair had said, but those words confused him because was very much alive and breathing, to the point that he was able to handle the devlair and check on Rosella.

Curiosity started to take over, so he felt different parts of his body over the undershirt he was wearing for cuts or slashes. When he found none, he remembered the devlair seemed to favor the throat, so he placed his fingers on his own and started to move around. Within seconds of feeling his skin, he froze, dread drowning his chest as his heart rate soared sky high, and his breath caught in his throat.

Under his fingers, he could feel a raised new and tender scar that stretched from one side of his lower neck to the other in a perfect line, and due to the height of the scar tissue, he could tell it was a deep cut.

How did Elaras survive, though? Could he now heal himself unconsciously, or did some outside force help him? The voice he heard in his dream before waking up? Without realizing he was doing it, his other hand started his healing incantations, and blue smoke poured out his fingertips in smooth waves. After a few minutes, however, the scar did not subside and remained on his neck unchanged.

What the fuck? he thought to himself, and he gathered his leathers and put everything on. Once he buckled the top of his torso leathers around his neck, he felt that they covered the scar effortlessly. Letting a small amount of relief fill his body, he turned back to the ember-filled fire and started to make breakfast from things in his pack. The thought of what could have happened filled his morning thoughts, but he also knew he couldn't do anything else. Now he needed to figure out who sent the devlair to kill him and Rosella, and he had an idea of who.

11
Rotten Skittles

"Wait, what?" Rosella said as she ate a blue apple. She was sitting up and despite still feeling exhausted, she was listening intently to Elaras' retelling of last night's events down to the crushed night queen flower. Elaras had just finished explaining how he discovered the cut on his throat just an hour before and even unbuckled his collar to show her.

"I'm not sure, but what I'm more worried about is who is after me, and in turn you. We need to be careful about where we go and who we talk to. Rion is a few days' travel, but I think it'll take us about a week from now to get there safely, and that's cutting it closer than I would like to. Are you okay with that?" he asked, slicing up a pink pear with one of his smooth-sided daggers.

"I don't have magic and still can't use a dagger, so I'd rather be safe. I can only do so much with a bow," she said as she finished off her apple, feeling nervous now.

Elaras regarded her through his lashes and tilted his head as he chewed on a piece of pear. "That's better than nothing. Let's get going in a few minutes," he said, finishing his pear and packing up his items.

She thought of his cut and went to feel her own neck. Elaras was correct that there was no scar to be felt, and her mind drifted to Akuna.

"Did you heal him so he could protect me?" Rosella asked him, thinking she knew the answer already but wanting to confirm.

After a moment of silence, Akuna responded, *"Yes. I got to him before the devlair placed the dagger to your throat, so the devlair Slayer did not see me. I could have taken care of the devlair myself, but we need Elaras, and I could not let him die. I healed you while he was taking care of the devlair, though."*

"Wait. So if I die, you could bring me back to life?" she asked, shocked again at the power of Akuna's magic.

"Yes, ideally within a few minutes of your heart stopping. Elaras was only four seconds into death when I woke him, but I did not have time to heal him completely. The scar will remain, unfortunately."

"He tried to heal his own scar away, but he couldn't. Why?"

"Because my magic is more powerful, and if another's magic is weaker and is used against the same thing for the same purpose, it will be ineffective. Since he was trying to cover the scar made by my magic with his own, it would not work, hence his frustration with it."

"Whoa. Well, thank you for saving him, no matter how frustrating he is to be around."

"Frustrating mentally or sexually?"

"Rosella, are you almost ready?" came Elaras' voice from near the entrance of the cave just as she gasped and clapped her hand over her mouth.

In her head, Akuna was laughing maniacally so much that her chest was rumbling with his laughter.

"Yeah, just another minute or so!" she said as she scrambled to shove the rest of her things in her pouch. *"AKUNA!"* she yelled at him telepathically, and he laughed even harder.

After a few more minutes, they left the cave and headed toward the border of Arja. They walked through the lingering morning fog, and dew splattered onto their boots. The air was filled with moss and wet earth, morning flowers and weathered wood. Birds chirped merrily, and bugs sang their dreary songs as they continued on over a hill where the land lit up.

The low-hanging sun pierced the land between the trees, and each ray of light was sharply defined by the fog that clung to the ground. She could feel the heat of each ray she walked into and the cold of the shadows behind the trees. Her hand drifted up and her fingers played in a sunbeam and the shadows, a smile spreading across her face at the simple beauty. Numerous photos of what she was looking at were captured on Earth, but none of those compared to seeing and feeling the rays themselves dance on her own skin. Soft crunches sounded near her, and she looked away from her hand to see Elaras approaching her. A hand appeared near hers, and he shared her sunbeam, his fingers dancing to imaginary music. Chilly shadows obscured his face, but his smiling gray eyes reflected the warm sunlight.

"I always love the morning," Elaras said quietly, soft enough so if others were around only Rosella could hear.

"I can understand. It's beautiful," Rosella said as softly as she spoke, and his eyes drifted to hers.

A sweet smile spread across his lips, and he lowered his hand, encasing all of him back in the shadows. They stared at each other for a few moments before she lowered her own hand, and they simultaneously walked back onto the path toward Arja.

After a few hours, they were climbing a hill that was sporadically covered in flowers. Elaras halted them near the peak. When Rosella was about to question him, he held a hand up.

"When was the last time you were here, and be honest with me?" Elaras said, a look of cold determination on his face. She met his gray eyes and had to swallow a tense knot which had formed in her throat.

"Say, 'It's been too long to remember details.' That is the best you can say right now," came Akuna's calm voice, but she could feel him getting nervous in the fold of her hood.

"It's been too long to remember the details. Why?"

The look that crossed his face made her instantly concerned, and she tilted her head.

"What you're going to see will not be easy to comprehend. We'll take it slow, and I know of a small place some distance from here to rest in case it is overwhelming. Are you ready?" he asked, his cool and smooth tone slower than normal.

She nodded and took in a breath, unsure what she was going to see.

He nodded back and trekked forward. Once he reached the arch of the hill, he stopped once more, and she could visibly see him take in a deep breath. "It's worse than I thought," he said solemnly, and upon hearing those words, she hurried to meet him at the peak with him on her left side.

At the top, she froze, and her heart dropped, unable to take her eyes off the land before her.

The lively green and purple grass with a rainbow of flowers and trees that were behind her met a hard line in the ground before them. Beyond that line lay brown and black wilting grass with dead flowers in small patches. There were still white and pink clouds, but further into the land were dark blue clouds with various storms spilling orange rain and red lightning. There were hardly any animals around, and the air was silent, as if the wind did not dare sing here. The trees that she could see hardly held leaves on their branches and were similar to those from horror movies.

She had known the land was suffering, but not like this. Akuna took over her vision, and with the blurry purple hue washing over her sight, she felt her eyes frantically scanning over every inch of the landscape. After a minute or so of this, he released her sight, and she felt him tremble on her back, unsure of the emotion he was feeling.

"How does this happen? How are people still alive here?" she asked, not able to take her eyes off the land. For a reason she wasn't sure about, her chest tightened, and her ears grew hot. She removed her hood to let the stiff air cool her skin, and Akuna dove down her back. Before she could determine why she was feeling like this, she heard a loud exhale of breath, and Elaras took a step forward to enter her peripheral vision.

"The land relied on the Nightstones, as there was something in their palace that helped the land thrive, and only the Nightstones and their Clerics knew how. The Clerics can only do so much, but it was the Nightstones that powered and protected this land. Something in their bloodline, perhaps. The people of Arja that are still alive were forced to move inland, as the radius of the magic decreases every year. Since Rion is the epicenter of the magic, that is the safest and will last the longest. Before long, though, Rion will be gone too," he said more solemnly than Rosella had ever heard from him.

"It's as if the magic was literally seeped from the ground," she said and instantly felt stupid for stating something so obvious.

Elaras chuckled and turned to her. "You're understanding, so that's good. Let's go in, and we'll find that safe place I know about," he said as he took a tentative step forward then stopped.

A second later, she felt his fingers on the helix of her ear, startling her with the sudden touch.

"Why are you touching my ears?" she asked, her hand swatting him away.

Despite the swatting, he reached back out and pulled her ear and head toward him, making her yelp and Akuna growl softly. His face was within inches of the side of her head, and she realized what he was looking at. Her ears were still human-like, and no other race she had seen had ears similar to her, not even the dwarves.

"Your ears. Why are they like this?" he asked as he felt the skin and cartilage of her ear so tightly that she couldn't move her head.

"Fuck," she said to Akuna before speaking out to Elaras. "Deformity as a baby, I think. I don't know. Completely normal and actually rare," she lied, hoping he would believe her. She was not ready to tell him she was from another universe.

"Hmm. Well, they're quite...cute, your ears. So...small and soft," he murmured while finally taking his hand off her ear. He cleared his throat and turned away from her once again. "Ready?"

"Yes, and thanks?" she said, touching her now very hot ear and rubbing it gently.

The transition from the healthy grass to the wilted and dried grass was louder than silence. The grass underneath her crunched hard and the air truly stilled.

"Nice cover. I think he believes you for now," Akuna reassured. She took in a deep breath while the crunching continued below her feet.

"Thanks. Do you think eventually I'll have to tell him?" she asked, her anxiety from the land and from the interaction intertwining her words.

"I would hope that by the time you do tell him, it will be

because you want to and not because you have to," Akuna said wisely.

They were silent the rest of the trip until they reached a vacant farmhouse two hours later. The dark clouds hung in the air nearby, and the clashing of thunder and rain was loud enough to not allow whispers to be heard.

"Oh god, this is like we're in a zombie apocalypse movie, or that zombie show that has been going on forever," she said to Akuna, then realized something worse. *"This is probably what my world looks like, isn't it?"*

The only response she received was a deep, body-rumbling sigh filled with dread and sadness. Looking around, she imagined her world as this one, with flattened buildings and everything around them dead. She imagined a red sheen from the bombs covering the sun completely and the rain to be made of acid. The world grew cold and heartless, no life anywhere except for that dome in Kansas. This world, Dorthos, was doing better than Earth, but was there really a difference between the two?

Rosella's breath quickened as her vision started to fog, and her gaze darted around for somewhere to go, where the grass was healthy and the clouds were pink.

"Rosella, are you alright?" came a hollow voice from nearby.

Without looking to see who asked the question, she started walking the way she came. A few hours' walk was worth getting out of this literal hell if it meant she would be safe. Her heart rate spiked, and her eyes grew wide, finding the path of their crunched footprints. A burning sensation grew in her lungs as her breath quickened.

"Rosella!" came the voice again, hollower than before but more rushed and seemingly panicked.

"I need to go. I need to get to a shelter!" came Rosella's loud voice, but she was unaware of what she was saying. She did not care. Her priority was to get to safety, or to land that was safe. Her vision was now a foggy tunnel as she grew more frantic and ran. She was on Earth, and she was going to die. She was going to be blown up or her skin would melt from the radiation. A bunker would be safe. There had to be one where the land was still healthy that she could go to.

"Rosella, stop!" came a loud, stern voice, but this time in her head.

She screamed and ran faster to escape. Looking around, she realized she was missing something, something that was really important, and she couldn't believe she left them behind. All sounds were muted except for the bombs hitting the ground, the tree bark cracking from the heat and the air's remaining moisture sizzling.

"Wren? Wren, where are you? Wren, we have to go before the bombs hit!" she screamed at the top of her lungs, still running forward but sporadically turning in different directions to find her friend. The thought of leaving her friend behind terrified her. She couldn't leave her again. Her brain worked hard to try and see where Wren was so they could escape this wasteland, this new hell on Earth, to get to the bunker.

"Rosella, please stop running!" the first voice said again, but this time from in front of her. A figure she could not distinguish appeared and held their hands out to stop Rosella. This figure was not Wren, so she had to keep running. She could not stop. Her legs would need to fall off before she stopped.

"I need to find Wren before more bombs drop!" she screamed at the voice. The cape from her cloak flew behind her from the speed she was running, the belt with pouches and Shadow Breaker bouncing against her strides. Her boots thudded on the dead ground and the wind now blowing by her ears, her panic rising faster than ever.

"Wren!" she screamed one more time, not able to hear herself, as if her eardrums were blown out. Her lungs felt like they were simultaneously on fire and tearing apart, and she struggled to take in air as she ran. Before she could scream for her friend one more time, her body stopped dead in its tracks.

Her aching lungs began to forcibly breathe in a steady but quick deep rhythm, and her heart rate slowed the more breaths she took. She had lost all control of her body as her tunneled vision became purple and her entire body tensed up to the point that even her fingers were stiff. Wren's name froze in her throat.

"Rosella, you're safe. You are on Dorthos, not on Earth. You cannot find Wren. She is not on this plane of existence. There are no bombs here, and there never will be. You. Are. Safe, Rosella. You are safe with me, now and forever. You're okay, I promise," a voice as calm as a cool stream said into her mind that she felt in the deepest part of her soul.

He repeated his words until they sank in, and she felt her own body relax. Her breaths slowed and became lighter, and she flexed and curled her fingers to release the remaining tension her own mind imprinted on her body. She remembered how his voice always relaxed her when they first spoke telepathically, and now she was grateful for his peaceful and soothing presence more than ever. The nightmares had plagued her for the last few nights, but now she was unnerved that they were invading her time awake.

"I'm okay. I'm safe?" she asked hesitantly to Akuna, almost scared of the answer in case he was just telling fibs she needed to hear so she would stop running.

"Yes, I promise you're okay, and that you're safe. I have you. You're on Dorthos, not Earth," he said, and she began to cry. The purple hue left her vision, and she fell to her knees in a ball, her face in her hands. Before she could scream from frustration, fear,

and sadness, she felt a body against her and hands wrap
around her.

"Oh my gods, Rosella. What just happened?" came Elaras'
panicked voice from where he rested his head on her, trying to
hold her as close as possible.

Rosella released a painful whimper, and Elaras hugged her
tighter. Rosella felt her body rumble softly, like a large cat was
purring on her chest, and realized Akuna was comforting her as
best as he could while staying hidden. They sat there for some
time before her tears subsided. She lifted her face out of her
hands and sat up, forcing Elaras to move and unwrap himself
from her.

"Vikshae—"

His rumble interrupted her as he said, *"Of course, my dear.
You will get through this, I promise."*

Rosella looked to Elaras, who seemed shaken himself but did
not speak. She gave a weak smile and wiped a tear from her face.

"I have...trauma in my past, and it snuck up on me," she said
simply. She was growing dizzier by the second and just wanted to
lie down and rest. "This land just reminded me of that trauma. I'm
sorry I ran away. I need to rest, but I'll be okay."

He gave a soft half-smile, then frowned once more before
asking, "Are you sure you're going to be alright, Rosella?"

"I think so, but I do wish we could make soup," she said as
confidently as possible.

When he nodded in response and began to stand up, she felt
a shiver of adrenaline flow through her body. He helped her to her
feet, and pain stabbed at her lungs as she walked, forcing her to
go slowly. Together they trudged to the farmhouse to rest for the
remainder of the night.

As she lay on her sleeping pad, she saw a faint puff of silky
soft blue smoke before her eyes drooped.

Besides the day she came to Dorthos, that night was one of the first nights where she did not have nightmares. Instead, she dreamed of different hues of blues and purples with white and gold sparkles floating around in mesmerizing swirls, and when she awoke, she was saddened the colors were gone, but happy to be awake and alive.

12
Yesterday's Sorrow Is Today's Warning

"Aim for that bigger knot in the panel," Akuna said, resting in her downed hood but peeking out from the lip of the fabric. He had decided to change his color again to deep red scales with amber-colored eyes, his Swiss-cheese frilled ears still prevalent with whatever scale color he took.

Rosella raised her Penobscot bow after nocking an arrow, pulled back, and fired within a span of three seconds. The arrow flew and hit the dead center of a knot with a loud and satisfying *thud*, causing the panels of the farmhouse to shake.

She was still getting used to the style of bow since it was stronger and heavier than her own barebow from home. Since it was double the size and double the strength, she had to adjust herself every time she pulled back the bowstring. As Rosella was reaching for another arrow, little taps on her shoulder told her that Akuna was happy she made the shot. Since yesterday, Akuna had been more encouraging and less catty than usual, which unnerved her, but was nonetheless appreciated.

"Good, again. This time, take a few steps back and aim for the

knot that is higher up, the small one. Yes, that one. Great, you got it! Now, aim for the elf's head."

Rosella turned as Akuna dipped back into the hood and saw Elaras ambling up to her, a wry smile on his face with two cups of something hot. "Tea. I hope you like molasses," he said calmly as he handed one to Rosella and before taking a sip from his own cup.

She raised an eyebrow before flinging her bow on her back, then took the cup and examined it. The cup was wooden but was painted blue with small circles encircling it, and the tea was earthy yet harsh. The molasses helped sweeten the drink, but the tea itself was stiff and unlike any tea she had ever tasted.

"Bitter," she said shortly, but still took another sip.

Elaras smiled and shrugged. "Now I know you like your tea sweet. I'll make tomorrow's to your liking. Ready to go? You can practice hunting on the road too, if you like," he said, peering at her over the lip of his cup.

She lowered the cup and gave him a slightly mortified look. "I've never shot anything alive, only targets," she admitted sheepishly.

"Well, you get to practice! We can start with bigger targets then go to small ones. Deer first, then squirrels," he said, downing the rest of his tea before placing the cup back in his backpack. "It will take time to even find an animal out here, but when we see one, we'll go for it. If we shoot something big, we can feed it to villagers and farmers that are nearby, if there are any."

Rosella gave a half smile and chugged her drink, the harsh taste attacking the back of her throat. She handed the cup back and waited on Elaras before walking down the path toward Rion. The fact that she was standing in Arja now, the land that she was supposed to rule in weeks' time, horrified her. Thinking back to her life on Earth, she would have never believed this would become her real life and not her in a fantasy dream. Instead, she was here, partnered with a dragon and an elf, set to be queen of a land that she still did not know. She shook the thought away and put her hood up, feeling Akuna crawl up to her shoulder.

"*How's your chest, Rosella?*" Akuna asked, and she mentally scraped over her body.

"*I feel more panic than pain, so I'll take it. My lungs are sore every day, but yesterday made them worse,*" Rosella replied, rubbing her hand along her ribs.

"*I apologize for not being able to heal them more.*"

"*It's alright, Akuna. This is better than nothing, or being dead.*"

"*True,*" Akuna said, and he dipped back into her hood.

An hour passed in the morning light before Elaras held out a hand for her to stop. Pointing ahead of them, she saw a massive buck with antlers that were triple the size of deer back on Earth and a bright yellow tail that swished to swap bugs away. Instantly, she crouched down behind a wide tree while taking out her bow and an arrow, Elaras following closely behind.

"Aim for the eye," Elaras whispered to Rosella.

"Shush," Rosella said, side-eying him. If she was going to shoot something alive for the first time, she needed to focus and remember that they were killing it for food, for survival.

She channeled a huntress she read about in a dystopian book and nocked the arrow. She pulled back and aimed, waiting for the head to rise from eating grass. Within a second of the head rising, she released the arrow, and it went straight into the deer's eye and out the other side of the head.

The deer fell with a loud *thud,* and Elaras ran over to the body to examine it. "Gods, Rosella, that was great! Yes, this will do nicely. Let's set up a fire and a place to break this deer down."

Without arguing, she followed him, and after a few hours of prep, cleaning, draining, and breaking down, they had large slabs of meat and two massive antlers. She stored the meat and antlers into her magic pouch, then snuck a few pieces to Akuna. They did not wait long after they were done before they set off again, snacking on cooked pieces of the venison while they walked. Rosella, feeling exhausted physically and mentally, did not say much, and Elaras seemed to notice but did not say or ask anything, and she was thankful. She was not in the mood to talk as her mind spun and grew in pain, throbbing harder the further they went.

"Tylenol!" she said telepathically, and opened her magic pouch to stick her hand in. As soon as her hand passed the threshold, a small packet of Tylenol fell into her fingers, and a sigh of relief escaped her throat. *"Oh my god, I've never been so thankful for painkillers."*

"What's that?" asked Elaras, as Rosella had been so focused on getting the Tylenol that she did not notice he had looked over at the exact moment she tore open the packet.

She crunched the small packet in her hand and pulled her canteen around. "Just a bag of medicinal herbs. My head is really hurting, so I figured I'd grab something for it," she quipped before lifting the packet to her mouth and dropping the pills in, quickly followed by a swig of water. Before he could question more, she shoved the empty blister packet into her pouch and swung her canteen back to her side. "Nothing to be concerned about. How much further until we get to another resting stop?" she asked as casually as ever, but Elaras was staring at her pouch and moved to her right side to get closer to it.

"I knew you had a magic pouch, but what kind of magic is it? Conjuring? Transmutation? Extradimensional? " he asked as he started to open the pouch and look inside. Before she could answer, he stuck his arm elbow deep into it and wildly moved it around searching for anything.

"Dude! Boundaries much?" she exclaimed at him.

Right before she could reach for his arm, he yanked it out with a loud yelp of pain, holding his arm in front of his face. His arm had turned black and red, the skin smoking from the bright embers still making the skin audibly sizzle.

"Holy shit! Elaras!" she yelled, trying her best to look at the arm, but Elaras had started to scream and wave his arm around to extinguish the embers.

"He shouldn't have tried to enter a space that is only attuned to you and me," Akuna said, a slight chuckle in his tone.

"Why didn't you tell me to stop him?" she demanded close to yelling at Akuna in her head.

"Because I thought it would be funny, but mostly because I wanted to confirm that no other speaking kind could enter the bag. Your true identity, your human identity, needs to be protected, and the items in that bag would raise many unpleasant questions. The spell I cast on it worked marvelously, if I do say so myself."

"Yes, wonderful. I love whenever you cast magic and shit, but goddamn, Akuna. It looks like he doesn't even have muscles now."

"He'll be fine. He can heal himself," Akuna said with a laugh.

Rosella realized that Akuna was right, though she had not seen Elaras heal himself yet. Elaras had told her that he was going to heal her, so why wouldn't he heal himself now?

"Elaras! Start healing yourself!" she yelled to Elaras, who was on his knees staring at his arm. "Come on, magic man!"

"It fucking hurts!" he cried, and Rosella rolled her eyes.

"Of course it hurts, but it'll feel better when you heal yourself! I shouldn't have to tell you to do that, goodness gracious," she said, faintly annoyed while getting her canteen out. She walked over and poured some water gently onto his arm to burn out the remaining embers and to stop the smoking. "Now, let's get off the path and work your magic. We aren't going anywhere until your arm is a normal purple again."

As an hour passed, Rosella sat and watched Elaras heal his arm with his silky smoke magic, and after some time she realized that Akuna, in fact, had much stronger magic than Elaras.

"Told you, human," Akuna's voice sneaked in as she thought of all the times Akuna cast magic compared to Elaras.

"Want me to tell you you're pretty, too? That way we know your ego is fully inflated?" Rosella asked, trying her best to hide a snort.

"Why yes, that would be lovely. I need to reinflate a little," Akuna said, and she could feel him straighten out his back from the way he moved in the hood.

"You're pretty...annoying," Rosella said, hiding a smile behind her hand so Elaras wouldn't see if he looked over.

Akuna's body deflated, and she felt steam rise on the back of her neck. A laugh croaked from her throat behind the clapped hand, and Elaras finally glanced over, his magic still working on his arm.

"What?" he asked in a tired voice that edged on annoyed.

"Thinking back on a story where I almost scared a crush to death with my archery," Rosella said, coming up with an excuse. Lying was becoming too easy for her, but she knew it was important to keep her identity secret for as long as possible, even with Elaras.

Elaras' eyebrows rose sharply, and he adjusted himself so he was facing her, his magic still pouring into his arm. By now, his arm was almost fully healed, but the skin was still cracked and angry. "Tell me, so I can laugh too," he said, his half-smile making an appearance.

"Let's see if your storytelling is as good as the god of stories, Vehab," came Akuna's amused voice. *"See if you can arouse him with your lies."*

"You're not gonna help me?"

"Nope, not this time. This is your story to fabricate."

Rosella cleared her throat, giving her a moment to find a way to tell a real story that would be plausible in this fantasy world that was Dorthos.

"So, a few years ago or so back, there was a boy that had just come to live in the village with his parents. Handsome, green-skinned half-orc, half-elf, big and strong too. Everyone our age flocked to him except for me. I was busy all the time, so I never gave him the time of day, but you bet I was crushing on him hard. One day he came to my stall and asked me for an apple. He must have gotten used to getting what he wanted, because when I said no, he just looked at me and asked again, 'Can I have an apple, sweet lady?' and again I said no. When he demanded I give him two apples, my crush blew away faster than a feather in the wind, and I told him he could have it on one condition. He would have to hit an apple off his mother's head. Oh man, the look on his face was super hilarious."

Rosella told the story animatedly and with vigor, hoping to play off the awkwardness that she was mixing the truth as she went. "After a little while, he came back with his mother. Well, he set his mother up like...twenty meters away. He grabbed a bow, set the arrow, and released it. The arrow landed like five feet in front of him. So he said, 'I didn't practice. I'm a bit rusty.' I told him, 'Too bad. Looks like you're not getting those apples you're so desperate for.' So he challenged me, and even volunteered to set the apple on his head. I obliged, and of course I shot the apple clean off his head.

"Oh man, the way he got so angry and embarrassed was more hilarious than before, until he grabbed a dagger and ran toward me. I nocked two arrows this time and aimed it at him. The only reason I didn't shoot was because his mother was yelling at me, and we had gathered a crowd. You bet that when I nocked those two arrows though, he halted and was terrified. He never came to my stall again after that, and he never got his apples. He was lucky that the only thing that got hurt that day was his big, fat ego."

"Ah, so you're a menace, is what you're saying. I knew it," Elaras said, a wide smile on his face. His arm was only a few minutes away from being healed, so he had become more relaxed the more his skin returned to its normal color.

"Excuse me?" she retorted.

"Please, Rosella. There is more to you than meets the eye, and I have known you were a menace since I first laid eyes on you. Your first words confirmed that for me, how you were basically stabbing me with your eyes for even sitting down at your table."

"Well, you do have an issue with boundaries. It's fucking annoying!" she said while gesturing to his injured arm.

Elaras laughed harder than she had heard him before, and she smiled to herself. When he was done, he got up and held out a hand for her to pull her up. They made their back way to the path and traveled on to another farmhouse that was also abandoned. The day went by with nothing of interest, and that night Elaras put her under another sleeping spell like the night before.

This time, however, she could faintly hear things that she had not heard last night when the dream was silent. There were voices singing, the tone and melody tranquil and beautiful, and Rosella wished for them to never stop, despite not understanding the words. Two other unfamiliar voices spoke words that she could not make out, and the tone of the words were quick yet gentle. The voices were speaking as if a problem had arisen, but then an answer came, and all was well again.

After some time of her hearing and never understanding a single word, one of the voices quieted the others, making the singers stop. Then, all of the voices whispered six words in unison, unmistakably directed at Rosella.

"Rosella Nightstone, find us. Save us."

13
Heavy is the Mind that Bears the Pain

The grand halls of Nocturnal Manor lay silent as High Cleric Varran Daldrack walked, whispering blessings of protection and peace. As each blessing was made, small wisps of singing white smoke would shoot out of his free hand and go in a direction through the familiar walls around him. The housekeeper and their servants rested, and the cats were on the prowl for vermin, moving soundlessly between the walls and up corridors. The guards and Paladins, the ones that were left, either rested or stood sentry at the entrances to the manor.

High Cleric Varran, a dwarf of one hundred and twenty-five years of age with no gray in sight among his blond hair and neat beard, strode as quietly as possible. He knew there was no Nightstone alive to wake, that the house had lain devoid of a true Nightstone family member for almost thirty years. The ghosts of this home kept to their own, and Varran let them be, knowing no good came from waking or disturbing the dead. What good came from reminding those that left this world prematurely that they, in fact, were dead and mourned?

Most nights he could not sleep because of this. Most nights he lay awake, afraid of seeing the dead faces of the Nightstones, afraid of seeing the Rockshires that took them from this world, afraid of the devastation on his Goddess Elyphr, the goddess of night. His face and body bore the signs of dramatic exhaustion, and without the help of the housekeeper making sleep elixirs, his mind too would be exhausted.

How long was this manor, this city, this land, this people, willing to wait for another Nightstone? For someone to take over and bring order to this land, to help the citizens be able to go to their homes and to be able to work again? To live? To raise children without the fear of starvation? Arja had been waiting long enough. Arja and all of Dorthos needed a Nightstone. Thoughts of this land and its suffering plagued him every day, as it did for almost everyone in Arja.

As Varran was about to turn the corner to the dining room, he looked up to see a faint glow of light that was not from his own candle. Quickly but silently, he pressed himself against the shared wall of the dining room, and he did not need to wait long to hear hushed voices. The voices were of those he did not recognize, as he knew every voice of every person in this manor.

"Wow, that bitch was ugly. What do you think, Lycilla?" came a male voice that was nasally and had the essence of someone young.

"Oh yeah, I mean look at her hair. Why would someone think that style was a good idea? And the white streak? Come on, that was obviously dyed to seem special," came a harsh and unfriendly female voice.

"Oh, gods, you're right! The rest of the family have white streaks, too! Did you notice that? How stupid of them, really, to dye their hair like that," the male voice said in an unforgiving tone. "Okay, enough staring at disgusting portraits. I'm getting nauseated looking at them. Let's find that vault and get what we came here for."

The female giggled, and two sets of footsteps began to walk away from where Varran stood, the light they had disappearing from the walls. They were heading into the kitchens which then led to the other wing of the manor that contained the throne room, chapel, and stairwells to the other levels. The grand Nightstone vault also stood hidden in the opposite wing.

Varran set down his candle and began whispering an incantation and moving his fingers in precise movements. A second later, a wisp of white smoke in the shape of a sparrow shot out of his hand and split into many smaller birds once it exited the hallway. He waited only moments before he heard footsteps round the corner and saw magically lightened Nightstone crests on their armor.

Six guards and two Paladins approached in grand blue, white and silver armor that echoed against the walls of the manor. Varran pointed in the direction the intruders were, and all but one of the Paladins went towards the opposite wing. When their footsteps became lighter and their lights faded away, the Paladin that stood with Varran knelt and grabbed the candle from the ground.

"Did you get a look at the intruders?" High Paladin Joss Bildow asked as he handed Varran the candle, as Varran was half his height.

"No, only heard them. They were insulting Queen Kayline's portrait, so I know they were not welcome strangers with good intentions," Varran said, letting nervousness weave into his words.

High Paladin Joss was a half-orc, half-goliath man with angry green eyes that complemented his darker complexion, and he had been on the Nightstone post just as long as Varran at close to sixty years. They had both worked up to their positions, and currently they were the highest-ranked members of the house along with the housekeeper, who had also been with the Nightstones for as long as Varran and Joss. Joss' long beard showed white strands, but his strength was unmatched, along with his loyalty to the Nightstone name.

"Hmm. I had been hearing rumors of a Rockshire that lived. Was one a female voice?" asked Joss, adjusting his stance.

"Yes, she was very cruel in nature. The other was a male that seemed to have a young spirit but was unkind. They said they were looking for something."

"Looking for something?" Joss asked with a raised eyebrow, crossing his massive arms. "Like what?"

"My only guess is riches, and possibly the night stone jewelry."

"Night stone jewelry? Do they think that if they possess a night stone that they can rule?"

"Well, it would certainly help their claim. The Rockshires, by Dorthos law, usurped the Nightstones. If this Rockshire were to get their hands on a night stone somehow, the Rockshire would take rule despite the lack of the true Nightstone name. The emperor is growing impatient, especially at the rate of decay of the land, so I believe he would allow anyone with probable cause at this point."

"To Hells with the emperor! There has to be a Nightstone out there. If there is a Rockshire alive, there has to be a Nightstone!" Joss said, his anger rising and his eyes growing wild.

Varran raised his hands, and as he wiggled his fingers with a soft incantation on his lips, his hand glowed white and drifted toward Joss. Within seconds, Joss' tense muscles relaxed, and he heaved a great sigh that shook the walls.

"Thanks, Varran."

"Of course. What we can be thankful for is that there is no way for them to get the night stones. If they leave here with their lives, they will most likely leave here empty-handed," Varran said, looking toward the kitchen entrance and waiting to hear footsteps of the guards and second Paladin.

"Aren't they in the vault with everything else, if those intruders can somehow even get in the vault? I thought you put them there after that night?" Joss asked, not being vague about his curiosity.

At this, Varran glanced up with a raised forehead and eyebrows, his eyes wide, before straightening his face. "Ah, you aren't aware."

"Aware of what? Shouldn't I be aware of whatever goes on in this home?"

"Yes, and I had believed I had told you that day when...well, I'll tell you now," Varran said before clearing his throat softly. "As you know, each birthed family member after a certain age is given a new night stone to place in whatever holder they want: necklace, bracelet, ring, or earring. Married-in members also receive a stone the same night as the marriage ceremony. Sometimes the stones themselves are passed down from a dying family member to the newest born. If a stone is not passed down to anyone, the stone itself vanishes, leaving behind the metal that held it. Since the entire family all passed at once, the stones are nowhere to be found, and there is no way to find them," Varran finished, straightening his black tunic to distract himself from getting emotional.

"Wait, so, they just vanished into thin air, and no one knows where they went? How did I not notice this?" Joss asked, his bushy eyebrows furrowed and head tilted to one side.

"Yes. Goddess Elyphr seems to know, but even she will not tell me. The crowns bear no stones, and the throne... Besides, there was a lot that happened that night, so I understand you not noticing something like that."

"Of course your goddess knows—she's a goddess! A pretty

one at that," Joss said, laughing a little at the side-eye he received from Varran.

Varran coughed slightly before continuing. "I'm not surprised she will not tell me, but if there is a night stone out there, I do wish that somehow one will not fall into that Rockshire's hands. That is, if she is in fact a Rockshire."

Just then, various footsteps could be heard coming toward them. Joss placed his thumb on the guard of his sword and popped the sword out slightly, ready to attack if the footsteps did not belong to the guards and Paladin. Thankfully, the light from their crest flashed on the walls, and Varran breathed a sigh of relief. When they rounded the corner, they stood at attention in front of Varran and Joss.

Joss let his sword fall back into its sheath. "Well?"

"We had the two in hand, but the girl whispered something, and they both disappeared in red smoke. We do believe that the girl is in fact a Rockshire, and the man is a Moonshadow from the stone pendant he wore," said the other Paladin, Gerrart Hamsturg, who was also half-orc, half-goliath but with blue eyes and a shorter beard.

"Did they take anything?" asked Joss, anger lacing his tone.

"No, we caught them outside the vault trying to enter," Gerrart said. "The woman seemed furious and was saying something about the stones and how they needed to get in there."

Varran pondered and looked up at Joss. "Do we know the name of the Rockshire by chance?" he asked, and when Joss shook his head, Varran felt nervous. "Joss, you have this handled?"

"Yes. I'll relay more information if we get any, High Cleric Varran," Joss said formally, and Varran nodded his gratitude to the guards and Gerrart in front of him.

He turned and headed to the other side of the manor toward

the Elyphr chapel. Once inside, he lit incense and a candle before kneeling at the altar, a grand and ornate statue of Elyphr.

"Lady of the Night and of the Stars and Moon, hear me. We, the people of Arja, need your answers. Please provide, and I shall continue to serve in your name," Varran chanted, drooping his head and clasping his hands, closing his eyes and mind.

Before long, he felt a rush of air and light appear from behind his eyelids, a soft and deep song ringing in his ears. He opened his eyes and before him stood a woman dressed in white glowing fabric with piercing blue and black eyes.

"My favorite child, you have called upon me once again," came the voice of Elyphr. Her voice was strong but beautiful, the very sound that gave peace and tranquility when heard. The singing came from behind her now as a chorus sang of the stars of the night and the creatures that lurked in the darkest of shadows.

"Yes, My Goddess. A Rockshire is alive and is seeking the throne of Arja. I do not believe she is looking to save this land and is only thirsting for and craving power. She is searching for a night stone, perhaps to show that she is the true ruler, despite her usurper method of obtaining the throne. Is there guidance you can give, My Goddess?" Varran asked, not afraid to show his apprehension and fear.

A minute or so went by, and during that time Elyphr raised her head and closed her eyes, singing along with the chorus behind her. When she looked back down, he was surprised to see that she had a smile on her face.

"Need not worry, my child. Since our last communication, the next Nightstone queen has appeared in this world, shepherded by a trusted ally to the Nightstone family. Rosella Nightstone is her name. She is on her way here now, accompanied by a third, an elf. She shall take the throne, and when she does, you shall be by her side to help her," she said in a sing-song voice that made the room glow brighter and yet not blinding.

Varran stood astonished by the words she had said. There was another Nightstone? And who were the two she was with?

"My Goddess, where was this Nightstone before? Why are they now making an appearance?" Varran asked, letting shock show through his words as he spoke.

Elyphr hummed a few notes before waving her hands in the air in front of Varran. The chorus that was behind her started singing and chanting, *"Rosella Nightstone, find us. Save us."*

"Rosella is not of this world, though her line and blood are true. Seek her, find her, and bring her here. You shall not judge her as our world is new to her, and soon she will understand her place and her responsibilities. She wears a night stone necklace and bears the Nightstone symbol on her skin. Her appearance is unique and cannot be missed, as the ears that hear and the skin she bears tell the truth you seek. Need not worry—only she can wear the necklace without harm. That will be your true tell. You will know who she is once you lay your eyes on her. Protect her, my child. Help her."

As she did this, she raised her hands in front of her, and a flash of light erupted from her palms. Words were spoken that Varran could not understand, and he felt the force from Elphyr's light hit his face. Varran blocked his eyes, and a moment later he felt the hard stone under his knees once more. He looked up to the archway embossed with moons and stars and saw the incense and candle had blown out, as they usually did when he communicated with Elyphr. Tears began to well up as the words of his goddess cemented into his mind.

"Rosella Nightstone, I will find you, and I will help you, and in turn help Arja."

14
Haunting Serenity

"Just like that. Good. Again. Not that hard. You'll take my eye out, woman!" Elaras said as they practiced hand-to-hand with two sticks.

The Shadow Breaker rested on her belt as Elaras had insisted he did not want to heal himself two days in a row, as well as further insisting she was not ready to wield its power. Since Rosella's dream the night before of someone begging her to save them, she had been determined to strengthen up and to be as prepared as possible. She demanded Elaras show her hand-to-hand today before traveling further, and to disclose Shadow Breaker's magical properties, but he was still holding back on giving information. Thankfully, Elaras was more than happy and willing to train her, as he did not take the dream lightly after she told him the details. However, the entire morning after she told him about the dream, he had been acting slightly distant and hollow, giving fake smiles and not moving with vigor.

They were slashing and blocking, moving to avoid or for better vantage points, and occasionally stabbing. After some time in a sequence, Elaras let his guard down, and Rosella was able to easily approach his throat with her stick pressed against his skin. They froze, staring at each other and breathing heavily, a foot of space between their faces.

Elaras' face spread into a wide smile that looked odd, and he held his hands up in defeat. Rosella lowered the stick dagger but did not take a step back.

"What's on your mind?" she asked, tilting her head.

Elaras' eyebrows furrowed, and he matched her head tilt. "What makes you think something is on my mind?" he asked, his oily, sly voice coming back with full force.

Rosella shook her head, her eyes holding his gaze. "You seem a little off. You're not your annoying self, so what's going on in your head?" she asked, and she decided to match his tone, making her voice low and slick.

His eyebrows rose, and he gave a small, genuine laugh. "You're imitating me now, Rosella?"

"Answer the question, Cricket. What is going on in that pretty little head of yours?"

The laugh he gave made his head fling back slightly, breaking their gaze, and Rosella took that moment to take a silent panicked breath. He looked back at her, and his smile became too intoxicating, and she wanted this conversation to finish.

"You, Rosella, are on my pretty little mind. Not for the ways you think, though, so don't get your hopes up," he said, moving his head back and forth like a serpent and keeping his voice smooth like silk. "You are an...interesting creature, and I have learned much more than I anticipated since I have met you. You also seem to be hiding a lot, and the only true things about you that you have told me are that you are a Nightstone and that you can use a bow." Suddenly, the backs of his fingers were gently stroking her cheek, and her skin tingled so fiercely that she grew warm. "Tell me one of your secrets, Rosella, and I'll tell you one of mine."

A ball of anxiety dropped in her stomach as she swallowed, her mind working furiously on what she could tell him. He had proven that he could be trustworthy and protective, so why was finding a simple truth about herself so difficult? He hardly raised questions, and when he did with no honest answer, he never pushed. Still, she had to be careful with what she said and how she said it.

"Is there something you had in mind that you wanted to know more about?" she asked, her voice wavering a little.

"Who is Wren?" he asked, as simple as could be.

Hearing her name on his lips shocked her to her core, and she finally took a step back. She swallowed hard and looked down to the ground, now afraid to meet his eyes and see the expression on his face.

"Wren was...a good friend of mine. She died not long ago suddenly and tragically," she said solemnly, and tears heated her face as her throat burned. "I saw her almost every day, and she always made my day brighter. So when she died, it felt like a light had gone out of my life. Sometimes it still feels that way in the quietest of nights and the silence that sits between conversations. When I was running I—I thought I had lost her again. I thought she had died again."

Elaras took a step toward her but did not reach for her. "My father killed my mother's father after they married so that he could fully take on her family's title and become wealthier and more prominent in the underworld's society," he said in a manner that seemed to let go of something inside of him, as if saying this lifted a weight off his shoulders. "My mother doesn't even know; she just thinks that her father died of natural causes a week after she married my father. Now they're topside, and my father is doing what he can to get whatever power he can, even if it means someone else is left to starve or perish. That means that he will do what he can to take Arja away from you because that is the only place that can give him power and has vacancy."

Shocked, she asked, "How did you find out about your father murdering your grandfather?"

"Because he told his brother, my uncle. I overheard them reminiscing on their past in the drinking parlor, and he was *bragging* about the look on his father-in-law's face when he killed him," he said, taking another step toward the sniffling Rosella. "My father has always done what he could for power, and I wish to stay as far away from him as possible. At least my mother is a wonderful person. I think she's the only reason the Moonshadow name hasn't been completely tarnished."

"That's horrible, truly," she said, and that was all she was able to get out before having to sniffle again.

"Yes, well, he has always been controlling of *everything*. So we just have to stop him and the Rockshire girl before they succeed."

"*And kill them,*" piped up Akuna, who had been sleeping minutes before in her cloak that was resting on a log.

"Yes," she said to both Akuna and Elaras.

Elaras nodded, then heaved a sigh that Rosella felt in her bones. One of his hands rose in the air between them but turned into a fist and returned to his side, and he grimaced.

"I'm sorry about your friend Wren. There must have been a special bond between the two of you," Elaras managed to say with a smile, but his eyes flashed something sad, something hollow.

"She called me Rose, same with my mother. So, yeah...a really special bond. I'm sorry for getting angry about it before," Rosella said softly, and Elaras' smile disappeared.

"It's quite alright, and there is nothing to apologize for. Okay?"

Rosella nodded and reached to squeeze his hand for a moment before walking to grab her cloak and Akuna.

They traveled for two more days, going the safest and most discreet route with Elaras' direction. They discussed small details like the animals and birds, dragons and their hordes, and societal dynamics around Dorthos. Elaras kept to his word and did not judge Rosella for asking various basic and simple questions that she knew she should already know. They trained with sticks, and Elaras still did not reveal Shadow Breaker's magic, and she started to grow annoyed that he was being secretive about the black dagger's power.

Despite him being annoying about many things, Rosella started to realize that the tension between them was not something she could ignore. Every time he smiled, laughed, or even looked her way, her heart fluttered, and she couldn't help but smile. There was a stray thought of him leaving for whatever reason, and she grew pained at the thought of him not being by her side. A determination grew inside her that she would keep him at her side no matter what, for however long possible.

Akuna stayed in her hood and was given food and drink in secret, and he observed and made snarky comments. The closer they drew to Rion, the more serious he became. More often than not while they were walking, Rosella would see her vision turn purple and her control relinquished to Akuna, who wanted to look around for himself. This was something Rosella got used to, not arguing or questioning whenever Akuna did it. She knew this area seemed important to him, so she let him do this whenever he wanted.

When they were another two days' worth of travel from Rion due to the discreet path, Elaras pointed out a cave that he said led to a gigantic cavern. While entering the cave, Rosella thought she saw someone in the corner of her eye watching them from behind a tree but left it alone when Elaras kept calling for her to enter.

Something felt off, and anticipation was twisting her gut, but she pushed the feeling aside and decided to trust the location and Elaras. She was going to ask Akuna, but he seemed to be asleep, so she left him alone. They made camp, and within an hour, they were all asleep soundlessly.

15
Smoldering Tungsten

Lycilla Rockshire crept toward the massive cave's opening, a large red dagger palmed. They were outside the opening when Alryo Moonshadow sniffled softly. She whipped her head around and stared at him.

"Are you going to make noises all the time, Al?" she asked with a bite to her tone.

"What? No, I just had to sniffle a little. Pollen got in my nose or something," Alryo said quietly, grabbing one dagger from his belt and a lantern with the other hand.

She rolled her eyes and gave a disapproving look before lighting the lantern with a simple flame incantation. "Do you at least remember the plan, or do I need to remind your stupid brain again?" she asked, not afraid of letting her annoyance show through her words. He gave a thumbs up so she wouldn't get irritated about him speaking again, and she turned back toward the mouth of the cave. "It's a fucking miracle that you haven't died as a Slayer yet."

Lycilla knew that she could do this on her own, this mission.

She knew she could get to the throne herself if she really tried. By right, the throne belonged to her since her father killed the king and queen of Arja, and her mother slayed their children, and Lycilla watched everything. Her immediate and extended family brutalized the entire Nightstone family, making sure that their line was truly extinct. When it came time for her own family to die, she listened as her parents begged and pleaded for their lives, screaming apologetic words as they fell to their agonizing deaths.

Only being ten at the time, Lycilla had been playing hide and seek with her mother, and she was hiding in a small cabinet. She never laid eyes on the thing that killed them, but she knew that whatever it was, her parents and family had no chance of survival. The thing had informed her parents before their deaths that just like what they did to the Nightstones, they would do to them. Her family name would become extinct.

Except Lycilla survived, merely because she had been playing a game.

After careful planning and spying, Lycilla and Alryo crept further toward the cave mouth. No firelight was in sight within the tunnel, so they walked forward, their breaths slow and steady. After a long downward dip and after a curve, an open cavern lay before them. The cavern had a space as big as a ballroom with extremely high ceilings and a small opening on the ceiling that allowed soft moonlight in.

Elaras Moonshadow could be seen, propped up and asleep against a wall, head on his chest and arms crossed. To his right and deeper into the cave was the girl, and in the faint light from the fire Lycilla could see the glint of two stone pendants around her neck. The girl had her hood over her head, and her cloak wrapped tightly around her body, as if she was cold, or the cloak possibly held protective magical properties.

Seeking the opportunity, Lycilla growled quietly and shot

Elaras with a puff of red smoke like a dart. Red smoke wrapped him tightly as his eyes shot open and body froze in place. While Lycilla knew she could kill Elaras, she wanted him to watch his companion die. From everything Alryo and Kaine Moonshadow had told her, he was as good as a traitor in her eyes. In this moment, however, her desire to make him suffer outweighed the desire to kill him.

"I'm sorry, brother," Lycilla heard Alryo say in a malignant tone. "If it means anything to you, you probably won't die today. We just need something from your little, weird-looking girlfriend. By the way, I'm hurt that you didn't tell me about her last time I saw you! I knew you were hiding something."

Lycilla let out a soft chuckle before striding over to the sleeping girl. "I told you, he's the worst brother."

She glanced over at Alryo once more as Alryo's eyes drifted down to his brother's neck and landed on the long scar that resided there. "Ah, I guess Father was being honest. He did send an assassin to kill you so you would be out of the way. No wonder Father was furious when the assassin didn't come back. He must have known you killed him instead."

A wave of dark blue smoke exploded from Elaras, and the red smoke that surrounded his body shifted slightly, then fell back into place as the blue smoke dissipated. Lycilla let a piercing smile cross her face as Alryo laughed and continued to take daggers from his brother's body. "That won't do anything, brother. I have always loved you, but now you're an inconvenience to my love. Without you around, I get to be the best son," he whispered and sat down next to Elaras so he could watch Lycilla. He looked over at Elaras one more time and held a dagger over his carotid. "You know, I have to take precautions in case you somehow escape."

With a wide smile on her face, Lycilla turned and shot the

same red smoke onto the girl. Something flashed in her peripheral, but she kept her eyes on the girl.

The girl's eyes shot open, but as she was trying to prop herself up to see what was going on, her body froze in place just like Elaras'.

Lycilla stored her dagger and walked toward the girl and crouched in front of her, shock and confusion written all over her face. This girl had black hair with a white streak, just like the rest of the Nightstones.

"Don't worry, it's nothing personal. You just have something I want that you don't need. Besides, you're obviously playing pretend with that hair and this fake stone," Lycilla said, the words sliding out of her mouth like a cool breeze. She waved her fingers to release both necklaces from her magic, and the chains yielded to her commands, the pendants swinging back and forth slightly. She picked up the moonstone and pulled it to her face, straining the chain around Rosella's neck. "The brother gave you his stone? How romantic, and disgustingly pathetic," she mocked before dropping the stone. Unclasping the night stone necklace gently and removing it from the girl's neck, she examined the black and white stone. "My, my, this is a near replica of an actual night stone necklace. Quite immaculate, too. No blemish to be seen and no chinks in the chain. I almost feel bad taking this from you. Alas, I need it to rule Arja. Thank you for serving your future queen, girl."

She stood up, and with the chain still in her hand, she smiled down at the girl. As she took in a deep breath, she realized something was wrong. Turning toward Elaras, she saw the lantern was now on the ground with Alryo's body splayed out next to it on the cave floor, his skin turning green and his face in an eternal scream. Small choking sounds she now heard were coming from his throat while his body shriveled up.

"Alryo!" she yelled while running to him. When she got close to him, she stopped in her tracks. The smell coming from his body was blindingly putrid, something no one should ever have to smell or experience. "Oh, gods, Alryo," she whispered.

Looking up to Elaras, she knew he could not have done anything as he was still frozen in place, but with a tear running down his cheek as he stared down at his brother's body.

A ground and wall-quaking growl came from behind her that made her eardrums ring. A quick stream of purple smoke flew past her, and moments later she could hear rocks falling and somehow knew it was the entrance of the cave being blocked in.

Another deep and low growl erupted and rang around the room as a massive rush of air blew onto her back and made her hair fly into her face. For some reason, she raised her arms in the air with the necklace in hand and started to turn around, eyes on the ground. When she could raise her gaze, she grew more terrified than she ever had in her entire life.

Before her stood a massive white and red dragon that she could only see the shape of due to the faint fire and lantern light. The dragon was as tall as the ceiling, and his body and wings completely filled out the room in front of her. She had to crane her neck back to even see the entirety of his head as it breathed out massive puffs of hot steam through his nostrils. His vibrant red eyes were so bright they completely illuminated the room, and they leered at her with malice and fury. His four heavily scarred wings were slightly spread, and his sharp tail swished back and forth, knocking dust and rocks into the air.

He took a step toward her and over the still-paralyzed girl, standing over her protectively. When she saw the unmistakable and universally recognizable four wings and the holes in his head frills, she felt her knees beg to give way as she realized who and what this dragon was.

"The Great Wrath of Dorthos," Lycilla whimpered, her hands still raised in the air despite feeling extremely weak with fear. Her body felt like it was shutting down, as if her muscles were suddenly loose and her blood was not racing through her body, as if she was losing control of everything.

This dragon was rumored to be unkillable and to be the living god of dragons in Dorthos due to his power, magic, and strength. Even Slayers collectively would only play with the idea of hunting him, as there were stories that the Great Wrath could kill someone just by looking at them. Rumors flew that the steam he breathed alone would torch one's skin or set one's lungs on fire. There were stories that were told to children to fear this dragon, as he would not show mercy if someone wronged him or even stepped near him. Now, horribly, she was standing face to face with him, and she felt like she was deteriorating under the piercing gaze.

"Lycilla Rockshire," came his voice, and Lycilla let out a small yelp, terrified at the idea of the Great Wrath knowing her name. His voice made her ears ring and the ground tremble slightly. He lowered his head so she could look into his eyes easier, the steam from his nostrils warming the air around her. "You are not worthy of the Arja throne, and you never were or will be. Drop the stone and surrender, and your life will be spared. If you do not, your last moments of life will be lived like your friend, but worse."

Even though she wanted to do what he said, her fingers would not let go of the chain. She was so tense with fear that her fingers locked. In that moment, she realized that this must be a true night stone if this dragon was demanding its return. If that were to be true, then was the girl somehow a member of the Nightstone family?

With these thoughts running through her head, her mind flew to focus on the Moonshadow drawing room. Her eyes were locked on the dragon as she pictured the couch and ornate table, the decorations around the room and biscuits on the table, saying the teleportation incantation in her head at the same time. She whipped her hand in a circle so that the chain of the necklace wrapped itself around her palm to stay secured.

"Drop it, or I will end your life, Lycilla Rockshire. This is your final chance," he said, his booming voice louder than ever as he took another step forward, a bellow of purple smoke gathering in his mouth.

As she was finishing the incantation in her head, she started feeling an intense burning sensation in the hand that held the necklace. Was he using his magic to force her to drop it? She was terrified to even look at her hand, as dropping eye contact might make the Great Wrath react.

"Stop it!" she yelled at him, and in a quick puff of red smoke that filled her vision, she landed on the hardwood of the drawing room in Moonshadow manor. Feeling a small moment of relief from the fear and the burning feeling, she heard a tiny thud on the ground followed by a bigger thud.

Looking down, she saw the necklace had landed on the wood, and next to it was the top half of a burnt and blacked palm with burnt fingers still attached. Confused, she saw that only the lower half of her palm and her thumb were left behind. The night stone necklace had burned clean through her hand and lay unblemished on the ground, as if it was simply dropped.

Part 2

Part 2

16
Life Under a Paper Sky

Purple smoke enveloped Rosella, and her muscles released their tight hold, Lycilla's magic quickly ebbing away. Two loud thuds could be heard, and a moment later Akuna was at her side but was the same size as when she first met him. Panic settled slightly in her veins as she felt an emptiness on her neck where her necklace had been before, the same necklace that had never left her neck in three years. She glanced over at Elaras and she saw he was slumped over and breathing deeply.

"You knocked him out?" she asked, looking back at Akuna. His red eyes had lost the vibrant glow they had before and he looked simply like Akuna.

"Yes, because I believe we should talk before he wakes up," he said, and he lay down in front of her on all fours, his head still arched up. Even in his normal small size, this position made him eye to eye with Rosella, who was sitting on her pad. She crossed her legs like a child waiting for an explanation from their parents, the panic ever steady in her chest.

"I did not give myself that nickname. I was named the 'Great

Wrath' because over the hundreds and thousands of years that I have been alive, I have never been captured or successfully killed," Akuna said, holding his head high in a pompous way. "Many have tried, as you can see with the scars I bear, but every attempt has, obviously, failed. Some call me the Protector of Dorthos, some call me the Wise, or even the Father of Dorthos. I am, in fact, the oldest dragon in Dorthos and the oldest to ever live. I am aware of every dragon that is born and every dragon that dies, that gets sick or is injured. No, I am not a god of dragons, but I might as well be."

Rosella smiled as she watched him. She was not entirely surprised he was an incredibly powerful dragon and considered a god. This same dragon pulled her from Earth to Dorthos and waved it off after like it was no big deal. Countless times she had seen him do magic that seemed difficult, but he did it all so effortlessly. It was no wonder why he did not want to be seen by anyone, especially Elaras. He would still be recognizable by his characteristics even in the darkness of this cavern. Before Rosella could ask any questions, Akuna continued.

"I knew the Nightstones in a way that dragons should not know speaking kinds. I am almost as old as the Nightstones themselves, but I only interacted with them towards the end of their reign. Close to a hundred years ago, the king then, King Purtdrell, asked for assistance concerning the magic of the land. It seemed something was blocking the flow of the night stones' magic to the land itself when there had been two thousand years without issue. Possibly the sphere that houses the magic, the stones themselves, or the people wielding the magic.

"Nonetheless, with the king's ingenuity and my magic, we solved the issue by creating conduits for the magic to flow and expand effortlessly. Because of this new show of power from the conduits, the citizens became aware that the stones themselves bore power that was special. Before, they believed the rulers of Arja were the ones providing nourishment to the fields and overall well-being of the citizens. While that is true, the consistent power came from the stones the family wore, giving an aura of magic that healed the land.

"Though I helped with the conduits, I did not stay. I checked in, and when new members of the family were brought into ranks, I met them. Over time, I became part of the family, as I would visit and help them when they needed it. The family and the staff all knew me as Akuna, rather than Vikshae or Great Wrath. One day, I had left to check on a dragon who had injured their wing in the east. While I was gone, that was when the Nightstones were murdered.

"When I found out who killed them, I slaughtered the entire line myself. I did not succeed, it seems. When Elaras told us a Rockshire was alive, I grew furious. I had worked to protect the Nightstones, to help them aid others, to bring peace into this world. The Rockshire girl was here, and I could have ended all of this, but you, the last Nightstone, needed protecting more than my fury needed to be unleashed. We will find your night stone, and we will get your throne, I promise you that."

She had to take a moment to process it all, so she sat quietly with her eyes focused on his sharp blood-red claws. Questions flew around in her mind and only grew as more information sank in, making her confused and slightly disoriented. There was one question that stuck out among the rest, and if it was the only question she could ask, then that was the one that mattered most. Looking back into Akuna's eyes, she saw that he was still regarding her with unwavering attention.

"Is this why you will be with me for the rest of my lifetime, so that what happened to the Nightstones doesn't happen to me?"

she asked. The answer seemed obvious, but she wanted to hear it from him and to not be told "revealed in due time."

"Yes. I will not allow what happened to them and to Arja happen again. Some Cleric with some speaking kind god may say it was prophesied or that it was destiny, but I am doing this for my own sanity and for your well-being. There is not a grand answer to this question besides that—selfish motives. I have, however, grown fond of you, and I know you will make a great queen and ruler." He lurched backward to avoid Rosella's hurried movement to stand up.

"You keep saying I'll be a great ruler and that you'll be by my side, but I know *nothing* of ruling anything!" Rosella yelled, pacing in the cavern in front of Akuna. "I wasn't even a lead or manager at my job. I have never had a leading position in my entire life! All my dreams that involve me being the queen result in me and all of Arja dying in bombings and of cursed lands! How the *fuck* am I supposed to know exactly what I'm supposed to do or just flawlessly take over? I've only read about royal politics in fantasy books and seen it in television shows."

Rosella heaved a deep breath as she grabbed the sleeves of her dress, twisting the fabric between her fingers. Loose stones crunched under her feet as she paced, the sound echoing in the large cavern. She turned to Akuna's unrelenting gaze, his eyes now only illuminated by the dim fire.

"How am I supposed to do this, Akuna? I know I have no choice in the matter and that I *have* to do this, but I'm going to fucking fail and these people are not going to trust me. Why would they trust me in the first place? Because my mom gave me her necklace on her cancerous deathbed and told me to protect it at all costs? She told me of the value and that it was special, but she did not tell me it was so important that one day I would be pushed into royalty! What if these people that I rule over die by my hand because of a choice I made, or they hate me because I am not like them? I'm a fucking *human*, Akuna. I'm not like any of them. I'm an outsider with a stone. How am I even qualified for this? How can I rule a fucking nation?"

They had talked about this before, but Rosella still felt like the responsibility was crushing her like a mountain on her back. The pressure now was enough to make her feel like she was crumbling, falling apart at the seams and there was no way to patch her up. Thoughts of her on the throne and being a queen was horrifying and almost laughable if she was still on Earth. To be transported to a different world and be thrust the keys to a land was not something she ever dreamed of, wanted, or wished. Images of tossing the necklace into a lake crossed her mind, or giving the necklace to Elaras came up as he was from this world and would be better suited. Besides her true name and necklace, what authority did she truly hold?

Akuna stood up and without a word or slight hesitation, he pushed his head against her cheek, and she felt his chest press against her stomach. His scales felt rough and smooth at the same time, and she could feel his breathing from his throat against her torso. Shocked by the sudden wave of kindness and the feeling of something or someone comforting her, she began to tear up.

"I am terrified, Vikshae. What am I supposed to do? And how am I supposed to get my necklace back?" she whimpered, pressing her head against his scaly face. As she did this, she realized she was shaking so much that she could see Akuna's spine spikes moving back and forth slightly.

"I know this is not the life you expected to have. Going from a normal, simple, easy life to one that comparatively is more difficult and stranger is distressing. From a place that you had routine, a home, things you grew up with, this new life is difficult to adjust to," Akuna said softly and as comfortingly as possible. His voice wavered as he spoke. "I'm truly sorry for taking you out of that place, for bringing you to a world that is not your own in any way that is thinkable. I believe in you because I have seen what this world will turn into without you in it. I thrust you into royalty, and that is my fault, Rosella. It is also my fault that the Rockshire got away with your necklace, and I promise we will get it back."

Rosella was thankful for the words he was saying. She realized that he did this because he knew she needed this, and that he could still feel her emotions and hear her thoughts.

Without a second thought, she wrapped her arms around his neck and squeezed him with as much strength as she had, and Akuna gave a gasp then let out a deep breath. They stood there for a few moments, waiting for Rosella's tears to subside and for her breathing to return to normal.

"What will happen if I don't make a good queen, Akuna?" she asked softly.

"Then we will work on how to make you the best queen. You will only fail if you let yourself. Mistakes are not the same as failures," he said wisely.

Nodding, she stroked his neck and felt the texture under her fingers, feeling the bumps and ridges of each scale and scar. When she let go of him and he took a step back, he looked over to Elaras.

"Shall I release him?" he asked, almost amused.

She glanced at Elaras as well, his body still slumped with an unmistakable line of drool on his face.

"Sure, but don't tell him about the drool," she said while letting out a chuckle.

Akuna inhaled before gazing expectantly at Rosella. "Shall I wipe his memory? Wipe me, and possibly his brother from his mind?"

Rosella looked over to the burnt body of Alryo. She now recognized him and Lycilla as the two who had slayed Salista the week before.

"No. We need to tell him something, and he needs to see that his brother was a victim of Lycilla in the end, and what he died for. Besides, if the connection he has with his mother is true, I believe she would like to hear from Elaras about Alryo's death."

"Very well."

Elaras, unparalyzed yet frozen, sat over his brother's ruined body and stared. Since Akuna released him from Lycilla's magic, he had not said a word to either Rosella or Akuna. He did not cry. He did not yell. He did not even look upset. He simply stared at the rotted remains of his little brother and breathed in rhythmic breaths.

"You think he's going to be okay?" Rosella asked Akuna while observing Elaras. She sat on her pad that was a far distance away from Elaras to give him space, and Akuna was poised like a cat examining a fish.

"He will have to be okay. Over time the loss will get more difficult, but he will heal. His brother made his choices," Akuna said, letting steam roll out of his mouth as he watched Elaras as well.

"What if he's upset at you for killing his brother?" Rosella asked, growing nervous because she had not thought of the implications of Akuna killing Alryo until now, and how Elaras might react to Akuna overall. How would Elaras react to Rosella when she

took Akuna's side if Elaras was upset? Would he try and kill her, or would he leave and never be seen again? She looked up to Akuna who, while sitting, was taller than she was. The sight of Elaras and his brother was nauseating her with concern and sadness.

"No matter what, Alryo made his choices, and I made mine. I made my choice to protect the both of you. Besides, Alryo was a Slayer, and I am happy to rid them from the world," Akuna said with defiance, holding his scaly head up high.

Rosella brought her legs to her chest and hugged them, putting her chin on her knees in contemplation, and they sat in silence.

Before long, Rosella saw movement from the corner of her eye. Elaras had raised his arm. His fingers moved with such finesse and ease that the pure blue smoke slithered from them with grace. Whispered incantations could be heard from his lips as the smoke wrapped around his brother's body.

Without any warning, Alryo's body became engulfed with black flames, and smoke from the fire flew out of the cavern toward the cave entrance. Elaras had not moved despite the heat from the flames, and he sat like a stone while his brother's body deteriorated before their eyes. In less than a minute, the body was gone and what was left was a pile of ashes and the family moonstone necklace.

"Whoa..." Rosella said to Akuna, as she could not help but stare at Elaras. She watched as he pulled out something from his bag, and without a break in his movements, he used his magic to make the ashes fly into the small, possibly magically enhanced, pouch. When all the ashes were in, he gingerly grabbed the necklace, and he wrapped the chain around the top of the bag to secure it, the pendant hanging on the side. He held the pouch in his hand and stared at it, and Rosella could see that his muscles

were loosening with each breath he took, giving into the emotions.

As if he could sense her eyes on him, he looked up to her, and she could see trails of tears on his cheeks that she had not noticed before. "It's interesting, isn't it? Seeing someone you have known most of your life and growing up with them. Making mistakes, making goals, pretending to be kings or soldiers. Having someone you can teach and someone you can learn from. Thinking you know every aspect of them, down to the hairs on their back. Then the next thing you know, they're completely different. They change their views, their values, their priorities," Elaras said, looking to Rosella and to the pouch. Tears were streaming steadily from his eyes, but his voice did not waver, nor did it break. "Then, one day, they die in front of you as a shadow of a person you once knew. On that same day, they become only ashes and a necklace. No face, no laugh, no smile, no more choices to be made. Nothing. Just...dust. Gone."

Rosella wanted nothing more than to go over to him and wrap her arms around him to give comfort. Everything inside her was telling her to help ease his pain and his thoughts, but her brain told her to wait. The knot in her throat gave her pause as well, because despite being saddened for Elaras, it was her companion, Akuna, that ended his brother's life. She knew she needed to wait until Elaras came to her, whenever he was ready to receive comfort or to talk. So, she stayed where she was and waited patiently, keeping an eye on him from afar.

Soon enough, she saw him draw up more smoke, and a large royal blue sparrow appeared in front of him. He took the string from the pouch and tied it to the leg of the sparrow, whispered a few things to the bird, and sat back. The bird gazed around for a moment, then flew out of the cavern and toward the entrance.

Rosella watched the bird fly away and didn't realize Elaras had started to walk over to her. Slightly startled, she moved to one side of the pad so he could sit on the other end, and he sat down without a word. Akuna got up and moved to the other side of Rosella, so that Rosella sat in between the two, and he let his gaze sit on the entrance to the cavern. Rosella adjusted her body so that she faced Elaras' right side, waiting patiently for him to speak or to even move.

After a few moments, he let his eyes drift to hers. His face was dry, and there was a look of determination placed upon it. "I understand why he had to kill my brother, and I'm not upset with him. In a way, he saved our lives because I do not think either of us would have walked out of this cavern alive if he had not intervened. So, it was either us or them. I'm just...shocked by many things right now, so I apologize for taking longer to come to words." He beheld Akuna for a moment and nodded, and she understood that as pure acceptance of Akuna's actions. Elaras leaned in close to her. "However, I am a little upset with you."

"What? Why?" she asked in a panicked tone, her eyes growing wide.

Akuna growled softly, and Elaras raised his hand to Akuna in a "wait" motion.

"You didn't tell me you had a dragon by your side. You know how much easier our traveling could have been? Quite selfish to keep him to yourself, Rosella," he said, and a soft, sly smile spread across his lips.

Rosella's chest had tightened significantly since Lycilla and Alryo arrived, and seeing his smile began to relax her muscles. She smacked his arm and pointed two fingers in his face.

"Don't do that to me, Elaras!" she exclaimed and laughed, smiling deeply.

Elaras laughed lightly, as if still weighted down by the

emotions he was feeling earlier but doing his best to break out of them.

When their laughter subsided, he looked to Akuna with great interest. "So, the Great Wrath of Dorthos. How did this start?" he asked simply, turning his body to finally face Rosella. She grew sheepish, and he saw the apprehension cross her face. "Or just tell me later. I have had enough emotion and mind-boggling shit for one night. Tomorrow, we can talk about you two," he said, pointing a finger toward both Rosella and Akuna, "and we can also plan how to get your necklace back. Together."

17
Reveries of the Heart

"So, when were you originally going to tell me that you were best friends with not just any dragon, but the living god of dragons, no less?" Elaras asked while they emerged from the cave the next morning.

They were only able to sleep for a few hours until they needed to make their way to Rion. The few hours Rosella slept were restless, and the emptiness she felt with her necklace grew stronger with every passing moment. She did her best to keep her spirits up nonetheless, even if it meant answering Elaras' now endless questions. Thankfully he had waited until they started their travel to ask anything of real importance.

"Ideally, I wasn't going to tell you for a while or at all, given that people and dragons don't associate with one another," she said simply as she fiddled with the moonstone.

Akuna chose to have yellow scales and green eyes, and instead of hiding in her hood, he rested on her shoulder.

"Really? So if he never made an appearance, you may have never told me?" Elaras asked, leading them to the path ahead.

"Pretty much, unless Akuna said it was okay to tell you, of course."

"Hmm. So you do what he says, then?"

"Yeah, pretty much whenever I need guidance."

"And you're okay with that?"

"Of course."

"Interesting," Elaras said coolly and stayed silent for a moment. "Why is he helping you, anyways?"

"Well, because he helped the Nightstones and now he is helping me," she said with a shrug.

"Okay. Well, how did he find you? You never really told me where you were from or your general history. I'd like to get to know you before things get more out of hand," he said, stepping in front of her to force her to stop walking.

This time she caught herself and did not run into him like he did the last time he pulled this move on her. His gray eyes bore into hers with vigor, and she felt her chest flutter like it always did when he looked at her, especially in this manner. The stare would surely intimidate anyone else, but it only made her fall a little harder for him. She could not think of that now, though, as she knew Elaras needed answers, and she was tired of skipping around the subject.

"Tell him. If he does not accept you, I will silence him so he cannot speak your secrets," Akuna said, and she felt her chest plummet into her stomach. Ice filled her veins, and she had to take a shuddering breath to keep her composure.

"Will you do what you said you would do, keep what I tell you about myself to yourself?" she asked, keeping her hand on the moonstone and holding his gaze.

"Of course," Elaras said, taking a step toward her and once again, they were only inches apart.

"Do you promise?"

"Yes, Rosella, I promise."

"You must promise me something else," she said, realizing that she needed more assurance about something she never expected to have toward Elaras.

"Okay, what is it?" he asked with a head tilt, a half-smile that was full of curiosity.

She took in a heaving breath, hoping the quake in her chest would cease long enough for her to get the words out. "You have to promise that you will remain by my side, despite what I say. I know that it is incredibly selfish of me to ask this of you before you even know what I'm going to say, but I don't have anyone else in this world. Besides Akuna, I'm alone. And, more selfishly, I'm beginning to trust you."

Elaras' eyebrows rose so high that his face seemed to elongate. He pursed his lips as his eyebrows fell, and he shifted his feet before saying, "All right, I promise that I will remain by your side, no matter what you will say."

Feeling a little bit of needed assurance, she took in another deep breath that did nothing to help her body from shaking. Elaras seemed to notice, and he placed his hands on her elbows. He gave a small nod, and she felt a thread of encouragement float through her.

"I'm not from this world. I'm from a place called Earth, and my birth name is Rosella Smith. I am a Nightstone, but from another universe, I think. Even though time feels longer, I was brought here by Akuna almost two weeks ago, because he knew that I would be able to save Arja. When he pulled me from Earth, I was very close to dying, and I should have died. I didn't, though. He saved me," she said as calmly as she possibly could, and given the look on Elaras' face she knew that what she was saying did not make sense. "On Earth, during my time, the Nightstones were not rulers. I was just a simple woman living my day-to-day life, and that world is so vastly different from Dorthos that I'm still trying to understand everything here. That is why I asked you not to judge me for things I ask that I should know. I know this is a lot, and I can prove that I'm not from Dorthos if you don't believe me. But please, know that I really am a Nightstone and that I plan on saving Arja. It may not be what I pictured for myself a year ago, but I am here now, and I plan on doing what I can."

Elaras stared at her with his mouth agape, and she realized he was digging his fingers into her skin. He looked away, confusion written all over his face while he processed the information. Instead of being angry or walking away, he started to laugh. The laugh was airy and hollow, and it filled the air with a sharpness to her ears that was unsettling.

Had she said too much, or not enough? Was he going to break the promise she should have never asked him to make and walk away? She began to stare out at the mountains to distract herself from his laughter, clutching the stone harder in her hand.

When she tried to take a few steps away, he gripped her elbows tighter, and she was pulled back forward, closer to him than before. His laugh vanished, but his enchanting smile remained, wider than it had been since his brother died.

"Oh, Rosella, I knew you were something special; I just didn't realize *how* special you were. All your questions and naivety makes complete sense now. My gods, Rosella Nightstone. I would like proof, though, if you don't mind. It's not that I don't trust your words while you're being vulnerable; I just want to make sure I can confirm my instincts to trust you," he said in his classic smooth tone that reminded her of the first day they met.

She smiled at him and heaved a sigh, hoping that would be the final deep breath she would have to take that day. Wiggling out of his hands reluctantly, she reached into her magic pouch and whispered, "Cell phone."

With wide eyes, he followed the cell phone in her hands as she removed it out of her pouch and held it out between them. The look Elaras had on his face was like a baby seeing a large stuffed animal, curiosity with a hint of fear.

"This is a cell phone. We use this to communicate with other people instantly, anywhere. We can also look information up, take pictures, play games or music, track time, and even create art. Our world is technologically advanced, but we don't have magic. We make up for it with things like this," she explained as she sort of waved it around and showed all angles of the device. When she pressed the lock button and the screen lit up, Elaras gasped and looked closer at the screen. The background was a picture of the Grand Teton mountains in Wyoming from a trip Rosella and her mother took a year before her mother passed.

"Mountains," Elaras said simply, while staring at the screen.

"Yep. The lands look similar enough on Earth compared to Dorthos, but there are more colors here," she said while constantly clicking the lock button to keep the screen illuminated. Rosella swiped her finger to unlock the phone, and the home screen showed the various apps that now seemed ancient. She tried to hand the phone to him so he could look through it himself, but he shook his head and held his hands up.

"Oh no, I may trust you, but this thing is...weird. So wait, you can call anyone on this, like how you can call me with my stone?" he asked with furrowed eyebrows and squinting eyes. She nodded, and his mouth fell open.

"Instead of just saying your name though and you come running, we can have a conversation. As long as you have one of these, though. Here on Dorthos, I can't call anyone. This phone is basically useless here, but I can still take photos."

"Photos?"

"Like realistic paintings."

"What?"

"Here, let me show you," she said with a chuckle while opening the camera app. The app opened with ease, and the screen filled with the trees that were next to them. She adjusted her phone to the front-facing camera and posed with an unamused Akuna still on her shoulder. After she took a photo, she opened the folder and showed it to Elaras. He immediately and gently lifted the phone from her hands and examined the photo, astonishment written all over his face.

"What the actual fuck!" he exclaimed, and Rosella giggled from the oddity of the situation in front of her. An elven man from a still-strange world, examining her cell phone from her world. The roles were reversed in this situation, and she was thankful that she was not the one learning something for once, and seeing someone else going through the same brain maze as her was interesting to watch.

"So, you believe me?" she asked, not able to wipe the smile from her face while watching him.

He looked up, and his face was still like a surprised child's, but this time gleeful. "Oh, gods, yes. Take a photo of me!" he said excitedly, handing her phone back to her.

She opened the camera again and aimed the back camera to him. "Pose like you would for a painting," she said, and he posed in a regal way. She took the photo and knew immediately that this would be her new background screen photo. When she showed him, he gasped and admired himself.

"That's how I look nowadays? Damn, I look good," he said while stroking his hair and tracing his sharp chin with his fingers.

Rosella rolled her eyes and averted her gaze, hoping he would not see her blush. She turned back and saw he was still looking at the photo. "You can go through them by swiping the screen left or right. Just touch the screen and it'll do what you want. I guess you can learn a lot about me if you want to look through my photos, and I can answer whatever questions you have," she said as she took a step away from him and started down the path a little.

He glanced up at her and grabbed her hand before she could get too far, suddenly serious. "Wait, Rosella. Since you aren't of Dorthos and you look like no being I have ever seen, what are you?" he asked, letting the hand that held her phone drop to his side, his other still holding onto hers.

The notorious lump that had appeared numerous times with Elaras came up again, and she had to swallow it down. "I'm what you would call a human," she said quietly and in a straightforward manner.

His head tilted in confusion, and she closed her eyes for a second, realizing that she was going to have to explain the entirety of the human race to someone that had never heard of them. Another thing that was so normal to her was not normal to him.

"Humans are not magical, and our skin tones range from pale white or albino, tans, to very dark brown. Mine isn't pale nor is it dark. It's more tanned like I've been in the sun for some time. We aren't blue or green, we don't grow scales or horns, and our ears are like mine: curved and boring. There are no other people-like species on our planet, and if there are, they are things of legends. So really, overall, humans are more dull compared to those here on Dorthos."

The grip grew tighter on her hand as Elaras stared at her. The look he had made her feel something she had never thought she would ever need to feel in her entire life. She felt *seen*, fully and completely.

"You aren't boring to me, Rosella Nightstone. My sweet, you are extraordinary," he said in a soft tone, and in that moment, she knew that she was falling hard for him and that there was no going back.

18
One of Your Many Toys

Lycilla Rockshire lay on a sanitary medical bed as a Cleric examined her severed palm. When she landed back at the Moonshadow manor, she rushed to the hospital wing with her fingers and the night stone necklace and berated the Clerics to connect the two halves again. The head Cleric told her that there was no way to fully heal this severe a burn and cut, and few magic users could heal such a severe bodily trauma. She resorted to just having the Clerics healing the remaining palm and thumb and placing her under a sleeping spell to accelerate the healing process. The night stone necklace resided in her pocket, and she did not dare touch it, afraid it would burn her again.

Now, two days after retrieving the necklace, Kaine Moonshadow stood by her bedside with an upturned nose and narrowed eyes while the Clerics tended to her. Whatever magic that was contained in the necklace proved to be extremely powerful, as her skin was still blackened and painful.

"You retrieved the necklace, but my son was killed. The idiot boy, he should have never grown so cocky. Now my eldest is somehow still alive because, what, you wanted him to watch his little girlfriend die?" he said in a bored voice, arms crossed in front of him. He wore all black as a formality for his son's death, but he still had an air of indifference at the loss of Alryo.

"You said you wanted Elaras dead. Well, I wanted him to suffer first. If that fucking dragon hadn't showed up, then they would have been dead and you would still have Alryo. I know how much you hate Elaras. I just wanted you to be satisfied," she said, making her voice strong as she spoke.

Kaine shook his head, and he squeezed the bridge of his nose. "I'm not satisfied because Elaras is still alive. I don't care for his little girlfriend. I only cared that she had a stone similar to the Nightstones'. The dragon will be a problem, though. No matter, you have the necklace, yes?" he said as he held out a palm.

Lycilla paused as she looked at him, stunned that he would want to touch the necklace after seeing the damage it had done to her hand. His eyes narrowed at her before she could respond, and she fished the chain out of her pocket then placed it in his palm as gingerly as possible.

He picked it up by the chain's clasp and watched it sway back and forth in the air in front of him. "Marvelous. This will make a suitable replacement."

"You should know, Kaine, that stone has powers. I—I think she's truly a Nightstone," Lycilla said, starting to grow nervous by his presence.

He shifted his eyes to her before gazing back at the night stone. "Impossible for her to be of Nightstone blood, stupid girl. Your family saw to that, remember? Besides, most stones like these have powers, but it is impossible that this is a real Nightstone pendant. Those have all disappeared, and you would have known this if you asked me before you broke into their manor. Therefore, this will have to do. Is the pendant the reason for your mangled hand?"

"Yes. I wrapped the chain around my hand so I wouldn't drop it while teleporting," she said, speaking quietly and turning sheepish.

"You wrapped the chain around your hand, and the chain cut it off?" he asked, his tone changing slightly to interest. He took the chain in his other hand and wound it around his index finger. Instantly, the skin began to sizzle and blacken. As quickly as he wrapped the chain, he unwrapped it and let it hang while grasping the clasp gently. "My, how interesting this has become. Clearly, you will not be able to wear this unless you want to become decapitated. I have never seen a stone hold such power, and the chain itself is immaculate, no burnt flesh on the chain, and there is no tarnishing."

"What are we going to do?" she asked, eyes wide with astonishment to see the ring of burnt skin on his finger where the chain wrapped around it.

Kaine took the necklace and pocketed it swiftly, then placed his hands behind his back. "I always come up with a plan, and I have yet to fail. That is why, for now on, you will stay here and only do as I say. While this is not a Nightstone's necklace, it's equally powerful."

"I was already staying here. I'm not sure what else you mean," she said, and she noticed that the Cleric had disappeared. She was now alone with Kaine for the first time ever, as she had always been with Alryo when they were in the same room.

Kaine turned to regard Lycilla, and she immediately felt more unnerved than she had ever felt. The look he had on his face was one of malice and disdain, and Lycilla was afraid of what he was going to do next. A grin slowly appeared on his face, and he leaned into her as close as he could without touching.

"You will become my wife. We will take over Arja, and then Dorthos. You are now mine to own. You will not tell anyone of this. You only say and do what I want. Do you understand, Lycilla Rockshire?" he said quietly, and as he spoke, subtle orange smoke leaked from the corners of his mouth.

As she looked at him and listened, her vision became covered in a blurry orange hue, and her ears muffled. Her muscles grew rigid, and when she tried to move a finger, extreme sharp pain shot through her body, and though she wanted to scream, her lungs seized. The only thing she could control herself were her eyes, and she blinked furiously through the pain at Kaine's malicious smile. Her thoughts silenced, and the only thing she could hear was a heartbeat that was not her own. When she tried to say something in her mind to herself, no words came. The only thing that could be heard was Kaine's voice in her head.

"Good girl. I'm glad you understand."

19
The Dark Side of the Moon

Rosella and Elaras traveled for another day before they reached a decently populated town. Elaras asked Rosella so many questions about Earth, humans, and other various things that spurred from her answers. They talked about how there were no dragons in her world and those were purely legend and fantasy creatures, how each country had different forms of currency, and even mundane things like Chapstick and chewing gum. The fascination on Elaras' face whenever she described anything must have been the same look she held when he described his world to her, and she couldn't deny that she enjoyed talking about Earth to someone who would never see it.

Elaras was trying to understand Earth's medicine as they were walking through a medium-sized town's gates. The decay stopped at the border of this town, the brown and black flora meeting green and lively glass. Rosella noticed that the land within the town looked very much like Earth, simply grass and leafy trees, blue skies and white clouds. The colorful lands that were precious to Dorthos and to Arja were still being sapped from the soil and the air, but slower than Rosella expected. Rosella gazed up toward the sky, and for a brief, intangible moment, she thought she was on Earth once again, and she simply woke up from an awful, lucid dream.

"So you're saying if your head throbs, you take a little block, and the pain goes away? You don't have to just deal with the throbbing or lie down—you can block the pain altogether?" Elaras' voice sounded, breaking Rosella from her thoughts and forcibly landing her back in her reality. She turned and saw his head was tilted quizzically, watching her as they walked.

"Yeah, it's pretty simple. It took years to develop Tylenol, and now it's part of everyday life for many people on Earth, depending on what they need it for," she said, shrugging as she reached into her pouch to grab the packet of Tylenol. She opened the packet and let the little pills drop in her palm.

Elaras stopped and peered closer at the pills. "Wicked gods be damned! Why can't we have this on Dorthos?" he asked, taking one and rotating it in his fingers.

"We have lots of issues that make Dorthos look like a dream, especially now," she said in a slightly somber tone. Elaras handed the pill back to Rosella, and she took both to ebb her own headache that had started to form.

"Well, clearly you have never heard of leshin's lament!"

"Leshin's lament? What's that?"

"Ah, well, it's absolutely grotesque! First you start to grow lesions, then your brain starts to eat itself, and even worse your skin starts to—"

"*Put your hood up,*" came Akuna's voice, blocking out the rest of Elaras' list of symptoms.

She immediately obliged and continued forward further into town, listening to Elaras ramble about the leshin's lament disease.

"*What's up?*" she asked as she started to look around.

"We're in a town that was forgotten from my memory. We can hurry through, and we'll be in Rion in a day or so," Akuna said with a tone that sounded similar to nervousness.

"Why? Is this town bad?" Rosella asked, and before she could get an answer, her eyes fell upon a large statue in what must have been the city center. Perched on what must be a mountain peak carved from green fluorite was a dragon of white and red stone. The dragon had holes in the frills, and all four of its wings were spread, and the mouth was wide open to mimic a loud roar. Rosella stood, gasping as she could feel Akuna rumbling in her hood, and beside her Elaras let out a hearty chuckle.

"Oh, gods, I forgot this town was here! And," he said before lowering his voice to a whisper, "this town would lose their collective shit if they knew Akuna was here. That would be so entertaining to watch."

Akuna climbed up Rosella's back and peered through her braids and hood. From the corner of her eye, she could see steam flowing through the air.

Elaras looked down to meet Akuna's eyes, a wide smile on his face. "What? You're a god; of course you'd have a town dedicated to you. If you saved them from some catastrophic event, I wouldn't be surprised if they worship you as well. You can't be mad at me for pointing out the obvious, *Great Wrath*."

Rosella tried and failed to hide a smile as a small growl came from Akuna's tiny chest, his eyes narrowed at Elaras. "He's right. They would lose their collective shit, but we won't tell anyone. Don't worry," she said as she lifted a finger to Akuna and gently poked his nose.

"I will not hesitate to skin him alive," Akuna said with a huff before moving to Rosella's other shoulder to be out of sight of Elaras.

"Oh, I know, Great Wrath of Dorthos," Rosella said, chuckling

as she looked around the city center, ignoring another growl from Akuna.

This town was larger than any town or village that Rosella had been in so far. Buildings were painted various colors, and there were cobblestone paths that weaved around the buildings. White and red flowers bloomed in patches around buildings and homes, and the trees that were littered through town had white and red leaves. The city center had three large buildings that were ornate and sturdy, made of massive stones of natural colors. The building on the left looked like a temple, and while she couldn't read the sign on the front from the angle they were standing in, she knew immediately that the church was for Akuna.

"They really love Akuna here. What'd he do to have a town dedicated to him?" Elaras asked as they both surveyed their surroundings.

"Oh hello, visitors!" came a tiny voice from behind Rosella. She whirled around and saw two young children standing, gazing up at Rosella with wide smiles.

"Hello! What are your names?" she asked, trying her best to match their excitement.

"I'm Drex!" said the devlair boy with light green skin and black horns, his yellow eyes reflecting the sun.

"I'm Drix!" said the other boy, a dwarf with tanned skin with a green beard already growing in, his blue eyes as bright as crystals.

"Hello, Drex and Drix, I'm Rosella. This is my friend, uh, Ethan" Rosella said while gesturing to Elaras. She ignored the tilt of his head and continued talking to the two boys. "Where can we find the tavern in this lovely town? We just need to rest for the night."

"This is your first time in Ye' Ol' Daltorys?" said Drex excitedly, jumping around in place.

"We have to show you around!" said Drix, holding a fist in the air and turning around.

Both Drex and Drix started walking away, and Rosella pulled Elaras along to follow.

"Ye' Ol' Daltorys? Isn't that Akuna's last name? Gods, what did he do for this town?" Elaras asked in a whisper as both Drex and Drix skipped ahead.

Rosella looked at Elaras, but before she could answer, her vision turned purple within the blink of her eyes. If she had a mental palace where she could sit back in a chair and let Akuna do his thing, she would. However, she had to let him control her, and she had to watch everything.

"Yes, it is my last name, and the town was *renamed* after me. However, I do not appreciate being called *old*," Akuna said with her voice.

Elaras' eyes grew extremely wide, and he got close to Rosella's face. He roughly grabbed a hold of her jaw and jerked her head up to examine her eyes, his face inches from hers. In the same instant he grabbed her face, Akuna made Rosella's hand fly up and grabbed Elaras' wrist in response.

"Do anything, and I'll snap your hand off your body," Akuna said, and with a combination of his words and her tone, she sounded menacing, and in her own mind, terrifying. Rosella's entire body began to bristle as Akuna's anger rose, her nerves tingling and her hair standing on end.

Elaras glanced at Rosella's hand gripping his wrist then looked back into her eyes before exhaling a deep breath. As he did so, an explosion of smoke burst from his body as he exhaled a second time.

The world around them turned dark and cold. Her skin prickled with ice, and she could barely see in front of her. The only thing that stood out was Elaras' bright gray eyes, as if his eyes acted like lanterns. Rosella wanted to ask what was going on, but no words came out. She could feel Akuna's anger skyrocketed as he readjusted himself to stand on her shoulder.

"Release us, elf," Akuna said with malice spitting through his words, and this time he was speaking in both his and Rosella's voices.

"Release her first, *dragon*," Elaras spat, his fury etched on his face. This was a ruthless rage that changed the lines of his face and the shape of his eyes. The scars on his face and neck became prominent, and his nose flared with each breath. He was taking sharp breaths as his hand squeezed her chin harder, his fingers spreading to her neck. The heat coming from Elaras' angry body was warming the air around them, but the inky blackness still remained.

She began to understand that Elaras, in fact, was not just a regular traveler and that the scars alone told a much bigger story than she was aware of. This was a side of Elaras she had never seen, and despite knowing his wrath was not directed at her, she still grew fearful because this was not the Elaras she had come to know.

"I will release her when you let go. She never has and never will be harmed by my hand. If you harm her under my care, you will not live the following hour," Akuna growled deeply with her and his joined voices. His growl reverberated throughout the space and in her ears as he inched forward on her shoulder, and Elaras finally broke his steely gaze with Rosella's eyes to regard Akuna.

A moment later, he let go of her chin but traced her body down to her hand to grab, the magic around them still holding strong. Akuna released Rosella from his mental grip, her vision turned to normal, and she regained control of her limbs. The dragon moved off her shoulder and into her hood once more without another word. Once she felt her fingers stop tingling from nerves and how tightly Akuna held onto Elaras, she stepped closer to the elf and stood in front of his heaving chest.

"Elaras..." she whispered, and when she reached to grab his other hand, he pulled away.

"How often does he do that?" he asked without looking at her.

"Besides the few times he's used my eyes to look around for a few seconds, five times. Fourth time with you," she said as she started to fiddle with the moon stone pendant, missing her own. He looked at her, but his face was serious, with hard lines and dark eyes.

"When?" he asked simply, but his tone was harsh and unforgiving.

"First time was in the tavern where we met, before you came to the table. Second time was when you told me about Lycilla. He talked through me for a bit. Third was when we first saw Arja, but he was just looking around. He used me to look around because he was hiding," she said, rubbing the moon stone in her fingers more than ever. "Fourth was when I had the panic attack when we first walked to the farmhouse in Arja. He stopped me in my tracks and talked me through my panic. He only does that to help me or to look around if he can't see himself, or in this case to answer you. I have never told him to not do it, as he doesn't take advantage of me in that way."

Elaras breathed in deeply, and he raised his head up to stare above her head. "My father does that, the controlling thing. He has been doing it all my life and that is how he is able to climb the ranks and gain power easily. Akuna can do it without his magic showing up, but with my father it doesn't matter if anyone sees it. Everyone is too scared to defy or challenge him. For a moment, I thought Akuna was controlling you more than you said he would. Controlling everything you say, or only allowing you to do or say certain things. I was concerned, and I was trying to find the purple in your eyes, but they weren't there. All I saw was you," he said softly, harshness still lacing his words, but his tone was slowly losing its sharp edge. He grabbed her other hand and released the hand that had grasped Rosella's face and flexed it, as if making his hand do something else would dull the memory.

"Sometimes he'll tell me what to say if I don't know how to answer something, or something that I should know he'll give me the answer to. From the flora to the laws that control the land, this world is nothing like Earth. I am out of my element and would not survive if not for Akuna," Rosella said, feeling her shoulders rise. Elaras' eyes landed on hers, and her shoulders lowered, seeing concern in them. "I trust him, and all he has done is help me. You don't need to trust him, but you also don't have to worry about being the only thing protecting me."

Elaras' lips pursed in thought as his toe tapped softly on the gravel. His eyes drifted to his feet, and the tapping ceased. "I don't trust him, but I think we can at least get on the same page. I don't like that he can control you, but as long as it's to keep you safe, then I can be as okay with it as possible."

"That's the best I can hope for, I think. Thank you, Elaras," she said softly, and he flinched. She realized that she had grabbed his moon stone with her other hand and said his name. "Oh, I'm sorry! I won't do that again. I didn't realize it would be so loud."

"No, it's not that," he said as he lifted his head again and took in a quivering breath. "You can do that whenever you need to, regardless of how close we stand."

"Oh, alright then," she said, confused, but still laying the necklace on her chest.

"Rosella, I'm sorry I handled you in that manner. I shouldn't have laid a hand on you, and I'm so sorry you had to see that side of me. I just—I got scared," he admitted, his eyes softening and taking a step closer. She took that as a sign of him calming down and reached to grab his other hand. Thankfully, he did not pull away this time.

"I forgive you, Elaras. Just, don't let the roughness be a normal thing between us, alright?" she asked, squeezing both sets of his large yet nimble fingers.

He squeezed hers back and nodded. "I promise," he said softly, smiling for the first time since Akuna took over her mind. "Are you alright, truly?"

"Yes, I'm alright," Rosella responded, though she could still feel heat and tenderness where his hand gripped her face and neck moments before. Before he could say something in response, she asked, "Okay, now, can you please take us out of this thing? I think Drex and Drix will wonder where we are, if they can even see this?"

Elaras looked around, and his sly grin came back. He let go of Rosella's hands, then whipped his hand in a flourish, and when deep blue smoke slithered out of his fingers, the black walls fell straight into the ground and bright sunlight pierced her eyes.

"There you are! We were looking everywhere for you!" Drex and Drix said simultaneously, both with hands on their hips.

"You both disappeared for a whole minute!" Drex said exaggeratedly, his hands flying in the air.

"So now we have to start over!" Drix said, mimicking Drex perfectly.

"Let's go! And no more running off!" they both said before turning around and walking.

Rosella and Elaras glanced at each other, and Rosella could tell that the usual gleam in his eyes had disappeared.

"I'm sorry," she said simply to him as she started to follow the two boys.

"What for?" Elaras said, his arm bumping gently into hers. She forgot that she always had to look higher up when they stood this close together.

"For the trauma your father caused you. He sounds like an evil man, and I'm sorry that you have to call him Father," she said softly. She decided to maintain eye contact and to match his stride and movements, trusting in his steps to not guide her off Drex's and Drix's path.

However, he stopped in his tracks and took in a deep breath. After holding a finger to Drex and Drix, who had turned around to say something, he turned to Rosella. "That is very kind of you to say. I...have never had anyone tell me something like that before. Not even my mother. Thank you for making me feel seen," he said in the softest tone she had ever heard him use.

"You make me feel seen, and you don't judge me. I'm happy I can make you feel the same as me," she said, smiling.

Elaras gave a sweet and genuine grin, then grabbed her hand, intertwining his fingers with hers. "My sweet, it's the least we can do for each other—make each other feel seen when no one else can. However, I do judge you."

"What? What for?" she said, shock and slight panic filling her voice.

"Darling, your hair is a mess. It's no wonder you leave the hood up! You really need to fix those braids of yours. Or better yet, match my hair," he said, laughing, gesturing to his long, neatly half pulled back blue and black hair. He tugged her forward, leading them on to follow Drex and Drix once more.

"My hair? *That* is what you're choosing to judge me over?" she said, trying her best to not smack him with her free hand.

Elaras, however, poked his free finger into her hair, and a large strand of hair fell into her face. "Yes, re-braid it soon, or they'll assume their new queen is a complete imbecile," he said with a hearty laugh as he watched Rosella stroke the disheveled braids.

As she did so, a flash of silver caught her eye. Turning in its direction, she thought she saw a black-furred head with a pair of green eyes observing them. A house blocked her view for a moment, but when they passed it, the person was gone.

20

Everything Looks the Same When Everything's Changing

Drex and Drix skipped ahead and pointed at each building, stating who lived in each home and what various buildings were, like an apothecary, a bookstore, and a textile shop. An hour later they made it back to the city center and pointed down a central busy road and reminded them that the tavern was halfway down.

"Bye, Rosella!" said Drex

"Bye, Ethan!" said Drix, and both scurried away from Rosella and Elaras.

They turned and went down the road toward the tavern.

"Are you going to tell me why you said my name was Ethan?" asked Elaras, who was considerably more cheerful as the tour went on.

Rosella and Elaras barely spoke during the tour, the silence seeming to calm his heightened nerves. On the other hand, Rosella had grown more anxious because the people she was seeing and waving to were people she was going to one day rule over, and the thought of that alone made her heart rate spike. She was in something of a trance when Elaras spoke, and she had to shake herself out of it.

"Oh, because I'm not sure how popular you are, and with the upcoming conflict with your family and the Rockshire girl, I didn't want people here to connect you to them. I wanted people to see you in a positive light, plus Ethan is a fun name from back home."

Elaras gave a small look of approval and nodded. She looked up at him and saw his sharp profile, and she studied his face and his features. The man she had seen less than two hours ago was terrifying, and she knew that she never wanted him to look at her the way he did then. Right now, he appeared calm and content, walking with purpose but also with an air of newfound peace. Meanwhile, Akuna had been hidden and silent since his and Elaras' exchange.

They made it to the tavern, the White Dragon Inn, and made their way to an open table. A pink lizgon was behind the bar, and a green-skinned female forest elf was walking around taking orders and passing out meals and drinks. They ordered food and asked for a night in the inn, and Rosella fished out chips for the server.

After they finished eating and drinking, they made their way to their own rooms for the night. As Rosella was in bed, she realized that her mind was too busy to fall asleep. Countless questions were flying around, and her eyes refused to shut, so she sat up in bed and placed her head into her hands. Akuna was curled up like a kitten and was fast asleep on the pillow next to where her head was moments ago.

Her body was moving before she realized what was happening. She slipped on her boots and made sure her dress was tightened, then she gently scooped up Akuna and stepped lightly to the door. When she opened the door, she expected to see at least one other person in the hall, but the only noises made were distant snores and creaking wood. She shut the door behind her and went to Elaras', knocking gently so she didn't wake Akuna in her hand.

As she waited, she gazed down at Akuna, his chest rising and falling with each breath and warm steam occasionally coming out of his nostrils. His scales were rough, and his sharp claws poked her palm, but the hair tufts on his head were incredibly soft like kitten fur. The Great Wrath of Dorthos, a living dragon god, Vikshae Akuna Daltorys, rested peacefully in the palm of her hand, and she couldn't help but be humbled by the trust he showed her.

Rosella raised her gaze and saw that Elaras had opened his door, and she could tell he was fully awake like her. He wore a black ruffled tunic and loose black pants. His black boots were still on, and the edge of one of his dagger's hilts sticking out from the boot. He clutched a dagger in his hand, but the blade was not facing her, as if he was casually walking around with it at the ready. His long hair was in a tight bun on the back of his head, and she could fully see his neck and ears. She had never seen him out of his leathers as he had changed when she fell asleep, or with his hair fully up, and she had to calm herself as she felt something tingling in her chest at the sight of him like this.

He looked down at her questioningly for a moment before opening the door further to let her and Akuna in. As she went to sit on his bed, a bit of blue smoke drifted from his fingers and flowed into Akuna. Seeing him do this to herself, she knew he was putting Akuna into a deeper sleep, so now she thankfully did not have to worry about waking him up. She placed her hands in her lap, still holding the tiny sleeping dragon before getting the courage to say anything.

"I couldn't sleep. I have so many questions I need answered. You couldn't sleep either?" Rosella asked, letting her gaze fall once more to Akuna. Now he was snoring so deeply that she had to cup her hands together to prevent from dropping him.

Elaras sat on the bed next to her. "No. It's hard for me to sleep most of the time. I'm always moving, always looking out, always... So, even though we're in a tavern and not a cave, I still don't feel safe,"

"Why are you always moving, anyways? Is it really that you have to figure out who killed the Rockshires and learn from them, or are you running from or to something else?" she asked, shifting her gaze to his but not outright staring at him. In this moment, she knew by the look on his face that this was not a simple question.

He took a moment, fidgeting with his nails and taking in a soft, quaking breath. "I do want to find out more about the magic user that took out the Rockshires, but that is just a cover. In reality, I'm staying away from my father. While I love my mother very much and would die for her, I cannot be in the same room as my father for more than five minutes. He controls every room he's in and ones that are miles away. He can control bodies and minds, a puppet master, and that is how he was able to rise through the ranks of nobility over the last hundred years or so. He would use his powers to abuse me and Alryo, and after so long I just left and only returned when my mother called for me, and sometimes Alryo. He was my brother, after all."

When he looked back at Rosella, he chuckled slightly. "What's got you looking like you just saw a redcap, Rosella?"

"A hundred years?" she asked simply.

"Ah, I guess humans don't live for long?" he asked with a laugh, seemingly thankful for the light conversation. "Elves can live for about two hundred years. I'm forty-six myself, but I'm probably closer to your age when it comes to maturing and growing since we have long lifespans. What about humans?"

"Humans can live for about a hundred years if they're lucky and take care of themselves. We're still considered children until we're eighteen, but our brains don't fully develop until we're about twenty-five."

"Wow, it sounds awful being a human."

"You're telling me. So, you're running from your father, and yet we're probably going to have to deal with him when we find my necklace. Lycilla was with your brother and was betrothed to him, so your father is definitely involved. Are you going to be okay facing him in that nature?" Rosella asked nervously. She wanted to know as much about him as possible, and she thought that if they talked about his father that it might help him somehow.

He grimaced and looked away again. "Yes, we'll have to face him. He's just...abusive and fucking awful. I feel horrible for my mother, and I'm not sure why she's with him. When I was a kid and I learned that I could use magic, I did everything I could to learn as much as possible and be just like him. My magic, however, was opposite of what he could do. His magic is purely for controlling anything he wants, and mine is to create and to move myself or anything else. I learned all that I could, especially from Mystrias, but it was never enough.

"One day when I was eight, he was yelling at Alryo about something, and I became so scared that I just wanted a place to hide. Next thing I knew I was in the black shrouded place, the world outside of it slowed down. I hid in my haven for about two hours, and he didn't know where I was the entire time. Whenever I needed to hide or to calm down, I would make my haven pop up, and eventually I learned I could move around in it. I'll be in one place one second, and far away the next. It's not teleportation. I think it's just freezing time and moving around, even though I can't interact with anything outside of my haven if I don't bring anything in it first. I used my haven to run away from home after Mystrias died, because I didn't want him to find me. Even though I tried for years to improve my magic for him, I learned I was doing it for myself the entire time."

Rosella let her gaze drift all over his face, taking in every detail she could. The furrowed brows when he spoke of his dad, the airiness of his tone when he spoke of his mom. Speaking of his haven made him light with his movements and his breath. When he was finished, he let out a sigh, and his shoulders drooped.

"Are you still wanting to learn from the one that killed the Rockshires?" Rosella asked simply.

"Yes, eventually," he said, shrugging.

Rosella smiled and poked Elaras' arm, and when he turned to face her, she pointed down at Akuna. His eyes grew wide like saucers. When she smiled and nodded, he stood up and placed his hands on his head in shock. He was pacing back and forth, and Rosella couldn't help but grin at his surprise.

"I'm not surprised, if I'm being honest. He was connected to the Nightstones, so of course he would be the one responsible for the Rockshires' demise," Rosella said, her eyes still following Elaras pace around the room.

He stopped and faced her, his hands now on his hips. "Rosella, I could learn *so much* from him, but my gods, I doubt he'll ever talk to me again. My search is over, and of course it ends with *him*. This is so cool, though. The Great Wrath, avenging a whole family."

"You'll have to get used to him, Elaras. He'll be with me for the rest of my life. If you're going to be with me for the rest of my life as well, you'll have to get used to being around him," Rosella said, and she quickly realized that her words likely sounded more than what she had meant.

Elaras caught on to the implication, however, and his eyebrows shot up to his forehead. A wide, genuine smile spread across his face.

Wanting to avoid any awkward conversations and to prevent anything happening, she got up and scurried out of the room.

Oh my god, I'm such a child! I'm twenty-eight years old, not a fucking teenager. Stupid, stupid, stupid, she said to herself as she ran to her room and locked the door behind her. She placed Akuna on the pillow next to hers and covered her whole body with blankets, hiding from the world in her own non-magical haven.

The next morning, she was afraid to leave her bed, knowing she would have to face Elaras and potentially face questioning for what she could have possibly meant the night before. Akuna had other ideas as he started tapping her still-blanketed head. For a creature so small, his paws—hands?—were quite strong as he rapped her head with measurable force.

"Get up, silly human. You'll have to face him sooner than later," Akuna mocked.

Rosella groaned and smacked him from under the blanket. *"How'd you know I was avoiding Elaras?"* Rosella retorted, though she already knew the answer.

"I can read your mind, remember? Now get up, or he'll come find you himself."

"Fuck no. I'll rather live under here and be a child than have him ask me if I like him or not."

"You obviously like him. It's obnoxious. Just tell him you do and move on. Stop embarrassing us."

"Me, embarrassing *us*?" Rosella yelled as she flung the blanket off her head and twisted around in bed until she locked eyes with Akuna, who had been tossed with the blanket and was now hovering in front of her. "I might as well have told him we were going to be married and have lots of children to continue the Nightstone line! I only embarrassed myself. You were asleep the whole time! I'll act like a child right now if I want to. I won't be able to when I'm queen."

"Ah, so you're slowly accepting becoming queen?" Akuna said with a toothy grin, his tiny chest puffed out and head held high.

"Really, that's all you got out of that?"

"Well, yes, because it was the most important thing to hear. Everything else is exhausting. Now, you're going to be queen soon, so you need to start practicing being queen. Start by telling Elaras you like him and that you want to make Nightstone babies together."

"*Akuna*!" Rosella yelled before grabbing a pillow to toss at him.

When the pillow went airborne towards him, he shot purple smoke at it, and purple bubbles burst into the air where the pillow once was. Rosella scowled at him while Akuna laughed heartily.

After getting ready for the day and leaving her room, she talked herself through the speech she was going to give to Elaras. She was going to ask him to be hers and to be by her side when she became queen. When things settled down after a year or so, they would think about where they wanted their relationship to go, if it got that far. They could become married and have kids sometime after, or they could have no kids at all. She liked him, and she guessed he liked her too, so why hesitate any longer and why not set up the plan for them, or make a resemblance of one?

However, when she made it downstairs to the tavern, she saw that Elaras was sitting with someone wearing sparkling silver armor. They were chatting animatedly, and Elaras had a wide smile on his face as he spoke, and he was not hiding his face at all. As she walked closer, Elaras saw Rosella and stood up in haste, which was odd for him as he never reacted that way to seeing her before. Then he gestured toward the person with the armor, who stood up quickly and turned around.

Rosella saw this was a cat-like person with black fur and shining green eyes and one heavily scarred ear. The undercloth of their armor was a royal blue and white patterned fabric, and the close-to-black chainmail on top of the fabric had a deep purple sheen. They wore the same bracers and greaves as Rosella, but she noticed that they were not wearing boots. The armor's coat of arms itself was what caught Rosella's eye, as the exact pattern of her tattoo was reflected on the chest plate, right above the cat-person's sternum. Three stars surrounding a crescent moon gleamed brightly from the morning sunlight that poured into the tavern. The sight reminded her of the dreams she would have on Earth, her tattoo glowing silver, remembering the warmth she felt from them.

This shook Rosella to her core until the person fell to a knee and placed their paw-like hand in the shape of a crescent moon over their chest, their head bowed low. The next thing they said were words that Rosella would never forget, and would forever solidify the truth that she was, in fact, to be queen.

"Pleasure to make your acquaintance, Future Queen Nightstone."

21
Be Careful, Icarus

High Cleric Varran Daldrack paced the entry hall of the Nightstone manor, the morning sun spilling in from the moon and star-stained glass that rested above the grand mahogany doors. He was whispering incantations, and small puffs of white light were shooting from his fingers so quickly that only the trail of each puff could be seen. Each light shot into walls and into the guards, the housekeeper and their staff, the Clerics, and the Paladins who all stood to the side of the entry hall. High Paladin Joss Bildow stood sentry near the doors themselves and watched Varran pace back and forth, letting the white puffs of smoke enter his body without flinching.

"Varran, you're going to wear a hole in your boots," Joss said, loud enough so Varran could hear him over the incantations.

Varran was wearing his normal garb of black bracers and greaves that showed the Nightstone symbol of a crescent moon and three stars, blue and white patterned undershirt with a long purple hauberk that stretched to the mid-thigh, and a silver chest plate with the Nightstone coat of arms. Everyone around him wore the same uniform and armor, but the Clerics did not wear helmets, and the guards did, adorned with a white flowing plume on top that waved in the air every time the wearer moved. Varran and Joss' were varied as well, as they had black leather and steel-armored skirts adorning moons and stars splitting in the front to show the hauberk that fell to their mid-thigh.

"Joss, my boots are the least of my concerns right now," Varran said without looking up at him. "These...people...are coming to tell us that they have the right to take over Arja because they have something that deems them worthy. What could they possibly have? And how is the emperor not involved? Then again, we shouldn't want him involved because the emperor is desperate for someone to take over Arja. We have yet to find Rosella. None of my Clerics have sent word that they found her."

"We have to trust that things will work out and that the Rockshire girl will not be able to take over for whatever silly reason they think they have," Joss said, shifting his stance. "Besides, at the end of the day, the emperor should know that only a Nightstone can hold the Arja throne."

"I'm not sure, but I know for a fact that they do not have the night stone, as they cannot properly possess it. As for the emperor, remember that he is growing restless after thirty years so he may say that it is time to go the traditional route of ruling. Because the Rockshires successfully ended the Nightstone line, they would take over the throne. I do not believe the emperor will care that the land is not healing, and they will just tell the Rockshire girl to figure something out."

"That is unjust and will only create chaos," Joss said loudly in his boisterous orcish and goliath tone.

Varran stopped in his tracks as the last incantation was shot into a manor cat that was strolling the back hall. "I know, Joss. I believe I speak for everyone here that we do not want this girl and whoever her companion is that is supposed to solidify the throne for her to take over. They will have to go to the emperor no matter what to make their case, but they wanted to lay 'claim' to the manor first," Varran said, walking up to Joss and having to look straight up at him. "I'm not sure what else they plan to do while they're here. Prove to us somehow she belongs on the throne? Tell us to not leave until they come back? Control us somehow, make us believe them? All of this is odd, and I have a twinge in my chest about this."

Joss kneeled in front of Varran and placed a massive hand on his shoulder. "We'll figure it out. Worst case scenario, me and my guards will kill them. I know, I know, you don't condone violence, but I believe it is warranted here," Joss said with a chuckle.

Behind them, Varran could hear quiet agreements from the entire staff, the other Clerics, and guards. Varran smiled in response and placed a gentle, smaller hand on Joss'.

A loud knock echoed throughout the room that originated from the front doors. Varran and Joss separated, and Varran moved to the center of the hall, nodding at the guards closest to the door. The sunlight spilled into the hall and two silhouettes appeared at the threshold. One was a tall male elf in what looked like lavish purple and black robes with accents of gold, and the other a female devlair with similar robes and stood considerably shorter than the man. They walked toe to toe with each other up to Varran and stopped once they were in front of him.

"Hello, you must be the High Cleric of the Nightstones. I'm Lord Kaine Moonshadow, and this is my betrothed, Lycilla Rockshire," Kaine said, his deep blue skin soaking in the light so that only his eyes radiated along with his shining teeth. He held out a hand for Varran to shake, and Varran took it politely.

"High Cleric Varran Daldrack. How may I help you today? We received your sparrow, but we are still unclear as to what you were needing or requesting," Varran said simply but professionally. He let his eyes wander briefly between the two of them and saw the orange-skinned devlair with black horns was quite expressionless. Considering this was the same devlair that had broken into the manor about a week or more ago, he had expected a grander, more energetic entrance. Instead, she stood with her eyes straight ahead and her right hand clasped over her left in front of her robes.

"As you and this household may be aware, the Rockshires are the rightful heir to the Arja throne. This Rockshire," Kaine said as he placed a hand on her lower back, "is ready to claim her rightful throne, and I am to be her king consort. We just need to know from you all how to proceed with her claiming the throne, after we meet with the emperor in a week's time, of course. Oh, I would also like to be wed in this estate, to make succeeding the throne as smooth as possible."

Varran stood stock still and simply stared at Kaine Moonshadow. Kaine had the face of arrogance and of someone that was hungry for power, and Varran had seen this look enough to know that this was not something that would end well for anyone. Joss took a step closer to the pair and growled softly, staring daggers into Kaine.

Varran cleared his throat and placed his hand on his own chest over the Nightstone coat of arms. "Lord Moonshadow, unfortunately only a Nightstone can claim the throne. The magic the family held was one that would heal the lands, and without a Nightstone, this land would die, and all of Dorthos will suffer. While I appreciate your effort and your presence, I cannot allow you or the Rockshire girl to ascend the throne. I will also not have you wed in this manor, as this home simply does not belong to you."

Who knew, maybe this Moonshadow man believed this would

work and that they could take the throne. Varran was also not going to allow him to know that a Nightstone was alive, and that he was waiting for her to appear.

Kaine, however, stood straighter and stared down his nose at Varran, looking more arrogant than before. "High Cleric Daldrack, we are to ascend the throne. You say Arja needs a Nightstone, but is it truly that you need a Nightstone or just that you need the stone of night to power the land? Because I have the stone, and Lycilla shall use it to heal this land on the throne that belongs to her," he said, then he fished out a pendant and chain from his pocket.

Unmistakably, it was the black stone with star-like speckles, and the pendant itself hung from a pristine chain. A few gasps in the hall rang out from behind Varran, and he raised a hand out to silence them, keeping his eyes on the pendant and on Kaine.

"Lord Moonshadow, I believe that is meant to be worn as a necklace. I will believe you or the Rockshire are meant for the throne when you put it on. Not any time before that, unfortunately," Varran said with a strong voice.

He knew these two could never wear the necklace, and he wanted everyone around him to see that these two did not belong on the throne. Yes, the name Nightstone powered the land, but they used the stones to keep the land alive and to ensure the land was right with minerals and remained healthy. If a plague began, the Nightstones used their own magic and that of the stone to vanquish the virus before it could spread. The stone and the family were one and the same, and someone married into the family that received the name could use the family power. Someone that usurped the throne completely could not take over and use the same power. Rosella Nightstone appearing after so long was a miracle, and the Nocturnal Manor waited with bated breath for her arrival.

Kaine gave a half smile and pocketed the necklace once more and placed his hands behind his back and leaned down stiff-backed toward Varran. "I do not need to put this on to show we belong on the throne. We shall go to the emperor, and he shall give us the throne himself. We simply came here out of courtesy, *Cleric*."

"You may get your permission, but you will never be allowed in this home again. Now, *Lord*, please leave," Varran said, gesturing to the door and nodding to the guards around him.

Joss took another step forward and placed his war hammer in both hands at the ready.

The Rockshire, suspiciously, had not moved once since entering the entry hall. Finding this odd, Varran closed his eyes for just a second to cast an incantation in his mind, and when he opened them, he saw the various magical properties around him. He saw his staff around him glowing white from the magic he placed on them, and he saw a blue and white light shine from Kaine's pocket where the necklace resided. When he looked at the Rockshire girl, he saw a bright orange hue all over her body, and her eyes shone so bright that the glow burned his sight.

The spell faded, and he took a step back from Kaine and pointed at the girl. Before he could do anything, however, Kaine raised his hands and shouted two words of an incantation.

The room filled with a bright orange light that was similar to the glow coming from the Rockshire girl, and the smoke from the magic shot out like a shockwave. Varran held his bracers in front of his face to block the magic and the light as much as possible, and when he put his arms down, he saw Kaine had a malicious smile on his face and his hand raised with orange smoke cuffed around it.

"High Cleric Daldrack, I wish you the best of luck, even though you will probably not be here when we take the throne. Toodaloo.

Lycilla, teleport us back to our manor, now," Kaine said, and the Rockshire girl raised her hand in the air.

With a few flicks of her wrist, red, shaky smoke twisting around her fingers, they were gone. Before she vanished, however, Varran saw that her left hand had been blackened and half of her hand was gone. Varran knew instantly that at some point the necklace had once been wrapped around her hand, and that was how they knew putting on the necklace was dangerous. Confirmation that the necklace was a true night stone and had been stolen from Rosella was reassuring, but that feeling only lasted a moment as he realized that everyone, including Joss, was encroaching on Varran.

Everyone that was surrounding him had an orange hue to their eyes that he did not need magic to see, and every single face had their teeth bared and were whispering insults and threats. Two of the guards closed the doors, then were stalking to Varran, their swords drawn. Kaine must have cast a controlling spell on them, and his goal was to take out the one person that had current control of the Nightstone home.

First, Varran waved his hands in front of him with a few words that sounded like a song. A large white, opaque bubble was placed around him so that he could be shielded from the staff, not wanting to risk getting hurt. Then, he closed his eyes and held his palms up, whispering a string of words and rhymes that made the shield glow a blinding white shining through his eyelids. Slowly, he turned his palms to face out and stretched to each side of his body. He completed the words of the spell, and when he opened his eyes, he saw the shield explode outward in white smoke similar to Kaine's magic moments before.

An echo of groans and screams rang out loudly in the halls all around him, and the people staggered in place, grasping their heads or rubbing their eyes.

Joss was the first to come to and shake off the magic smoke.

"Varran! Did Kaine cast a spell on us?" he asked. Varran noticed a tinge of panic enter Joss' tone for the first time in a very long time.

When Varran nodded, Joss grabbed his war hammer with both hands once more and charged toward the door.

"No, Joss! They teleported out of here, I'm sure, back to his home. You can't do anything right now," Varran said, stepping toward Joss.

Joss turned around, panting and sweat beading on his forehead.

"He cast that spell for us to kill you, didn't he?" said Gerrart from behind Varran, the other younger half-orc, half-goliath Paladin.

Varran turned to him and nodded. "Everyone, we have to be vigilant. We in this manor know Kaine and Lycilla cannot truly take the throne, and we also know that a true Nightstone is out there. We are not sure where, but we know that she is the one to save us. As I have told each and every one of you, we have to be on the lookout for her and do what we can for her. My other Clerics are out there waiting for her, searching. We cannot control what the emperor says or does, but what we can do is make sure they do not come back with force. For now, we *must* protect the Nocturnal Manor, the throne, and most importantly, the Nightstone name. Do you all understand?"

Everyone in the manor concurred, and they all placed their hand to their chest with their fingers in the shape of a crescent moon. Varran smiled, turning to Joss and setting a gentle hand on his hand that held the hammer. He whispered the same words he used the other week and sent calm emotions into Joss. A deep sigh escaped Joss' throat, and he nodded in thanks, letting his war hammer fall into its sheath on his back.

A yellow mystical sparrow flew through the wall of the manor and landed on Varran's shoulder. A scroll of paper was clamped in its mouth, and he did not wait a second taking the scroll and unwrapping it. His eyes scanned the paper, and when he looked up, he saw that everyone was staring at him expectantly. A smile spread on his face, and he held up the letter in a sign of victory.

"Ezralious found her. She is in Ye Ol' Daltorys! He is going to bring her here in two days' time after he meets with her. We must prepare for her arrival!" Varran said, ecstatic for the positive news. He turned to the housekeeper, a lizgon with bright purple scales and blue eyes, and asked, "Please connect with Alizstar and their guild. I need to know everything about the Moonshadows, but they cannot be connected to this manor. Kaine knows who we all are, and I guarantee we will now be watched. Stay on guard and let me know if you need anything."

The lizgon nodded and headed toward the back entry, their staff following them. A smile formed on his face again, and he knew it had been some time since he smiled because his face muscles strained and resisted. In the back of his mind, he hoped that this would be the first of many smiles after this hopeful news.

22
Spinning Heads and Broken Darkness

Rosella stared at the cat-person with pure shock, and in a moment of panic she rushed forward and grabbed their elbows to lift them up. Their green eyes flashed in confusion, but they stood at Rosella's command. They were easily a foot taller than Rosella as well as skinnier, but their nature and presence were calm.

"No, please, try and not be outright about it. I, uh, thank you for your courtesy but please, let's keep this quiet for now. What's your name?" Rosella asked them, doing what she saw Princess Diana do many times and hold their paw-like hand, not breaking eye contact.

"Cleric Ezralious, my future Queen," they said quietly as they shook her hand. Hearing someone call her "*Queen*" was odd, especially from someone other than Akuna or Elaras. She knew this was something she would have to get used to, but the shock was still in her veins.

"*That is a felinette. They are rare but inherently loyal,*" came Akuna's voice from her head, and there was a sense of fascination from Akuna she did not expect.

"Ezralious, pleasure to meet you. Please, sit so we can talk?" Rosella asked, letting go of his paw and gesturing to the table.

He nodded gratefully and sat down across from her, Elaras sitting closely to her left side. The realization hit her that Elaras always chose her left side when sitting or walking next to her, and while it struck her as a little odd, she brushed it off.

"So, were you out looking for me? How'd you know who I was? I don't even have my necklace."

"Our—your—High Cleric told us your description that was given to him by the Goddess Elyphr, and you and your friend here matched what was given. However, we were told there were three, but I have only met you two. Did you lose someone on your journey?" Ezralious said in an almost hasty manner.

"The goddess of night told them I was here?" Rosella asked Akuna, whom she knew couldn't give a straight answer.

"Seems so," he replied. *"The gods work in ways that are hard to explain. She seems to want you in this world and to be on the throne."*

"Uh, our third is away at the moment, but there is no need for concern. They will meet with us in Rion, I presume," Rosella said, sending a shifty look toward Elaras, who was smiling to himself.

"Alright, well, do you need an escort to Rion? I can take you there as quickly as possible," Ezralious said, placing his paws on the table.

"Oh, no, we should be good on our own. Don't worry, we should get there in a day or two if we leave here in a bit," Rosella said, hoping she was sounding confident. Having an escort would be nice, but she was not keen on the idea of having a stranger with Akuna still wanting to be hidden. The other thought she had was if she could have a few more moments of alone time with Elaras, they could discuss their future properly.

"Yes, Your Majesty. I'll send a sparrow to High Cleric Varran and tell him you're on the way. He'll be ready for your arrival! I sent one earlier this morning telling him I found you, so he knows where you are already, for now at least," Ezralious said before standing up. They bowed their head once more and placed the hand moon symbol to their chest quickly, Rosella thankful that they did not kneel this time. They straightened and bounded out of the tavern.

Elaras turned in his chair and faced Rosella, a smirk on his face. "Well, how did it feel giving your first order as a future queen?"

"Do you want to die? Because that is what will happen if you keep being annoying."

"If I die by your hands, I wouldn't be upset. However, I will haunt you for the remainder of your human life," Elaras said, laughing and waving a server over to order food.

Per Akuna's request, they headed out of the town once they were finished eating and onto the path toward Rion. An hour outside of Ye Ol' Daltorys, the lands were colorfully vibrant like they were in Cupridale. Rosella watched the pink clouds above billow into swirls and felt the cool breeze on her skin. The purple grass crunched under her feet and the rainbow leaves of trees danced in the healthy wind. They walked for most of the day without much discussion, and they also agreed that fight training could wait until after she was crowned, given the time needed to get to Rion.

Toward the end of the day, they found an abandoned cabin a half day's travel away from Rion and decided to stay there. They ate dinner, and both Elaras and Akuna were quick to fall asleep. Rosella was not so lucky, as she tossed and turned on her sleeping pad for what seemed like hours. Supposedly, she was to be in the town and the castle she would spend the rest of her life in a matter of a day. Being called "queen" by a Cleric that served the Nightstones—served her—gave her a feeling of shocked sensory overload. Processing what they said, their armor, the coat of arms that matched her tattoo exactly, was overwhelming and made everything real. She sometimes thought this was a strange fever dream, or some fake reality that someone pulled her consciously into. No, this was very real and was actually happening.

Deciding she needed air and to stretch, she got up quietly and headed to the door after putting on her boots but leaving the bracers and cuirass behind. Her hand hesitated above the door handle, and she felt frozen. Her body was telling her to not leave, though her mind needed an escape. She walked back and grabbed her bow, her belt with Shadow Breaker and quiver, before trying the handle again. Her hand hovered for a second before she grabbed the handle and turned, walking out silently into the cool air.

The night was bright from the full moon, and shadows were cast from the trees and the cabin itself. Elaras' last name started to make sense, as this moon was so massive that she could almost see clearly between the trees in the moonlight, but the shadows were as dark as a new moon night.

Close to where she stood, she heard soft footsteps stepping on snapping twigs and hard dirt, so she knelt and grabbed her bow and an arrow. Creeping forward, she saw movement ahead of her, but due to them being in the shadow, she could not make out a shape. Nonetheless, she moved forward and nocked the arrow into the string and kept moving forward as quietly as possible. Within a minute, the shape started to take form, and she noticed that instead of a deer or some sort of wildlife, the creature was standing tall and was wearing all black with a hood.

Their eyes met hers for a split second before the creature charged forward, laughing maniacally. She pulled back the string, aimed, and fired at the creature that charged at her, thankful they were a distance away. The arrow flew into the creature's nose and out the back of the head, the arrow squelching as it sliced through the skull and landed in a tree trunk behind the creature.

The creature's now lifeless form fell forward with a *thunk*, and all was quiet again.

Wanting to retrieve the arrow and to see the creature she just struck down, she crept through the trees toward the body. She noticed immediately that it was a devlair man with light yellow skin, and the blood that spilled onto their skin contracted drastically.

Rosella covered her mouth to hide a scream, realizing that this was a person, and she just killed them. Feeling her knees and legs give way, she fell back and scrambled backward, trying her best to get away from the body of the unknown assailant. She rushed to get her belt off in hopes that even the small amount of pressure that was on her torso being released would help her breathe as deeply as possible.

Elaras. She needed Elaras. Maybe he knew this person and who they worked for, or they possibly worked for his father. Who else would come after her in the dead of night for a third time? When that realization came to mind, she decided that she would never sleep anywhere without Akuna locking the door or putting a trap in place. No more trusting that no one would come after her or her companions. No more walking outside alone, especially in the brightest of nights. She reached for the moonstone and grasped it in her hand, her hands shaking violently.

"Elaras Moons—" she said, and before she could say any more, she felt something hit her from the side, and her body was pinned to the ground.

Someone big and strong sat on her chest and had pinned her legs with their own. The weight of their body was immeasurable as she struggled to breathe from the tackle and from the pressure on her chest. She dropped the necklace back to her chest as grabbed her bow with both hands and wailed the assailant on top of her.

"Now, now, pretty, little, pathetic *queen*. If you struggle, this will be more painful," said the voice, and the only features she could make out were tusks protruding from their lower lip and long braided hair that was a deep green.

"Why are you—trying to—kill me?" Rosella said between useless whacks of her bow and shallow breaths.

"Because you're in the way, that's all. Without you and that handsome, idiotic elf, my master's job will become a lot easier," the orc teased, their arms crossed as they stared down with an evil smile on their face, ignoring Rosella's hits completely.

"Lycilla will never become queen, and Dorthos will suffer if she does," Rosella struggled to say. Each whack was now taking the last remaining oxygen she had, her vision growing blurry and her arms growing weaker. She let the bow fall next to her, and the orc laughed.

"See, isn't it better to just let go? Give it a few more minutes, and you'll be with the gods," she said in a mocking tone, laughing between her words.

Rosella stared back up at her, wishing Akuna or Elaras was there. Then a thought struck her like a brick, and she used the remaining few breaths she had left.

"Great Wrath of Dorthos, save me from this turmoil! I see you now flying above! Save me!" she said, pointing to the sky.

Pleasantly surprised, the orc looked up toward the treetops and tried to peer through the branches. While the orc was distracted, Rosella grabbed Shadow Breaker from her belt that ended up by her head and stabbed it into the orc's stomach, the red glow of the ruby lighting up the area around them. A moment later, she glared down at Rosella with pure shock and displeasure.

"You pathetic waste of time!" the orc cried and ripped Rosella's hand away. The orc then grasped the handle to pull the blade out of her stomach but the dagger remained in place no matter how much the female orc pulled and tugged at the handle. The ruby had dimmed when Rosella released the dagger and now the dagger became unwavering, unmoving. "What is this?"

"Shadow Breaker. Now get off me, you fucking bitch!" Rosella said with conviction, smiling and watching the blood drain out of the orc's stomach. Rosella reached up to grab the handle with both hands, and they watched as the ruby glowed brightly again.

The female orc's face twisted in fear as Rosella took a rattling breath before twisting the dagger in her hands with her remaining strength and energy.

One moment the orc was still sitting on her, seemingly afraid of what was about to happen, and another she was completely gone. Rosella sat on the ground completely covered in blood and viscera. As she gasped for air, she felt the orc's blood trickle down her throat, tasting strong metal on her tongue and in between her teeth. She lay there for some time, catching her breath and wiping her eyes as much as possible to stop the stinging. Was it blood that was stinging her eyes, or was it sweat, or even tears she didn't realize had escaped?

"Rosella!" came Elaras' voice from nearby the cabin.

"Over here, lying down. Too weak, too tired," Rosella said as best as possible, still breathless and weak. She could fall asleep right now, and she would probably get the best rest of her life.

"Rosella, I can't find you!" came his voice again. She heard his footsteps shuffling through the leaves and branches, but he was getting further away.

As a last-ditch effort before falling asleep, she grabbed the moonstone.

"Elaras Moonshadow," she whispered into the pendant before dropping it to her chest.

In the time it took for the moonstone to land on her chest, Elaras was at her side. His eyes wildly scanned her whole body and the scene around her, taking in every detail.

"I killed two people. They tried to kill me first, so I think it's reasonable," she said breathlessly before she had a coughing fit. Her throat cleared, and she felt the need to sit up to cough more.

Elaras helped her lean forward, and she puked immediately upon sitting upright. Her coughing resumed once she hacked up her entire stomach. Days had passed since she felt the need to cough, and the returning sensation was not welcome.

"Gods, Rosella. Why were you out here alone?" Elaras asked, brushing her now loose hair out of her face and rubbing her back.

She looked at him and gave a weak smile. "I couldn't sleep. I figured I was fine. Nope, your father sent assassins *again*," she said, pointing to the blood and the gut-filled spray that covered the grass and trees around her and to the body she shot with an arrow. "These fuckers tried, but I got them. I'm *not* pathetic."

"Who said you were?"

"Orc lady. Now orc lady is the...mist. This dagger is insane," Rosella said, her fingers tapping the blade that had dropped from her hands.

Elaras smiled and grabbed the dagger to place it back into its sheath. "And now you understand why it's called Shadow Breaker," he said in an amused way, then he grabbed her bow and placed it around himself to carry along with her belt on one shoulder.

Once those were in place and secured, he picked her up under her knees and behind her back, her head falling to his shoulder. She watched as he navigated through the trees and around shrubs, hardly making any noise despite carrying her. As he entered the cabin, he placed her on her sleeping pad next to Akuna's slumbering form and set down her bow and belt with her remaining clothing.

"Go to sleep now. I'll whisk this carnage away. You did great defending yourself, even though it must have been difficult. Just rest now," he said softly as his hands produced blue smoke.

Her eyes drooped closed, and as she started to drift off, she could feel her skin becoming clean and dry. The last thing she felt was a kiss to her forehead before Elaras' own forehead was pressed to hers. When he spoke next, his words were quiet and echoed in her ears.

"You are not pathetic, my sweet."

23
Welcome to Your Unfamiliar Home

"So you shot one assailant with an arrow and another became mist from that dagger? And you were walking around because...?" Akuna questioned Rosella the next morning while Elaras cooked some breakfast. She was sitting on her sleeping pad, and Akuna perched on the pillow in front of her.

"I couldn't sleep, so I walked around. And yeah, the arrow shot was one of my best because he went down super quickly, so I think the arrow went through his brain stem. The other, well, I almost died because they were sitting on me, crushing me, and I could only move my arms," Rosella said in between sips of tea. More than ever she was missing coffee as tea never made her feel awake, and she preferred the taste of coffee.

"I'm glad you made it out and that you could defend yourself. Next time, please go with one of us or have a bit more training so you can defend yourself more efficiently. You dying prematurely would be useless for us all." Akuna said, placing a paw on her knee.

"I'll be more prepared next time, Dad," Rosella joked, and the annoyed sneer she got from Akuna satisfied her. She looked over to Elaras and she caught him giving her a smiling side glance. When their eyes met, he returned to cooking, and Rosella turned back to Akuna, who had started hovering in front of her, his wings flapping rapidly to keep himself in the air.

"Don't worry, I'll be having a 'fatherly' talking-to with him. He should have woken me," Akuna said telepathically in a drawling voice. *"Are you truly all right, Rosella?"*

Rosella gave a half-smile and shrugged. *"I have to be, don't I? I'm sure I'll cry about it all later on,"* she said as confidently as possible. She knew keeping emotions and stress packed down was not healthy, but she knew in the next few days she would have to be as strong as possible.

To distract herself for the moment, she raised her palm and held it below Akuna. He gently dropped into her hand and folded his wings neatly, staring up at her. She raised her other hand and stroked the top of his head, and a gentle stream of steam flowed out of his nostrils as he closed his eyes. In this moment, he truly was like a cat, and she was thankful that he let her pet his head, feeling comfort in the steady and repetitive rhythm of stroking his scales and tufts.

"When I'm done, would you like me to braid your hair?" Elaras asked, and Rosella shot her eyes up to find a cheeky grin on his face.

"You know how to braid hair?" she asked, dumbfounded.

"My hair may not be as long as yours, but I still know how to make mine pretty and utilitarian!" Elaras said as he shook his head, making his hair swish back and forth. "What, do men on Earth not know how to braid hair?"

"Most men don't have long hair like yours! In history they did, but not many in my time in 2042. Even then, those with long hair may not know how to braid! Well, except those in indigenous cultures. Their braids are always perfect," Rosella said, laughing.

Elaras laughed as well and looked back at the filets of meat he was sautéing. "Well, I'm not like most men, then."

She giggled and smiled, agreeing with that statement tenfold.

"Okay, wait, hold on, you're telling me that on Earth there was something called a 'car,' and these 'cars' took you from one place to another without a horse or an ox?" Elaras asked, flabbergasted.

Rosella had told him about a few technological things on Earth that did not seem possible on Dorthos. They had been walking for a few hours, and around midday they were about an hour away from Rion. Anxious to get to Rion, they snacked on fruits and jerky for lunch as they walked. Elaras had braided her hair into an intricate style that took up both sides of her hair and met in the middle, then split at the back of her head so her hair could rest on her chest to make room for Akuna in her hood. She had to stop herself from feeling the soft ridges and bumps of the braids as they hugged her head.

As they walked closer, Rosella's anxiety climbed as the distance shortened. She was talking to distract herself, and thankfully discussing mundane things to Elaras was entertaining and was the perfect distraction for her. Akuna came out of her hood periodically to see the path they were taking and their surroundings, once or twice even coming out and flying around them but staying in sight.

"Oh, yeah, and they were made of metal, wires, electricity, and the tires were rubber. They were simple in the beginning and evolved to pure ingenuity and became crazy advanced. A car came out a few months ago that could drive from side to side to park easier," Rosella said enthusiastically, and when Elaras tilted his head and she chuckled a little. "Cars drive similar to horses and carts, except you can reverse easier in a car. They didn't drive sideways, so it was a crazy invention, and people were excited for it. I don't believe any were officially released by the time the bombs fell."

"What are bombs, anyways?" Elaras asked, and Rosella felt her heart sink.

"Bombs are things of human design that are...awful," Rosella said while rubbing her skin under her long sleeved dress. "They were simple in the beginning, only spraying metal and fire. For the last hundred years on Earth, they used nuclear power in the bombs, ranging from small cluster bombs to large ones that wiped out entire cities. Nuclear bombs, to my understanding, cause sickness and spread material that is highly harmful to everything it touches. The use of nuclear bombs won wars and also prevented others from starting. Where I was, they used smaller bombs, my guess to spread the radiation—uh, the sickening substance—because buildings weren't being destroyed. Just fires and poisoned air. The threat of them, the bombs, was more terrifying than dragon fire, in a simple way to compare it to you."

The feeling of her skin burning and the radiation in her lungs was unforgettable, and as she spoke she could feel her skin prickle and her throat tighten. Tinges of pain would still occasionally fill her lungs in moments she least expected the pain to arise. The radiation left damage in her lungs that Akuna could not heal, but she understood that something was better than nothing. However, she also knew that if anything else damaged her lungs, that she would suffer and there would not be much to repair the damage.

"I'm happy I live in a world without that, despite all the things humans developed compared to what we have here," Elaras said simply, watching Rosella rubbing her skin and also reaching to her throat to soothe the tightness.

After some time passed with silence, her skin calmed, and her throat eased, the pain in her chest subsiding. Her anxiety slowed to a crawl, and she felt words wanting to escape.

"I'm happy I live here now, too," she said, smiling but keeping her eyes on the path.

She noticed something silver flying directly towards them quickly. Before Rosella could try to make out what the thing was, Elaras stepped in front of her and snatched the silver object out of the air. As the item froze in his hand, she saw that it was a large sparrow with an envelope in its beak, and Elaras held out the shining silver sparrow to her.

"It's for you. Only you can grab the envelope," he said, an eyebrow raised.

She gently took the envelope and opened it hastily. The sparrow remained in his hand but did not move, and she knew that this must be the same magic Elaras used to send his brother's ashes back home.

Dear Future Queen Rosella Nightstone,

My name is High Cleric Varran Daldrack, and I serve the Nightstone family as the head of house under the family and Nocturnal Manor. I cannot write for long so I will be quick.

There are spies watching the house, and they are waiting for you to arrive and are probably watching your path here, thanks to the description the Rockshire gave. We were unaware of them by the time you met with Ezralious, and we regret not sending you with an escort. When you arrive, please enter the tunnel that is a mile southeast of the manor entrance. One of my Clerics will be waiting for you there.

Please hurry. We have much to discuss. May Goddess Elyphr guide your path.

Yours kindly,
High Cleric Varran Daldrick

"Well, what does it say?" asked Elaras from next to her.

Before she could answer, Akuna took over her vision, the purple hue washing over her sight as her eyes involuntarily scanned the page. When Akuna was done reading, he released her and burrowed further into her hood. Rosella looked up to Elaras as she handed him the note, watching him read it as the sparrow puffed into silver vapor. Swiftly, he handed back the letter, and she pocketed it in the magic pouch while exchanging silent glances with Elaras.

Without a warning, without a word exchanged, Elaras stepped up to Rosella and intertwined his fingers with hers, rubbing the back of her hand with his thumb. He took in a deep breath, and when he exhaled, they entered his haven, the swirls of black and blue magic surrounding them in an instant. The world grew cold, dim, and solitary, calmness poured into her muscles and into her lungs. She was starting to understand why he loved being in this patch of the world when she felt a tug on her hand.

"Come on, we must get to that tunnel. I think I know where it is, and this is the safest way to travel so the spies don't see us.

Are you comfortable running?" Elaras asked, looking down at her boots.

"I haven't run in them yet, but I'm sure it's fine," she replied, doing small stretches with her legs.

"Good, start running, but do not let go of me," he said. "You may want to hold onto Akuna."

"I'll go in the pouch. I can cushion myself better, and I don't have to feel your clammy hands," Akuna said in a mockingly, disdainful tone. Making sure he kept consistent contact on Rosella, he crawled his way down her arm and into the pouch that Rosella held open for him.

Once he was secure, she felt Elaras pull her. They ran for almost an hour, only taking one break to drink water and to catch their breaths. Elaras being in all leathers and Rosella not having the stamina to run, it was difficult, and they were worn out by the time they made it to the edge of a wooded area.

"I never want to do that again," Rosella said between panting breaths. She was hunched over with a hand on her knee, the other hand still attached to Elaras'. Her chest was on fire, and every breath felt like knives were repeatedly stabbing her lungs.

Elaras, like Rosella, was bent over and simply gave a thumbs up to her for assent. After they were done catching their breaths, Elaras stood up straight and pointed toward the wooded area.

"We have to go through here. If it is the same tunnel I am remembering, then it isn't too far, and we can drop the haven," Elaras said as he walked between the trees, dragging Rosella behind him. The magic smoke in front of him acted as a constant barrier that was being pushed through, the smoke flowing backward but being replaced by new smoke. They truly were in a bubble, but the bubble moved around them effortlessly with no resistance.

Seeing him move with no hesitation while pulling her along

was comforting, despite the situation. However, she was not sure how he knew where they were going as seeing details of the world outside was difficult, and she could only see the vague shapes of trees but not their leaves. He came to an abrupt stop after close to ten minutes of walking.

"Crouch," he whispered, and she followed his direction.

When they were both crouched low, he dropped the haven, and the sunlight from the afternoon sun broke through the trees and pierced her eyes through the breaks in the branches above. She grabbed her hood to place over her head to try and block the bright sun that splintered the ground, and Elaras copied her.

"Just up here a little ways. I think I see a sparrow waiting for us," came Elaras' voice as she blinked the blindness away.

"Lead the way," she whispered, and they both walked as stealthy as possible while still keeping hold of the other's hands.

After another five minutes, they came upon a blue and white sparrow that was perched on a low-hanging branch. Curiously, it gazed down at the pair of them and flapped its wings to fluff its iridescent feathers.

"Put your hood down so it can see you," Elaras whispered.

"How do we know this is a Nightstone sparrow?" Rosella asked sharply, and Elaras gave a sly smile.

"Because my father's are orange," he said softly as he looked down at her. "Trust me, that isn't one of his."

Rosella looked back up at the sparrow, then took her free hand to push back her hood. The sparrow tilted its shiny head and flew away from them. Confused, Rosella glanced at Elaras again.

"Do we follow it or something?" she asked.

Elaras adjusted his stance to a more comfortable position and squeezed her aching hand. "We should stay here and wait. I think someone will come from the tunnel and let us in. How's your hand?"

Rosella followed suit and adjusted her stance as well, but she did not squeeze his hand. "Honestly? It's sore and clammy."

"*Gross,*" Akuna chimed in, and Rosella tried her best to not roll her eyes.

"*Sweating is better than molting, I would think,*" she quipped back at him.

She heard a huff come from his pouch and smiled. Elaras, not privy to the conversation, had let go of her hand and was now massaging her joints in silence.

They did not have to wait long in the trees, as a few minutes later they heard what sounded like metal grinding and locks turning. Part of the ground itself tilted upward and revealed a trapdoor. The rocks, twigs, and dirt that were resting on top of the door spilled backward to the ground as someone in shining armor poked their helmeted head through the door.

"State your names," came the gruff voice, whose eyes shone a bright orange from the little bits of sun that peeked through the trees.

"Rosella Nightstone and Elaras Moonshadow," Rosella said, clearing her throat.

The orange eyes grew wide, and they proceeded to push the door wider so Rosella and Elaras could slip into the tight opening.

Once the door was closed, torches magically lit themselves, and before them were two rows of guards, with the one that opened the door leading one of the rows. Every single one was armed with either swords, axes, or morningstar maces, and they wore the same armor as Ezralious with the addition of helmets that had an extravagant white plume on top.

As she was examining all the guards and taking in her scenery, a large creature walked up and stood in front of her. They slammed the staff of their massive war-axe into the ground before they kneeled in front of her, bowing their head and making the moon symbol on their chest. When the guard did this, the rest followed suit in complete unison and with impeccable accuracy.

"Future Queen Nightstone," the guard in front said, and the rest of the guards repeated after him.

"*Oh, fuck me,*" Rosella said to Akuna as all the guards stood up in one swift movement and readjusted their weapons.

The guard in front took a step forward, and Rosella noticed that this must be an orc mixed with another large race as they towered over the other orcs she had seen.

"My name is Gerrart Hamstrug, Paladin of the Nightstones. These are members of your Queens Guard. Please follow me, Your Majesty," Gerrart said before turning and walking down the wide tunnel.

Rosella followed him, hearing the trapdoor lock into place with loud clicks and groans. As she passed by every guard, they each bowed their heads and placed the moon symbol to their chest. While she had seen this with Ezralious, she began to understand that this was the salute to Nightstone royalty, like the royalty in England. This was something she would have to get used to, though the thought of having people other than Akuna and Elaras protect her was comforting.

After almost twenty minutes of walking, they reached a large metal door with bolts and heavy-looking hinges. Gerrart tapped in a rhythmic pattern, and after only a moment the weighted door swung inward, bright white light pouring into the torch-lit tunnel. Gerrart walked through and stepped to the side, holding a hand out for Rosella to grab onto as she stepped over the threshold.

Before her was a small room with boxes lining the walls and a single portrait of a mountain range that resembled the one in Arja. Before she could take in more details of the room, the door opposite the trapdoor darkened, and a large silhouette stepped up to the entryway.

A person similar to Gerrart but older with a longer beard and green eyes instead of blue stood and examined Rosella. His eyes swept over her in swift, studying movements before he himself knelt in salute, his massive hand making a crescent moon over his strong chest.

"Future Queen Nightstone, welcome home."

24
A Home of Lost, Unresting Souls

Just like with Ezralious, Rosella was shocked, but she maintained her composure and thankfully, the large orc did not stay kneeled for long. He stood up more nimbly than she would have expected for someone of his size, and he stepped back out of the small room and to the side of the door.

"This way, Your Majesty. High Cleric Varran is waiting for you in your study," he said as he strode to the right.

Rosella nodded and followed, realizing she was afraid to say anything. For some reason, she started to tremble, and her teeth chattered slightly despite the air not being cold. Maybe it was him saying "your study" or because this place was now hers. A manor, a home, that now she had every right to and yet she felt like she did not belong to yet. The dark stones of her new home closed in on her, but she pressed forward.

Most of the guards went off in different directions in pairs, and only two guards and the Paladin Gerrart stayed behind her and Elaras, following in stride. The orc man led her through various halls with tall walls of blue, purple, white, and black tapestries and various portraits of what must have been past Nightstones, along with many art fixtures like statues and vases set on pedestals. Occasionally they would pass murals that depicted constellations and moon phases. One hallway had a gargantuan family tree that showed generations upon generations of Nightstones and stretched from one end of the long hall to another, so she had to turn her head completely to see both ends of the tree. At this, she stopped walking and read through the various names and saw how far back the entire line went.

"What year is it in this world?" she asked Akuna.

"3532 S.C.," he replied quickly.

At this, she squinted at the far left of the family tree, and saw the earliest year was 1096, with Nelven Night and Sukia Stone. To the right was Rubious Nightstone and Twilla Nightstone, who must be their children, and next to them must have been their respective spouses and children, continuing the tree beyond that. Quickly, she did the math in her head, and she let out a small gasp when she reached the calculation.

"Two thousand, four hundred thirty-six years this family has been around, and they all died at the hands of the Rockshires. An entire family line and history, gone in one night," she said to Akuna, and she felt a dreary rumble in her chest.

"Hey, you okay?" Elaras murmured in her ear, breaking into her subconsciousness.

Despite this, she did not look at him and only released a quaking exhale and nodded from the sudden weight of being here and being responsible for restarting the over two-thousand-year-long family line. She felt his hand slip into hers and give a gentle squeeze, and that alone was what broke her eyes away from the family tree.

Squeezing back as a thank you, she released his hand and followed the armored orc once more, who had graciously waited for her to finish reading the tree before continuing. She tried her best to think of herself in one of the many television shows or movies where royalty was on the screen. Claire Foy came to mind, and she straightened her back, feeling her muscles creak and her bones pop as she did so. The last thing she wanted was to embarrass herself in front of those in this manor and the High Cleric.

What seemed like hours of walking ended at the end of one of the many halls with a grand double-door entryway. As the orc reached for the door handles, she cleared her throat and brushed the few strands of loose hair that had fallen out while they were running.

When the doors swung open, she saw ceiling-high black bookshelves that were filled with a colorful assortment of spines that spread from wall to wall. In the center of the room was a large central coffee table with a purple couch and cushioned chairs surrounding it, as well as more cushioned chairs and smaller tables spread across the room. The orc walked in and stood by the doorway inside the study, and Rosella stepped inside, taking in as much as possible.

In one of the chairs by a curtained window that matched the height of the bookshelves was an older dwarf man dressed in black and blue robes with metal armor pieces on his belt and around his neck. Noticeably, his bracers and greaves were the same as all the others she had seen on the guards and Ezralious, though his seemed more decorative and on the comfortable side.

When she entered the room, he stood up immediately and strode across the room to her. Expecting him to kneel and salute, she was pleasantly surprised when he walked right up to her and held out a hand for her to shake.

"Rosella Nightstone?" he asked curtly.

"Hello. Are you High Cleric Daldrack?" she asked, trying to not let her awkwardness at the gesture show. She noted that he was about a head and a half shorter than her, but his presence was unmistakably powerful and commanding.

"Yes, Your Majesty. You may call me Varran if you would like and if that would make you more comfortable. That," he said as he gestured to the orc who was now stone-still at the doorway, "is your High Paladin Joss Bildow, and you may call him Joss. He is in charge of your Queens Guard, and Gerrart Hamstrug is the second in command after him. He is also a Paladin under your rule. You will meet your housekeeper soon. They are finishing up dinner. However, I would like to talk with you before then, if that is alright with you?"

"Of course. That would be nice, I think," Rosella said almost sheepishly. Her mind was beginning to become overwhelmed, though she knew now was not the time to let those emotions get to her.

Varran smiled, then looked at the High Paladin Joss and nodded at him. At that small command, Joss grabbed the door and began to shut it closed. Rosella followed his gaze and saw Elaras taking a step further into the room but stopping when he saw the look Joss shot in his direction. He pivoted on his heel and walked out of the room as Joss shut the door. Rosella felt the silence hit her as hard as when her eardrums blew out weeks before, and the room began to spin.

"Are you alright, Your Majesty?" Varran's voice rang in her ears, breaking the silence loudly like a shockwave.

She met his eyes as best as she could, but her head spun faster and her vision tunneled so narrowly that everything grew fuzzy. Her breath grew rapid and shaky at the same time her throat tightened, so much that she felt like she was choking. Her muscles wanted to give way and buckle, but she was determined to stay upright and not show weakness in front of this authoritative person. Trying desperately to say that she was all right, she only managed to let out a panicked breath.

At the point of feeling like she was about to collapse, a soft white light filled her vision, and as quickly as the light appeared, she felt her body calm. Her vision cleared, and her muscles felt stronger, her throat and breath returning to their normal state. Astonished, she looked at Varran, who just lowered his hands and had a kind smile on his face.

"I understand this must be a lot to take in. Please, sit. Would you rather me call you Rosella? Would that help?" he asked gently, gesturing to a large, cushioned chair that had constellations stitched into purple plush fabric.

"Yes, I believe so. I'm so sorry," Rosella admitted, sitting down on the comfortable chair and welcoming the hug of the cushioning.

Varran sat down opposite her in a similar chair, and he placed his hands in his lap. "You have nothing to apologize for, Rosella, though I apologize for the questions I'm about to ask you."

"Oh?" Rosella said, feeling slightly nervous for a moment before the feeling drifted away. Varran's magic must last for some time, because she felt the calmest she had ever been since coming to Dorthos.

"Yes. I know your night stone was stolen by Lycilla Rockshire, but I am also aware you bear the Nightstone symbol upon your skin," Varran said, becoming serious and professional.

Rosella, without hesitating, took off her cloak and began to unlace the cuirass. The need for someone to see her tattoo, to see the resemblance to the Nightstone coat of arms, was intense, and she realized she needed this validation to confirm her role in this world. Varran seemed to also require the validation as he did not question her removing the leather cuirass and unlacing the front of her dress. Thankfully the dress was split far down enough in the front that she did not need to pull down the fabric and only needed to slightly pull apart the laced slit.

The tattoo itself was three golden stars surrounding a white crescent moon with a blue swirl background. As tall and wide as her small hand, the tattoo sat in the middle of her chest from halfway down her chest to the bottom of the sternum bone between her breasts. At the time of getting the tattoo at eighteen, her breasts were considerably smaller, so the tattoo was easily noticeable. Now, she had to awkwardly spread her breasts so Varran could see the tattoo fully. Unphased by the potential exposure or awkwardness, Varran leaned in and stared at the tattoo with little to no expression except for his raised eyebrows.

"My Goddess spoke true as always. You truly are a Nightstone," he said, his voice laced with astonishment. "It's just like your coat of arms. What inspired you to get this?" he asked, leaning back in his chair, his eyes back on her face.

She laced her dress back up but did not put her cuirass back on, letting her lungs breathe freely. "When I was younger, my mother and I would always draw the moon and stars. My mom was obsessed with the galaxy, so she filled our home with as many moons and stars as possible. Most kids would probably get annoyed, but I loved it. I would see the design in my dreams, and no matter how many times I drew them, I couldn't get it out of my head. Always a crescent moon and three stars. Since something drew me to them, I knew for my eighteenth birthday I wanted the tattoo as close to my heart as possible. I guess, now that I'm saying it, I always knew I was a Nightstone before I was aware of the Nightstones' existence."

When she finished, she saw the kind smile on Varran's face again.

"May I ask your mother and father's names?" he asked as simply as asking if she wanted a glass of water.

"My mother was Olympe. Sometimes people would call her Olly. As for my father, I'm not sure who my father is since I have never met him, and my mother never mentioned him," she said, and she noticed Varran's eyes grew wide just for a split second before his face returned to contentment.

"I was told you had a third ally. Where are they?" he asked, and before she could answer, she felt Akuna's pouch move.

Instinctively, she opened the pouch and saw Akuna crawl out, but he donned his normal colors of white and red.

Varran's eyes shot down to the pouch, and his face exploded with excitement. "Akuna! My Goddess, it has been too long!"

Akuna flew to hover in front of Varran, and in a puff of purple smoke, he grew so that he stood at eye level with Rosella and Varran. "Varran, it's grand to see you alive and well," Akuna said in a happy tone, his lips curling into a smile she had not seen before, and she knew that was the smile of seeing an old friend.

"So it was you that brought Rosella to us?" Varran asked, all of his attention on Akuna now.

"Yes, now was the correct time for both her and for Arja. I have been with her ever since, and I do not plan on leaving her side. I must make up for my mistake for leaving the Nightstones before, and I hope this pleases your goddess."

"She has no bad thoughts or intentions of you, old friend. Thank you for bringing her. We have a long road ahead of us, but we are prepared and willing to do what we can. What of the Moonshadow son, though?"

At Varran's words, Rosella's smile dimmed, and she began to grow anxious of Akuna's potential choice of words regarding Elaras.

"Elaras Moonshadow has good intentions and had many chances to end Rosella's life. I do believe he is true to his word and is wanting to protect her alongside us," Akuna said confidently with no harshness found in his tone. Rosella let out a strained breath, and Akuna shot her a side-eye. "He's proven himself enough, though he is still under the threat of flaying."

Rosella smacked her hand to her face and let out an anxious giggle, smiling at this dragon that kept surprising her. When she raised her head off her hand, she saw the two in front of her were looking at each other intently, now and then reacting with small movements. Was this how it looked when Akuna talked telepathically to her? It was no wonder Elaras questioned her. If she was not aware of what was going on, she would ask questions too.

She sat there letting her eyes wander around the room as they spoke to themselves, seeing the titles of books she knew she wanted to read immediately, like *History of Dragons and Why They Are Considered Gods*, *The Making of Castles: Nightstone Edition*, and *The Story of Vehab, God of Stories*. When she heard Varran and Akuna both laugh, she risked looking over, and Varran was slapping his knee and Akuna's head was raised back in a toothy smile. Grinning herself, she continued to examine the room while the two maintained their quiet conversation.

After a few more minutes, it was Varran who broke the silence.

"Rosella, are you aware of what would happen if someone was to put on your necklace, or have the chain encircle or wrap a body part?"

Rosella shook her head as she grew perplexed, and she had to admit she was unsure.

Varran leaned forward in his chair and looked at her square in the eye. "The chain itself would burn so quickly and so badly that the skin would not be able to heal, and if the chain was not removed quickly enough, then the chain would burn completely through muscle and bone until it was no longer making contact."

Rosella's mind flew a million different directions at these words. If the necklace was around a neck that did not bear the Nightstone name, it would do what it could to make sure it did not stay on said neck. Therefore, Lycilla would never be able to wear the necklace because then, otherwise and simply, she would no longer have a head. Self-gratitude rose in her chest as she remembered never allowing anyone back on Earth to put on the necklace or even hold it.

"So, since it has not done that with me..." Rosella started to say, and she saw both Varran and Akuna nodding, satisfaction on their faces. "She would not be able to wear it, obviously, but they could still hold onto my necklace, and just make sure it did not wrap around their skin, like their hand or something?"

"Correct," Varran said. "I did notice that Lycilla's hand looked odd when they were here, and she was hiding it for the entire encounter until they teleported away. She must have wrapped the chain around her hand at one point because it was blackened, and only half of the hand was remaining."

"Yes, she did wrap it around her hand, just before she teleported herself out of the cavern. I saw her skin start to sizzle, so I'm not surprised to hear the chain successfully cut through her hand and wounded her badly," sneered Akuna with almost a growl.

"I really am a Nightstone," Rosella said to herself.

Varran and Akuna regarded her with something like sympathy or apprehension.

"Yes, and I can already tell you're going to be a wonderful queen. Would you like to see your manor?" Varran asked.

Rosella smiled sheepishly and nodded.

As she was about to stand to exit the study, a purple sparrow flew through the wall and landed on Varran's knee. Instead of a letter in its beak or a scroll wrapped around its ankle, it opened its small mouth and began to speak, repeating words that must have been recorded somehow.

"Dinner is ready to be served!" said a cheerful voice.

When the recording was finished, the sparrow burst into purple smoke that drifted to the high ceiling.

Varran smiled and stood up, Akuna following suit.

"I apologize. We shall take a tour after dinner. Mellis, the housekeeper, loves to host meals, and she never fails to disappoint. Knowing you're here, this dinner will be spectacular. Akuna, do you require a plate?"

"Yes, I'll take my small form," Akuna said before letting out more purple smoke and returning to his tiny form but keeping his scale color. He flew next to Rosella, and she was oddly feeling extreme gratitude toward him more than ever.

Rosella gave him a wide smile before following Varran to the dining room.

25
Eyes Sing, Nerves Scream

The six horse-drawn carriage wound down the cobblestone path into the Sidosa border, the capital of Dorthos. With each bump that shook the carriage, Lycilla winced sharply but remained frozen, still held by Kaine's power.

"Enough of that, or I'll muzzle your face so I don't have to see it," Kaine said, annoyed as he tried to read the scroll of parchment on his lap. The scroll had been delivered by a footman for Emperor Harporous and stated that the emperor would accept the request for an audience. According to intel given to Kaine by his spies, the emperor was eager to put Lycilla into power due to the need for a governing power in Arja.

The magic decay that tore through Arja was now affecting the capital's food supply, and citizens were beginning to starve. Intel also said that while the emperor knew the Rockshire girl was not a Nightstone, her family did usurp the throne and therefore was the most rightful heir. Having the stone in hand would solidify the emperor's decision, so by this time next week Kaine would take the throne. However, he knew he would have to take care of Lycilla once she was sworn in and they were married. Have her produce a few heirs for him, then have her disappear, just like Evanora. As Kaine smiled to himself about the prospects of his plans, the carriage came to an abrupt halt. Kaine threw the parchment to the side and opened the carriage door.

"What is going on?" he snapped in the open air. He saw that his footmen and guards were spreading into the trees around them with their weapons drawn, scanning the land around them. His head guard, Tordias, a burly, gray-furred minotaurus with sturdy black horns, walked to Kaine's front with his longsword drawn, shielding Kaine from the potential danger.

"There is a blockage in the road that was deliberately placed. We saw someone dash into the woods wearing black with a small moon and stars coat of arms on the bracers," said Tordias to Kaine, his black and purple armored back to Kaine and rotating his body to search the trees around them. The black plumes on Tordias' helmet resembling a mohawk rustled in the wind, and the black cape he wore with a cream-colored moon flapped against Kaine's legs.

"Remove the blockage, and let's go!" Kaine yelled, furious that his men were more concerned about finding the assailants than removing the roadblock.

Tordias pivoted to give him an exasperated look. His green eyes narrowed toward his leader, a large thick scar cutting down his face toward his torso wrinkling as his face twisted with annoyance.

"My lord, the block is too significant and would take hours. I'll have your men search the grounds around us before starting on the blockage. We need to make sure you and the lady will be safe."

Kaine narrowed his eyes and strode around Tordias to look at the roadblock. After passing all six of the horses, he saw that the path had tree trunks piled as far as he could see and as high as the carriage itself. The sides of the road were locked in with more trees, so the carriage was stuck and there were no other paths to the capital. A spark of inspiration filled Kaine's mind, and he went back to the carriage and swung the door open with such force that the door handle dented the wall of the carriage.

"You, come," he said to Lycilla, and watched as she mindlessly followed his instruction.

She stepped out of the carriage and followed him around the blockade through the trees, flanked by two guards that saw the pair outside the carriage. When they reached the end of the blockade, Kaine stopped and examined the clear path ahead before looking to Lycilla. "Remember this, and teleport the carriage to this spot."

Lycilla obediently bowed her head before being led by the two guards back to the carriage. After about five minutes of waiting on the cleared side of the roadblock, dark red smoke splintered the air, and the carriage along with the six horses appeared in front of him. The guards around them that were in the trees echoed their surprise, and hurried footsteps approached Kaine. Kaine himself was unable to hide his own surprise as he entered the carriage but left the door open to speak to the guards.

"Let's go. Forget the assailants. We need to be in the capital and in front of the emperor by three, and it is eleven right now," Kaine directed to Tordias, who was closest to him while standing outside the carriage door.

"Let me gather the men, and we will leave, my lord," Tordias said obediently before meeting with another pair of guards. After ten minutes with Kaine impatiently waiting, Tordias returned and heaved a sigh. "We are missing a man, my lord. They flew after the criminal, and they have not made it back."

Kaine rolled his eyes and waved him off. "That is yours and his problem. He should have stayed close, and you should have trained him better. I will not waste my energy telling you all that we need to go again," Kaine said, annoyed and now facing forward into the carriage, ignoring Tordias.

Tordias, however, did not move or close the carriage door. "Sir, that is one of your men. He is sworn to you. I suggest we wait for him. Now is not the time to be losing your men or staff given the circumstances. We do not need the information going out to anyone. You know we have spies on us," Tordias whispered, leaning his massive head into the threshold of the carriage.

Kaine scowled at Tordias with pure malice and rage, and Tordias leaned back out of the carriage doorway.

"Go find him, then fall on your sword. You, lanky lizgon guard. Herus?" Kaine said, pointing to the guard that stood behind Tordias, and orange smoke slinked out of the tip of his finger. "You are now head guard. Take Tordias' cape and take Tordias' post as driver."

Without question, Herus stood shocked for a moment before stiffly reaching up and grabbing the black cape that rested on Tordias' shoulders before hooking it to his own armor. Tordias stared at Kaine, his face filled with resentment.

"I have been with you since your children were born, and this is how you repay my dedication to your family?" Tordias spat out.

Kaine smiled at Tordias and waved an orange smoky finger in Tordias' direction. "Do as I told you, cow."

Tordias, however, puffed out his chest and straightened his back defiantly, his green eyes remaining green instead of gaining an orange hue. "After all these decades, you still forget magic does not work on minotauruses, elf," he said, his face showing that he relished in the glory of the look on Kaine Moonshadow's face. "I'll be on my way to find the missing man, then, and we will return to your estate to await you there."

"No, you will do as I say! Find the man and kill him and yourself!" Kaine barked.

"I'd rather go to the estate, thanks. I'll be on my way now."

"You will do no such thing! I will have you killed where you stand by your own men!"

"*Your* men, you mean? Your mind is so narrow that you cannot see the fuller landscape and see reason," Tordias mocked, tilting his head and letting a sneer fall on his face. "I am giving you a logical option to our situation, and you still demand for me to end my life because a man went to try and find the spy *for you*?"

"I did not ask for your opinion. Do as I have told you and get out of my sight before I have you speared and cut!"

"You killed your wife and took control of another woman to force her to wed you. You did not bat an eye when your son died and your other son, your oldest and your heir, is off in the wind with the unknown girl. Will you really let your men kill me with your commanding hand because you're so desperate to keep your frail secrets at bay from the world around you, all for power that does not belong to you?"

"SILENCE, FILTHY COW!" Kaine yelled, jumping from his seat and grabbing the edge of the carriage door.

Tordias took a step back and straightened his spine to his full height, double Kaine's stature. "Your days are coming to an end, Kaine. No one with honor or dignity will serve you in time," Tordias said with defiance. As Tordias turned away from the carriage, Kaine screamed with pure anger and shouted at his back.

With no effect, Kaine turned to his other guards except for Herus and told them to chase after him. Kaine despised admitting that Tordias was right in that he had been guarding the family since his children were born, and since he was head of the guard, he knew every secret that the Moonshadows held. Panic masked itself as rage, and Kaine made orange commanding magic explode out of him to the guards that stood stock-still, staring at their lord.

As the magic shot into each of them, they stiffly turned and ran toward Tordias, swords drawn and war cries growing dim as they ventured further into the forest around them. Kaine breathed deeply and sat back in his seat in the carriage, straightening his robes and looking at the still-paralyzed Lycilla.

"Herus, let's go," Kaine said lazily, feeling the lurch of the carriage that Herus now led.

———

Emperor Harporous Dreadtrell, a pompous and wide-sided felinette with solid ginger fur and yellow eyes, laughed heartily at a joke Kaine had just told him. Empress Loka Dreadtrell, a skinny gray-striped felinette with orange eyes, politely smiled and watched as her laughing husband spewed chunks of chicken out of his mouth and onto his plate and into his wine. Princess Temel, a ginger-striped felinette with purple eyes, and Prince Zaas, a black and white felinette with blue eyes, watched on, eyes wide at the presence of Kaine and the frozen and silent Lycilla.

"Kaine, you must tell that joke at the upcoming gathering. Everyone will get a hoot out of it!" Emperor Harporous smiled and smacked Kaine on the back. "Though I know you are not here to tell jokes. Please tell me your plan for Arja with your beautiful new bride."

Kaine cleared his throat and set down his wine goblet, leaning forward in his chair. "Emperor Harporous, I plan on putting Lycilla Rockshire on the Arja throne, as her family name is the rightful heir. I do plan to help her with understanding the politics and nobility of it all, and I was going to do it as a father-in-law, but, as you know..." Kaine said before he had to clear his throat again. "My son was killed by the Great Wrath of Dorthos. He, the Great Wrath, somehow possessed a night stone pendant in his horde, and as my son was taking it for his beautiful bride so she could earn her rightful place, the Great Wrath killed him. It was a miracle that I was there so I could stop the Great Wrath with my magic to keep him from killing me while I grabbed the necklace. That dragon must have stolen the necklace decades ago.

"As for my wife, well, she passed away just a few days ago due to ever-declining health," Kaine said, a small sniffle that helped cover the blatant lies. "A few days before her death, she told me she wished for me to help her would-be daughter-in-law, as she believed that Lycilla was the next true queen of Arja. When I came home from retrieving the night stone for Lycilla without my son, I discovered she had passed while I and Alryo were gone. She never got to see her son before she passed, and my son did not get to see his mother again. My wish is to avenge and to make right their deaths by helping Lycilla, and I do believe the best course of action is to marry her, purely to continue the line and to help her every step of the way."

"That is very valiant of you, Kaine. Do you have the night stone necklace with you now?" the emperor asked, his eyes becoming wide as saucers with curiosity.

Kaine pulled out the pendant but did not offer it to the emperor. The last thing he wanted was for the emperor to cut off his own finger and immediately get suspicious about the stone.

"It's a genuine night stone. It holds great power, and we believe the Great Wrath stole it to become more powerful. I am holding onto it until I wed Lycilla, and she will receive it as a wedding gift," Kaine said unapologetically.

While Emperor Harporous smiled and wagged his finger at him, he saw Prince Zaas wave his fingers in the air. Small wisps of pink smoke flew from the tips of his paws, and his eyes that were locked on the pendant glowed a bright shimmering pink. For a moment, Kaine thought the prince's eyes glanced in Lycilla's direction, but the only thing he did when his eyes returned to normal was give a curt nod to his mother.

"Good lad, Kaine. Frankly, I am happy the Nightstones are long gone. They were too...what word am I looking for, Loka?" the emperor asked, turning toward his wife. She leaned in and whispered something into his large, fluffy ear. The emperor exclaimed and snapped his fingers before saying, "Virtuous and righteous! Over two thousand years, and they were too good and too kind, letting rules be bent and letting criminals be free. Ridiculous. I trust Lycilla Rockshire will make a grand queen with you by her side commanding her what to do, and I trust that she will also comply obediently." The emperor smiled and gave a side-eyed glance to Lycilla, who had not eaten or drunk anything all night, and Kaine thought he could hear her stomach growling.

"Eat, you stupid girl," Kaine said telepathically to her, and instantly she began to eat in a polite manner and only taking small sips of wine. Satisfied, Kaine turned his attention back to the emperor, who was waving over an elf server to fill his goblet with more wine. "Emperor Harporous, I was curious if Lycilla and myself should marry here or at the Nightstone estate."

The emperor looked up, and his face fell slightly. Empress Loka leaned in once more and whispered in his ear for quite some time. After a few minutes, the emperor waved her away and looked back at Kaine with a slightly solemn look that was replaced by a smile with food-covered teeth. "I believe getting married at the Nightstone estate will be most appropriate. The Arja people can be invited, and it can be a grand affair! We'll bring lots of food and merriment for the party! Let's set the date for three weeks from now? Given that the travel from here to there is about a week at a slow pace and that will give plenty of time for my and the Nightstone staff to set up everything for the wedding and the coronation. We'll teleport there the day before the wedding. How does that sound, my good lad?"

While Kaine wished to not wait three weeks, he understood the emperor's wants, so he did not argue. He would have to tell what was left of his staff to be vigilant and unwavering in their protection and to keep their eyes and ears open. Kaine raised his goblet in the air before looking to Lycilla. *"Raise your goblet and thank your emperor,"* he told her, and was pleased when she did exactly what she was told.

"Thank you, Your High Excellency, for the throne that is owed to my family and for granting the privilege of being here in your home," Lycilla said in a weak and cracking voice. Kaine noted that she had not spoken in two days, so her voice sounded less than appealing.

"My dear girl, are you alright?" the emperor asked while lowering his goblet, and even Empress Loka took interest, her eyes roaming over Lycilla's body.

"You are weary from our travels," Kaine commanded her to say.

"Your High Excellency, I am just weary from our travels," Lycilla said more confidently, and Kaine smirked.

"I insist you both stay here for as long as you both need! After all, you both can help decide what to take with you for the wedding and coronation. How does that sound?" the emperor asked jovially.

"No, Emperor Harporous, I believe we should be on our way after this lovely meal. Thank you for the offer. We are honored," Kaine said, not wanting to be at risk under the emperor's roof.

"We insist, Lord Moonshadow," came a voice that was demanding and strong.

Kaine's eardrums rang, and his chest vibrated. An orange and green hue flooded his vision, and he froze in place, feeling his muscles constrict and his nerves tingle.

"Please, at least stay for the night and organize the arrangements. Besides, I'd love to get to know our new queen of Arja," said the voice, and he was able to shift his eyes toward where it came from. As soon as his eyes landed on the smiling, sly face of Empress Loka, she released him from her grip.

"That sounds lovely after all," Kaine choked out, and the emperor yelled with excitement, clapping his hands to call for dessert. Kaine's eyes drifted to the Empress Loka once more, and her slit eyes bore down on him as she leaned back in her chair, shaking her head at him with a cocky smile.

For the first time in quite a long time, Kaine grew fearful of his company, and he knew that first thing in the morning Lycilla and his staff would leave to return to his manor.

26
A Dog Among Wolves

The halls of Nocturnal Manor were silent, the curtained windows allowing light to spill from the edges and giving a soft atmosphere. There was a noticeable lack of life that haunted the air, and Elaras gave a quivering breath while glancing at the walls around him. He had been in these halls twice before, once when Mystrias held a private magic class when he was younger, and the second when the Nightstones held a feast for the birth of twins. The twins, Calus and Talus, were the youngest members of the family to die at the hands of the Rockshires, and the thought made Elaras shiver.

Elaras paced slowly back and forth near the study, being watched closely by the High Paladin Joss. Admittedly, Elaras did not like being separated from Rosella, especially since she was in a new place, and he knew she must be overwhelmed. He wanted to be near her to make sure she was okay and to help calm her if needed, but she needed to meet with the High Cleric Varran. They could not travel and sleep in caves for the rest of their lives, and he knew that eventually she would not solely rely on him and Akuna as she got used to this world.

"Moonshadow," came the gruff voice of Joss that broke Elaras' focus.

Elaras looked at the High Paladin and took a few steps toward him. "Yes?"

"How'd you meet Our Majesty?" Joss asked with a straight face.

Elaras was slightly taken aback by the question, but he understood that this was Rosella's new protection, and they needed and wanted to know as much about Rosella and those that interacted with her.

"I saw her in a tavern a few weeks ago, and she had the Nightstone family necklace. She was by herself, and I grew interested because I hadn't seen the night stone on anyone since the family died. Mystrias taught me magic, so I was familiar with the family," Elaras said, adding the last detail about Princess Mystrias in hopes that Joss would not see him as a complete stranger. Elaras also did not want to give the full truth as Joss might find Elaras dreaming of her before they even met suspicious.

"So you just stayed with her?"

"Oh, no. I actually met with her, gave her a dagger, then left," Elaras said with a shrug. He felt a smile spread on his face at the thought of her on the day he first set eyes on her. His eyes met Joss', and he cleared his throat before saying, "I saw her again twice the next day, then I joined her a few days later after I realized that she needed protection and guidance. I have been by her side ever since."

"Was your protection needed?"

Before Elaras answered, he cleared his throat again and shifted his feet. Rosella's new High Paladin made him nervous, like a fatherly figure questioning his intentions with his daughter. "Yes, actually, a few times. I would recommend training her more on hand-to-hand. I trained her a bit, but she needs more. Ranged, she's perfect at, but her dagger hands need refining."

"She has been attacked under your care?" Joss said, slamming the staff of his war hammer on the ground.

"Uh, yeah. First time was my fault. My father sent an assassin to kill me and in turn threatened her. I took care of him, so that is no issue. The second time was when the Rockshire girl and my brother stole Rosella's necklace, but my brother died, and the girl teleported away. The last time was last night, when two Moonshadow assassins came after her, and Rosella took one out with an arrow and the other with Shadow Breaker," Elaras said quickly and defensively. The last few weeks of travel had been quite eventful, and he realized that sharing this information with the heaving and angry half-orc, half-goliath might have not been the best idea.

"I should throw you out of this manor just for putting our future queen in danger," Joss growled.

Elaras swallowed a lump that had lodged in his throat.

Joss stepped forward and picked up his massive war hammer in both hands. Just as Elaras was about to say something, the doors of the study opened with quiet creaks. High Cleric Daldrack walked out with Akuna flying by his head, both chatting with each other in hushed voices.

Joss turned to look at the pair, and when he saw Akuna, his entire mood changed to excitement and glee. "Akuna! Great to see you, buddy! I was wondering how this elf and Rosella were able to survive for weeks without help, and being attacked three times!"

As Elaras cringed at the stab towards him, Akuna said, "Ah, well, he tried his best, and he actually did well watching over our future queen. She trusts him, so for now I do too. Wonderful to see you again, Joss." Akuna hovered in Joss' eye line, and the sight of Akuna's tiny body in front of Joss' massive one was like a bug flying in front of a mountain.

Before Elaras could say anything, his eyes fell onto Rosella, who had slowly emerged from the study and headed toward him. She had a different composure about her, more confident and relaxed. Her face was softer and less lined from stress, and her lips were spread into a small smile that was directed at Elaras. The world around him muffled, and his vision hyper-focused on her.

"Hey, you," she said softly to Elaras before grabbing his hand and lacing her fingers with his.

"Hello. Are you feeling better? Things are becoming easier?" Elaras asked, matching her tone. He took their hands with his free one and massaged the back of hers, being it was the same hand he held onto for over an hour while running. He moved two of his fingers to her wrist and pressed, feeling her strong and quickened heartbeat against his skin.

"Yes, I think so. I know I'll feel overwhelmed again later, but that is for future Rosella to figure out," she said with a smile, her eyes gleaming and happy.

He smiled back at her before a distant voice interrupted their conversation.

"Let's head to dinner, all. Mellis is excited for this meal, and we shall not disappoint them!" High Cleric Varran said, ushering the group toward the direction of the dining room.

Rosella glanced up at Elaras, giving him another quick smile. "I'm going to walk with Joss, if that's okay?"

"Of course, my sweet. I'll be right behind you," Elaras said softly, and she slipped her hand out of his to follow the High Paladin and Akuna to the dining room. In the few moments when her hand left his, the coldness in the air around his hands made him feel completely and utterly alone. The absence of her, this woman he had just met but was growing extremely fond of, and the woman that would soon become a queen, made him realize that his feelings toward her were nothing to ignore. He knew something was special about her, and he even told her so, but he admitted that he still was not sure if what they had was something outside of mere flirtation and close proximity. He wanted to be next to her and feel her warmth, to protect her, to do what he could to be at her side at all times.

Suddenly, he was hit in the chest with another realization that was merely a simple suspicion before: if he was to stay by her side, what would that make him? Would he work for her and the Nightstone family, possibly as a spy or as a guard of some sort? Would he possibly just be someone to have around because they could not live without the other even if the feelings were platonic? Or—and his heart skipped a beat when the thought came to mind—would he marry her and help restore the Nightstone family line? Of the choices that floated in his head, the last was the most desirable but also, for some reason, the most difficult to see come to fruition, because what if the feelings were not mutual? What if he was correct and she was just flirtatious with him and close proximity made the other more appealing?

"Elaras?" came the High Cleric's voice. He was waiting on Elaras as he was lost in thought, standing in the same spot Rosella had left him in.

Elaras snapped his attention to the High Cleric and flattened out the hood of his cloak to keep his hands busy. "Yes, my apologies, High Cleric," Elaras said, having to clear his throat slightly. He walked in the same steps Rosella and the High Paladin took and wrung his sore fingers, letting the pain distract him from his skyrocketing heartbeat.

The grand dining hall was large and lavish. The tall ceilings had sparkling lights that twinkled like stars, and one central chandelier was a large sphere to look like the moon. Unlike the rest of the house, the room had silver accents, and the walls had a mix of blue and yellow tapestries and paintings of the country sides of Arja. Two long tables sat side by side decorated with candles and flowers. At the head of the two tables stood one smaller perpendicular table which sat seven chairs with only six of the seats filled.

Rosella sat in the central seat in an ornate blue and white chair with High Cleric Varran and High Paladin Joss sitting on either side of her. Elaras sat on one end next to Akuna, who was next to Varran. Mellis, the housekeeper, sat next to Joss, and Mellis, like everyone else, was smiling widely and periodically glancing toward Rosella for her approval. The two long tables were filled with close to fifty Nightstone staff members, and everyone was eating joyfully and in high spirits. At this moment, no one was working as this was a moment of celebration.

Their future queen was home.

With the ecstasy-filled air and loud conversations from the staff and those that shared his table, Elaras kept to himself as he enjoyed the exquisite food and atmosphere. Mellis made a dish with elk steak and smashed brown butter potatoes, and the rainbow vegetables were seasoned with citrus and peppers, and he admitted that this meal was one of the best he had had in quite some time.

Thousands of thoughts were running through his head, and he felt moments of anxiety thinking of what would happen after this meal. He knew they would have to face his father and Lycilla to retrieve Rosella's night stone, and he knew for a fact that his father would not be an easy man to negotiate with. There were concerns for his mother as he had not heard from her since he joined Rosella. He found it odd that there was no word sent back about Alryo's death, no funeral notice or condolences. Unfortunately, it took eating this meal to make him realize he had not thought of his mother.

"What's going on in your little elf brain, Elaras?" Akuna's voice broke into his thoughts.

He looked at the tiny form of Akuna, who was sitting politely with a clean plate. He was given a mound of fresh raw meat as his meal.

Elaras smiled and held his fork lazily in his fingers. "I'll be honest with you and say that I'm thinking of my mother. My father is not a kind man, and he has simply put up with my mother for the time they have been together. I'm worried for her safety as she cannot use magic, and I hope she is alright considering the circumstances." Letting this voracious dragon in on something vulnerable was difficult, though he had grown fond of Akuna despite the spat they had the other day.

"You could let Varran know, and he can inform the spies to keep a lookout for her and to check for her safety," Akuna said simply, as if this information was purely conversational.

Elaras' eyes grew wide, but then he shook his head. He leaned into Akuna's space until he was about a foot away from him. He almost expected Akuna to take a step back or even bristle, but the tiny dragon stayed rooted to the spot.

"As amazing as that idea is, I'm not one with the Nightstones, nor am I even really familiar enough to ask such a thing. Besides, Akuna, my *father* is essentially their number one enemy. How can I ask that of the Nightstone staff?" Elaras asked, allowing his vulnerability to show.

Akuna, surprisingly, rolled his eyes and turned away from

Elaras to face Varran. They exchanged a few hushed voices, Varran glancing toward Elaras once or twice before returning to their conversation. When they finished, Akuna pivoted and placed a clawed paw on Elaras' hand.

"Varran will let the spies know to get your mother's status," Akuna said calmly. "If your father has done something to harm your mother, that will only solidify Rosella as the rightful heir to the throne to not only Arja, but to all of Dorthos."

Elaras, too stunned to talk, looked up at Varran, who happened to be staring at Elaras. "High Cleric Varran, thank you," Elaras managed to choke out toward him.

Varran gave a kind and reassuring smile and nodded before turning to Rosella to continue a conversation they were having.

Elaras gazed toward Akuna, who was still looking at Elaras but had taken his paw away. "And thank you, Akuna. Also I—I truly am sorry for..." Elaras started before Akuna narrowed his eyes at him, making Elaras stop his words.

"There is nothing more to be sorry for. Continue to prove yourself, as my trust does not come easily. Rosella cares for you as I care for her. Do not hurt her again," Akuna said stiffly, but with an attitude of a father berating their child's significant other.

Elaras nodded and let out a stressed breath, unaware he was holding one. "I promise I won't hurt her again. I care too much for her," Elaras admitted, placing his chin on a closed fist.

"That has become blatantly obvious, elf," Akuna said with a chuckle before spreading his wings and flying to Mellis on the other end of the table.

After about another hour of finishing dinner and dessert, Varran stood from his chair and cast a small incantation to amplify his voice so the entirety of the room could hear.

"Our future queen is home, and soon the Nightstone line and the land of Arja will be restored. However, as we are all aware,

Kaine Moonshadow and Lycilla Rockshire possess Our Majesty's night stone. Tomorrow, we will make the plan for retrieving the stone and restoring this home completely. Tonight, we shall rest and give Our Majesty the time she needs to adjust herself to her new home. Before giving her a tour of the manor, Rosella has asked for each and every one of her staff to come to her and to introduce yourselves with your name, your rank, and your position before returning to your regular routines. Thank you all, and long live the Nightstones."

The room was filled with scraping chairs as everyone from the two long tables stood up and filed into a single line in front of the table. Rosella stood up and walked around the table to stand in front of the spot she was just sitting at.

Each member of the staff did exactly as Varran asked of them, and each person that walked up to Rosella shook her hand and introduced themselves accordingly. Elaras was astonished by the politeness of the staff, and also by the fact that every single person seemed absolutely delighted to meet her. Elaras leaned toward Varran, who was watching on with an observing eye.

"High Cleric, are these the same staff that were here during the Nightstones' time?" he asked, letting his thoughts flow into his words.

Varran glanced at him from the side before leaning further into Elaras' space so as to not be overheard by Rosella or the staff. "Yes. We have only hired a few members of staff since their demise, and the members that have been here the longest are High Paladin Joss, Mellis, and myself. Many joined about five or ten years before with the rest joining after and have stuck around because they have believed a Nightstone will return. So the joy they feel is immeasurable, as it is for the three of us at this table."

Elaras leaned back, watching Rosella greet the last few members with the same enthusiasm as the first one she met. Her comfort was becoming clearer, and his heart soared seeing her embrace these moments, the first of many here at the Nightstone castle.

As the last member left, Rosella turned and smiled at those sitting at the table behind her.

"I'm ready for that tour now, Varran, if you're still up for it?" Rosella asked politely.

Despite her not addressing him, Elaras grinned at the happy sight of her. Whatever the future held for them, he was happy to just be here with her for her journey.

27

If the Walls Could Speak

Rosella kept pace with Varran, Joss, Akuna, and Elaras as they walked the entirety of the Nocturnal Manor, peering into rooms and onto the hundreds of paintings and tapestries that lined the walls. Varran filled her mind with everything he seemed to know about the Nightstones, and asked her various questions like her time so far in Dorthos, her thoughts on the food here, and even her opinion on changes she would like to make. Rosella told him everything she could as well, but when it came to the changes, she did not have any for the moment because by this point she had only been in the manor for about three hours.

The only room that Varran could not show her was the throne room, as all the doors to the large room had been locked for thirty years. The doors needed a family member with a night stone to open the doors or for a member to already be inside, so no one on staff had been able to enter. Not far from the throne room and the adjourned chapel was a small hidden space that only had a large vault door that was double the size of her inside. She looked on curiously as Varran explained that this was the Nightstone vault, and only members of the family could open this door.

"Oh, so I need my necklace for the door just like the throne room?" she asked, realizing the question came off as stupid. Varran graciously did not give her a questioning look before turning to her.

"Yes, or you have to be wearing a crown," Varran said, setting a gentle hand on the door as he spoke to Rosella. "The Nightstone riches and valuables are kept here, as the stones themselves only appear for a Nightstone themselves to lay claim to it. You will be able to access your chips once we have your stone in hand."

Before Rosella could reply, Akuna flew up in between them "Varran, I should tell you that her magic pouch has access to the vault. She needed a way to pay for things when she came to Dorthos, so I made a small portal from inside the vault to the pouch."

Varran looked taken aback for a moment before laughing deeply. "Akuna, I always forget how powerful you are! Though I must ask just for my own peace of mind, did you enchant the pouch to ward off unwanted hands?"

"Oh, yeah, he definitely did," came Elaras' chuckling voice, and Rosella turned to see he was rubbing his arm that he had stuck into her pouch.

At this comment, Joss grunted toward Elaras. Varran, however, laughed more and ushered them out of the room, shaking his head in amusement. As Rosella passed Elaras, he gave a sly smile and a wink, and Rosella felt her chest flutter at the sight. After only a few more rooms among the massive manor, they entered a hallway and approached grand double doors on the third level that were at the end of a hallway. Varran stepped forward and opened both doors simultaneously.

Inside was a gigantic room that was washed over with gentle pastel blues and whites, and each corner of the room was lit with candles. From the doorway she could not see a bed, but she could see double windowed doors that led to a balcony with moonlight spilling into the room, and to the right was an ornate desk with a lit fire in the fireplace. For a moment, Rosella stood frozen in the doorway, and only moved inside when she felt a gentle hand on her elbow from Varran.

She slowly walked in and saw that both sides of the room stretched wide, and on the far-left side was a large bed with four poster posts and a canopy over the bed. The bed itself was covered in a thick dark blue comforter and a variety of pillows, and as she stepped closer, she realized the bed could easily fit four people side by side. Side tables on each side of the bed held bright lanterns, and further on her left were two doors, assumingly one for the bathroom and one for the closet. Astounded, she turned around and saw that behind the desk was in fact a fireplace along with four floor-to ceiling bookshelves filled with colorful spines. Two plush chairs and a loveseat were situated around a dark brown coffee table in front of the bookshelves and opposite the desk.

"Is this...?" Rosella asked no one in particular.

"This is your room, Rosella," Varran said, his hands clasped together and a genuine smile on his face. "Let me introduce you to your lady's maids. They are responsible for tidying your room, helping you dress, organize what you need, and much more. I know you met them, but we have Lodmora, Mija, Qax, and Nimue."

After he said this, four people—a female dwarf, a brown cow-like person, a blue lizgon, and a red-skinned androgynous elf—walked in. Rosella recognized them all, though she did not realize they would be her maids as they simply said "housekeeping" earlier when they all introduced themselves.

Lodmora, the female dwarf with dark skin and long braided hair, led the other three in a line and stopped just short of her, bowing their heads and saluting the moon symbol to her. "We are honored to be given the position of your maids, Your Majesty. Please let us know whatever you need, and we shall oblige!" she said, and when she looked up, she, along with the other three, had giddy smiles on their faces.

Despite her thinking this would be a dreary job, they seemed to believe the opposite and that the work they did was something they genuinely enjoyed.

"I'm honored to have you with me. I apologize now for some confusion on my end in the beginning as this is something for me to get used to, so please bear with me," Rosella said as kindly as possible.

At once, all of them spoke in reassuring tones and gestures, stopping when Varran cleared his throat.

"Rosella, is there anything you need before you head to bed for the night?" Varran asked politely.

She thought for a moment, trying to think through all the knowledge and information she had gained over the last few hours. For some reason, now was the time when her anxiety started to appear, and she had to take a quick and slightly quavering breath.

"I believe a bath and a glass of juice will do nicely. What do you think, Rosella?" came Elaras' voice into her subconscious, and she glanced over to see that he had taken a step forward and was regarding her with a raised brow and a smirk. Rosella, astounded by the thoughtfulness of this, nodded and looked to Lodmora.

"Yes, actually. It has been some time since I have had a bath, and I think that would be lovely," Rosella said, and the four maids smiled at her.

"Yes, Your Majesty, right away!" Lodmora said before the four hurried to the bathroom. Noises of running water and rummaging around cabinets filled the room.

Rosella faced Varran. "Thank you, and I believe that is all for tonight."

"Sounds good. You can ring the silent bell on either side of your bed if you need anything at all. Your maids are down the hall from you. We shall leave you now so you can decompress," Varran said before turning towards the door.

Elaras held a finger up to his mouth and approached Rosella. "If I may, I'd like to have a moment with you, please," he said, and Rosella felt more fluttering in her chest.

Varran and Joss, however, did not look happy at the request.

"I believe Our Majesty needs some rest, Elaras. She has been through enough today," Joss suggested in a menacing tone.

Rosella wanted to talk and be with Elaras alone, but she also wanted to respect those of this home, especially given that she did not know the dynamics and rules of this manor entirely. She was still new, and the last thing she wanted was to be disrespectful. Thankfully, Akuna was the one to speak up.

"Give them a few minutes, Joss. They have much to discuss. We will be outside the doors when Elaras is ready to be shown to his room," Akuna said authoritatively.

Joss nodded and took a step back, letting out a grunt-filled exhale.

"Um, lady's maids?" Rosella called out toward the bathroom.

Qax, the blue lizgon with vibrant yellow eyes, emerged from the bathroom. "Yes, Your Majesty?"

"I would like a few minutes alone with Elaras. Could you all give us some privacy, please? Just a few minutes."

"Yes, Your Majesty! And you can just call us 'ladies' if you need all of us!"

"Sounds good, Qax, thank you," Rosella said, nodding gently.

Qax returned to the bathroom and gathered the other three, then they left the bathroom and followed Varran, Joss, and Akuna out the door.

When the door snapped shut, Rosella's body relaxed completely, and she let out a deep exhale. Elaras' eyebrows raised, and he let out a soft chuckle.

"Yeah? I bet your brain hurts from everything that was told to you today," Elaras said, folding his arms to his chest and watching her as she stretched.

"It hurts a little already, but I know it'll hurt a lot more tomorrow. Like, it's all still hitting me hard, and I thought I would have fully accepted it by now, you know?" Rosella said, taking rhythmic breaths and looking to the ceiling which was covered in embossed stars and the stages of the moon.

"I don't think this will stop being overwhelming until about a year or so from now, when you're comfortable and everything is as normal as possible," Elaras said intelligently, not taking his eyes off Rosella. "I believe this world will always surprise you since it seems so different from Earth, but at least you came here in the best possible position you could have."

"Yeah, true. Thank you for sticking by me this whole time. You've helped me more than I could ever thank you for," Rosella said, rolling her neck and shoulders.

When their eyes met, his smile grew wide, and his gray eyes sparkled in the candle and moonlight. She herself could not help but match his smile, and her heart skipped a beat. He drew closer to her and gently caressed her cheek, his eyes not letting go of hers.

"It'll always be my pleasure to help you, Rosella. This may sound cheesy, but I hope I never have to leave your side because my dark world is better when you're there to light up the shadows around me," Elaras murmured, vulnerable and yet full of longing.

She pulled herself into his space until their chests were pressed together, the leathers they both wore rubbing and squeaking quietly against each other. She knew that in this delicate moment where they stood so close that they could kiss, or confess their fondness for the other, but Rosella realized she wanted one thing, and she knew she could only get that from Elaras.

Freeing her face from his hand, she launched herself into his body, wrapping him in a tight and deep hug. Her face pressed hard against his black leather, her forehead barely touching his collarbone and her cheek and ear pressed where his heart was. She shut her eyes and held him so tight that if he wasn't wearing the armor, she knew he would bruise.

Elaras did not hesitate and hugged her back, but he wrapped one arm around her waist as the other held her head closer to his chest. He leaned his cheek down to touch the top of her head, and they stood there like stones, the only movements being their chests rising and falling. The silence around them was only interrupted by the fireplace and the beating of his heart in her ear.

Rosella felt warm and safe, protected and validated in his arms, and she wanted to stay for as long as possible. After a few minutes passed, Elaras took his cheek off her head and pressed a kiss to her hair, then moved the hand that was on her head to her cheek and lifted her face up toward his.

"Would you like me to stay in this room with you tonight, my sweet?" he asked so softly that no one but themselves could possibly ever hear.

She smiled up at him, and instead of responding right away,

she stood up on her toes to close the space between them. "I would love that, Elaras," she whispered.

He gave a rumbling exhale that sounded like a gentle growl before he leaned in further into her. This was the closest they had ever been, and her heart was pounding to the point of explosion. Their lips were barely brushing against each other as they breathed the same air, her mind only focused on him. Everything faded around her, and she welcomed it wholeheartedly. She felt his hand move to the nape of her neck and into her hair.

Just as she was about to look into his eyes one more time to see those gray pearls shining back at her, he pressed his lips against hers. Her eyes fell shut, and she saw swirls of blues and purples, silver and gold glitter, and stars sparkling and shimmering. She had to take in a deep breath, and he did the same as they kissed deeply and passionately, their hands never letting go of the other as they moved up each other's bodies, gripping tighter so the other could not escape. Her back arched, and she stood up higher on her toes, the need to be as close as possible to him taking over every instinct she had. It was the only thing she wanted along with never tearing her lips from his.

She had kissed many men in her time on Earth, but none were ever like this. This was a kiss with someone, anyone, she only ever dreamed about and a kiss she knew that once she let go, it would be the saddest feeling in the world. The air around her would feel empty and cold, and the only way to feel that warmth was to kiss the one she adored most.

Everything felt right, and she craved every part of Elaras, not just romantically but every part of who he was as a person. This kiss would ruin her in the best possible way, and she hoped selfishly that this kiss would ruin him too so that it would give him more reason to stay with her, to never leave, to be hers and she to be his. To be her king and husband. To be her love. At the thought, she kissed him even harder, sliding her hand into his hair and gripping, hoping that was enough of a clue to not let her go anytime soon.

Through their overwhelmingly shared bliss and hunger for the other came a noise that shocked her, the beautiful colors in her closed eyes exploding away. She felt Elaras break their lips apart, but his hands never left contact with her body, his hand still on her lower back and his hand in her hair. She opened her eyes to see where the repeated loud noise was coming from, angry the moment came to an abrupt stop.

What looked like an odd version of a medieval fire alarm on the wall was making the siren noise and was flashing out puffs of yellow smoke.

Varran burst through the door, and his eyes landed on her and Elaras, his eyes hardened like ice. Elaras shoved her behind him while he reached for a dagger at his waistband, but he eased up when he realized it was Varran. She also noticed Joss and Akuna were not behind him, and the maids were standing to the side huddled together.

"We have unexpected guests. Elaras, do not let her go in case you need to displace yourself and our queen," Varran ordered Elaras.

Elaras grabbed her hand tightly as the three of them ran down to the main floor where guards and the two Paladins stood by the back entry. When Rosella, Elaras, and Varran reached Gerrart and Joss, Gerrart stood in front of Rosella so she had to peer around at who was at the doors. Akuna was noticeably out of sight, and Rosella assumed that he was hiding to not be exposed.

"*That is correct. I cannot let these guests see me. I'm on Joss' back in case you need me,*" came Akuna's voice, and she looked to Joss' upper back and saw a small bump of silver that was the tiny form of Akuna, who had changed his scale color to match Joss' armor.

Before them out of the light of the overhead lanterns stood a larger, gray, and burlier version of Mija, the cow-like person who she now realized must be Dorthos' version of a minotaur, as well as six other men wearing armor of black and purple behind them. They were all panting as they stood in front of Joss, who was interrogating them.

"Why would you come here instead of your estate that you are responsible for?" Joss questioned the minotaur. He had his weapon at the ready, baring his teeth in a snarl.

"Because the head of the Moonshadow family has failed us for the final time. Twen, one of the Moonshadow guards, teleported us here. We heard whispers of a Nightstone returning, and we would like to give ourselves to the future king or queen to serve or to be punished, if they would have us. I have information about the Moonshadows that will help the cause," the minotaur said, almost exhaustedly, but he took a step forward into the light.

At these words and the clear sight of the minotaur, Elaras, who was still holding onto Rosella's hand, let go and strode to the front of the Nightstone guards.

"Tordias?" Elaras questioned, surprise lacing his tone.

Tordias turned his attention away from Joss, and his eyes landed on Elaras, growing wide with a light that was lost returned to them.

"Young Elaras, how good it is to see you! I knew you were with a woman, though I was not aware you would be here at the manor. Wait, does that mean...?" he asked before he trailed off.

The Nightstone guards all shifted forward as Joss did, and the Moonshadow guards took a step back, raising their arms in the air to show they were unarmed. Tordias, on the other hand, remained where he stood, unmoving and unwavering. Rosella felt something squirm with anticipation in her gut, and without a second thought, she stepped around Gerrart and placed her hand into Elaras' again in case her plan did not work.

The minotaur, Tordias, met her eyes, and his grew as large as saucers. When she stopped by Elaras' side, he heaved heavy breaths before kneeling before her. He bowed his head that was now at eye level with her, his horns tipping forward. "Future Queen Nightstone, I resent the Moonshadow post and their family and wish to serve under you, your Paladins, your guards, and your name. I wish to be at your service as you will do justice to Arja and save the citizens of Dorthos."

After he was done, the guards behind him copied his movements and his words in unison, similar to how the Nightstone guards did in the tunnel when she arrived. Rosella glanced to Varran for guidance, and after a moment he gave a simple nod. She looked back to see Tordias and the guards had not moved, awaiting her word.

"I don't recommend threatening them, but tell them they will need to be in the dungeons tonight and they can be integrated tomorrow," Akuna said to her quickly. *"We need to be sure they are on our side and to see what information they have."*

"Okay," she said to Akuna. Rosella gently cleared her throat before telling Tordias, "Tordias, you and your men shall serve the Nightstone name given what you say is true and when you prove yourself. Tonight, you will be given a meal and drink, and you will spend the night in the dungeons. Soon, we shall determine your honor and dignity."

"Yes, Your Majesty. Thank you for your generosity," Tordias said, and the guards copied him once again.

"Rise," she said with finality, and at once the Moonshadow guards and Tordias stood up in unison, Tordias towering over Rosella. They were filed away by Gerrart toward the dungeons, and Rosella saw a flash of Mellis heading in the opposite direction, undoubtedly heading to the kitchen to prepare something for the newcomers.

Rosella turned to Varran, and she saw he was giving a reassuring smile.

"Please, head to bed, and we can discuss in the morning. You did well, as I would have done the same. Goodnight, Rosella," he said and he gestured in the direction of her bedroom three flights above.

"Thank you, Varran, and thank you all for your protection. Goodnight," she said to everyone that stood around her before turning to Elaras. She leaned in and whispered, "Sit with me while I finally take my bath, Cricket?"

"Sounds absolutely lovely, my sweet," he said with a sly smile.

28
Trust in Thyself, Trust in Thine Enemies

The beginning of Rihanna's song "Disturbia" rang out in the bathroom, making Rosella open her eyes to see Elaras' child-like face examining her cellphone in his hands. He was sitting next to her large bathtub facing her and was wearing the same clothes she saw him in at the inn the other night. The water in the tub was so cloudy with a flower milky substance and soapy bubbles that no more than an inch could be seen under the water's surface. Because of the cloudy water, Rosella felt fully comfortable having Elaras sit with her and keep her company without risking him seeing more of her than she was comfortable with yet.

"What do you —" she tried to ask Elaras, but he stuck a quick finger in the air and made a shushing sound.

Rosella let out a chuckle and watched him move his body back and forth to the music, his eyes never leaving the screen. When the song finished, his blazing eyes landed on hers, and she felt her eyes go wide in reaction to his face, which looked perplexed and full of curiosity.

"So this is normal music on Earth? Not just strings, horns, and vocals?" he asked, scooting his chair slightly forward.

"Oh, there are all types of music. There are computer-generated songs, ones made purely of strings like an orchestra, and depending on your region and culture, there may be beautiful tribal music with or without vocals. I have a lot of various musical types downloaded on that phone so you can listen whenever you want. I needed music for when I practiced archery or worked out, and I had many phases," Rosella said as Elaras scanned through the long list of music that was stored, feeling extremely grateful that her phone worked and played music, so she did not feel completely homesick.

"You said combuer earlier?" Elaras asked without looking up.

Rosella blew a raspberry realizing, once again, that this world would not have those and that was something else she would have to explain. "A *computer*? Think of it as a machine made of metal and other materials and is a much bigger and more efficient version of my phone," she said, and Elaras let out a gentle gasp.

He tapped the screen and waited for a new song to play. After a few drumbeats, an unknown language played, and the vocals sounded like multiple sounds were being performed by the same singer or by two. The sound was harsh to the ear. Elaras tilted his head in surprise and confusion, and he simply stared at her.

Rosella smiled at him in amusement. "'Sugaan Essena' by the HU. They're a metal Mongolian throat singing group. They're quite good."

"Throat singing?"

"Yes, using your throat to create multiple sounds at once. It's quite hard, but the Mongolians are quite good at it."

"Your world still amazes me."

"As does yours. I'd rather be here than on Earth, to be honest," Rosella said, and Elaras' expression softened.

He reached his hand over the edge of the tub and waited for her to grab it so it did not have to enter the water. They smiled at each other, then she closed her eyes and leaned her head back while Elaras scrolled through her phone more, soon finding the thousands of stored photos on her camera roll, not letting go of each other's hands.

———

"You have to understand, as I'm sure Young Elaras knows, Kaine is not someone that can easily be contained. He does not like being in one spot for too long or at the whims of others. He took in Lycilla Rockshire a few months ago after Young Alryo brought her home. Two months ago, they became engaged, and they set out on missions of a nature I was not aware of. I know a few missions were to slay dragons and to bring in money to the family and to give to the Rockshire girl. The last dragon they brought in was a pink one, and that was enough to supply the both of them with equipment —"

"Salista. Her name was Salista Dila Brentious, the singing pink dragon," Rosella cut in quietly, and everyone grew silent at once. She looked up and saw all eyes were on her, and she cleared her throat and faced Tordias. "My apologies, the words came out, and they should have stayed as thoughts and not as spoken words. Please, continue."

Varran nodded approvingly like a proud father as Tordias accepted her apology.

They were seated in a dark yet decadent room that had a long table and professional cushioned chairs that were a simple dark blue but had a symbol designating the position of the person.

Around the table was Rosella at the head with a simple crown embroidered on the chair; Elaras on her left in a chair with a single star; Varran on her right with what looked like the symbol of Elyphr with a crescent moon, five stars and clouds; Joss on his right with the head of a war hammer; and Akuna sat inside Rosella's pouch at her waist.

Tordias, whom Rosella was told was a minotaurus in Dorthos, sat at the very end of the table and was seated between two standing guards, his chair having no embroidery. He was in simple tunics, and Rosella saw that the muscles Tordias had were what gave him his bulk and not the armor he wore the night before. She also saw that the scar on his face continued down into the neck of his tunic, and he had medium-length dark gray dreadlocks that were pulled back between his horns.

"After Lycilla came back with your night stone and without Alryo, that was when Kaine took advantage of her. He began his control of her mind and body, and I do not believe he has released her in many days," Tordias said with careful words to the group before him. "When someone under his control gets far away enough, they can break out of control like my men did last night, but she is by his side at all times. While I do not agree with her motives and desires for the Arja throne, I do believe we need to remove her from his clutches."

"What of my mother, Tordias?" Elaras blurted out.

The look Tordias gave him was grim. "Young Elaras, I'm so sorry. Kaine told his men that she fell ill, but her lady's maid informed me in secret that she was in fact poisoned. I—I carried her body to the carriage heading to the House of Passing myself to prepare her body. She's dead, my young lord, and I'm truly sorry. She was a wonderful woman."

When Rosella looked at Elaras, her heart completely dropped, a lump forming in her throat. She reached for his hand, and he took it with a shaky grip. His skin grew hot and was beginning to clam up from shock.

"Was all of this why you left your post at the Moonshadow residence?" Varran asked cautiously.

"Yes. I was with the family for about fifty years, and over time I came to know the true nature of Kaine Moonshadow," Tordias said while periodically shifting his gaze from Varran to Elaras. "Yesterday was the breaking point when he ordered one of his men to die by my hand and for me to fall on my own sword after one of his guards ran after one of your Nightstone spies. The blockade was great, but the Lycilla girl was able to teleport the carriage and horses around it so they proceeded to the capital with only a ten-minute delay. I will say I am not sure how long they will be there in the capital before heading back to the Moonshadow estate or even to here."

Joss and Varran exchanged silent words. After a moment of silence between them, Varran conjured a silver sparrow and sent it through the wall.

A few more minutes of silence and waiting, Mellis swept through the door and walked directly to Varran. They exchanged more words that the rest of the room was not privy to, then Mellis left out the door with haste.

Rosella, curious about the interactions that just took place, leaned back in her chair and observed Tordias at the other end of the table. His presence was calm and unashamed, as if this was just another conversation and not a meeting to determine his place in this home. She glanced at Elaras, who was breathing heavily, but she squeezed his hand tighter in hopes that it would help ease his pain. Looking back to Tordias, she saw that he was smiling at Elaras and herself. This guard saw Elaras grow up, so it must feel wondrous to see how far Elaras had come and also to see him in the rival of his previous post's home.

"Tordias," she said simply, and he straightened his back. "Can we trust you and your men? My concern is that one of your men is a spy and will somehow relay information to Kaine."

He regarded her in a way that made her squirm in an unpleasant way. This person was quite intimidating, and she understood why he had overseen the Moonshadow guard. Even if Tordias didn't intend to be menacing, he stared at her with such an angry but determined look.

Then he put the crescent moon hand symbol to his chest before saying, "You can trust in all of us that we will serve and protect you and your name, and we have no plans to relay any information at all or to be in contact with Kaine or Lycilla. I know you or your home may not trust us, but me and my men agreed that the only good remaining member of the Moonshadow household was Elaras, and he was in the wind. You have our strength, our swords, and our minds, wherever you see fit for us."

Bowing his head at the end then looking up, she realized what expression he was giving and how best to describe him: unwavering stoicism.

She nodded at him and turned to Varran and Joss. "I trust that you both will be able to make a wise decision based on your expertise and knowledge. I do believe Tordias has good intentions, and I also believe that Elaras would have told us right away if he or his men were not to be trusted. Am I right in presuming that, Elaras?"

While he was still somber and silent, he nodded and looked at her with eyes that were filled with sadness, but no tears. "Tordias has always been loyal and noble. It must have taken a lot for him to leave. He pledged himself to the Nightstone name. I say give him a chance to prove himself," Elaras said, his voice clear of sadness, contrasting his expression.

Varran and Joss looked at each other once more and nodded

before Varran turned to the guards behind Tordias. "Please place him and his men in the additional barracks and have the blacksmith rework their armor to bear the Nightstone coat of arms. Tordias, please report to Gerrart for duties for you and your men. You are excused, and thank you."

Tordias stood up and saluted Rosella.

Once he and the guards were gone, Varran and Joss turned their attention to Rosella. "Now, we must plan for how to get your stone back. We know that Kaine and Lycilla are at Keene, the capital, and those that can use teleportation on staff cannot teleport that far. Remind me, Akuna, can you teleport?"

Akuna crawled out of Rosella's pouch and flew up to sit on her shoulder before saying, "I can, but dragon transportation is different than speaking-kind teleportation. We need to create portals, and a portal in this instance would take great power and time. Besides, I have wings to take me anywhere I need to go."

Varran sighed and twiddled his fingers. However, his train of thought was interrupted when a blue and yellow sparrow flew through the wall and landed in front of him. He grabbed the letter in its beak and read through as the sparrow dissipated. When he was finished, he gave the letter to Joss and turned back to Rosella.

"Kaine and Lycilla were granted the Arja throne by the emperor, and they are meant to remain in Keene for three weeks before returning for the approved wedding and coronation. It seems that Kaine and Lycilla tried to leave this morning, but they and their remaining party were restricted from leaving by the empress. As far as this letter says, Kaine and Lycilla are still within the emperor's castle," he said, his voice stern and sharp. "Three weeks would give us plenty of time to go to Keene to convince the emperor that Rosella is the rightful heir, and we also have a chance to get the stone."

Joss grunted in response as he finished reading, handing the letter to Rosella and Elaras, who read it in unison. When they finished, they looked at each other, Elaras apprehensive.

"What is it, Elaras?" Rosella asked quietly, but she knew the other three in the room could hear her.

Elaras gripped her hand harder and took in a deep breath. "I don't think you should interact with him. He can do a lot of harm, and if he can kill my mother, who knows what he would do with you. He can control you with a whisper, and you would have no way out of it," he said, slight fear lacing his tone. He turned to Varran and Joss. "Would we send a group with her, or would we need to do this stealthily?"

"I believe stealth will be best. No need to send a calvary when some of our best fighters and defenders are our spies. We're thankful that the same person that sent that letter is very close to the emperor, so they can let us in and help," Varran said, almost in a reassuring tone.

"How close, though?" asked Elaras, leaning forward toward him.

"Familial."

"Familial? Okay, so, we travel there off-road in hopes Moonshadow spies don't catch us, and when we get there, sneak into the castle. After that, berate the emperor until he gives Rosella the throne and steal the stone from my father?"

"That seems like the best bet if we were to do something now rather than later," Varran said, and Rosella was able to see the gears whirling in his head as he spoke. "Arja has lost the majority of the standing military presence since the Nightstones' passing, so what you have seen is what we have. Stealth will be best if we are to act now."

"Well, I am good at stealth and sneaking," Elaras said, leaning back in his chair and mindlessly rubbing Rosella's knuckles.

"Your displacer magic, yes. Can you do that over long distances with multiple people?" Varran asked, and when Elaras nodded, Varran placed a finger to his lips to think.

"The capital is a five-day trip, and I know a route with many caves and hiding spots along the way. You will have to get with Mellis to confirm this, as they're Mellis' spies that will lead you," Joss said to both Rosella and Elaras.

"Joss, with Elaras' displacing magic, they can be there in half the time. Do we want that?" said Varran, still lost in thought. "Or should we add on someone that can help them move stealthily? Decktor knows how to cloak, along with Flitch, but I do not believe they can do more than four people."

"Four should be enough, and I'm sure Akuna can also cloak us if need be, right, Akuna?" Rosella finally said to the group.

"Yes, I can if necessary," Akuna said simply.

"So we have options. When do we leave?" asked Elaras, and both Varran and Joss regarded him before looking at each other. Rosella grew slightly envious of their connection.

"Tomorrow? And we'll have you two meet with Mellis before the end of the night to plan further," Varran said, turning back to Rosella and Elaras. They both nodded, and Varran let out a sigh of relief. "Either way and no matter how you and the spies go about it, we need the stone before the end of the three weeks is up. Pack what you both will need, and Rosella, you will find that new clothes have been made for you. The armor being made for you is being rushed and will be ready before you leave tomorrow. Let me or Joss know if you need anything else in the meantime. Good day to you three."

Rosella nodded, and she noticed that no one stood up to leave the table. She looked to Elaras, who raised his eyebrows expectantly. All the shows she had seen of royals came to mind, showing her that the head royal had to stand up from any table before the group could stand or adjourn. With this in mind, she stood up, and the effect was immediate as Varran and Joss stood up after her and left the room.

"Ready for an adventure with a hint of espionage?" Elaras teased in her ear as he moved to stand next to her.

"Hell yeah," she said, smiling up at him before they exited the room after Varran and Joss, Akuna still on her shoulder.

29

Lust Intertwined with Stardust

"Tell me about the underworld, Elaras," Rosella said as the two meandered hand in hand through the halls of the Nocturnal Manor. They passed by what seemed like hundreds of rooms and people going about their duties, each stopping to salute her as she passed.

"Dark, gloomy, no sun, but alive with creatures that could never dwell on the surface. Winged creatures that are said to be undead devlairs, giant spiders and skin-eating moths, and creatures that look like humans but actually eat your brains if they get the chance, just to name a few," Elaras said, starting to walk to the second floor. "If any of those creatures came to the surface, they would burn in the sun before they even took a breath. There is also beautiful flora that glow on their own and are plentiful, along with mushrooms and spores everywhere you step."

"Sounds, yeah, gloomy and also dangerous. Is the surface better?"

"In many ways, yes, though I do miss the ambiance of the underworld, and sometimes the simplicity of it. The whole of the underworld is ruled by one family, and each generation brings a mixed bag of a person. Some rulers are great, while others are worse than the emperor."

"Oh no, no thank you."

"It's okay, the king down there now is cool. He did his best to be better than his father, and his father was so bad that even my father wanted nothing to do with him, hence why he moved us all up to the surface. I'll take you there sometime, with an entourage everywhere we go, of course," Elaras promised with a chuckle.

"I'll only go if you go with me. I'll consider it a vacation," Rosella said with a smile, and she was glad to see Elaras smile back.

"What about you? What part of Earth are you from?" Elaras asked excitedly.

Rosella laughed and had to think of how to best describe her home. "Well, Earth is big. From what I've seen of Dorthos, Earth's continents are bigger and within those continents are different countries, states, and provinces. I came from a place called North America in a state called Texas. Blazing hot in the summer, freezing in the winter. Big food portions full of grease and carbs, and the people had big personalities and were unlike any other state."

"Sounds welcoming and different from anything in Dorthos."

"Truly, Texas is its own world sometimes," Rosella said, feeling a little homesick and a sudden craving for sweet tea.

They talked more about Texas and of the different parts of Earth as they strolled around the manor, saying hello to staff members and occasionally peeking out of a curtain-covered window. Eventually they ended up back on the first floor and came across the massive mural of the family tree. Rosella walked the length of the tree, peering at the different names and years of the Nightstones now that she had more time to look closely. She felt that same weight fall onto her chest that came yesterday when first looking at this, and she instantly felt a mix of feelings she couldn't describe.

When the lines of names ended, she stopped and gazed at the last branches on the tree. King Raynne and Queen Kayline topped this particular branch that spread to fifteen separate limbs. Their four children—Princess Mystrias, Prince Kildo, Princess Luvu, and Prince Pirkac—all had spouses. Only Prince Kildo and Princess Luvu had children, the youngest being the twin princes Calus and Talus.

All fifteen family members shared the same death year: 3502.

"It's a lot, isn't it?" Elaras asked quietly, looking up at the family tree alongside her, squeezing her hand gently.

"Yeah," she said, sighing, unsure of what else to say at this moment. Five children died at the hands of the Rockshires. Did they even know what was happening when the massacre started? Were they comforted? Who would hurt *children* with such barbarity? Rosella's heart lurched, and her eyes burned with tears. Though this was not her birth family, her soul screamed with despair, louder each moment she gazed upon the tree. To see so many family members die at once, possibly together in the same room, shook her to her core.

Elaras wrapped his arm around her shoulders, and she reciprocated by wrapping her now free arm around his waist. They stood there for a while reading and taking in all of the information. Her heart grew heavier as she reread the last names to be added to the tree, and she did her best to hold back the building tears.

"Rosella, it's time to meet with Mellis' speaking kind. They're waiting on you and Elaras. You can make Nightstone babies later," came Akuna's voice, and she wiped a tear that had begun to spill out of her eye.

"On the way, and we're not—nevermind," she responded curtly.

The pull the tree had was strong, and it took more willpower than she expected to rip her eyes away and to turn her back on it. Elaras watched her as she did so, and when she faced him, he wrapped his arms around her in the same way he hugged her the night before. She reciprocated and did her best to be defiant despite knowing she did not have to pretend to be strong with Elaras.

"I'm sorry, Rosella, and I'm sorry for the almost impossible position you have been put into," Elaras said close to her ear, bending his head so his lips gently brushed the top of her ear.

"This is going to be really fucking hard," she managed to say before tears dripped onto his leathers where her face was pressed against it.

In response, he squeezed her tighter and kissed the top of her head, gently swaying side to side. "I know. You'll learn, and you have people beside you that will help you. You are not alone. I've got you, and you're not going anywhere."

"Always?" she asked in a whimper. Asking for a promise was difficult, but in this moment, she needed assurance more than anything else. She felt his chest expand between her arms, and her cheeks slid up the leathers from the tears as his chest rose.

"Always. I'm here to stay, and I will protect you and help you however I can," he said, his voice almost cooing, and she was thankful.

She raised her cheek off his chest and kissed him gently, unabashed by the warm tears that were now on their lips. The screaming in her soul was ebbing, her heart slowing to a steady beat with each kiss they shared.

When they broke away, he smiled and brushed her hair back with a finger before gripping the side of her face. "I—I promise, my sweet," he said, stuttering. He seemed like he wanted to say more but stopped himself, so she did not push him.

"Thank you, Cricket. And I promise I've always got you, at least as best I can," she said, giggling a little but nonetheless smiling and not breaking eye contact.

He smiled deeply and kissed her again, softly and tenderly. The kiss was like gentle rainfall on the skin, a refreshing gust of wind, or that perfect last bite of a great dessert. She was not sure how to describe the kiss exactly; all she knew was that this kiss was just as good as their first, and she felt herself swooning down to her knees. Just as she felt like she was going to fall into a blissful bath of flowers and pine, he broke away and pecked her on the nose.

"Come on, let's leave this hall. Maybe we can find a window that shows the garden. Maybe check out that archery range?" he said, keeping his arms around her a little longer, not moving or taking steps away from her. She wanted to agree and go with him, but she sighed, and his expression changed. "What?"

"Akuna told me Mellis' people are ready to see us," she said, feeling a pit form in her stomach. She did not want to go just yet. She did not want to be with anyone else at that moment. The need to be with just him was powerful, but she knew she needed to escape the fantasy and rejoin reality.

Elaras, however, looked outright disappointed. "Ah, well, we'll have to save the garden and archery for another time. For now, though, we can make them wait another five minutes," Elaras said, mischief alighting on his face. His smile turned purely sly and cocky, eyes darting all around them for anyone else.

Rosella was about to ask what he meant until she saw him squat and felt his hands grip her thighs and lifted her up, pressed her against the wall, and she yelped in surprise. She was now above him looking down. He held her there with an arm, and his body was pressed against hers. She had to wrap her legs around his torso to help hold herself up and held his face in her hands. He took a hand and dug it into the back of her head, grabbing her hair, and he brought her lips to his in another kiss.

This kiss was similar to their first but with more passion than she had ever experienced with any other. They groaned into each other's mouths, and their tongues collided playfully, their lips rubbing wonderfully raw, and the desire of wanting more growing ever more powerful. She moved a hand into his hair, and the other was wrapped around his neck, trying her best to pull him in closer to satisfy the overwhelming hunger she had for him.

What only seemed like a few seconds was actually a few minutes, and when she came up for air, she saw on one end of the hall a few staff members hiding behind the corner, giggling and scurrying away when Rosella saw them.

Elaras had his face pressed against her neck, about to kiss her when he heard the giggling. He looked right as the staff had disappeared, then back up at Rosella. He chuckled deeply before kissing her again, with a grand tenderness she least expected of him.

Before he set her down, Rosella's eyes grew wide, and she felt her heart sink slightly. Now she was the one that was disappointed because she wanted more, and she wanted to say something before this moment had to come to an end.

"Wait!" she said a little too loudly, and he froze, looking back up at her with confusion. "I just... You're great, and I hate not—uh —" she said sheepishly, unable to form more words as his eyebrows rose and his smile turned into one that was sly, his eyes so focused on her that Rosella thought he was peering into her soul. She loved that smile, and his eyes, and his attentiveness to her, and she grew speechless. He pushed her back up onto the wall and pressed his body against hers again, but he looked relaxed as both of his hands ended up under her thighs just holding her up.

"You hate not, what, kissing me?" Elaras murmured tilting his head to the side. His demeanor and the way he looked at her made her want to drool like a teenager crushing hard on the jock.

She nodded through the mesmerizing look he was giving her, moving her fingers to the scars on his cheeks and lips as well as gently tracing his sharp jawline with her fingertips. She needed confirmation she was not dreaming this moment with him, that this world was real and that he was with her like in the hundreds of dreams she had of him before she came to Dorthos.

As she was feeling the sensation of his skin under her fingertips, he said, "Well, my sweet, I hate not kissing you too. I always have to touch you, or I feel —"

"Cold?" she interrupted him, and she felt his fingertips dig deeply into her thighs. "Hold me, kiss me, so I don't have to feel the cold anymore. Make me believe that this is not a dream and that this moment with you is true, that I'm not making this up. I need to believe that you're real and that you're not a figment of my imagination just to keep me warm at night."

He kissed her again for who knew how long, possibly to stop her from talking, or his only appropriate response was to kiss her in agreement. The urge to say something else was making her heart race even more, and she felt the lump get stuck in her throat, so she broke apart from him again. He bit his lip while sucking in air, his eyes staring deeply into hers.

"Elaras, I—I think I—" she started to say, but he pressed a hand to her lips.

"If you're going to say what I can assume you're going to say, just wait a little longer for that specific word. But, if you want to say something similar besides that one word, I won't stop you,"

Elaras said in his silky tone, leaning his head forward toward hers, staring at her through his long eyelashes.

She pursed her lips and raised her eyebrows, exhaling something deep from her core. He was right. Now was not the time to admit to feelings that might not be completely true or might not be fully realized, the meaning of the word being moot. The moment was strong, and she had let her heart and body tell her brain otherwise, to not think completely logically.

"Elaras, I really like you," she whispered as she pushed her lips into his, and kissed him gently for just a moment before he broke them apart.

"Rosella, I really like you too," he said and kissed her again.

The thought came to her that if she watched this moment in a movie, she would have thought it would be cheesy, but that feeling washed away because now she understood the cheesy moment. She understood why cheesy rom-coms were so successful, and she wished she had appreciated them more in life before they all disappeared from her world.

"Rosella, they're waiting for you," Akuna's voice came through, laced with irritation, and for the first time since she met Akuna, she was not happy to hear him speak. Despite this though, she was also thankful for the reminder because there were responsibilities to uphold and something outside of her and Elaras was bigger than themselves. She broke off from Elaras once again, and she sighed deeply, not afraid of showing disappointment at their moment ending.

"We have to go. Akuna called me again," she said softly, and he set her down as he himself let out a deep exhale.

He pressed his forehead hard against hers, and they stood there until their heartbeats returned to as good as a normal pace. "Fine, let's go see what your guard dog wants," Elaras said, and they chuckled as they separated.

He grabbed her left hand, and they walked together to the entrance of the housekeeper's section of the home and into a secret door that led to where the spies would meet. There waiting for them was Akuna in his small form, sitting on Mellis' shoulder and still silver from yesterday. Mellis was standing next to a solid brown-furred felinette and a shorter person with deep red hair, smaller than a dwarf in height but clearly an adult. Both of the spies were dressed in sleek, skin-tight and well-worn black leather armor, and they both had knee-length black cloaks. The hoods were down and they both had a black scarf wrapped around their necks to hide their faces if need be. Both, despite their races, wore the same expression of cold fearlessness and looked intimidating in their own right, and interestingly, neither were wearing boots. As expected, all but Akuna saluted Rosella as she entered, and they took their seats after she did.

"Future Queen Rosella, this is Paton and Flitch, my spies that will accompany you on your journey to the capital," Mellis said, pointing to the two, Paton being the felinette and Flitch being the shorter person. Rosella noted that Flitch was one of the people she was told that could cloak them if need be, and so she grew curious if Paton could use magic as well or if they were more of a fighter.

"*Hobdrig,*" Akuna said to her telepathically, and she knew that it was him telling her what race Flitch was.

"Lovely to meet you both," Rosella said, and they both saluted her again.

"Alright, everyone situated?" Mellis asked everyone in the room, and when all heads nodded, they smiled. "Good. Let's get our queen's stone and put her on the throne."

Part 3

30

The Innocents Are Falling for Me

Early the next morning, Rosella stood on a small pedestal as two older devlairs danced around her stitching pieces of leather and fabric together onto her body and fitting pieces of armor into place with leather strings and straps. The two devlairs were two older twin sisters with milky white skin and silver hair, and they continuously finished the other's sentence or train of thought, and they quite literally pranced around her as they completed their work of art. The armor was done by the time she got to the stitchers' room, but they still had to make adjustments due to her "unexpected physique". The days in the gym, archery on Earth, the continuous walking on Dorthos, and hand-to-hand combat training only continued to tone her muscles.

"Almost finished, my high lady!" Avy said with a happy squeal, moving the metal chest plate into place on top of a leather one.

"Just a few more pieces, My Queen!" Bebbie said with a similar happy squeal, adjusting the leather and metal armor skirt.

Rosella was constantly being jostled around by the two, but she was enjoying seeing them do their work. The pieces that she had seen consisted of black metal pieces of shaped armor which was covered by very dark black leather. A few details she noticed were crescent moons and stars, and even a few smaller pieces had constellations pressed into the leather. She was thankful that Avy and Bebbie left the bracers and boots that Akuna gave to her, though she was going to miss the cuirass she had been wearing.

Lodmora, Mija, Qax, and Nimue were all in the stitchers' as well, watching and listening intently as Avy and Bebbie finished up the armor. Avy and Bebbie had started coaching them on how to put on the armor and how to take care of the leather, and they stood like statues soaking in every word. Elaras was in his room, possibly bathing or cleaning his weapons, though she felt coldness in his absence.

"Are you ready to see?" Avy said excitedly.

"Are you ready to squeal?" Bebbie said even more excitedly.

Rosella smiled and turned around on the pedestal to face a mirror, and she stared open-mouthed at her reflection.

The armor looked like it was only made of leather, but she knew the metal was hidden underneath. The only pieces of fabric that showed was a deep blue at her elbows and the back of her knees. Every other part of her body had decorative leather, the bigger pieces like the pauldrons and the kneecaps with the moon on it and stars in various spots. The torso extended down her front about halfway down her thighs, with the armored skirt in the front and back, the sides arching up to expose the side of her thigh. Her pants had metal pieces in the front and back of her thighs, and the devlair sisters attached greaves on top of her boots that covered the front and back as well, covering her Achilles, thankfully. Her chest piece had the coat of arms embedded into the leather like the other moons, stars, and constellations. On her stomach were leather belts that wrapped from her back to her front, and she knew these were what held the armor together in one piece and tight to her body. Her muscles groaned under the tight armor, but she had to admit that she looked entirely different in all black and form-fitting armor. The confidence she had for herself soared through the roof, and she grinned to herself.

Lodmora walked up behind her and fastened her black cloak to a few hooks on her shoulders, then she handed Rosella a head wrap that could be used to cover her mouth and nose. When Rosella put the hood up and put the scarf over her face, her lady's maids and the sisters all gasped in unison. Rosella turned around, and all six of the people in front of her covered their mouths with their hands, eyes wide.

"You look great!" exclaimed Mija.

"You look *hot*!" shouted Nimue, the red-skinned elf.

"*Nimue*!" yelled Qax, but Rosella laughed.

"How do you feel, Your Majesty?" asked Lodmora, talking through her fingers.

"I feel fucking amazing. This is great, Avy and Bebbie, thank you so much," Rosella said, turning to the sisters and lowering the scarf and hood.

"It was our pleasure, our lovely Night Queen!" the sisters said while bowing exaggeratedly and placing their moon-shaped hands above their chests.

Rosella's brain pinged a memory, and her thoughts were filled with Elaras giving her the night queen flower weeks ago, and how the same flower was crushed hours later. He told her the flower would bloom on the anniversary of the queen's coronation, and she let her mind wonder if that would happen with her. Rosella gave a small curtsy and went to gather her clothes, but the maids stopped her.

"We shall take these and launder them, Your Majesty!" Qax said, raising her hands up to stop Rosella.

"No need to worry! We shall see you in a week or two's time, Your Majesty. Be safe!" Nimue said, and the other maids gave similar sentiments that made Rosella blush.

"I appreciate you all. I'll see you soon," she said, then she grabbed her belt and attached it to her waist as she walked the short distance to the entrance of the tunnel she used to get into the castle the other day.

There awaited Akuna on top of Varran's shoulder, Joss propped up on his war hammer, Mellis with Paton and Flitch, and Elaras, who was dressed in his black leathers. However, as she approached the group, she noticed on Elaras' chest piece was the Nightstone coat of arms, and her heart swelled at the sight. When his eyes sat upon Rosella, his face exploded with admiration as his eyes scanned every inch of her, his hands on his hips.

"Ah, good, you're here. Avy and Bebbie did another fantastic job, I see!" Varran said when his eyes fell on Rosella too.

Rosella stopped in front of them all and gave a small curtsy, grabbing the edges of the armored skirt and raising it to the sides like it was a dress.

"We're ready?" asked Paton, and Rosella noted that their voice was quiet and stern with a hint of suave. Neither Paton nor Flitch spoke the night before when they came up with their plan with Mellis, and Rosella wondered if they were always quiet or if they respected Mellis enough to not feel the need to speak.

"I'm ready if Rosella is," Elaras said, and when Rosella looked at him again, she saw that he seemed flustered. His eyes darted to her then away, his face turning redder every time he peeked in her direction.

"I'm ready. Let's go," Rosella, smirking to herself, said to the group. She wanted to give Varran, Joss, and Mellis hugs, but she held off and simply inclined her head to each of them as they filed out the tunnel door. Before she could step through, Varran stopped her with a gentle hand on the elbow.

"Be careful, Rosella. Have any of the others send a sparrow if you need us. May Elyphr guide your path," Varran said before saluting her.

Despite telling herself not even a moment ago she would not hug any of the three, she launched herself at Varran and hugged him tightly. Varran let out a small gasp of surprise but reciprocated the hug. After a few moments, she released him and smiled down at him.

"Thank you, Varran, and to the rest of you, of course. See you all soon," Rosella said to the group before stepping through the door behind Elaras.

Akuna flew onto Rosella's shoulder as she raised the hood up onto her head and stepped into the dank, dark tunnel. They walked the twenty minutes it took to get to the other side, according to Mellis, and before they reached the end, Flitch cast an incantation onto the group that appeared as soft yellow smoke in the air around their bodies. Rosella glanced down and she saw herself glitching in and out of focus, and when she peered at the others they looked the same as her.

"Let's go," Flitch said shortly, and his voice was surprisingly deep for someone so small.

Paton opened the trapdoor, and they darted through it and into the surrounding forest. They ran for quite some time, and she was thankful she could see fragments of their cloaks flapping behind them dramatically so she never got lost.

Once they entered another forest area that had extremely dense, dying trees, Flitch dropped the incantation and turned to Elaras, who put up his haven before Flitch could say anything to him. Nodding approvingly, Flitch turned back toward the path, and they walked with a haste to their step, hand in hand to stay in the haven. They would walk for a few hours, and every now and then they would switch to jogging. When Elaras grew wary, he would switch with Flitch, and they would run during that time of being cloaked.

With Elaras' haven, Rosella calculated that the time slowed down to about a minute for every ten that passed in the haven. So in the haven, if they walked for three hours, only eighteen minutes passed in the outside world. The idea of this was to only spend about two days traveling in this method, and the rest of the plan would go into effect when they got to the capital and to the emperor's castle. They would only need to rest one night during their travel, and Rosella already stated she wanted Akuna to set up the protection for that so Flitch and Elaras could rest. She was still unaware of the limit of power magic users had, so she did not want to risk them becoming more tired than necessary.

After about fourteen hours of switching from the haven and cloaking, Paton located a cave, and they made their way inside. They ate and established guard duty amongst Elaras, Akuna, Paton, and Flitch. Rosella was immediately excluded per all of their demands, and she didn't feel the need to argue. Paton took the first watch, and Elaras brought out a sleeping pad and blanket that could fit two people. They fell asleep to the sound of Paton sharpening something, and Rosella let her mind wonder if Paton was sharpening their claws.

Sounds of scrambling footsteps and whispered voices roused her from her sleep hours later, and she opened her eyes just in time to see Elaras jump out of the pad like an acrobat and fist two daggers. She saw Akuna was small and still on her pillow, but he was at full attention facing the cave entrance. Paton and Flitch both had daggers or swords in hand.

What sounded like bullets being fired from a large gun was echoing through the cave as blast after blast rang out. From where they were, they could not see what was causing the noise as there was a small curve in the cavern. If someone in her party stepped away and poked their head around the bend, they could see who was at the magically concealed entrance.

"Are you sure that block will hold?" came Flitch's voice, still facing the bend in the cave.

"Are you doubting my abilities?" Akuna said almost catty.

A grunt came from Flitch's throat, and he adjusted his fighting stance.

After a few minutes, the blasting stopped, and indistinguishable yells were heard. When the voices themselves died away and they waited a few minutes, Paton and Flitch lowered their weapons. Elaras, who had not relaxed for a moment, sheathed his weapons as well.

"I'd say it's safe to resume our nightly planned slumber. We will see what the commotion was in the morning," Elaras said, trying to sound jovial.

Paton gave him a raised-whisker look before returning to their bed. "Your turn, Akuna, then Elaras. Flitch just finished his watch."

Rosella, not looking forward to Akuna or Elaras leaving her side, lay back down. Elaras climbed in after and wrapped her in his arms without saying a word.

The next morning, Rosella woke up to the sound of sizzling meat and cut up fruit. She roused Akuna and carried him over to the small fire. Akuna, thankfully, had created a vent in the ceiling to the outside for the smoke as he had done in every cave they stayed in thus far. After everyone ate and cleaned their teeth, they packed up everything, and Flitch cloaked everyone. Flitch took the lead, and right as he was about to walk out of the cave, he stopped everyone and called for Akuna.

"What is it?" Rosella asked as Akuna flew to Flitch's shoulder.

From where Rosella stood, she could see his scaly face change demeanor.

"Wait here," he said before flying through the barrier.

Rosella, ignoring Akuna's demand, ran to the front and peered outside despite hands grabbing at her.

There was a sign that was staked into the ground that read, *Nightstones needeth stay dead!* The words were written in a dark red substance, and there was a trail from the sign to somewhere to the right.

Panic filled her chest, and she pushed through the barrier, knowing it would be safe to come out of but not go in. Her eyes landed on the trail, and she followed it into the brown, crunchy grass. Sooner than expected, she found a large pool of the substance, and she saw the liquid drip from above her head. Looking up, three snow-white foxes hung lifelessly by their tails.

Before she could react, Elaras grabbed her from behind and whirled her around so she no longer faced the carnage.

"Let me look!" she yelled and ripped herself out of his arms to see the poor creatures' limp bodies.

Akuna flew over and landed on her shoulder. "The snow fox is the animal that represents the Nightstones. While not represented in the manor, citizens from all over know that the snow fox is the animal of your family," he said quietly and calmly.

She felt his eyes on her but ignored him, and she walked back to the sign. After standing there for a moment, she grabbed her phone from the pouch and turned on the camera app. Angling herself so that both the sign's words and the foxes were in frame, she took a photo. Satisfied, she stowed her camera and looked into the glitching, confused, and fearful bodies of her party.

"Proof to show to the emperor. Kaine finally knows I'm a real Nightstone, and he intended to kill me last night," Rosella said to the group. "Cut them down and bury them. Elaras, make a night queen flower and place it on their grave, please."

Paton and Flitch did not hesitate and did as Rosella commanded. Paton cut the rope holding the foxes while Flitch used his magic to dig a hole. Once the dead earth covered the three bodies, Elaras grew three night queens and handed them to Rosella. Shaking with fury, she stalked to the fresh mound and placed the flowers on top.

Goddess Elyphr, if you can hear me, please watch over these innocent souls. I know I have never asked for anything before, from any god, but please. Do this for me.

A gentle warmth washed over her as she stood up, contrasting with her ire-filled veins. Any fear she felt before of her future, Arja's future, disappeared as she stared at the three now glowing flowers. Elyphr's message was loud and clear.

Rosella knew that she could not be fearful any longer. This man, Kaine, could not take the throne and let more lives suffer and die because of his greed for power. If she was to become queen as destiny intended, she would now have to fight her way to it, even if it meant guilty blood would be shed.

31
Secret Tunnels!

The withered grass crunched hard under their feet the closer to the border they got, and Rosella had to push back her memories of the panic attack she suffered when first entering Arja. The anger had ebbed away, but she found a new confident determination that helped her body continue forward. After almost six hours, the grass met the hard border of Sidosa with green and purple dancing around her feet and the rainbow trees greeting her with glee. Birds sang overhead while large-winged dragons flew high above, deer roaming between the trees. Mountains reached for the sky in front of them, and they traversed through a tunnel that connected Sidosa and Arja.

Not long after traveling in the tunnel, they found the sun and met a small wooded area where the trees were glittering like golden stars in the sunlight. In the near distance stood a grand, gated city inside a massif where the buildings towered and glimmered, mesmerizing and intimidating. The city itself was massive and stretched so far on either side that she had to turn her head both ways to see the edges. Even at a distance, she could tell that the walls that surrounded the city were massive and climbing up or down would never be an option. The tops of most buildings seemed to peek over the walls edges, and she saw hundreds of them, knowing that there were probably over a thousand unseen buildings. In the middle of the city was a towering castle whose gold and white surface shines brightly in the sun and reflected beams of light into the city itself. One grand tower in the middle of the castle seemed to act like a beacon or a marker in the sky, while the two towers on either side rose only halfway in the air but were adorned with bells at the top of those towers.

"Gigantic," Rosella said simply, staring at the blinding buildings and the blue mountains around them.

"Come on, we know a way inside without entering the gates," said Flitch, and they started to lead the party off to the left.

They traveled inside the haven for about twenty minutes until they reached a trapdoor, similar to the one for the Nocturnal Manor. Elaras dropped the haven as Flitch knocked on the trapdoor, waiting with bated breath.

The trapdoor cracked open, and Rosella saw a person with extremely wide eyes peering out and shutting the door again when they saw Flitch. After a moment, the trapdoor swung up and out, revealing a passageway underground that was lit with torches. Flitch led the way into the soft dirt tunnel, and Rosella's eyes were unable to adjust quickly enough to see a small person crouching by the trapdoor when they passed. When everyone was inside, the door slammed behind her, and she whirled around to see another hobdrig but with bright pink hair and round blue eyes, a smile as big as a child in a candy shop.

"Hello!" the female hobdrig whispered to the group but bouncing on the balls of her feet.

"Raya, this is Rosella, future queen of Arja," Flitch said sternly and slightly annoyed.

Raya seemed to take no notice as she gasped, and they bowed with the moon symbol to their chest.

"Your Majesty! Lovely to meet you!" she said, and she stood up straight to look at Rosella. "Are you going to save the world now that you can use your magic to make crops grow tall and help animals live?" she asked excitedly, despite the weight of the question itself.

Rosella straightened and coughed a tiny bit, wishing she could have some water before she had to answer. "That is my goal, yes. There are some steps before we get to that point, though," Rosella said as confidently as she could.

Raya exclaimed more excitedly than ever, and she jumped in place. "I knew it! You're gonna save the world!" she yelled, her voice echoing through the vast tunnel.

"Hey, keep it down, Raya, or I'll sic Paton on you!" Flitch said in his stern tone but with a wide smile on his face.

Raya stopped and stared at Paton, who did not miss a step and unleashed their claws, a sneering smile on their face.

"Noooo!" Raya yelled, and she ran down the tunnel that was in the direction of the city.

Rosella looked at Paton and Flitch with raised eyebrows but she saw they were both laughing, which shocked Rosella even more.

"So, who is she to you, if I may ask?" Rosella asked Flitch as they traveled down the dark yet warm tunnel.

"That's my little sister. She knows Paton would never hurt her. I just love using Paton's claws as a threat," Flitch said humorously, and Rosella smiled as they continued forward.

"My sweet?" Elaras' voice sounded in her ear, and she looked up at him. He looked like he was concerned but also in a way relieved, and Rosellla could not pinpoint which emotion was the stronger of the two.

"Yes, Cricket?" Rosella asked, and she saw his smile again.

"Are you getting nervous?"

"I have been, but I'm more angry and on edge than anything. I can feel myself getting antsy."

"I understand. Let's hope this goes by quickly once we get to the castle."

"Agreed," Rosella said and saw the tunnel was coming to an end at a tall staircase.

They walked up steps upon steps until they reached another trapdoor, Flitch knocking on the underside. When the door cracked, bright yellow eyes peered from the crack, but they immediately disappeared as the door was flung open. The four stepped inside, Akuna still in her hood, and entered a similarly dark room full of lit fireplaces and people walking around.

Paton turned to Elaras and Rosella as Flitch walked off to find Raya and said, "Welcome to the Nocturnal Stalkers' Guild, a group of mercenaries and spies that run all throughout Dorthos to aid the Nightstones and worthy allies."

Around them were all sorts of races and even a few Rosella had never seen before, and every single one was dressed in black with a knee-length cloak and a black scarf, all just like Paton and Flitch. There were paintings along the wall that varied from what must be the underworld landscape to portraits of the Nightstones themselves. There were weapon racks, potion bottle racks, herbs hanging from wires, and even a blacksmith in the far corner. Everyone was moving at their own pace, yet Rosella feared being in someone's way as every single person had a look of determination on their face.

There was a red-skinned elf in a far corner that was poring over parchment that caught Rosella's attention. The elf seemed to shimmer slightly with gold glitter wrapped itself around their whole body in streams of gray smoke, not dissimilar to Flitch's cloaking. As the elf adjusted the parchment, the glitter vibrated violently, and the smoke wrapped itself about their fingers and arms, moving the glitter like a river. Rosella took a step toward the person but was gently pulled back by Elaras, giving her a small quizzical look.

"Nocturnal Stalkers? All of this for the Nightstones?" Rosella asked simply as she examined the room, letting her eyes linger on the elf with the glitter and smoke.

"Yep. Mellis inherited the guild, and Ladroth is the second leader-in-command of this post, which is the hub of the organization," Paton said informatively before lowering their voice. "I understand this is still new for you, and I'll tell you this, even if you already know. Much longer without a Nightstone on the throne to aid the land of Arja, all of Dorthos will collapse. Also, the Nightstones were the longest reigning family, so there are many allies of the family and only a few enemies because of how beloved they were. Therefore, you have more people on your side than you could ever imagine."

"Whoa. What about the enemies besides Kaine? Should I be concerned?" Rosella asked.

"Oh no, as most of them do not make themselves known and most of them can't do real harm. Most people, even the enemies, understand the severity of the Arja situation. The kingdoms tried to ignore the problem and just let Arja go leaderless, but then they saw the deterioration of the land and have now begun to panic. It is no wonder the emperor is so eager to find someone to sit the throne, and the easiest choice for him was the usurper."

"Is he even aware of me yet?"

"He has to be by now, but we are not sure if he believes you are a true Nightstone or if you just happened to have a necklace that matches the night stone," Paton said, shrugging. The felinette's whiskers bristled, and their eyes narrowed before continuing, "Kaine could have also shared a completely different story, and the emperor will be surprised you are a true Nightstone. When we meet with Ladroth, we'll get more information. Also, the emperor is not one to go back on his word, so the fact that he has already given the throne to Lycilla is concerning. It may be difficult to change his mind. He's a greedy fucker, so we'll have to see how things go tomorrow."

"Not stressful at all," Rosella said simply, taking in the information from Paton in stride.

"Yeah. Let's go find Ladroth and confirm the plan we have is still doable. Flitch, come on!" Paton said, yelling toward Flitch, who was letting Raya squish his cheeks and forcing him to make raspberry noises. Rosella noticed that four sharp teeth in Paton's mouth were all coated in a silver-colored metal.

The remaining three walked through the open space and down a hall toward a heavy wooden door that had an extravagant brass knocker and a rudimentary peephole. Paton knocked twice, scratched once, and knocked twice again and waited. The peephole opened, and a single purple eye appeared, looked at the three standing at the door, then turned the locks on their side.

A waft of citrus and bergamot rushed into Rosella's nose, and the warm air that washed over her face made her nerves tingle. The room itself was a decent size and contained a few bookshelves, a large desk and chair, and a table with three normal-sized chairs and one massive one off to the side. There were also a few chests lining the walls that looked extremely heavy and ornate, the keyholes to each of them looking intricate.

Near the fireplace was a felinette with orange-striped fur and the same purple eyes that had just peered through the peep-hole, and just like any other felinette, they were not wearing boots. They stood prim and proper, wearing a purple cuirass and a gold dress underneath with long sleeves. There was a purple cloak attached at their shoulders to the cuirass, but their hood was down.

At the large desk sat a strongly built creature with long fur all over their body that was a chestnut brown. The armor they wore was a shining dark metal that was rough around the edges and had many smaller dents. This person, who must have been Ladroth, seemed extremely tall like Joss or Tordias, and when they saw the group enter, this theory was confirmed as they stood to greet them.

"*Berhog,*" Akuna stated simply as the berhog took long steps to meet the group with a large smile on their face.

"Paton! Ah this must be the crew Mellis mentioned with their sparrow. My Queen, Rosella Nightstone, how wonderful it is to meet you. I'm Ladroth!" the berhog said as they held out a hand to her instead of bowing.

While she was just getting used to people bowing and saluting her, she was thankful to do something familiar from Earth. She gladly took Ladroth's oversized rough hand, and she had to crane her neck to look at his face.

He turned and looked at Elaras, his eyes wide with surprise. "Ah, you must be the abandoned and forgotten Moonshadow boy, the eldest. Elaras, yes?"

"Yep, that's me," Elaras said shortly, holding out his own hand for Ladroth to shake.

Ladroth took it immediately and gave Elaras a hearty shake. "If your queen accepts you as her own, then you are an ally to me! Where is Flitch?" Ladroth asked just as light-as-air footsteps could be heard behind them.

"My apologies. I had to remind Raya that I am, in fact, the older sibling," Flitch said as he seemed his way into the room.

Rosella noticed that Paton had made their way silently to

stand next to the ginger felinette that was by the fire, and they were conversing quietly and holding each other's paws. Seeing a different side to both Paton and Flitch while in these headquarters made her appreciate their professionalism but also showed that they themselves had their own lives outside this guild.

"Ah, Raya, she's a valuable asset to this guild, and I appreciate her enthusiasm every day that she is here! Queen Nightstone, please sit while we discuss the plans." Ladroth, sounding genuine, gestured to the table with the four chairs on the other end of the room.

Everyone except Paton and the ginger felinette sat down, but they had moved to the edge of the table to listen in. Rosella noticed that the ginger with purple eyes truly looked elegant, and the few times she caught her voice it sounded light and sweet, opposite of Paton's stern, suave tone.

Flitch took the lead of reciting the plans to Ladroth, letting the rest listen intently and never interrupting him. He stated how Paton and Flitch planned on getting Rosella and Elaras to the front gates of the castle during a citizen hearing council, and they would stick around and talk to the emperor then. They would demand a private audience with the emperor, and Rosella would plead her case with him. Paton and Flitch would stay close by in case things went south and if they needed to make sure they got out.

With the two remaining close by, they would also locate Kaine and Lycilla and try to retrieve the necklace from their grasp. While the meeting with the emperor would probably not succeed, Paton and Flitch would do what they could to get the necklace back without the emperor's knowledge. Once both groups were done, they would meet back up in a neutral location.

When Flitch was finished, Ladroth just looked between the three sitting at the table.

"That could possibly work, but things never go according to plan," he said with concern lacing his boisterous tone.

"We're aware. That's why Mellis picked Paton and myself," Flitch stated, leaning back in his chair.

Ladroth smiled at this and tapped his forehead. "You two are the best at impromptu plans, this is true. They picked the best for this mission, that is clear. When will you all be heading out? The next hearing is tomorrow morning."

"Early morning if possible, then."

"Wait," said the calm voice of the ginger felinette from behind Ladroth. Everyone looked to her, and Rosella saw she was fidgeting with her paws, her ears twitching. "What if I grant you both an audience tonight? Would it not be less risky to have less eyes on you in the council?"

Ladroth and Flitch both put their fingers to their chins like twins and thought on this idea. Elaras, however, asked exactly what was on Rosella's mind.

"How could you grant us an audience tonight?"

The ginger felinette glanced hesitantly at Paton, and Paton nodded, stroking the ginger's back before whispering, "It's okay, tell them."

The ginger nodded at Paton and looked back at Elaras with her wide purple eyes, taking a step forward. "Because I'm Princess Temel Dreadtrell, daughter of the emperor. If I say you two are my friends and wish for you two to come to dinner, he will not say no."

"Wait, you're part of this guild *and* the emperor's daughter? You must really not like your father." Elaras laughed, and Rosella couldn't help but agree with him.

The princess to the current ruler of all of Dorthos being

revealed as a spy for the Nightstones was not something she had expected, and she knew that Temel was taking a huge risk being here. If she was willing to be a part of something as dangerous as espionage on a potentially daily basis, she knew that Temel truly wanted to be here despite the risk.

"Fuck, no. I think he's a destructive glutton that only craves power and wealth. If you were to ask him, he would tell you that I'm his favorite child and that I could never do wrong. I, on the other hand, despise every part of him, and I wish to see him off the throne. I'm tired of his abuse of power, and I grow angry whenever I see anyone else abuse any power over anyone that is innocent," Princess Temel said quickly and sharply, her serene tone disappearing. Her claws began to show, and her whiskers stood on end, her eyes wide and her ears flattened. The elegance that once graced her face was now full of beautiful fury.

"That settles it then, I think! Temel, will you be able to take them there in a few hours for dinner?" Ladroth asked Temel, who was now wrapped in a loving and supportive embrace with Paton. "That may be the best time since his favorite meal is dinner."

"Yes, dinner is at seven, so if we leave in a few minutes, we can get there within two hours," Temel said, squeezing Paton back. Her whiskers calmed, and her claws retracted, but her ears were still flattened.

"Good! Send a sparrow when you arrive at the castle. Flitch and Paton, still seek the necklace while Temel, Rosella, and Elaras meet with the emperor to plead their case. If things go well and you tell him you're the true heir, he may revoke Kaine and Lycilla's grant," Ladroth jeered before turning to the heated princess. "Remind me, Temel, what does the emperor know of Rosella?"

"Nothing," Temel said, and the room fell into an odd silence. "Oh, I thought I mentioned this to you earlier, Ladroth. Kaine told the family that he got the necklace from the Great Wrath of

Dorthos. He and his son went to retrieve the necklace because I guess they heard the dragon had it in its horde. They went, his son died, and Kaine used his magic to defend himself and got the necklace that way. I've been wanting to ask Lycilla if that was true, but Zaas told me she was under the control of Kaine. Zaas hasn't told Father that detail, though, but it made sense later why she was almost statue-like during dinner."

Rosella heard Akuna guffaw in her mind at the lie, and Rosella thought that the story was ridiculous as well, but she tried to remain serious.

"I believe she originally stole the necklace from me because she thought it mimicked the night stone, but they seem to have figured out it is a true stone and are using it to their advantage. You saw the necklace, but neither had it on, correct?" Rosella asked Temel.

"I saw him pull it out of his pocket, and Zaas confirmed it to be the true night stone by detecting the magic enveloping it." Temel said while Paton loosened their grip on her. Paton's ears were now flattened, but they continued to hold Temel's hand. "I thought it was odd that he did not put it on, but I had been hearing rumors that if you are not a Nightstone, you cannot wear jewelry with a night stone pendant."

"It's true. If someone was to put on my necklace and they weren't a Nightstone, the chain would burn through your skin like a hot knife cutting butter. If either one were to wear it, they would get decapitated," Rosella said matter-of-factly, and she saw that this information must have not been public knowledge due to the look on everyone's faces.

Even Elaras' eyes were wide, and he had placed a hand to his cheek, making noises of comprehension.

"So the rumors are true, and the night stones are not only

insanely powerful—they're actually deadly. Good to know when we try and get it later," Flitch said, clearing his throat.

"No wrapping it. Just place it in a secure pocket. Got it," Paton said, mild shock still remaining on their furry face.

"Well, refill your canteens and grab supplies if need be, and meet back in ten minutes? You two meet the emperor," Ladroth said, pointing to Rosella and Elaras. "You two sneak around and get the night stone and *do not* wrap it around *anything*," he said, pointing to Paton and Flitch. "And you, please stay safe. You remember your training?" he asked Temel, and she nodded weakly. Unsure of the training he meant, Rosella hoped that it was training that could help defend Temel if need be.

When Rosella stood up, everyone else followed suit, and they went their separate ways. However, a moment later, she felt a tap on her shoulder as she began to walk out of the room. Rosella turned and saw a lone Temel, nervousness written all over her face.

"Yes, Temel?"

"Um, I wanted to ask you for something. You may not be able to, or want to, but I still wanted to ask," she said, that nervousness that etched her face emerging into her tone.

"It depends on what you're going to ask. Are you asking Rosella, or are you asking the future queen?" Rosella said, and Temel looked up at her wide-eyed. Rosella smiled and tilted her head, hoping the move came off as reassuring.

"Well, um, the future queen. When all of this is over, I'd like to renounce my nobility and live in Rion. Either under the Nightstone name as a spy, or even as a maid. If neither of those things work, I can find something else. I just—I just want to not be under my father's rule, and if you grant me a home under your name, it'll be harder for my father to take me back without your permission or my wanting to go back. Yes, he's the emperor, but the kingdoms still have their own jurisdictions and armies, their own laws and cultures. So, if I seek refuge in Rion under your protection, my father can't do anything about it," she said, and Rosella could tell this was a lot to ask of her. She appreciated the risk this took to say the words.

"I'm still new to all of this...politics stuff...so I guess I'm not understanding how if he's the emperor, why he can't take you away? What does he rule if the separate kingdoms have their own power?"

"He rules the empire. The queens and kings rule their province," Temel said, wringing her paws and taking short breathes. "If the nobility of those kingdoms enact a law or demand something within their land, the emperor must abide by those laws put in place by that queen or king. If the nobility cannot make a decision, the emperor steps in."

"They act as equals then, in a way? Queens, kings, and the emperor?" Rosella asked, and when Temel nodded enthusiastically, she continued. "So you are willing to leave your family and your name behind just to get away from your father? What is your desire, for when you leave the capital? What would you like to do with your life?"

Temel looked at the patiently waiting Paton, who was examining a red-stoned pendant necklace Rosella had not noticed before. Temel turned back around, and she had a sweet smile on her face before she said, "Wherever Paton is, I want to be. I know they reside at the Nocturnal Manor most nights, and if I was there serving you or serving the guild, my father could never get me back since I would be under another's direct rule. I would be safe, useful, and in a place where Paton knew where I was."

Rosella looked at her, and she felt empathy for her desires and wished for only the best for this princess. "I'll see what I can do.

After all, I'm new to this, so I will have to consult with my High Cleric and my High Paladin. I'll have Elaras send a sparrow in regard to the request. If I'm able, I'd love for you to be with Paton, whatever way possible," she said, grabbing Temel's paws gently and squeezing.

The smile that broke on Temel's face was pure joy, and she even squealed softly. She let go of Rosella's hands and bowed, saluting with vigor before going to Paton, hugging them tightly. When Paton wrapped their arms around Temel, they looked up and smiled at Rosella, and Rosella nodded in response with a smile.

It was not hard to find Elaras as he was standing alone in the next room gathering various tools that Rosella did not know the names of.

"Hey, could you send a sparrow to Varran and Joss for me, please?" she asked, and Elaras looked up and grinned at her.

"Of course. I was going to send one here in a bit anyway to let him know we were here. What else would you like me to say?" he asked, and after Rosella explained Temel's request, his eyebrows shot up and his mouth fell agape.

"That may be difficult, but smart to ask before giving her a definite answer," Elaras said as he pulled out paper and found a quill and ink on a nearby table. He wrote the note and summoned a blue and black sparrow, giving it the note. In a light whoosh of air from its wings, it disappeared through the ceiling and out of sight.

Rosella looked back to Elaras and was immediately met with his lips on hers, his hands cupping her face. She wrapped her arms around his neck and let the satisfying feelings of happiness flow through her. After a few seconds of passionate kissing that made her crave more, he withdrew and he gently pecked her nose.

"I could do that all day," she whispered, and he smiled deeply and warmly.

"Agreed. I just want to feel your warmth all the time, especially before it gets intense," Elaras said before giving her a deep kiss followed by a long hug.

Rosella wrapped her arms around his back as she listened to his heartbeat, wanting to stay there forever. However, they were called over by Flitch moments later, and both Elaras and Rosella put on faces of stoic determination as they met the group and climbed through a new tunnel.

32

Oh, My Sweetest Suffering

Princess Temel and Paton led the way down a tunnel that was cleaner and had torches every ten feet or so. The path was paved, and there were only a few rats scurrying away as they walked, and the width and height of the tunnel made Rosella believe that bigger things than people would traverse it. After about an hour of walking, Temel told them to wait a moment before she and Paton took a few tentative steps around a small bend. Distant voices could be heard discussing something while they were waiting, and after a few minutes, Temel came back and beckoned them forward.

Meeting up with Paton, they were met with a large tarnished-looking metal door that was extremely large, which had a wheel and numerous locks. Temel walked up to the metal, grabbed a necklace chain around her neck, and placed the stone of the pendant to the door. All it took was a soft tap of the stone to the metal before the locks started to disengage and the wheel spun rapidly.

When Temel looked back to the group, Rosella saw that the stone that was attached to the pendant was very distinctly a tiger's eye stone. The door swung open quietly, and before them was what looked like a dark basement with very little furniture and decorative pieces. They stepped through the threshold, and their noses were met with the strong scent of decay and rot.

"Gods, Temel, where are we?" Elaras muttered while plugging his nose and walking through the space.

"We're in the only space that is considered off-limits to anyone, purely because it is believed that if anyone enters this area, you will be cursed by the god of gluttony, Nurguttel," Temel said, unaffected by the smell and moving through the space as if it was simply another room.

Rosella looked at Elaras, and she giggled at his disgusted expression. Elaras gave her a "stop laughing at me or you'll regret it" look, making her laugh harder.

"In reality, this is where all the food goes to finish rotting for composting. Only the servants and myself come down here, and sometimes Zaas," Temel said, who was now next to a door on the opposite end of the room.

Flitch observed Temel. Rosella could tell his mind was working on piecing together information she was not privy to.

"So wait, food comes down here to *rot*? You mean to say that the emperor is eating his fill, and whatever isn't eaten just comes down here instead to the citizens of Sidosa?" he said, heading toward Temel.

"Correct. We get crates of food a day, and the leftovers come down here if they are not eaten by the staff. A lot is usually left over," Temel said.

Rosella noted the crates stacked up all along the walls, and she saw flies and other insects flying around and crawling in and out of the boxes. The walls were completely covered in crates of food, and they all lay abandoned until they deteriorated enough to be used in fertilizer.

"How much food do the lower class get per day? Do you know?" Rosella asked while still looking at all the crates.

"Families are lucky if they get a loaf of cheap bread a day. Typically those with children get priority. Everyone else has to be lucky," Temel said quietly.

Rosella felt fury building up in her bones at the injustice of the emperor's greed. "What was it like thirty years ago?" Rosella asked just as quietly, afraid of the answer.

"To my understanding, everyone in Dorthos ate well, even the homeless," Temel said. "As Arja deteriorated, so did the lower class. It's getting to the point that even my father can't get certain things he wants or craves because Arja's livestock is dying prematurely or crops are not growing."

Rosella did not respond. Instead, she resorted to deep breathing and quiet anger at the food here that could have been given to people who were dying of starvation. She strode to the door, and Temel opened it quietly and peered out before letting the others through. They walked a few minutes before they entered a storage room off a hallway, and Paton locked the door behind them.

"This is where we part. Any updates, I will send an invisible sparrow. Elaras, you do the same for you thr— all," Flitch said, hesitating on not giving away the fact that Akuna was with them to Temel.

"Invisible sparrow?" Rosella asked, and Elaras took her hand before explaining.

"Yes, you'll feel it on your shoulder before it whispers in your ear. Only you will be able to hear it, so it's great for secret communication."

"That's really cool," Rosella said, and Elaras smiled. She

looked and saw Temel and Paton were in a corner, hugging and licking each other's whiskers passionately. Feeling awkward, she turned her attention back to Elaras and Flitch. "So, do you have other siblings or just Raya?"

"Oh, I have eighteen other siblings. I'm third in line, and she's seventeenth, so she's considered a baby to me, but she's wicked smart in many fields," Flitch said, checking his daggers.

"Yeah? What does she specialize in?" Rosella asked curiously.

"Explosives," he said so casually that Rosella couldn't contain her amazement.

"Ready," Temel said, hand in hand with Paton.

"See you in a few hours," Elaras said to the group.

Everyone's eyes landed on Rosella as they stood stock-still, waiting for her to say or do something.

"Um. May the Goddess Elyphr guide your path, and may she protect you. Stay safe and good luck," Rosella said, and everyone smiled, everyone except Elaras bowing their heads and saluting the moon to their chests. Rosella had come to notice that not once had Elaras done this, and in a way she was extremely thankful because when she was with him, she did not feel like the queen version that she was getting used to. She felt purely like herself.

Temel walked out first with Rosella and Elaras in tow, and Rosella heard the soft footfalls of Paton and Flitch behind her heading in the opposite direction. Temel's demeanor changed so much that even her way of walking shifted, and the change made Rosella's hair stand on end. Her back grew extremely straight, her head was held so high that her jaw was parallel with the floor, and she walked like a Russian ballerina with her hands clasped in front of her, her arms also parallel with the floor.

"You remember your cover story?" Temel asked extremely

quietly, so much so that Rosella had to take a few quickened steps to lean into her.

"We're Slayers from Trihale, the ocean region. We are here as distant friends from your time visiting a few years ago. I'm still Rosella, and Elaras is Ethan," Rosella said, reciting the cover story her, Temel, and Elaras came up with while trekking through the tunnel to the castle.

"Yes, exactly. My father would believe you if you told them you were from another world and were here to tell everyone that you invented a way to fly," Temel said.

Rosella gave a half-smiling grimace look, Elaras covered his mouth to conceal laughter, and Akuna chuckled so hard that Rosella's chest vibrated. She had told Elaras the night before that on Earth there were a few ways to get around by flight like airplanes and helicopters, and Elaras refused to believe her until she showed him a video she had taken at an air show of various planes and jets flying around. That was when Elaras told her that he had looked at all of her photos and videos she had stored, and while he did not understand most of the things he was seeing like the airplanes, he still marveled at her life before coming to Dorthos. Strangely, she was not mad at all at him doing this, so she simply hugged him. They went through various other photos, and she explained each one he had questions about until they fell asleep.

As Rosella was reliving this memory, a light off to the side of her eye blinded her so greatly that she had to shield herself. When she looked around, she realized that everything around her was covered in gold or gemstones. The walls were painted gold, decorations were gold or were encrusted with stones, the floors seemed to be stitched with a golden fabric, and the flowers too were unmistakably gold.

"Jesus Christ," Rosella said before she could stop herself.

"Who?" Elaras asked quizzically as one of Temel's ears turned toward them.

Rosella screwed up her face, trying to think of the best way to describe to someone who wouldn't know of Christianity about one of the most well-known people in Earth's history.

"Uh, I'll explain later," she said almost dismissively as her head started to hurt. She herself did not belong to any religion on Earth, so she would have to remember what she learned from other people, and now was not the time to explain.

"*Good luck with that,* human," Akuna chortled, and Rosella resisted reaching back to smack him.

"We're here," Temel said quietly, her voice unwavering. Before two massive golden double doors were two gold-plated guards with halberds and bright red plumes on top of their full-face helmets. "Two guests. Sorry for the late notice," Temel said to the guard on the right as she was closest to that one, and Elaras, as always, was on Rosella's left.

The guard nodded and leaned toward the door handle along with the guard on the left. When they opened the doors, Rosella's eyes were attacked by bright lights, colorful mosaics that adorned every wall and the ceiling, and large chandeliers of gold lit up the room brilliantly.

"My girl!" came a boisterous voice from the end of the large golden table that sat in the middle of the room with thirty or forty chairs lining it. "And guests! Please, come in and sit!"

The boisterous voice came from a large, bowling-ball-shaped felinette with ginger fur that was sitting next to a sly and mischievous-looking gray-striped furred felinette, whose eyes fell immediately onto Rosella and did not leave or waver. The black and white felinette that sat next to the gray felinette looked slightly wary, and Rosella immediately figured that it must be Zaas, Temel's brother.

As they walked closer with Temel in the lead, servants could be seen scuttling back and forth along the side preparing plates and drinks for the princess and her guests. As Temel got to her seat, she bowed to her father then sat down, and Elaras and Rosella copied her before sitting down as well.

"Hello. These are my friends, Ethan and Rosella. They're Slayers from Trihale, and they were in town. I hope it's okay if they join us for dinner," Temel said, not looking at her father but at the sly felinette, which must be the empress.

The empress' orange eyes were still glued on Rosella when she leaned in toward the emperor and whispered a few words.

"Yes, of course, my dear! Please, enjoy yourselves!" the emperor said as he shoveled mouthfuls of steak and potatoes into his grease-lined lips.

Temel turned to the group and nodded, and Rosella and Elaras ate with no further comment when given food and drink. The thought of poisoning crossed her mind as she ate the delicious food, but she trusted Akuna to somehow help her if that were to happen.

"Of course I'll help you if you were poisoned. It's a royal's worst nightmare. Besides, I can smell poison, and I smell none in your food," Akuna said reassured. She was thankful he could read her thoughts.

"You've been quiet for a while. What happened to my grumpy lizard companion?"

"You've been doing queenly duties, and staying out of sight is my 'grumpy lizard' duty. For now," Akuna said coolly, and Rosella grinned while taking a bit of her roasted chicken.

"So, my lovely guests, what brings you into town?" the

emperor asked Rosella and Elaras after everyone was finished eating and they were all leaning back in their seats to let the food settle.

Rosella was grateful that the gluttonous emperor had the decency to wipe his face clean before speaking to them.

"Well, Father, they —" Temel started but was stopped with a raised hand from her father.

"I was not asking you. I was asking your friends," he said, interrupting her. He lowered his hand and clasped his paws over his voluminous belly. "As I was asking, what are you both doing in town?"

"Straight to the point. Tell them you are here to speak on the matter of the Nightstone throne," came Akuna's voice when both Elaras and Rosella looked at each other to see who would speak.

Rosella cleared her throat and sat up in her chair, facing the emperor. "We came here today to speak on the matter of the Nightstones. I —"

The emperor's jovial laugh interrupted her. The entire time they were speaking and since they had concluded eating, the empress had regarded Rosella with unwavering attention, her head propped on her paw.

"Oh, my dear, I have nothing to say on the matter! I don't care what you have to say or want to ask of me. It will not happen!" he said loudly with finality.

These words brought up all the anger Rosella was feeling since learning about the emperor's true nature and the fact that Kaine talked his way onto the throne that belonged to her. This man did not need to say more for Rosella to immediately understand why Temel wanted out of this family, and by the looks of Zaas, he felt the same way as his sister.

"Emperor, please. I'm —"

"I do not care! I give you great food, and you berate me on a

topic I care very little for? Whatever you say does not matter!" he yelled, and when he was finished, he was wheezing as he tried to take in deep breaths.

The empress leaned into the emperor once more, and his face turned from annoyance to contentment. He sighed as the empress leaned away from him, locking her eyes on Rosella again.

"It has been pointed out to me that I am tired, thus that is the reason for my behavior. Stay the night, and I will hear your inquiry about whatever you wish to discuss. That is all."

As the emperor said his final words, he stood up with surprising grace, and everyone else followed suit. The empress gave one last sly smile toward Rosella before following the emperor, paw in paw, leaving the group behind.

"Temel, what are you up to?" came Zaas' hushed voice as he rushed forward to Temel's side.

She looked around hurriedly and pulled him to a wall. "If you say anything, I'll flay you alive,"

Rosella's eyebrows shot up, as well as Zaas'.

"I swear by the sanity of my soul, please don't flay me," he said even quieter.

Temel shot a look at Rosella and Elaras, and Elaras simply shrugged.

"I have no issue helping you flay him if he hurts the future queen," Elaras said.

Zaas' eyes grew so wide that Rosella saw the whites of his eyes around the ocean blue irises, which was impressive for his felinette eyes. "Wait, she's...a Nightstone?" he said, his voice shaking and his ears pinning back.

When Temel nodded, his paws flew to his face, and he let out a silent scream.

"Oh my gods, get a hold of yourself. You act all tough around

Father and Mother, but now is when you make your whiskers quake?" Temel said, a confidence coming out that Rosella was surprised to see. "Where are Kaine and Lycilla?"

He relaxed for a moment before tilting his head toward his sister. "They left this morning. They have been wanting to leave since the day after they came, and Father grew wary of them fighting back on Kaine's request to leave, so he let them go. Oh gods, the necklace they had was yours! They lied to us about how they got it!"

"They left? Fuck. Back to the Moonshadow estate or to Nocturnal Manor?" Temel said, fur bristling and ears pinned.

"I'm not sure. I would guess the Moonshadow estate so they can get stuff they need before they go to Nocturnal Manor."

"Fine. We'll just have to leave once we meet with our father. You guys got here quickly. You will have to take the same method back. I'd recommend sending a sparrow to warn your staff," she said, facing Elaras. "Do it when I show you to your rooms. Thankfully, morning is not too far off, and they traveled here by carriage, so I think time is still on your side."

As they stood there, Elaras sent an invisible sparrow to both Paton and Flitch, and the moment it was sent off, he received one from them confirming that Kaine and Lycilla were not in the rooms they were staying in previously. Temel released Zaas from her anger and showed Elaras and Rosella to a room that was close to hers. She showed Elaras how to lock the door so that only a few magic users could get inside, but suggested placing other precautions on the door just in case.

Once inside the lavish and overly gold room, Rosella plopped on the bed as Akuna flew out of her hood, Elaras pacing back and forth. Akuna blew purple smoke around the door, window, and walls, a sheer barrier coming alive.

"He's going to Nocturnal Manor. I know it. He's going to

demand the public's favor and take over Rion," Elaras blurted out to the room, and Rosella lifted her head to look at him.

"'Take over Rion? What, by force?"

"Yes."

"That's a bit extreme. If the emperor already granted him the throne, why would he be forceful with it?"

"Rosella, he may have gotten the emperor's favor, but he has yet to be given Arja's favor. He needs to weasel his way into their lives and show that Lycilla is the rightful heir, and make them believe she will do good instead of making their lives worse and killing the world in the process," Elaras said in a frustrated tone, pacing a path into the golden carpet.

"So we'll do what Temel said: meet with the emperor and see if he can reverse his decision, and head back immediately. Joss said it takes about five normal days of travel with strong horses, so Kaine shouldn't have time to do much damage before we get back," Rosella said, trying to add positives to a really shitty situation. She knew she was just saying things to make herself and Elaras feel more confident, but she herself grew worried and concerned. The need to stay strong was powerful, but she only felt dread.

Elaras stopped pacing when he reached a desk and used the provided quill and ink to write a letter to Varran, updating him on the situation. When he was done sending off the letter with a sparrow, Elaras walked over and lay next to Rosella.

"You're right. It'll be fine, hopefully," he said, taking the ends of her braids and twirling them in his fingers.

Rosella kissed Elaras, then looked to Akuna, who was stock-still on the windowsill. "Akuna, is everything okay?"

"I can hear a cry, one reserved for pain and death," Akuna said, and Rosella bolted upright.

"A dragon?"

"Yes..."

"Then go. They need you. You put protective shields up. We'll be okay. *I'll* be okay. Go do your duty, grumpy lizard."

Akuna turned toward Rosella, his chest heaving. After a long, hard moment, he addressed Elaras, his haunting red eyes reminding Rosella of Akuna's fearsome presence. "Protect her."

"I promise, and I won't let anyone in," Elaras said firmly.

A nod of Akuna's tiny head and a long look at Rosella was all the Great Wrath did before flying off through the window.

Hours passed, and sleep was full of dreadful dreams, ones she was unsure were messages from a god or if they were her own self-conscious. Rosella saw herself scaling a plank on a pirate ship, being poked in the chest to keep walking to the edge. Someone was yelling, *"Just fall. No one will care! Die, and you will never be missed!"*

Rosella wanted to scream because despite wanting to move, wanting to jump, she was frozen. She kept getting poked and yelled at, no matter how much she wanted to cry out. Every time she moved, her nerves felt like they were being sliced open, her muscles tensing hard from the pain. Tears were falling, but she couldn't wipe them away.

"Let the girl die by your hand. Make yourself a true tragic story! Kill the queen, and you will be shamed like you deserve!" yelled someone from far away at the back of the watching group of pirates.

At the end of the long spear, she finally saw that it was Elaras holding the spear, his eyes filled with tears and silently screaming. He was being forced to kill Rosella, and there was nothing either could do for the other or for themselves. Where was Akuna? He had to be near. He had to know she was in trouble.

"Kill her, then kill yourself so you do not feel the shame, son!" yelled one more voice, and this time the voice was full of malice, full of greed, full of pure evil.

Wake up, wake up, wake up, Rosella said mentally to herself in the dream. This had to be a nightmare, and she wanted out of it. She did not want to see herself die at the hands of Elaras, being egged on by people who watched with glee. *Where the* fuck *is Akuna?*

Wind caught her dress in its grasp, and she flew off the plank. The drop to the ocean was further than she expected, and when she hit the water, it felt like she was immediately drowning. Her stomach dropped so hard that she felt like she fell down a flight of stairs, and she still couldn't move to swim to the surface to save herself.

"Wake up, you idiotic girl," came a strong, commanding voice that rang throughout her entire mind and in her nerves.

Her fingers tingled painfully, and she felt herself drift out of the water and into a lit room. Was she still dreaming? She couldn't be because she was now looking at Elaras next to her in the bed at the emperor's castle, but there was an odd orange hue to her vision along with red swirls of smoke, similar to Lycilla's magic when Lycilla paralyzed her in the cave.

The moment she tried to move her hands to touch Elaras' face however, pain shot through her entire body again, and she knew she was paralyzed. Elaras had tears in his eyes as he looked at Rosella, and she realized that there was also a faint orange hue in the whites of his eyes. When she tried to move her body closer to him, the pain soared through her body, and as she took a deep breath she felt something poke her below her sternum. Forcing her eyes to look down despite the immense pain, she saw that

Elaras was holding his sharpest and longest dagger to her chest, one she had only seen once before. This dagger was so long that she considered it a short sword.

"Ah, good, you're awake," came the same commanding voice that woke her up, and she realized it was the same one that had been taunting her and Elaras in her nightmare. "You took a while to wake up, enough time for me to tell Elaras here how much of a failure he is as an elder son. Tonight, he will at least succeed in one thing for me, and that is for him to kill you. You see, you stupid Nightstone bitch," the voice that must be Kaine said as he roughly grabbed her hair and turned her face to look upon his angry resentment, "I cannot kill you, nor can Lycilla. If either of us kill you, well, someone will eventually find out. I can make my son kill you, and make him the least trusted person in all of Dorthos. Killing the last and final Nightstone? Guaranteed to have his head on a spike outside of the gates of Sidosa if he doesnt kill himself from shame first. With his head on a spike, though, I will be given sympathy beyond belief, and people will mourn my son's death along with my wife's. That is the easiest way to gain sympathy, you see—the death of a loved one."

The wards. What happened to the wards? What happened to Akuna?

Kaine forced Rosella's body closer to the dagger in Elaras' hand. The tip pierced her skin, and even though she wanted to flinch, she couldn't even do that. With her face forcibly looking at Kaine, she could not see Elaras', and she wished more than anything she could be looking at him.

"I gained so much sympathy when I announced Evanora's passing that people did not bat an eye when I told them that I would be marrying Lycilla to help her," Kaine said with a gleeful sneer, poison dripping from his lips. "If you were to live, I'd give you this advice, but you won't live another five minutes. Maybe three, because your presence is pissing me off along with my childish son's pathetic mournful crying. Ah, and your *Great Wrath* savior? He's probably long dead after the trap we set for him. The stupid devlair girl was more useful than I anticipated, as it was she who set up the 'distress' call for your dragon. She learned his two weaknesses: a dragon in despair and *you*."

Kaine shoved her head back to where she was facing Elaras, and she saw that despite having tears running down his face to the pillows, his face was straight like a statue. Rosella wanted to scream, fight her way out of the orange control, scratch Kaine's eyes out, but she was stuck where she was. Then, unmistakably, Kaine's commanding voice rang out like a gunshot in the room but was now directed at Elaras.

"I taught you where a person's heart is, Elaras. For the first time in your life, make me proud and make her heart stop."

Sharp, undeniable, tearing and slicing pain shocked her body, and she screamed with no noise. Her vision tunneled from the agony as something warm started to race down her chest and onto the sheets. He ripped the dagger out of her, and more blood poured out, covering the golden-sheeted space between them.

Elaras did exactly as his father commanded of him. He had stabbed her successfully in the heart as well as her already damaged lung all the way through her collarbone. She could tell he tried to fight the command, but the voice of power was too strong to resist, and she would fall because of it, because of Kaine. Her vision began to fade as her muscles fully relaxed, but they became so weak that she knew if she wanted to stand up that she would fall.

Blackness started to block out her vision without even closing her eyes, and the need to scream seemed unnecessary. In the far, far distance she heard someone scream, a deafening roar, a chorus of yells from somewhere she did not see, nor did she care.

Peace overwhelmed her as dark, shadowed hands pulled her further into the water that she fell into in her nightmare. She welcomed the peace because she no longer felt pain, fear, anger. What it felt like to be a human was now an afterthought as she let a hand cover her mouth and her eyes, and she fell, fell, fell until there was nothing left but black.

33

Burn Your Name into My Throat

"I taught you where a person's heart is, Elaras. For the first time in your life, make me proud and make her heart stop," rang out in Elaras' ears, making his head dizzy. He pulled back the dagger, but the feeling of knives and needles pierced his skin and muscles, his nerves singing an ugly, mournful song as he tried his best to pull the tip out of Rosella's body. No matter how much he pulled, his body did not answer to his own command.

He had lost control. His father had taken him over, and the only thing that his body allowed him to do was plunge the dagger into Rosella. He fought harder, but he felt his elbow being pushed by an invisible hand deep into her chest, her mouth opening into a silent scream only heard by the gods as the dagger dove deeper. The hilt hit her skin with a thud, and the tip of the blade rammed into her collarbone and through her skin. Elaras wanted to scream, to cry harder, let go of the dagger that had already caused detrimental damage.

"Pull the dagger out, boy," came his father's voice, and his body instantly did as it was told. His hand gripped the handle

harder and yanked the blade out of her skin, her blood not hesitating to escape her body.

Elaras watched completely helpless as each breath she struggled to make made even more blood spill onto the tunic she still wore and onto the atrocious golden sheets, the crimson liquid pool growing larger by the second. His hand was still attached to the knife as slowly, ever so slowly, his body regained control and he was able to use his voice.

The orange hue of his father's control and the red, shaky smoke slowly dissipated, but too slowly it left his body, Kaine and Lycilla holding on to the last moment to release their grip on him.

Quietly, he screamed Rosella's name until his voice grew louder and louder, but with each time his voice grew in volume, the further Rosella fell. When his body was completely his own once again and his voice was under his control, he screamed Rosella's name at the top of his lungs. He dropped the blade off the side of the bed and scooped her up in his arms, tears from his eyes falling on to her face as her head fell back, eyes staring past him. One of his hands immediately went to her wrist to feel for a pulse, only to find that her skin was as still as a rock.

"Rosella! Wake up, *please!"* Elaras screamed once he found his full voice, not caring who heard. Panic filled his blood as he pressed harder into her wrist, waiting and hoping her blood would run and her heart would come back to life. He looked around and saw that both his father and Lycilla were gone, undoubtedly teleporting to some location where Elaras could never find them.

He turned back and saw Rosella's chest was still, her body completely limp in his now blood-soaked arms. "Rosella, please, please..." he whimpered as he let go of her wrist and raised his hand in the air.

He whispered incantations and saw his blue magic flow from his fingers into the holes his dagger made, by his own hand. His magic was slow, too slow. She would be dead for too long. He would lose her.

"AKUNA!" he yelled as his magic still flowed out of his shaking fingers.

The window was still open from when Akuna left earlier in the night, so he hoped to all the gods that somehow he would hear, that he could save her. Akuna was the most powerful being he had ever met, but he was not here. He was not able to save her. Of all the times for Akuna to leave, now was the worst. Just like the rest of the Nightstones, Akuna had failed Rosella by simply not being here.

Right as Elaras was about to give up, however, a flash caught the corner of his eye. A large mass of purple smoke covered Rosella. She was lifted into the air by the smoke, and it enveloped her entire body, swirling fiercely and relentlessly.

After a minute of her hovering and being swallowed by Akuna's magic, she was lowered onto the bed, and Elaras caught her as she gently landed in his arms. The wound that was supposed to be present on her chest and shoulder had closed. No scars were left where the dagger had been. Her tunic was still torn, but there was no blood or gaping holes in her skin, and her breathing had returned to normal.

"Rosella?" Elaras asked weakly, placing a hand on her cheek and feeling if her skin was warm.

Her neck was hot, but her cheeks barely radiated heat into his fingers. Ever so slowly color returned to her skin. His eyes never left her face as Elaras moved his hand to her wrist, waiting to feel the beat of life.

Akuna landed on the side of the bed, not saying a word and staring at Rosella.

Coughing echoed in the room as Rosella's body jerked with the motion, her lungs struggling to catch and hold on to air.

Without missing a beat, Akuna blew a thin stream of smoke into her nostrils, and the coughing ebbed as quickly as they came. Her eyes blinked furiously as they fell onto Elaras' tear-filled ones.

The second her eyes straightened out and came into focus, her own eyes began to fill with tears as she looked around. Her eyes landed on Akuna, and she ripped her wrist from Elaras' grasp so she could scoop Akuna up and hold him close to her chest. Then she pushed her head and body into Elaras' arms, and he wrapped one arm around her back, and the other held her face to his chest.

Elaras felt her body tremble violently as he held her, her breaths strained. They sat on the bed and cried together, letting out all the emotions of the night and the experience they just shared.

Akuna, oddly enough, seemed to vibrate in Rosella's grasp like he was purring, and Elaras felt the same frequency of rumbling when he stroked Rosella's back. After what seemed like an hour of holding each other, Rosella backed away enough so she could look Elaras in the face but not enough to force him to let go.

"Fuck your father," she said simply with a croak to her voice.

Of all the things Elaras expected her to say when she was brought back to life, that was not one of them, but he couldn't help but smile and laugh. His heart swelled, and he nodded, grinning down at her and stroking her face with his hand.

"Fuck my father," he said back to her, and she laughed weakly.

Still holding Akuna, she looked down at him, and he could see tears building up again in her eyes. "You resurrected me. Wait, are you all right? You're hurt..."

"I failed you by not being here. I promised I would be by your side, and I broke that promise. I was only gone for an hour, and that was enough time for you to... I'm fine. There is no need to worry about me," Akuna said, choking on his own words.

Tearing his eyes from Rosella, Elaras gazed upon the tiny dragon, and his mouth fell agape. The white, iridescent scales were covered in blood, and new cuts accompanied his aged scars. Rosella's palm was covered in blood that was not her own, and Akuna's chest was heaving. What trap did his father set for this powerful dragon, and how did Akuna escape?

"The wards..." Rosella choked out, a soft wheeze escaping her throat.

"Kaine and Lycilla set a fine trap, an excellent trap. Nothing like I've seen before," Akuna said through small gasps of air. "Escaping took most of my energy, and in turn..."

"Weakened the wards," Elaras finished. He gazed around the room at the invisible wards, hoping to find evidence of the fault, or a crack. Turning back, he could see Akuna's chest was heaving, blood trickling onto the bed. Elaras raised his hand and began flowing healing magic into Akuna, the blue smoke soaking into the open wounds. He knew his healing was nothing compared to the great dragon's, but something was better than nothing.

"What was the trap, and how did you escape?" Rosella said as clearly as possible after clearing her throat.

"Kislet, the dragon, was dead when I got there. A spiked mesh-lined cage sprung up from the ground, and a copper wire was wrapped around my neck. No matter what size I grew, the wire wrapped tighter, all while the spikes stabbed and sliced me. I—I had to animate Kislet's body to cut the wire from my neck."

"I'm sorry, *animate*?" Elaras said, his eyebrows shooting up.

"Yes. My draconic ability is necromancy. Manipulate the dead to do my bidding. So, I used Kislet to bit the wire free, then used his acid breath to melt the cage so I could get out," Akuna said, trembling slightly. "What happened here, exactly?"

"Lycilla paralyzed us, and Kaine took control of our bodies.

Kaine forced Elaras to...to kill me," Rosella said, unfazed by the revealed information Akuna gave.

Akuna's eyes started to glow a deadly red. "They did *what*?" he said, purple smoke and steam flowing out of his nostrils.

"Yeah. So, fuck his father," Rosella said defiantly, not even trying to calm Akuna down.

Akuna hovered in the air and twisted around, steadily flying around the room despite his injuries and examining the walls and doors, possibly for the faults in his wards. As he did this, Elaras brought Rosella's head to his chest again and stroked her hair.

"I'm so sorry I—" he started to say, but her hand flew to his mouth to stop him from talking.

"You had no control. You could not stop it from happening. I do not blame you, so you are not allowed to blame yourself," she said in a stern yet weak voice.

Elaras looked down at her beautiful face, always making his heart skip a beat.

"I'm serious. You do not get to blame yourself for this. If you do, I'll force myself to stop loving you."

There it was, the infamous L-word, and Elaras had no desire to fight her or disagree with her. In this moment, he wanted to blame himself for everything: Kaine being his father, for not staying awake until Akuna returned, for not protecting her. He stumbled for words because he truly wanted to place the blame, take fault, but she said words that he did not expect her to say so soon.

With his heart beating rapidly as he stared into her crystal blue eyes, he knew and had known for quite some time that he loved her. From the moment he saw her and gave her Shadow Breaker, he knew he was in love with her. The love he had for her was bigger than the moon itself, and he had never felt this way before about anyone.

"'Force yourself to stop loving me'? You could try, but you'd fail miserably," he quipped, trying to lighten the dark and heavy emotions off of them by chuckling a little.

She let out a soft chuckle and gave a half, weak smile, shaking her head in the annoyed way that only Elaras seemed to make her do.

"I love you, Rosella," he whispered to her, and her eyes twinkled so brightly that they resembled the fireflies he cherished so much, lighting a path for him.

"I love you too, and I could never stop loving you, no matter what," she whispered.

They both leaned in at the same time to kiss the other. They have had many kisses since that first time in her room, but this one was the most weighted of them all, and would be for some time in the future. This kiss would be remembered when they were old and telling the story to their kids, to their grandkids, the kiss that solidified their future completely with each other. From the shadows of the darkest nights to the stars that glittered in the night sky, nothing could compete with the beauty and significance of this kiss. It was Rosella's coughing that made them break apart, and there were small trickles of blood on the corners of her mouth.

"Akuna..." Elaras said, and Akuna was immediately on Elaras' shoulder, pouring his magic into her mouth and her nose.

"She will need healing throughout the night. I'll ward the room further and stay up with her, along with healing myself. Her lungs were damaged before she came to Dorthos, so I will try and do what I can to heal her lungs as much as possible. I can heal skin perfectly, but what I cannot see is difficult," Akuna said when he finished pushing magic into her.

Elaras stroked her hair, and she smiled up at him and Akuna.

"That sounds alright with me," Elaras said, and he pulled

Rosella down onto the bed and wrapped her in his arms in a tight embrace. Glancing at the dragon, Elaras added, "Thank you, Akuna. Truly. Will you be okay? Can you heal yourself?"

Akuna simply nodded.

"Wait, you're basically a necromancer?" Rosella piped up, looking over to Akuna.

An unmistakable smile spread his scaly face as he said, "Yes, my dear. And yes, it's pretty rare among dragons."

"Of course it is," Rosella said while laying back down, a small chuckle leaving her weak lungs.

As Elaras and Rosella drifted off to sleep, he saw flashes of purple in his blurry vision and felt small gusts of wind through his hair and against his ears from time to time.

34
Truth Condemns the Sinners

"We searched the entire castle for Kaine and Lycilla, but we found no trace of them here. It's as if they were never here," Flitch was saying the group, pacing back and forth. "Their carriage and horses were also gone, and none of his footmen or guards were here either. They must have teleported themselves here from somewhere nearby. How else would they have gotten into the room without being detected by any of the castle staff and through Akuna's wards?"

Paton was seated cross-legged on the table in the corner of the room, Elaras standing at the side of the bed while Rosella sat on the bed itself, with a healed and sleeping Akuna resting in her cupped hands. Rosella, despite the constant healing from Akuna throughout the night, still felt weak and would occasionally feel a pain spread through her chest for a moment or two.

When she was brought back to life by Akuna, the sensation was intense and overwhelming. She was in the dark place, surrounded by lively shadows and drowning by the pull of the hands she could not see, but she felt at peace. A light appeared from above, and she saw a large, purple, smoky clawed hand reach down into the depths for her. The moment she saw the hand, she realized that she did not want to be enveloped in darkness. She did not want to be held by shadows any longer. She wanted to live—she *needed* to live. People outside of herself needed her and depended on her.

Once the hand wrapped around her body, the hands and arms that were holding her down immediately disappeared and let her go. She was pulled so quickly that she grew dizzy, and pain she never believed would be possible coursed through her body like mercury in her veins. Her face broke the surface of the water that she fell into, and her chest exploded with agony accompanied by pure happiness she could not explain. When she opened her eyes, she saw Elaras' horrified face that broke into the same happiness she was feeling.

She was going to live.

"They have to be heading to Nocturnal Manor now, thinking they killed Rosella. They think they just made this whole thing easier for them, and that they now have a straight path to the throne," Paton said in their slick voice, examining their extended claws.

"Should we still talk to the emperor? Would that even help anymore? Or should we blaze our way back to Rion and confront him before he can do anything damaging?" Flitch asked the group, and Rosella felt herself shudder.

"We could try and talk to him, but I don't think it would go anywhere. Though, getting the throne granted to Rosella would be much easier politically, and a potential way to avoid bloodshed," Elaras said wisely as he stroked Rosella's back.

Rosella appreciated the motion as it helped her back feel less sore. She admittedly did not feel welcome in this castle anymore, and she wanted to leave, but she had to remember that politics were something she would have to familiarize herself with to when she became queen. Would a queen truly be a queen if she was perceived to steal the crown from someone that was already granted the throne? That was what the Rockshires did in a brutal manner, so if she did not talk to the emperor, how would she be any different from Lycilla?

"I need to speak with him. If it doesn't go well, then we'll leave immediately, and we'll force ourselves onto Kaine and Lycilla somehow," Rosella croaked, sitting up. She took a finger and prodded Akuna's wing, gently waking him up.

Halting his pacing, Flitch looked at her. Rosella locked her eyes onto him then onto Paton, feeling her face grow warm as her heart began to race.

"Are you sure you're alright, Rosella?" Flitch asked cautiously, and Rosella simply shrugged before straightening her spine.

"Paton and Flitch, get Temel and meet us in that room that is near the rotting room," Rosella said, nodding to both Paton and Flitch, and they nodded back, Paton standing up and retracting their claws. Rosella turned to Elaras and Akuna and said in a clearer tone, "Let's go talk to the emperor, do our best to convince him otherwise."

"Meet you soon. We will not leave without you," Paton said, and both Paton and Flitch stalked out the door.

Rosella grabbed her armor and took the few minutes it required to put the armor on, making sure there were no gaps or weak spots. Avy and Bebbie knew what they were doing, as each artery that could be punctured was covered with leather or metal. After her armor was situated, she grabbed her belt and cloak, placing her bow across her body, and made sure her quiver was within reach. Finally, she found the handle of Shadow Breaker and grabbed onto it to ensure the magic was still viable and became thankful when the ruby blinded her with its light.

Rosella waited as Elaras put on his armor, arranged his daggers, and grabbed his cloak and his own bag. When he was finished, he looked at Rosella, his eyebrows furrowed and his jaw clenched.

"I'm okay, I swear," she whispered, walking up to him and reaching for his face.

He immediately placed his hands over hers and leaned down to place his forehead against hers. "You're alive," he whispered.

Rosella felt heat in her face and a large lump forming in her throat. She had died, but he was the one who dealt the physical blow. After these next few days, she knew there would have to be conversations and a long road of healing for the both of them. Something like this was not simply forgotten or pushed down.

"I'm alive, and I love you," she said as softly as possible. Her thumbs stroked his cheeks and along the scars, feeling the slight bumps and irregularities in the stitched skin.

"I love you," he murmured back before kissing her. He hugged her so tightly, his fingertips squeaked against her armor.

When they broke apart, they smiled at each other and headed out of the room, wishing to never set foot in it again. Akuna flew into her hood and rested on the back of her neck, so Rosella pulled up her hood to conceal him. After having to ask a few guards and knights where the emperor was and how to navigate the massive castle, they found themselves outside gigantic golden double doors that were as wide as a house.

"Let us in," Rosella demanded to one of the guards, and they did not hesitate to reach over and push the doors wide open with the other guard.

Rosella strode in with haste, Elaras on her tail, and she did not look at the details of this extravagant room as it was so massive that it nauseated her. What she did catch was rows upon rows of bleacher-style seating along the walls that were made of wood painted with gold paint. There were paintings of what must have been previous emperors, as they varied from different pelts of felinettes, and their garbs changed in style the further down she walked toward an atrocious throne. The room, just like any other room she had been in and the castle itself, was painted completely gold, which easily reflected the golden chandeliers above.

Upon the throne at the very end of the unnecessarily long room sat the emperor, his fat spilling onto the sides of the elegant chair and his fur sagging so much that it covered parts of the edges of his clothing. He was eating something that resembled a large fish as his son, Zaas, sat to the right of him and his wife sat on his left and watched as Rosella and Elaras approached. When the emperor finally saw them, he placed the fish carcass on a small side table and wiped his mouth with a grubby paw.

"You're late, along with my daughter. Where is she?" the emperor asked in an unkind and impatient manner.

"I'm not sure, but I'm not here for her. I'm here to get what is rightfully mine," Rosella stated as she straightened her back and cupped her hands behind her back, mimicking all the times Elaras had done it. The look that crossed the emperor's face was hilarious to Rosella, as the fat in his face jiggled every time he blubbered in shock.

"Here to get what is rightfully yours? Preposterous. You stupid girl, nothing belongs to you. You are a mere commoner! Look at you! I don't even know what backwater village races you are supposed to be made of! You will get nothing from me!" the emperor yelled.

Rosella noticed that the empress' face slackened in response to the emperor's words. Did she know something he did not, and could she possibly already know that Rosella was more than a "backwater village race"? Rosella, however, took a few steps forward so that they were about ten feet apart from each other.

"You don't even remember my name," Rosella said, letting her irritation leak into her words.

"I do not need to know your name, stupid girl!" he blubbered on, and Rosella gave a half-cocked smile.

"My name is Rosella *Nightstone*, and you gave my usurper *my* throne. I am here to reclaim what was stolen from me, from my family. If you will not give it to me, I will take it by force."

The emperor's eyes grew wide, and the empress' face turned curious yet cunning. She looked satisfied and leaned forward in her smaller throne, her eyes narrowing in something that resembled excitement. The emperor, on the other hand, had his ears pinned back with bristled fur and was standing out of his throne and hobbling toward Rosella.

"You are *not* a Nightstone! It is not possible!" he yelled, getting closer and closer, all feline grace gone.

Like an archer who needed distance from their target, she stepped in stride with the emperor but backwards. Elaras copied her, and when she caught a quick glimpse of him, she saw that he was smirking.

"I am. Lycilla stole the necklace from me in my sleep, not thinking it was a true night stone. Did you notice how she or Kaine did not put on the necklace? Did you notice Lycilla's burnt and charred hand? That's because the stone *knows* that neither Lycilla nor Kaine belong on my throne. The necklace is mine, and I need it to save this world. You," she spat out and stopped in her tracks, pointing a sharp finger at the emperor as he stepped ever closer, "gave her *my* throne. So, give it back to me, and you will not have to suffer the consequences of denying a queen her throne."

The emperor stopped right in front of her, and he stared down, the size of his body casting a shadow onto her. She noticed that they only took maybe ten small steps from his throne, so she was still close enough to see that the empress was smirking and Zaas had narrowed eyes, both now standing up.

"Impossible. You just want the power for yourself. You have no right to the throne!" the emperor said, leaning down into her space. "Besides, where were you thirty years ago? Why are you coming here now?"

"I'm not from Dorthos. I'm from a world called Earth. I am a true Nightstone, of blood and progeny. Besides that fact, why would Kaine and Lycilla feel so threatened by me if I was not an actual Nightstone?" Rosella challenged, and she watched as the emperor's face fell into confusion, heaving so heavily that she could feel his fish-smelling breath on her face.

Reaching for the magic pouch, she thought of her cell phone and grabbed it, unlocking the screen and going to the photo album app. The emperor stepped back when he saw the device and screamed wildly, pointing at her as she was finding the photo of the hanging foxes and the sign that was left for them.

"Witch! Criminal! Hag!" he yelled, and the guards advanced toward Rosella with their halberds pointing toward her.

Surprisingly, it was the empress who walked past her husband and stood right in front of Rosella. They were the same height at five foot four, and her orange eyes bore down into Rosella's soul as she studied her body, scanning every inch. Rosella, feeling annoyed and uncomfortable, held her phone up to the empress' face, and she saw the empress' eyes dilate and focus on the screen.

She looked back at Rosella, let out a *hmph* noise, and walked back to the emperor and whispered in his ear. As she did so, her hands stretched out in the direction of the guards, and they immediately lowered their weapons and backed away. Once the emperor calmed down, the empress straightened up and stood next to her son.

"So, do you believe me now?" Rosella asked and watched the emperor's face think through an answer.

As this happened and they stood in silence, there was a distant whispering where Elaras stood. She looked over, and his face was locked in concentration as he stared intently toward the ground. Turning back, she waited for the emperor to answer, squeezing her phone in frustration. Elaras cut across her view of the emperor, partially blocked her it, and he grabbed her upper arm in a gentle yet firm grip.

"Rosella, Paton found out information from Temel's lady's maid. Thirty years ago, it was Emperor Harporous, this guy, that allowed and ordered the Rockshires to kill the Nightstones. He wants you dead," he whispered so softly that only she and Akuna could hear.

Akuna's body trembled with anger, and she felt her skin get hot with her own fury.

"He *ordered* the killing of the Nightstones? Why?" Rosella asked quietly and sharply.

"I'm not sure. That is all the invisible sparrow told me," Elaras said. Rosella looked up at him and his furious face matched her emotions. "Fuck this guy. We have to do this by force."

"What are you two whispering about? I do not have all day!" the emperor shouted, and Rosella's anger reached an all-time high, her chest fit to explode with pure malice.

"You ordered the Nightstones to be killed!" she accused. "You allowed the Rockshires to kill and usurp the throne! No fucking wonder you granted Lycilla the throne without hesitation! Any good ruler would see that as treacherous if someone that *belonged* on the throne and would actually save the country—and in turn the world—was alive after all. What possible fucking reason could you have to kill an entire family line, end the longest family rule of this whole world?"

"Tell the truth you so desire to keep quiet, my love," came the empress' voice, and she sounded just as sly as Rosella had expected.

This time, however, poison-green magic was pouring out of her fingertips from behind the emperor, and his eyes softened to lifeless orbs, his muscles relaxed, and he took even breaths. He did not look like he was being controlled, but it did look like some sort of mind spell calmed him and compelled him to tell the truth because he immediately started speaking rapidly yet calmly.

"I ordered their deaths because they learned we did not give the remaining food to the citizens of Sidosa, so they stopped sending extra food. I also ordered them to be killed because Princess Luvu refused to have her children Trusk and Brestia be betrothed to my children. The Rockshires wanted power, so I gave them power. You are supposed to be dead. Kaine told me just last night that he would kill you if I gave the order. I did. Finally end the Nightstone name once and for all." When he finished, his eyes came back to life. He whirled toward to his wife who had a wicked smile on her face, her arm wrapped around the now-seated and shocked Zaas.

"Not only did you order the Nightstones to die thirty years ago, but you also ordered my killing last night? How does it feel to see me alive and —" A hacking cough tore out of Rosella's throat so intensely that she fell to her knees.

Elaras was by her side instantly, rubbing her back.

Boisterous laughter from the emperor filled the room and rang in her ears, making her head spin from the noise and also from the lack of oxygen in her painful lungs. "What were you going to say? Alive and *well*? You don't look well to me!" the emperor said, and he seemed to fall into his throne from laughing because a loud thud made the floor vibrate.

Rosella had her eyes closed from the pain that was spreading further and deeper in her chest, and her coughing grew violent as spittles of saliva covered the floor in front of her. After a few moments, she felt the pain ease, and breathing became clearer and easier. When she opened her eyes, she saw thin streams of purple smoke flowing into her nose like a nasal cannula.

The emperor had stopped laughing as his eyes landed on the purple smoke, and the empress and Zaas had disappeared along with all the guards and staff that were lining the walls minutes before.

"You're a disgrace as an emperor, as a ruler, and as a leader," Rosella snarled. "I shall take back my throne and—"

"You can use magic? That means you could kill me! Do not harm me!" he was screaming at her, shielding his face from her. Taking advantage of his fear, she stepped forward while Akuna kept flowing magic into her lungs.

"I won't kill you. That wouldn't be very *queenly* of me. But I can have others kill you if I desire so," she said in a low tone, tilting her head as she walked closer to him. When she was at his throne, she propped one leg up on the arm rest and watched him flinch in his seat as she leaned into his space. "Give me my throne, and no harm will come to you, Harporous."

"Have mercy! Have mercy! Do not hurt me!"

"Give me my throne, then."

"I'll kill you before you leave my palace! Back away!"

"Yeah, all right, if this is how you're going to act, then I have no other choice," Rosella said, backing away from the throne and palming Shadow Breaker.

At this moment, Akuna's magic had disappeared, and she no

longer felt his claws on her back. Elaras had palmed two daggers as well, and he was creeping forward.

The emperor looked completely horror-struck as his eyes landed on Shadow Breaker's red gleam, pointing and gasping. "Shadow Breaker? How did you get Shadow Breaker?" He looked absolutely terrified, more so than she had ever seen thus far.

"Ah, this old thing? Got it from a friend. Nice to know you are aware of its reputation, so maybe you can take me seriously and give. Me. My. Throne," Rosella said, spinning the handle in her hand and making the bright red ruby's light fly around.

"Do not get close to me with that!" the emperor said.

Rosella rolled her eyes. "Elaras?" she called to him without looking in his direction.

She heard him chuckle as he approached the emperor. In a flash that was quicker than lightning, Elaras was behind the emperor with a blade to his throat, and the emperor thrashed, his claws scratching at Elaras' leathers.

"You killed my family line," Rosella snarled through gritted teeth. "You tried to kill me. This is your last chance to redeem yourself before you are killed with no witnesses."

"*No!*" the emperor said before his eyes drifted upward above her head, eyes wide with terror.

A large shadow was being cast on him and Elaras. Elaras' eyes were following the same thing the emperor was, so she turned and saw purple smoke filling the whole room.

What emerged from the smoke was the largest form she had ever seen of Akuna, as this was double the size of the cavern, and he was wearing his red and white coloration. His wings knocked down pillars, and his footsteps made indents in the floor, his claws stretching and pulling up the intricate gold carpet. Cracks could be heard along the walls, and distant, intelligible shouts were sounding in the halls. The rumble from his throat was much deeper than what she had heard before, and his eyes glowed brightly and menacingly.

"I will kill you as I killed the Rockshires if you do not comply," came the now extremely deep and ground-shaking voice of Akuna. He stepped forward, and she saw that the top of his foot was tall enough that Rosella could simply lower herself to sit on it. The world around Akuna shifted as he did, as if the air itself was afraid and moved frantically away from him.

Her hood flew off her head as she looked back at the emperor, who was staring like a statue up at Akuna. Elaras himself was surprised, but he kept his daggers in hand and against the emperor.

Akuna got as close as he could to the emperor, and when he blew steam out of his nostrils, the emperor yelped, too afraid to say or do much more.

"I told you I would have others kill you if you didn't give me my throne. Now, are we done showing hands, or can I leave to claim what is mine?" Rosella asked in an unapologetic, cocky manner.

The emperor simply nodded, and Akuna growled deeply, slightly opening his mouth.

"Say it, you filthy glutton," snapped Elaras, pushing the dagger closer to the emperor's neck.

"Arja is the true home of the Nightstone family, and therefore should be ruled by only the Nightstones," the emperor choked out. "No one shall fight for the throne, nor shall they be killed for their position again."

"Heard. Now, in payment of your ending the lives and line of the Nightstones, your daughter, Temel, shall live under my rule and shall only return with my permission. She is to work for me under the Nightstone name," Rosella said, taking advantage of this weakened moment for the emperor.

"Take her! Spare me! Have mercy on me, Great Wrath of Dorthos!" the emperor screamed and was now shielding his face.

Rosella backed off and smiled at the blubbering emperor. Elaras displaced himself to stand next to Rosella, and within a few seconds, Akuna had returned to his tiny form and flew into Rosella's hood, which she pulled back up. Elaras displaced them through a door that was off the side of the throne room, and they ran into Zaas and the empress.

While they were still in the haven, Rosella hauntingly noticed that no matter where they moved in the shadow pocket of reality, the empress followed in real time where they were. Elaras, noticing this too, pulled down the haven and stepped forward to her.

She was holding a rolled-up scroll and handed it to Elaras. He opened it while keeping his eyes on the empress, who was smirking but looked extremely satisfied. Zaas stood shocked and speechless, so Rosella ignored him and kept her eyes on the empress. When Elaras gave the scroll to Rosella, she was surprised to see what she read, and her whole attitude of the empress changed on that spot.

By decree of Emperor Harporous Dreadtrell and Empress Loka Dreadtrell:

Hereby from this day forth of Unei 26th, 3532, Rosella Elinor Nightstone shall sit and rule the throne of Arja for now until the remainder of her days, then shall her successor take the throne by birth or marriage.

Any future Emperor Dreadtrell or any empress in power shall no longer have the power to remove a Nightstone from the throne for any reason. If an emperor takes said actions, the Nightstone King, Queen, or Monarch shall use whatever force necessary to remind said emperor of what happened this day.

Princess Temel Dreadtrell must also serve under the Nightstone name for the remainder of her lifetime in return for the pain and suffering Emperor Harporous caused. Only the Nightstone ruler and Temel Dreadtrell may decide when she may leave Nightstone servitude.

Signed: Emperor Harporous and Empress Loka Dreadtrell.
Date: Rosday, Ueni 26th, 3532

Rosella looked up with a shocked gasp, rolling the scroll back up and placing it in her magic pouch. "Thank you," she managed to say, amazed at how quickly the empress was able to get this decree created.

Empress Loka bowed and gave Rosella the moon symbol salute. Before they walked away, she turned back toward Rosella and gave another examining look with a slick smile.

"Invite me and Zaas to the coronation and the wedding. You will make a *spectacular* queen, Rosella Nightstone," she said, shifting her eyes to Elaras for a moment before pivoting and walking away with her son in hand.

35
You Cannot Take the Sky From Me

Rosella and Elaras jogged through the castle to the room that was near the tunnel entrance and found that the door was locked. Thinking quickly, Rosella knocked twice, scratched once, then knocked twice again, mimicking the same knocking code as Paton did on Ladroth's door back at headquarters. The door swung open quickly, and Flitch, Paton, and Temel rushed out and sprinted toward the rotting room. Temel got to the metal door that led to the tunnel and unlocked it quickly, Paton glancing behind them all. Temel pushed through the door and Paton followed her in, along with the rest of the group, and when everyone was through, she took the door and locked it with her tiger's eye pendant. Panting, she looked at Rosella and Elaras.

"Well? What did my father say?" she asked.

Instead of responding, she reached into her magic pouch and brought out the scroll and handed it to Flitch. He held it up as high as he could so he could read it with Temel and Paton, and slowly their faces relaxed, with Temel's face breaking out in a wide smile. Paton's mouth fell agape, and they wrapped their arms around Temel, who was speechless and crying tears of joy.

"You asked him, and he said yes? For me to leave, I mean?" she asked, trembling as she spoke.

"Well, it wasn't hard to ask once we threatened him. It was really annoying and irritating having to constantly ask him for my throne, but we scared him into answering. Empress Loka gave us this once we left the throne room, so we no longer have to deal with the emperor. Now, we just have to find Kaine and Lycilla," Rosella said, and when she finished, Temel rushed forward with Paton still attached to her and flung an arm around Rosella's neck.

"Oh, thank you, thank you, thank you!" Temel squealed, crying through her words and shaking from the overwhelming emotions that must have been flooding through her.

Rosella did not hesitate to hug her back, hugging Paton in the process as they were still intertwined with Temel. After a few moments of hugging, Temel let go of Rosella, and she moved her arms to wrap around Paton, rubbing her cheeks into Paton's whiskers. In a way, Rosella realized that she brought two people who loved each other together, and her heart swelled with joy seeing the two giving each other affection.

"I'm all for the lovey-dovey shit, but we really need to move, guys," Flitch said as he walked a little ways down the tunnel.

Everyone agreed, and they hurried down the hour-long path through the tunnel and to the headquarters, Elaras holding Rosella's hand and Paton holding Temel's. When they reached the end and entered through the door, many people stopped what they were doing and stared at the group as they crawled through to the main room from the tunnel.

"Flitchy poo!" rang out a yell, and Raya came running forward. When the tiny form of Flitch's sister flew her arms around his neck, everyone else in the room relaxed and went about their day. The door to Ladroth's office opened, and he had to dip his head under the frame to see what the commotion was about. When his eyes landed on the group, his face broke out in a smile, and he raised his arms.

"Welcome back! Please, come in and give me a quick update on what happened!" he said, gesturing to the group to enter his office, having to bend down once more to enter himself.

The group with Raya latched onto Flitch's neck proceeded into the office and sat around the table. There, they each took turns explaining the events of the last day and a half. The information that neither part of the group were aware of was what happened while Rosella and Elaras were with the emperor. During that time, Paton and Flitch had to sneak their way into Temel's room, and they tried to pack as much as possible. Temel was given a magic pouch similar to Rosella's at one point years ago, so they were able to shove much more than planned into it, and she dressed in all black to match Paton and Flitch. She wore a scarf and a cloak to hide her appearance in case a guard caught sight of her. They had run through the maids' halls and trapdoors until they found the room near the rotting room.

When Rosella and Elaras told them of their events, excluding Akuna's appearance, everyone grew quiet.

"My lady's maid knew, but I still had no idea it was my father who ordered them to... I didn't realize he was that kind of person," Temel said, her ears flicking back and forth. "I'm glad I'm out of his clutches. He's an evil man. Killing a whole family just because he didn't get food and they didn't want young kids to be betrothed too early. Oh gods, that means that if they had accepted and the family lived, I would still be with the Nightstones."

Either way, Temel's life was going to lead to her being under the Nightstone name, whether it would be in employment or marriage. When Rosella was about to say something, Temel interrupted her politely and said, "I prefer this way. I get to be with Paton, not a royal that I would have to learn to love or tolerate."

Rosella smiled and nodded, agreeing with the sentiment.

"That's some real fucked-up shit right there. I'm so sorry, Rosella. How are you feeling?" Ladroth asked, real concern filling his vibrant green eyes.

"My chest hurts every now and then, but I can manage. Mentally and emotionally? Tired and worn out for sure. I just want all of this to be over with, and Kaine and Lycilla to be stopped. Once all of that is done, I think I will start to feel normal and be able to heal from all the traumatic events," Rosella said as casually as possible, but her anxiety made her chest tighten.

"Well, I suggest you all leave now so you can get there as soon as possible. Flitch, send a sparrow to your sister when all of this is over so I can be updated, alright?" Ladroth said to Flitch before turning to Temel. "Are you staying here until it's safe, or are you going with Paton?"

"Do you remember your training? Remember what I showed you to do in case things get intense?" Paton asked quietly to Temel, taking her hand and rubbing the back of it with their thumb. When Temel nodded, Paton smiled and looked back at Ladroth, saying with a smile they couldn't help but give, "She'll come with us. Her official training starts today."

"That settles it! Now go. I have wasted enough time keeping you all up. Resupply, then head out! I'll send a sparrow to Mellis and tell them what happened with the emperor," Ladroth said with vigor, and everyone stood up after Rosella and made their way out of the room.

As Rosella was about to leave, Ladroth stopped her and

beckoned her back in the room. "Take this and give one to each member of the party. From what you told us about last night, this will help make sure that never happens again," Ladroth said as he handed her five necklaces with a black, sharp-edged stone attached to a pendant. She was unfamiliar with the stone and found it odd that it was not polished or symmetrical like the others she had seen or even similar to her own.

"What is it?" she asked, feeling stupid but knowing clarification would benefit more than being embarrassed.

"That, My Queen, is black tourmaline. It'll protect your mind and body from control. Black tourmaline is rare, but so is the power to control someone else's body completely. Please, keep one for yourself and one for Elaras, but tell the others I need the other three back. Consider that a gift from me to the future queen of Arja," Ladroth said, bowing and saluting to her when he finished speaking.

Rosella smiled and went ahead to put one on, and she saw that the chain was just slightly smaller than the moonstone's chain, and bigger than her night stone's.

"Thank you for everything, Ladroth," she said, inclining her head in thanks before leaving.

Thankfully, everyone was ready to go and were standing together, so she gave them all a necklace to wear and explained to Paton, Flitch, and Temel that they were to return them after the mission. Rosella walked through the original tunnel door that they entered through, and they walked the twenty or so minutes it took to get through to the other side. Flitch took the initiative to open the trapdoor and peer out of it. He lowered the trapdoor and nodded to Elaras, who exhaled a deep breath and activated his haven, which shocked Temel slightly before Paton could reassure her that this was the displacer magic they had warned her about.

"Let's go. We can't waste any more time. Temel, if you have

any questions, ask Paton on the way," Flitch said as he pushed the door open, and they all walked out hand in hand.

They proceeded to travel in the haven for a few hours before Elaras needed a break, so they walked into a dense set of dead trees, and he dropped the haven. They were back in Arja, and Rosella had not noticed the change in flora when crossing the border. Temel's eyes had to adjust to the sudden brightness of the sun, but she looked like she was adapting well to her new life.

"Where are we?" she asked right as Flitch was casting the cloaking magic, yellow smoke filling the air around them.

"Arja. Another full day and a half or two days of travel," answered Paton as they started to run.

"Time slows down outside the haven. So really, that shortens the travel time?" Temel asked, already panting but keeping up, nonetheless.

"Yes," Paton said to Temel's glitchy form, and they ran in silence.

After only a few minutes, however, Rosella had to stop due to coughing deeply and as violently as she did in front of the emperor. This time, there were small droplets of blood that fell onto the withered grass where she had fallen to her knees. Everyone stopped and went back to her, seeing the small stream of magic come from Akuna from behind Rosella's hood.

"What's that?" Temel shouted. Flitch flinched at the sudden high-pitched voice.

For the second time in two days, Akuna walked onto Rosella's shoulder as smoke flowed like a stream into her nostrils, and Temel's ears perked with her mouth falling agape.

"The Great Wrath..." she said, refusing to tear her eyes away.

"I can't run like this, guys," Rosella managed to choke out. Elaras was on his knees next to her and had his arms loosely wrapped around her.

"We can't use the haven for too long, or Elaras will get wiped out, and if we walk, it'll take too much time," Paton said, almost sounding condescending, but Rosella knew the mission was on top of their mind.

"She can't run. That's that. Got any other ideas?" Elaras said sternly. Rosella had to put a hand on his arm to help calm his breathing.

The smoke was still flowing from Akuna to Rosella when she saw the magic stream break. Something from behind disturbed the air, and Rosella looked around her and the group. Flitch and Paton caught on quickly and palmed their weapons. Elaras helped Rosella stand up. Akuna, surprisingly, stayed on her shoulder and dug his claws into the leather on her shoulder, snarling at the air around them.

Thunk.

An arrow flew right in front of Rosella's face, the feathers making a small cut on her nose as it landed in a tree to her right. Rosella grabbed her bow and nocked an arrow, scanning the forest for anything out of place. Out of the corner of her eye, Flitch threw a dagger so quickly that she only saw where it landed, right in the eye of someone in purple and black-leathered armor with a full moon on the coat of arms.

Footsteps sounded all around them in the trees, surrounding her party as they closed in with daggers in hand and nocked bows. The first archer Rosella managed to see got shot square in the throat with Rosella's arrow and through the back of the neck, and before their body fell, she had nocked another arrow.

Elaras was standing with his back to hers, and someone came and tried to jump onto him, blades skidding off each other as they danced. It did not take long for Elaras to have the upper hand, and he stabbed his opponent through a split in their armor in their torso. Rosella's eyes caught on to someone that was running up to the distracted Paton, and Rosella released an arrow that landed inside and through the assailant's open mouth, cutting their battle cry short.

Four more assailants surrounded them, and one was now rushing toward Rosella, so she nocked an arrow and let it fly despite the close proximity. The arrow tore through the armor and landed in the grass behind the attacker, blood and shredded guts spilling into the grass as the attacker fell face-first, dead.

Another attacker managed to get on top of Flitch and raised their dagger in the air, but Rosella released another arrow, and it sliced the attacker's tendons, the dagger falling with a gentle clatter in the grass.

A loud growl sounded from where Paton and Temel once were, but before Rosella could look toward them, a towering and monstrous creature barreled through and tore the attacker off Flitch. When the attacker was pinned down, the creature tore and shred the armor and skin of the person, a husk left in a heap.

Rosella was about to nock an arrow to shoot the creature, afraid it would attack her group, but then she realized that this creature was wearing solid black *armor*. Not just that, but they were wearing a cloak, and neither Flitch nor Temel reacted to the creature tearing apart the person.

When the creature seemed satisfied, they turned around, teeth bared, and growled. That was when she noticed it—the creature had metal teeth.

"*Paton*?" Elaras gasped out, and Rosella knew that he had come to the same conclusion as she did.

The form Paton was in was remarkably like a prehistoric sabertooth tiger, their teeth sticking out past the lower jaw and muscles large and bulky. Paton's brown fur bristled at the hackles and vibrated with every heavy breath they took. They roared so loud that nearby birds took flight, and Rosella had to cover her ears.

The last two attackers rushed Paton with daggers palmed and screaming war cries. Paton swiftly took one of the Moonshadow attackers by the head with their jaws and flung the body toward the second attacker. When the second attacker struggled to get up, Paton pounced on top of them and tore their chest open in a quick motion that blurred in Rosella's vision.

Once their heart flew to land next to the lifeless body of the first attacker, Paton gave a deep huff and dug their claws into the dirt. Slowly, their breathing regulated, and they started to transform back to their normal size and shape, a regular felinette. They heaved a few heavy breaths and walked over to Temel's unscathed open arms.

"That's so sick, Paton! Is it that stone you have that gives you that power?" Rosella asked while putting her bow on her back.

"Yeah, I don't use it often, but it's pretty cool. Family heirloom," Paton said through haggard breaths but smiled widely, covered in blood.

Rosella grinned, and she turned toward Elaras, who stowed his daggers.

"The Moonshadow spies must know our route. This is about to get much harder to travel," Flitch said, almost as if the conversation never ended earlier or got interrupted, despite the numerous bodies that now lay around them. Flitch was also covered in blood, adding more to his clothes as he wiped his blades on his legs.

Rosella couldn't help but agree, feeling stress build up in her head. A groan vibrated through her ears, and she looked at Akuna, who had not moved from her shoulder.

"What, tiny lizard?" Rosella asked with a smirk, and Akuna gave her a side-eye that made Rosella chuckle.

"We'll fly there," Akuna said.

Everyone froze and stared at him.

"Wait, fly? People don't 'fly' on dragons. We avoid dragons as much as possible," Flitch said, his eyes locked on Akuna.

"Are you serious? What if we fall?" Temel asked warily.

"Yeah, how will we stay on?" Paton asked, piggybacking off Temel's question.

"Oh, gods..." Elaras said, staring up at the sky with fear in his eyes and running a hand through his now loose hair.

"Fuck yeah, dragon riders!" Rosella exclaimed. "Wait, we'll need goggles and a saddle! That way we can stay on!"

Everyone regarded her with exasperation and confusion. Akuna laughed and flew off Rosella's shoulder and toward a clearing in the batch of trees.

"At least someone is excited," Akuna said as he landed in a large clearing nearby.

Rosella followed, quickly pulling out her phone and pulling up a photo of a time she went skydiving and wore goggles. Akuna examined the photo for a moment, and he blew purple smoke on the ground. Before her were five pairs of goggles, and she handed one to each of them, showing them how to adjust the sides and how to wear them. Once those were situated on everyone's faces, Akuna blew out a large plume of smoke that surrounded his whole body.

His purple smoke grew larger and larger, and Rosella could tell that Akuna was growing bigger than she had ever seen him be. Akuna grew so large that only one foot was now able to fit into the clearing, and nearby they could hear crashing and snapping trees as he had to adjust and place himself on top of them. Birds and wildlife flew in opposite directions to avoid being crushed by Akuna's feet. His bright red claws were now a foot taller than her, and everyone had to crane their necks to even see his elbow. His white scales shone brightly in the sun, and they almost looked invisible against the sky above as they blended in. There were parts of him that looked unfamiliar to her; the size and quantity of the horns on his head were different than she had seen, and his body was riddled with more scars than she saw before.

"Is this your true form, your true size?" she asked just him. He moved his mountainous-sized head into the clearing and her eyes began scanning his two large horns that curved backward. As the horns stretched back, pieces like large thorns protruded out and curved with the larger piece of horn. The other two horns that poked out beneath the two larger horns also grew in size, but these curved out and away from his neck, making it so that they were parallel with his jaws. The frills showed more holes than before, and they fluttered in the wind along with the hair that lined the back of his head.

He spread his four wings out, casting giant dark shadows on the trees and onto the group themselves. His wings were bigger than she could comprehend, as when he stretched them, she could not see his wing thumb through the treetops. This form seemed extremely natural for him, and if he looked scary to others before, then that did not compare to how he looked now. He moved slowly due to his size, and the rumble of his lungs breathing shook the ground. This face was sharp and his scales told a thousand stories.

This was the Great Wrath of Dorthos.

"Yes," Akuna said defiantly.

"You're cuter in your tiny form," Rosella quipped, admitting to herself that if Akuna was not on her side, she would be scared shitless of him.

Deep and quaking laughter issued from Akuna's chest, and while his face remained reptilian and terrifying, the way he opened his jaws to laugh was the same as any other time that he had in the past. Rosella's heart swelled in appreciation of not just Akuna himself, but of the meaning of this moment with him.

"Climb," Akuna said when he was finished laughing, and his vocal voice was extremely deep and powerful, his voice rumbling the ground and trees as they moved forward to his foot.

"You're bigger than before, like the biggest creature I've ever seen!" Elaras said as he started to climb on Akuna's kneeling arm after Rosella, making the slope easier to ascend.

"Bigger wings, faster speed," Akuna said as the others situated themselves along his back.

Akuna was so wide, there was no possible way to wrap their legs around his body. Each person had to wrap themselves around a red spine spike, not dissimilar to wrapping their arms around a tree. Once everyone was secure between his wings, Akuna turned his head and blew purple magic onto all of them. What felt like invisible straps wrapped around their legs and torsos, and Rosella felt completely secure and much more confident about this ride.

"So you don't fall," he reassured. Rosella heard soft exhales of stress being released from her companions.

Akuna pointed his head to the sky and dipped his body, crouching his legs to help himself launch into the air, his wings pushing him up with a great force. Rosella's body felt like her stomach dropped from under her as he flung himself into the air, but the feeling of flying made her scream with delight. She became incredibly giddy, and everything else that was in the world remained on the ground, because in the air and riding on a dragon that was now her best friend was the best feeling on Earth or Dorthos.

36
Strawberry Snowflakes

__Thirty years earlier__

High Cleric Vannan Daldrack stood in the Elyphr chapel within the Nocturnal Manor with the entirety of the Nightstone family. The two youngest children, twins Talus and Calus, were held in the arms of their parents Prince Kildo and Princess Jukio, sound asleep and unaware of their surroundings. King Raynne and Queen Kayline stood by Kildo and Jukio's side, all anxiously awaiting for the inevitable blessing of the Goddess Elyphr to take place. The sacred ceremony for all Nightstone children and wedded spouses took place to receive a night stone from the goddess herself, and Talus and Calus had come of age to receive their own.

Before the stone ceremony could take place, several other smaller ceremonies had to happen: A water pouring to ask the water gods to protect the waters and rain of Arja, dirt rubbed in a crescent moon on their foreheads to show the gods of the earthly soil and rocks in the ground they stood on to remain healthy and viable, a cutting of hair burned to sacrifice a part of themselves to the fire and sun gods to appease them, and a holding of the nose and mouth for thirty seconds to signify to the gods of air that air was precious and shall be clean.

The twins did splendidly per Varran's eyes, and all that awaited the twins was the final blessing from Elyphr, the goddess of night. They had waited close to an hour for this blessing, and it was Prince Pirkac, the youngest of the king and queen, that was the first to speak.

"We have never had to wait this long for her. Is that correct, High Cleric?" he asked, walking over to Varran.

Varran looked up and saw there were lines of worry on Pirkac's face, and he looked around to see that every Nightstone family member wore the same expression.

"Yes, it is a little concerning. Gods and goddesses should not be rushed. Though, right now it seems to be a bit odd to have to wait long," Varran said, doing his best to not let his own worry dip into his voice.

"What was the longest you have had to wait for a blessing?" Pirkac asked, squatting next to Varran and rubbing his fingers to his forehead, his long black hair falling into his light green face.

"Ten minutes," Varran said shortly, letting out a stressed but quiet breath.

Pirkac looked up, and the worry that was once there was replaced with shock and surprise. "Ten minutes? Something has to be wrong. Maybe we didn't do something correctly. I remember Trusk's took a second but that was because he kept scratching Grancious' hands while he held his breath. Talus and Calus were good today. They were easy," Pirkac said, standing up and pacing in front of Varran.

"We have to remain calm, Prince Pirkac. We cannot let our

emotions get the best of us," Varran said, trying to sound strong. His nerves were getting to him. His goddess never wavered or made him or the Nightstones wait before. Varran could not help but agree with the young prince that something was wrong.

"Talk to her, then! See what's up!" Pirkac urged quietly, getting close to Varran's space to talk to him.

Varran sighed and turned away from Pirkac, looking to the Elyphr altar that towered over the group. *"Goddess of Night, please hear me. The family worries, and I must provide answers. They anxiously await your blessing and grow concerned for your absence. Please give a sign or word so I may ease their troubles,"* Varran said in his head, staring at the altar and raising a hand in the air, grasping his necklace with his other hand, which had the symbol for Elyphr on it. He held tight to the crescent moon, five stars, and clouds charm as he prayed, and his fingers dug into the corners of the stars as he concentrated, listening for anything from the goddess.

Instead of a voice ringing in his ears or a bright light shining from the altar itself, the necklace he held grew intensely hot, and Varran had to let go. He hastened to heal the surprisingly deep burn to his hand, and he opened his eyes to look at the altar once more, and pure horror that he never felt before consumed his body whole.

The altar, which was a statue of the Goddess Elyphr, had red liquid starkly similar to blood pouring from their eyes. The blood streamed so quickly and heavily that within moments the statue was completely covered in the bright red liquid, the excess pooling onto the ground.

The rest of the Nightstones seemed to have noticed too as screams of terror filled the room, and they congregated around the High Cleric.

"What does that mean?" Princess Luvu asked, choking out the words as she stared at the statue with her family and Varran.

Varran, having only read this in books and scrolls during his study, knew that this sign had only one possible meaning: death was upon them.

Almost as quickly as Varran came to the horrifying conclusion, a loud explosion sounded from the adjoining room, which happened to be the throne room. The Nightstones, except for King Raynne and Princess Mystrias, screamed and grouped together around Varran, looking in the direction of the sound.

Varran saw from the far windows a sheen of orange and red magic cover the stained-glass panes. Panic filled his lungs as he broke apart from the group, and he was met with cries of fear and hands reaching out to him.

"No, don't leave us!" Princess Jukio said, still holding a sleeping Calus.

"What if those are intruders? We can't fight against them with our children here!" Prince Kildo said while holding the other twin, Talus.

"Let him go and see what the commotion is about, children. All the guards are out there and will take care of the intruders, but our High Cleric needs to get a status report," Queen Kayline said, Varran hearing the familiar sound of her trying to sound reassuring.

"Then send a sparrow! We can only do so much here by ourselves with our children!" Prince Pirkac said, and Varran felt a pang of worry cross himself.

"What about Akuna, where is he? Can we call out to him?" cried Prince Asterion, who was holding tightly to Princess Mystrias' hand.

"The guards will be too busy to send a sparrow, but I will wait here with you all. Akuna is away, too far for us to call for him,"

Varran said, and as he finished, another loud explosion sound came from outside the chapel door. The older grandchildren, Princess Rebra, Princess Brestia, and Prince Trusk, immediately screamed and hid behind their parents' legs.

Without explanation, a red hue flooded Varran's vision, and his muscles grew rigid. His vision tunneled, and his mind grew quiet.

"Come outside. You will be safe. Leave the chapel," said a voice in the emptiness of his mind, and he obediently walked away from the Nightstone family and toward the door.

"Where are you going? You just said you would stay here! High Cleric!" sounded a voice in his ears that was so distant he could not make out who it came from.

Hands, several hands, grabbed onto him and started to pull him back, but the force that tugged him toward the doors was too powerful, too strong. Varran ripped out of their hands with ease, and he continued his path to the door without saying a word.

"That's it. Come closer, and come through the door," the voice said once more, and Varran quickened his step toward it through the long room.

"He's being controlled and we will not be able to break him out. We must act now, or all will fall, and we will not be able to live past this day. Come, family," came a strong, stoic voice from behind Varran.

Despite Varran being under the gaze of someone unseen and not having control of his body or mind, his skin prickled, and shockwaves ran over his skin. A loud chanting filled the room, and a flash of rainbow light from behind him blinded his sight for a moment as he stepped to the chapel's door. After the light dissipated, there were scuffling footsteps, and a door, one that led to the adjoining throne room by the sound of it, opened and closed after the footsteps died away. Without turning around to see what had happened, Varran went into the hallway.

"Good. Now go stand outside the throne room doors until I release you. There will be no need to talk or move," the voice said for the final time.

Varran walked to the grand double doors to the throne room and saw that they were being held locked by wood planks through the handles. He stood obediently outside them, head as empty as when the red hue first took over and muscles as relaxed as ever under the gripping control. No other living soul walked into the hallway where he stood, and he heard no other noises. No distant voices, no scuffing of feet or soft footsteps, no weapons clashing or explosions. Simple silence filled his ears.

Within minutes, screams beyond dreams or nightmares tore through the air from the room behind the doors he stood in front of. Pain and agony drenched his bones and his soul as he listened to the sounds of terror, the sounds of children crying for their parents, screams for a savior. The red hue still held strong as minutes passed, the screams not fading or letting up. The sounds only grew more intense when crashing sounds of furniture shattering and windows breaking open erupted in the air.

Hands pounded on the door behind Varran, the voices of the remaining Nighstones calling his name, calling for High Paladin Joss, for anyone, through the locked doors. Shortly after this, the sounds of fists and yelling faded. Metal hitting stone, then a distant explosion, were the last sounds Varran heard before the air quieted and grew heavy.

The world was silent once more, deafening and thundering heartbeats ringing in Varran's ears and mind. The red hue held for quite some time after the silence filled the air, and Varran could feel tears roll down his face. He needed to see what happened, needed to see who was alive in that room.

Soon, the orange and red magic that covered the windows faded along with the red hue in his vision. Varran crumbled to his knees, terror filling his eyes with burning tears as he sat on his hands and knees, the Elyphr necklace swinging back and forth from his heaving breaths.

Running footsteps, so many footsteps, came charging at him, and he saw shadows stand over his small and weakened form.

"High Cleric, what happened?" said a guard in a panicked tone.

He did not know the name of this guard, nor did he look up to see who spoke.

"High Cleric, we were all controlled, a red hue covering our visions. Were you controlled too?" came the familiar voice of the newly appointed Paladin, Gerrart Hamstrug.

Large footsteps approached him, and he saw the ornate pommel of a large weapon strike the ground. The shadow that was attached to the weapon grew larger as the person leaned down to him, trying their best to be face to face with Varran.

"Varran, is the family in the throne room?" came the unnusally soft, quizzical voice of High Paladin Joss.

All Varran could do was nod in response, and a heavy, worried sigh from Joss filled the air around Varran's body.

"Wait, they're in there? Why didn't you go in?" said another guard, and he recognized this voice to be Lucious, a long-time guard for the Nightstones.

"Because he was controlled too. We know that if he was with the family, they would have been protected," Joss' voice came, harsh and sharp towards Lucious.

Lucious seemed to take a few steps back because there was a sudden shuffle of footsteps, and Joss turned back toward Varran.

"You know what we need to do, Varran," he said quietly.

Varran took heaving breaths of air before holding out a hand so Joss could help him up. He straightened his armored skirt out and faced the door, tears still blinding him.

"Joss..." Varran said, standing and facing the wood of the doors, and his voice cracked uncharacteristically.

At this, Joss immediately turned around to address the guards and the Paladin.

"Gerrart, take the guards and inspect the rest of the manor. See where the intruders came from and see if you find anything odd. Do not come into the throne room or into the chapel until I give the word. Understood?"

Gerrart tapped the pommel of his war axe into the ground twice and turned to the rest of the guards, giving out orders for separate groups to investigate different parts of the manor. Varran waited patiently for all of the guards to leave, and when the footsteps receded far enough, he felt a large, strong hand clasp his shoulder.

"What awaits us in there, Varran?"

Varran took his time before answering. He wiped away tears and puffed out his chest slightly before saying with a mournful tone, "Carnage."

Joss nodded, and he took his hand off Varran. He lifted the wood planks off the door handles. Varran's heart raced as Joss reached for the handles, afraid of what would be seen once the doors were even cracked open.

The next hour was burned deeply into his mind with sheer clarity. The smell upon opening the door was putrid and sharp, metallic liquid burning the inside of his nose and lungs. Blood and guts effortlessly covered every inch of the walls, floors, and broken furniture. Three of the Nightstones were slumped against the doors, and their bodies fell lifelessly when the doors were swung open. Some family members' skulls were caved in or crushed completely, some had large gashes that split bodies apart and wide open, and one was stuck through a broken piece of furniture like a pig on a spit for display.

Varran took in everything he could, stepping carefully around each body he came across, noting who was where and what happened to them. A few bodies, including a few of the children, were so mangled that he could not determine who they were, and this was beginning to break every aspect of who he was.

Had his god warned him, or had his god failed him?

"Where is the throne?" Joss asked, but Varran could not speak, frozen by terror and misery.

The Astral Throne that was supposed to be at the end of the room was gone, only leaving an imprint of where the throne had sat for over two thousand years. As if he had been seated at the throne before his death, King Raynne's decapitated body lay slumped over with blood covering his lavish and ceremonial robes. The queen's chair on the left lay in splinters upon the ground with the lifeless queen lying next to it.

Varran silently stared at the empty space, his heart pounding painfully against his ribs.

"Varran, we are missing someone," Joss said some time later, breaking Varran's train of thought and shocking his shaken system.

Varran looked up at Joss and furrowed his brows at him. "Who?" Varran asked, concern filling his chest.

"I'm not sure, but the...body count is off. There are only fourteen; there should be fifteen," Joss said, and Varran immediately grimaced at the words.

That was what the Nightstone family had simply come to —bodies.

"Let's keep looking, and we'll figure out who is missing soon," Varran choked out, turning back to the carnage before him. The rainbow light and the chanting flashed in his mind again, and he grew curious if that moment had something to do with the missing Nightstone's disappearance.

As he gazed further at the bodies, he saw none of the Nightstones were wearing their night stone jewelry. Where had they gone? Were they stolen by the intruders? Did they take the throne as well, seeing as the throne itself was made of night stone? He started walking towards its original place through the blood, examining the ground for chipped stone and for the jewelry the stones resided in. He walked all the way to the trapdoor that was usually hidden behind the throne and saw no jewelry, but instead saw something that shocked his system again.

Death to the Nightstones. Long live the Rockshires!

The note was written in blood on the trapdoor, and when he opened it, he saw that the tunnel below was completely caved in. He had never heard of the Rockshires before this, nor was he aware of anyone at all becoming enemies to the Nightstones themselves. He let the trapdoor fall as he stood there, frozen and breathing heavily.

The Nightstones were dead, and there was nothing he could do.

The Goddess Elyphr remained silent.

37
Sometimes the Dreamers Wake Up

**Thirty years later—Present Day**

High Cleric Varran stood guard at the front entry with a few Queens Guards and Paladin Gerrart. He, along with all of Nocturnal Manor, were aware that Kaine Moonshadow and Lycilla Rockshire were on the way to claim the throne as their own. This time, he and the Nightstone staff were ready to face them both.

Mellis took the time to make Rion aware of what was going on by sending members of staff door-to-door with Ruler Beldris, warning them so they could leave to Ye' Ol' Daltorys if they had children or elderly. No one was sure if there would be a battle, but considering what Kaine and Lycilla did to Rosella, no chances were being taken this time.

In the next day or so, Rosella would arrive with Elaras, Paton, Flitch, and Akuna, and who knew what would happen when Kaine saw Rosella alive. It was later in the afternoon when High Paladin

Joss came up to Varran with a bowl of thick chicken soup and a slice of bread.

"You need to eat. You have been standing here for a while," Joss said, forcing the bowl into Varran's hands.

Varran took it despite only feeling knots in his stomach. "I've only been standing here an hour or so. I need to be ready for Kaine to show up, whenever that will be," Varran said, looking to the windows above the grand doors of the front entry of the manor.

"Honestly, I thought he would have been here by now!" Joss said, laughing amusedly.

"Agreed. It's been the better part of a day since the attempt on Rosella, so what is the hold up?" Varran wondered out loud.

Almost as if the gods were listening to their words, rhythmic sounds came from outside. Hooves and boots were marching on the cobblestone outside the doors, and a nearby guard took the uneaten soup from Varran and set it on a nearby table.

"*Arms*!" Joss yelled, followed by rushed footsteps and clattering metal echoing simultaneously around the manor.

Guards were heard moving to their posts, and a few more hurried into the entryway to stand behind Joss and Varran. After a few minutes, the hooves and boots stopped and settled, leaving the air quiet with only deep, anticipative breaths from everyone inside.

They did not have to wait long as within minutes there was polite knocking on the front doors. The two guards on either side of the frames looked to Varran and Joss for permission, and both of them nodded toward the guards. When the doors swung open, only two people stood on the steps: Kaine Moonshadow and Lycilla Rockshire.

Behind them, however, was a small army of people wearing purple and black armor wielding swords, spears, or bows. A six-horse drawn extravagant carriage was also behind them with piles of luggage, the horses periodically shaking their heads. Pure disappointment crossed Kaine's face when he made eye contact with both Varran and Joss, and he took a step forward before the threshold of the manor.

"Ah, High Cleric Daldrack, what an unpleasant surprise it is to see you," Kaine said with a sneer.

Varran smiled widely, remembering that Kaine had tried to kill him using the Nightstone staff with his mind control.

"Yes, and it is unpleasant to see you here on our doorstep. I hope you're not here thinking that you can take the throne? Oh, wait, that permission was revoked. Did you not hear, Kaine?" Varran taunted. Mellis had come to him early in the morning with a letter from Ladroth that explained what had happened with the emperor but did not give great detail.

Kaine's face grew dark as the words sunk in, his stature growing more rigid. Lycilla was unmistakably still under Kaine's control because she did not react to this news, and Varran wondered how her state of mind would be after so long under someone's influence.

"How?" Kaine bit out, and Varran's smile grew wide.

"He was...*convinced*...by another party," Varran said with his own sneer. While he had to admit that he was unsure if Akuna had done anything to help persuade the emperor to change his mind, Varran guessed that he had. Ladroth had still not been made aware of Akuna's presence as there was no mention of a dragon present with the emperor.

"Convinced? By whom? The throne is *ours*, and you will not take it away from me! We will force it from your hands even if we have to burn this manor down!" Kaine yelled.

Varran saw the small army advance, palming their weapons, yet Varran did not waver from his spot.

"You could try, but then you would have no manor to rule from," Varran said, smiling and shrugging.

"I will build on top of the ruins of this home, on top of all the history of the Nightstones and make one anew! I will bury you and everyone in this place to set the foundation of *my* dynasty!" Kaine yelled more furiously now, slowly taking steps forward. His army followed suit and approached the steps of the manor, leaving Lycilla where she stood.

"You could try, certainly, but you won't get far," Varran said.

Joss chuckled deeply, which made Kaine's eyes flare wide.

"Do not laugh at me, orc!" Kaine shouted, pointing his finger up at Joss.

At this, Joss and Varran stepped forward just a few feet from the doorframe of the manor, smiling and composed.

"I'll laugh if I want to laugh at you, puny, pathetic elf man!" Joss said.

Kaine, who had enough, twisted his fingers, and orange smoke spilled out of his fingers as his hands shook with anger. "We'll see who is laughing when you two are done killing each other!"

The magic shot out and stopped just short of their chests before it bounced back and floated aimlessly in the air. Seeing Kaine's wide eyes and slumped shoulders, Joss laughed as hard as ever, having to hold onto his war hammer to stay upright.

"Like I said, puny and pathetic!" Joss said through fits of laughter, and Varran couldn't help but chuckle.

By this point, citizens of Rion had started to gather on the other side of the carriage and were watching intently. There were easily a few hundred people watching on, and Varran was thankful to not see any children or elderly among the crowd. Most of the faces he saw were familiar, and seeing them only made him worried for their safety.

"How?" Kaine demanded, his hair growing wilder with the

trembling his body was doing. Admittedly Varran thought it was entertaining to watch a man like Kaine lose composure like this. As he was admiring the thought and basking in the satisfaction of Kaine's frustration, loud hoofed footsteps could be heard from behind Varran.

"Simple, Kaine. Black tourmaline, coated in minotaurus blood for extra measure," came the deep voice of Tordias. He was now wearing blue and black armor that matched all of the guards at Nocturnal Manor, accessorized by an expression of deep satisfaction. He was wielding a massive morningstar maul in one hand and a shield in the other, walking menacingly toward Varran and Joss to stand next to them.

Kaine's eyes flooded with malice as he closed the distance quickly.

"Tordias! You filthy c—" Kaine was shouting before he was cut short from running into and being pushed back by the invisible barrier in front of him. His skin and clothing sizzled and smoked as he tried to adjust himself, looking at the door then up to the windows around him that he could see.

An hour before taking his post, Varran had finished the extensive and meticulous shield that encased the entire castle and all of its entry points. Only residents of this manor and those associated with the Nightstones were allowed to pass, and only those that were inside the shielding could see the barrier. The entirety of the time Kaine was speaking to Varran, Joss, and Tordias, the three of them were looking at a sheer, shimmering wall made of white smoke, knowing they were protected. Kaine, realizing this, was at a loss for words as his army helped him to his feet and were trying to put out the sizzling skin and burns of their leader.

"You see, Kaine, we learn from history. Perhaps that is something you should learn how to do? You cannot make the future your own without learning of the past first. Here, at Nocturnal Manor, one thing stays the same," Varran said as he stepped within a few inches of the barrier. "A Nightstone will always be on Arja's throne."

Right as Kaine was about to approach the barrier again, a loud ground-trembling roar echoed throughout the air above them. Everyone turned in the direction of the sound, and as they looked up, many of the townspeople screamed and pointed at whatever was approaching.

Varran and those behind him were unable to see what was coming, but Varran had a good idea of who it was.

Kaine's men started to yell too, and Lycilla, surprisingly, could be seen shaking. The control over her must be fading as Kaine was losing his own self-control, and part of Varran wanted to release her from his grasp, but he did not trust her to not do something when she was given control of her body and mind back.

Many people in the crowd that had gathered backed up, eyes still in a trance on the sky, and Kaine's face went from shocked to furious as a massive shadow cast itself over the whole area. Large gusts of wind blew the leaves off nearby trees and made the plumes of the Moonshadow army's helmets dance in a crazy manner. The horses of the carriage that had a lone guard at the driver's seat were startled, rattling their harnesses and bridles with frequent agitation. When the shadow grew bigger and the wind picked up, the horses bolted away, taking the driver and the carriage along with it.

"Akuna?" Joss asked Varran quietly.

"I believe so," Varran agreed, and he could feel Tordias' palpable confusion and slight terror filling the air. "A dragon that is associated with the family," Varran said to Tordias, and the minotaurus' eyes grew wide, but he nodded and kept peering out the doorway.

The ground quaked and rumbled as something heavy landed upon it, and another roar issued from the creature assumed to be Akuna as well as screams echoing from the citizens and the army. The paintings vibrated, the chandeliers shook violently from their chains, and the uneaten bowl of Mellis' soup tipped and fell to the ground. The three of them had to hold their hands to their ears due to the volume.

A minute or so after the roar, a voice cut through the frightened silence, and Varran was pleasantly happy to hear that it was familiar and strong.

"My name is Rosella Nightstone, and I am to be your new queen of Arja."

38
As You Can See, I Am Not Dead

A few long hours with wind-burn and tired limbs later, Rosella felt Akuna start to lower in altitude. In the far distance, the Nocturnal Manor could be seen as a speck that rose sky-high among the other buildings and trees in Rion. Warmth and anticipation filled her chest when she saw the manor as she was excited to be back in a familiar place, but also worried what the next hour held if Kaine and Lycilla were there. She was glad she and her group wore armor and had scarves to help ease the pain of the wind-burn, but the wind was still harsh as it traveled through the small openings and around the goggles.

"Do you all remember the plan?" Akuna's boisterous voice said to the group.

A general sound of assent echoed among the group as Akuna lowered himself further, the manor coming ever closer.

"Are you sure you don't want me to stay with you the entire time?" Elaras yelled from behind her.

While Rosella was having the time of her life riding on Akuna, she could tell Elaras was struggling to enjoy the ride. She turned around to face him as he was attached to the spike behind hers and gave him a confident smile.

"Yes. This is something I need to do myself, and I need to prove myself to the people. I've got this!" she yelled back over the howling wind as she stretched out a hand to him.

He reached as far as he could without tipping over, and they managed to get their fingers to brush lightly.

"Okay, just call me if you need me!" Elaras said, his eyes shifting to the moonstone necklace.

"Kaine's here. We're about to land. Get ready and cover your ears," Akuna called out, and when Rosella turned around, she could now see the manor in its entirety. Shock filled her body as the realization that this was the first time she had seen the manor from the outside. It was far larger than she expected. The length and width seemed to match that of the massive national football stadium in New York Rosella went to once. The black stone masonry looked rough all the way to the spires that adorned all four corners of this manor, each spire with metal rods on their peaks of moons and stars.

Akuna launched downward, and smaller details came into view: an ornate purple and black carriage with black horses attached, citizens gathering around the front of the black manor, and a few people in reflective armor standing on the steps.

The group covered their ears. Right after they did so, Akuna roared voraciously. The air around them shook and his neck vibrated so violently that if he had not cast magic to keep them on his back, Rosella was sure they would have fallen off. Within a few minutes, they were extremely close to the ground, and he had slowed down tremendously, his four wings flapping to lower himself.

As this happened, Elaras climbed forward unsteadily and popped his haven around him and Rosella. Confused, she turned to him and was about to ask what he was doing until he pulled down her scarf and grabbed her waist, his lips crashing into hers. He kissed her deeply and passionately, his other hand running through her hair and holding on tightly. Sooner than she would have liked, he let go of her waist and smiled lovingly at her.

"Stay safe, my sweet," he said to her before letting go of her hair and backing away, popping her out of the haven.

When she saw him next, he was between Flitch and Paton, and Paton was holding onto Temel on the same spine spike. Rosella turned around and watched as the people's faces below grew in clarity.

Kaine, who seemed to have been burned by something, stared wide-eyed at her and Akuna, growing ever more furious at the sight. Lycilla remained where she was, her back facing the events that were happening behind her. The small Moonshadow army were staring like their leader, but they wore shocked faces that were full of fear. The citizens were also terrified, many gripping each other, and they were in a trance when Akuna approached.

A few moments later, Akuna landed with a visibly ground-shaking effect, and screams echoed around the area as he roared again. When standing tall, Akuna was double the height of the manor's corner rods, giving her visibility of the rooftop of the gigantic manor.

When he was done roaring, Rosella climbed from her spine spike and walked the length of his neck to his head, grasping the tall spikes for balance. The tips of his splintering horns were extremely sharp, so she navigated around the tips and only touched the flat surfaces. The tips of each horn were as wide as her and only grew in size the further down onto his head she went. Eventually, with what felt like hours instead of half a minute, she was standing between his two towering horns on top of his head. Akuna dropped his head low, giving her a better view of the sight below.

She heard a whirring airy noise and glanced down to see edges of purple magic from Akuna's mouth spilling out and drifting upward. She looked back up to the people below her, and she focused on the citizens in the crowd. Taking her goggles off, pulling her scarf down and putting down her hood, a few of the citizens in front of her let out small gasps of confusion.

"My name is Rosella Nightstone, and I am to be your new queen of Arja," she said, and as she did so, her voice was amplified by Akuna's magic, as if she was holding a microphone.

The crowd below her murmuring, many smiling while others were frozen in place. Some were still scared but their faces lit up the more she spoke.

"I am not of this world, but I am a true Nightstone. I was brought here to save the land of Arja and to bring back the Nightstone line. You may not believe me right now, and that is okay. However, if you are to believe something, it is that *that* woman," Rosella said while pointing at the back of Lycilla, "is not your true queen. Her family, the Rockshires, may have usurped my throne, but she is not worthy or deserving of the Arja throne. Help me, a true Nightstone, stop Kaine Moonshadow and Lycilla Rockshire from taking my throne, and help me bring Rion and Arja back to its original beauty."

Many of the citizens took her at her word and cheered loudly while a few others looked at one another with skepticism. A loud cry of anger struck the air, and everyone turned in the direction of the noise.

Elaras had displaced himself, Paton, Temel, and Flitch off of Akuna during her speech, and while the other three could not be seen, Elaras was standing behind his father. His goggles were off, and the scarf and hood were down, showing himself fully to his father and to the crowd. There was a tight grip around both of Kaine's arms, and Elaras had steadied himself so Kaine could not throw him off.

Varran had come out of the doorway of the manor and was digging through Kaine's pockets in search of the night stone necklace. Joss and surprisingly Tordias followed Varran and were standing guard menacingly, ready to attack any of the Moonshadow army if they decided to save their leader. Within a minute of searching, Varran pulled out the necklace by the chain and held it high in the air.

To Rosella it seemed that the citizens did not need to see the small white speckles on the pendant to know immediately that it was a necklace belonging to a Nightstone family member, as the air became electrified by their excitement. For good measure, Varran handed the necklace to Elaras, switching with Tordias on restraining Kaine.

"That," Rosella said to the crowd below her, "is *my* night stone necklace. Lycilla stole it from me in the darkest of night at my most vulnerable. I was trying to get here, to my new home, when she took it from me. She thought that if she had the stone, she could rule instead. Kaine has been helping her, and in turn he tried to kill me so Lycilla was guaranteed the throne. He had already killed his wife, so what was to stop him from killing me to make his and Lycilla's job easier?" Rosella asked the crowd, her voice ringing through the electrified air. Then she pointed toward the group on the steps, and the crowd of citizens followed her finger obediently.

Elaras went to Lycilla and forced her to turn around to face the crowd, grabbing onto her unblemished right hand. Knowing she would not move unless Kaine released her, he took the chain and wrapped it around her palm like she had done with her left all those weeks ago.

Instantly, the chain started to burn clean through, and the crowd and the Moonshadow army gasped in horror. Within seconds, the chain cut completely through her hand, and Elaras caught the necklace before it could fall to the ground. The top of her hand landed with a *splat,* a charred block onto the ground, and tears were streaming down Lycilla's face though it was still unmoving. Kaine, despite the state he was in, had still kept a firm grip on her.

Elaras held up the necklace triumphantly, then blue magic poured out of his hand and shot through the air toward Rosella, carrying the necklace to her. She caught it effortlessly, and she felt her whole body scream with joy when the necklace came in contact with her skin. Admiring it for only a moment in her fingers, she unclasped the chain and wrapped the necklace around her neck, clasped it closed, and let the pendant fall gently on top of her armor.

The crowd seemed to wait with bated breath, and when enough time passed, they screamed with joy at the sight of her wearing the necklace.

"All hail Queen Rosella!" one member of the town shouted, and soon the rest of the crowd was cheering the same tune.

Rosella's spirits soared at the sound, as this was the moment she knew that her future was solidified.

"*Enough!*" Kaine's voice rang out, and a startling wave of orange smoke soared over the crowd.

At once, everyone in the army and the citizens of Rion became silent and stared at Kaine, awaiting their next instruction.

Akuna swiveled his head and was now mere meters from him, growling deeply, and Rosella had to sink to one knee to keep balance. Kaine, seeing the massive dragon approach him, tried his best to scramble out of Tordias' grasp to escape.

Varran, who seemed to have anticipated Kaine taking control, had his eyes closed and was whispering words of an incantation. When his eyes opened and he opened his palms outward, another wave of singing magic that was white as snow burst from his hands and into the crowd in a bigger radius than Kaine's.

Kaine turned toward Varran and was about to shout at him, but Varran lazily shot a white ball of smoke into Kaine's mouth. Instantly, the crowd cheered wildly as they watched him mouth words with no audible sounds coming out, his charm fading from their faces. Kaine thrashed violently in Tordias' iron grip.

"You see what Kaine's capable of, Rion? Lycilla may be the Rockshire that tried to get my throne, but it was Kaine Moonshadow that orchestrated everything to get her to this point. He is not deserving of any ounce of power, nor is Lycilla. I do not believe that Lycilla is deserving of the harshest punishment, as her mind and body have been taken prisoner by a sadistic, evil man. She will, however, live and learn the error of her ways until she can be trusted by not only me, but by the people of Rion," Rosella said, standing back up and gesturing to Kaine and Lycilla. "Kaine, on the other hand, is not worthy of such kindness and mercy. He cannot be trusted, and he will never be trusted. He will never learn the error of his ways like I believe Lycilla will. Therefore, I order for the lifetime imprisonment of Kaine Moonshadow, for the crimes of murder, attempted murder of a royal-to-be, countless collusion of heinous crimes, and numerous other crimes that I'm sure will come to light after all of this is done."

The crowd cheered even louder.

Below, Elaras had palmed two daggers and was now facing his father eye to eye, and he leaned in to whisper something in his ear. When he backed away, he was inches from his father's face, placing the daggers below his father's chin in a crossed formation.

A flash of orange burst out from Kaine toward Elaras, but Elaras simply tilted his head in response. The black tourmaline worked, and she made a mental note to send a thank you gift to Ladroth the next chance she had.

Elaras leaned in extremely close to him again, Kaine's whole body rigid and tight as he did so. He said something directly to his father's face, and Kaine's face grew wide with fear. At once, Kaine dropped to a knee with Tordias still holding tight, his head drooped and defeat lining his shoulders.

Whatever Elaras said to his father to cause such a reaction, she could not be sure, but she rejoiced in the sight of Kaine kneeling in front of Elaras'. Towering over his father, Elaras still kept the daggers to his chin, but he backed up a foot or two, possibly admiring the view. Tordias was given some sort of tie or rudimentary handcuffs by a guard, and he did not wait to put on the restraints.

The crowd cheered merrily once more as Tordias and another guard roughly grabbed Kaine and started to drag him into the manor and through the barrier. Before crossing the threshold, Varran stopped them and seemed to tell them to bring Kaine to his knees again. They did so, and Varran walked right up to Kaine, now able to see eye to eye. He smacked the heel of his palm onto Kaine's forehead, and white magic burst out and into his face.

Kaine, noticeably and suddenly frustrated, silently yelled as Varran withdrew something from his own pocket and pulled out a long chain with a pendant attached to it. The moment Varran put the necklace around Kaine's neck, Kaine's body involuntarily convulsed for a few seconds, and he passed out in Tordias' and the guard's grasp. They hauled him inside and were out of sight, and Rosella started to relax.

"*What just happened?*" Rosella asked Akuna telepathically.

"*Varran temporarily blocked Kaine from performing magic,*

then placed a copper necklace on Kaine. Copper blocks all magic from exiting the user. Don't worry, he can't take it off," Akuna said jovially.

"Good."

Lycilla fell to her knees by her charred hand. Varran took out a similar necklace to the one he put onto Kaine and laid it gently on Lycilla's neck. Rosella could tell from on top of Akuna's head that Lycilla began crying, her body trembling violently from her sobs. She let out a scream that was loud enough for Rosella to hear from a distance, and it was one of relieving pain and pent-up stress.

The Moonshadow army stood shocked as their leader was dragged to the dungeons, and many of them dropped their weapons. A few of them looked around confused, flexing their fingers and stretching their jaws, and the remaining just stood paralyzed. One soldier broke from the group and bolted towards the direction of the carriage.

Rosella took out her bow, nocked an arrow, and shot at them within a few seconds. The arrow flew and landed in the soldier's leg, causing him to fall and land face-first on the cobblestone road.

"Hm, you truly are a wonderful archer. Maybe leave the daggers to Elaras," Akuna jeered, and Rosella smirked as she lowered her bow.

A cry released from the now injured soldier as Joss walked over to pick him up one-handed to take the him back to the line of the small Moonshadow army, who were now lined up and on their knees.

"I think it's time for me to get down," Rosella said to Akuna telepathically once more, and the whirring noise dissipated.

Akuna lowered his head and laid it flat on the ground so Rosella could slide off his nose. Before going to the crowds, she turned, stood on her toes, and kissed Akuna on his massive, scaly chin. His head was so gigantic that she might as well have kissed a wall because a single scale on his face was half the size of her, and his nose was four times her height. Akuna purred, and she felt the rumbling sensation in her chest through their connection before he blew purple smoke out, surrounding him. Within moments, he shrunk down back to the size of her palm, and she was happy that he had not changed the colors of his scales. He flew up and rubbed his face onto Rosella's cheek before flying off to set himself on Varran's shoulder.

Rosella turned, and instantly the few hundred citizens cheered for her, chanting, "All hail Queen Rosella!" She spent time greeting everyone she could, trying her best to remember names and the people themselves. During this time, she felt the presence of two Queens Guards behind her keeping watch, but they kept a good distance, nonetheless. She thanked the citizens for believing in her, and giving reassurances that she would do her best as their new queen.

After over an hour of this, she turned back to the steps and was thankful to see that the Moonshadow army was gone and that Nightstone guards were picking up the weapons the invading soldiers had deposited.

Lycilla was on her knees between two guards, tears streaming down her cheeks, but she also had a look of relief on her face. Another Cleric was tending to her right hand, casting healing magic onto it to the best of their abilities. Off to the side in the doorway, Elaras stood with Varran, Joss, and Tordias, and they were all grinning at her.

"Welcome home, Queen Rosella," Tordias said, saluting her and bowing his head.

Joss and Varran copied him, and when they raised their heads, Rosella saw that Joss had tears in his eyes.

"Are those tears for me, Joss?" Rosella asked in a cheerful tone while Elaras wrapped an arm around her and kissed the top of her head.

"Yes! I'm so happy this shit is over with and that you can finally be crowned! Varran, a Nightstone on the throne after thirty years! Can you believe it?" Joss said, bumping his fist onto Varran's shoulder, causing the High Cleric to stumble slightly but quickly regaining his composure.

Varran also wiped a tear from his eyes and walked up to Rosella, Akuna resting on his shoulder.

"It truly is amazing, Joss. Sometimes it's hard to comprehend that this is our reality, and that a Nightstone is home again," Varran said. He took Rosella's hand, dipped his head down, and pressed the back of her hand to his forehead. "Thank you, Rosella Nightstone."

When Varran raised his head, she gently took her hand out of his grasp and wrapped her arms around him in a deep embrace. Elaras and Joss followed suit with Rosella, all of them hugging and squeezing each other while Tordias looked on, unsure of what to do. Akuna, not wanting to be squished, flew above them and landed on top of Rosella's head. When they finally broke apart, everyone had tears in their eyes as they walked inside the manor.

39

Conquerors Giveth, Parasites Taketh

The song "Take It All" by Sawyer Fredricks filled the air, waking
Rosella from her deep slumber. When she opened her eyes, she
saw that Elaras was playing the music from her phone while next
to her on the bed. Ever since her group came back to Nocturnal
Manor almost two weeks ago, Elaras had stayed in Rosella's room
every day and had hardly left her side. Normally she would get
annoyed by such clinginess, but right now she was thankful.

Almost every night since that one stay in the capital had been
difficult for both of them, occasionally waking up from nightmares
or simply crying from the few minutes of mindless racing
thoughts that plagued them before falling asleep. She loved him,
and he loved her, and all they needed right now was to be with
each other to help wherever they could. What calmed her during
their time of healing and adjusting to their new life was that one
day, without a doubt in her mind, Elaras would be her husband
and in turn become the king consort of Arja. She would not want
anyone else by her side, for the rest of what she had left to

naturally live. For now, though, she was simply elated to listen to him wake her up with music from Earth.

"I love that song," Rosella said groggily, pushing her head back into the pillow and closing her eyes.

Elaras laughed and paused the music. He set the phone down and pulled Rosella to his chest, wrapping his arms tightly around her. "It's almost time for us to get up, my sweet, and you'll need your energy today," Elaras whispered into her hair, stroking her back over her tunic.

She opened her eyes slowly and only saw his tunic-covered chest and his arm wrapped around her shoulders. Today was not going to be a good day and might result in something she had come to despise deeply: blood and death.

Since the confrontation on the Nocturnal Manor entry steps, Kaine was still in the dungeons below the castle, wearing the same copper pendant and chain necklace that Varran had first put on him when he was arrested. She had later learned that along with the blocking magic, the necklace could not be removed until the person that put it on originally removed it, or until the wearer died.

Lycilla, given the same copper necklace as Kaine, was in the dungeons as well. When she was first taken down there after the Clerics did what they could for her hand, she screamed and burst into a pure panic when she saw Kaine in one of the cells. She was put in the other side of the dungeons; she had been silent and had not spoken to anyone. Varran offered his healing powers to her, but she simply sat and stared at the floor as far away from the iron gates as possible.

The Moonshadow soldiers that had been under the control of Kaine were put into the dungeon as well for a few days to adjust. Many of them had been in and out of his control, with a few being under control for months or years at a time. The hope for those that did not wish to serve under Kaine was that they could relax for a few days in a safe, restrained environment, and then the Nocturnal Council would decide what to do with them. Tordias had been helpful in the recuperation of the soldiers, helping them day to day and reminding them that if he could leave the Moonshadow rule, they could too. The soldiers that had not been under Kaine's control were sent to the capital to be prosecuted for their various crimes.

Today was the day that the Nocturnal Council would decide what to do with the groups below the manor. In the back of her mind, Rosella believed that Kaine would not go anywhere quietly, and she feared for those around her when it came time to decide his fate. The others, the soldiers and Lycilla, would more than likely be easier. Her coronation was set for two days from now, and Rosella knew that all of Arja, and possibly all of Dorthos, was waiting for her to take the throne so she could activate the ancient Nightstone magic and heal the land once again.

For now though, at this moment, she wanted to remain in this warm bed with her love.

"I know. Can we just stay here a little longer, please?" Rosella asked weakly, still tired as she stretched out below his arms.

"Ten more minutes. Mellis said they're making their favorite breakfast food, so we need to make an appearance to try it," Elaras whispered, snuggling closer to Rosella and closing his eyes.

"What are they making?"

"Something called pigs and blankets."

"Pigs in a blanket?"

"No, they said pigs and blankets," Elaras said, letting out a deep chuckle that vibrated her body, and she hugged him closer, wrapping her legs around his.

"We'll see, but I'm pretty sure it's supposed to be pigs in a blanket."

Soon enough, Rosella had to rip herself away from Elaras, and after bathing and dressing for the day, she chose a billowing blue and white dress embroidered with stars and moons. The dress had long sleeves and was floor-length, swishing with every step she took in satisfying movements, cut right below her collarbones. The belt Rosella had grown accustomed to wearing fit nicely along the skirt seam, the two pouches and Shadow Breaker still residing on it.

Rosella made her way down from her room and toward the kitchen two floors down. Elaras was no longer wearing armor as he followed her out of his room, wearing a white ruffled shirt, long cloak-like jacket that was midnight blue, and dark blue pants with black knee-high boots. Avy and Bebbie seemed to have been making new clothing for him, as all of his clothes before besides his armor were purple or black. Now he had a lot of clothes in different hues of blue, white, and a few in black, and he admitted he enjoyed having new clothes that reflected the life he wanted.

Now as Rosella and Elaras walked the halls to the casual dining area, every person they passed stopped in their tracks and gave the moon salute, bowing their heads in respect towards Rosella. This was still one of the many daily things Rosella had to grow used to just like every other part of her new role. She was thankful that this was something small, seemingly minuscule, though. There were times she had to wrap her head around the fact that they were doing these things and their jobs *for her*, and that alone made her want to be the best queen she could possibly be.

"Our queen and Elaras, just in time! I made a new batch of pigs and blankets!" Mellis called out and saluted as they entered the kitchen.

Varran and Gerrart were sitting at the six-seater table, and Rosella's heart swelled when she saw Akuna at the table with a plate of meat.

"Hello, Mellis! Hello, everyone!" Rosella called out.

Varran and Gerrart immediately stood up to salute and did not sit down until Rosella sat next to Gerrart. Gerrart handed her a few napkins, and gave a sweet smile as she took them.

"Trust me, you'll need these," Gerrart said mischievously.

Rosella's smiled back with a raised eyebrow as Mellis walked right over and dropped a plate of food and a scalding hot black tea with honey in front of her and Elaras. Pancakes with chunks of brown sausage were cooked into the batter, and there was a sheen of sausage grease on the tops of the pancakes. There were also links of sausage on the side that varied from pork to chicken.

Rosella cut a piece of pancake and stuffed it into her mouth, and the taste was magnificent as the salty and savory flavors of the sausage mixed with the sweet and buttery pancakes.

"Fuck, this is good, Mellis," Rosella said in between mouthfuls, and she saw Elaras give a thumbs up in agreement.

"Yay, good, I'm glad you think so, My Queen!" Mellis exclaimed then returned to work.

When all of their food and tea were gone, both Rosella and Elaras sat back in their seats to digest. Gerrart bid them all farewell and returned to his duties, and Varran and Akuna leaned in toward Rosella and Elaras.

"Rosella, are you ready to speak to them today?" Varran asked cautiously, and Rosella felt the food drop painfully in her stomach.

"Yes, we need to, then decide what to do with them," Rosella replied, and before anyone else could reply, loud footfalls could be heard from the hall.

Moments later, Joss strode in and moved to the oversized chair that Gerrart had vacated minutes prior, placing his war hammer against the wall. Mellis swiftly dropped a large plate of food, double the size of Rosella's or Elaras', and he immediately started eating.

"Pigs and blankets, my favorite!" Joss said excitedly, only pausing every few breaths and mouthfuls.

Varran, who must be used to this after many years working with Joss, turned back to Rosella and clasped his hands together on the table. "Speaking with them may be difficult. Would you like me to do the talking?" Varran asked, talking over Joss' munching.

"If need be, yes. However, I think this is something I have to do," Rosella responded with a quivering breath.

Varran gave a simple nod before leaning back in his chair and looking over to Joss. She peeked over to Joss and was surprised to see that he had already cleared his plate and was now sipping on a stein of tea.

"So, shall we go down there, then?" Elaras said after letting out a deep sigh.

Everyone agreed and started to get up, Joss grabbing his propped-up war hammer as they all left the room. Akuna flew up and dove into Rosella's belt pouch as she held open the flap for him.

"*Say the word, and I'll come out,*" Akuna said telepathically, and Rosella smiled.

"*Don't worry, I'll try to not disturb your nap time,*" Rosella replied, and she felt Akuna snort against her hip from inside the pouch.

The group walked down the expansive stairs to the dungeons, and the air around them grew heavy with every step. Once they reached the end of the stairs, Joss walked to the doors of the dungeons and unlocked the hatches. The air that rushed into their faces from the dungeons was musty and dank, just like the many tunnels Rosella had traveled in. This air, though, was heavy with stagnant stenches of prisoners past that could never truly be washed away.

Joss led the group in, and Rosella was surprised to see that the remaining uncontrolled Moonshadow soldiers that awaited transport were near the entrance. As she passed them, a few bowed their heads respectfully with one even saluting, but there were a few that glared daggers into her. A few spaces down were the Moonshadow soldiers that had been controlled by Kaine, and every single one stood up, bowed, and saluted to her. A few even voiced their gratitude towards her and her group, and she smiled and inclined her head in a small bow to them. Not far from this group was Lycilla in a considerably smaller dungeon cell than the groups of soldiers.

Lycilla's cell was orderly and clean, but she herself sat curled up in a disheveled state. Her hair was wild, and her clothes were tattered. Her orange skin looked shallow and pale with a few scabs that hung off or were reopened. Unblinking eyes stared deep into a corner of her cell that were wide and full of fear, her body rocking back and forth in a stemming motion. Her hands were in the worst state; thick black scabs covered what was left of her hands and wrists. The skin itself seemed to crack every time she moved as there was dried blood trickling down both arms. Rosella knew Lycilla had not sought treatment for her hands from Varran, but she did not realize the entire state of her well-being.

"Do you want to talk to her first?" Varran murmured to Rosella, who had stopped in front of Lycilla's cell.

Rosella nodded and took a few steps closer to Lycilla's cell bars, halting inches from the rusted, cold metal. When Rosella stopped, Lycilla's eyes snapped to Rosella's, she ceased rocking. Lycilla's face was grim with no smile or frown, her eyes fearful and yet full of thought, and Rosella could see that her chest was now trembling for breath. Her burnt hands remained motionless in her lap, the thumbs sticking up as if they were burnt into that position.

"Lycilla, please, let my High Cleric heal your hands. I cannot understand what you went through with that monster, but we can at least help you heal physically," Rosella said, slightly pleadingly because she could not imagine the pain Lycilla was going through purely from her hands and lack of fingers.

In a quick motion that shocked Rosella, Lycilla had stood up and rushed to the cell bars, sticking her arms straight through the metal. Rosella had to back up to avoid being hit by her arms, and she felt Joss and Elaras meet her by her side, Elaras grasping her hand in a vise-like grip. To Rosella's surprise, Lycilla teared up, and her face changed from grim to overwhelming sadness.

"Will you really heal my hands?" Lycilla asked Rosella through choking tears.

Rosella looked to Varran and saw his eyebrows were furrowed in concern, but he was slowly stepping forward toward Lycilla.

"Yes, my High Cleric can heal your hands. I don't know the extent of the —"

"*No*, you're *letting* my hands be healed?" Lycilla demanded.

Admittedly confused, Rosella simply nodded. Lycilla broke down crying, falling to her knees and putting her charred hands to her chest.

"I thought we told her you could heal them, and that you had asked to?" Rosella whispered to Varran before he stepped forward to the bars.

He whispered a few words in his soft sing-song voice, the white smoke flowing out of his fingers and into her hands. Slowly, her charred scabs began to fade away, and the skin underneath closed up and healed.

"My guess," Elaras leaned down and whispered, "is that she

waited for *your* direct permission to be healed. Despite Varran's rank, she wanted to hear from you that he could heal her."

Rosella's eyebrows shot up before nodding. Lycilla threatened both her and Elaras' lives, controlled them at their weakest, and yet Rosella could not help but feel pity and empathy for her. Did Kaine hurt her more than what was seen? Through that time, did Lycilla regret her actions and wished to be redeemed? Time would have to tell.

For now, as Varran's quick healing magic ebbed away, Lycilla looked down to her hands and gasped. She was still missing the tops of her hands, but despite that, her hands appeared normal, no redness or scabs to be seen. Lycilla's gaze darted between Varran and Rosella, and she gave a deep bow, her hands on the ground and her forehead and the curves of her horns pressed against the packed dirt.

"Thank you, future Queen Rosella and High Cleric Daldrack" she whimpered, tears and gratitude fueling her words.

"It's our pleasure, Lycilla. Please, get some rest," Rosella said, waiting for Lycilla to get up and to get to her bed.

However, Lycilla stood up and wiped a tear away. "I—I'm sorry, for everything. For trying to take your home, for stealing your necklace, for...for paralyzing you both in the capital. I'm sorry for your brother, Elaras," Lycilla said directly to Elaras before turning back to Rosella. "I have made mistakes, and I was narrow-minded. I wish to be redeemed for my actions, and I will accept whatever punishment you have for me. If you wish to keep me alive, I will serve under you in whatever capacity you wish. I do not have a home, and I had planned to make this manor mine in all the selfish ways one could think of. I know now that was the worst mistake I could have ever made with the little information I knew then. Now, I only have respect for this manor and its occupants, and most importantly for you,

Rosella." Lycilla sniffled but straightened her spine, her body trembling. "To be honest, if I knew you were a Nightstone in that cave and had the information that I know now, I would have aided you on your quest. I thought I wanted the throne because that is what my family wanted, but I was poisoned into believing it belonged to me. Kaine is...a monster, and his words influenced me and Alryo to make the worst choices imaginable. I do hope you can forgive me eventually, and I understand that will take time. Thank you for sparing my life and healing my hands."

Rosella had mixed emotions about Lycilla and her actions, though her words were comforting. There was an air of authenticity around Lycilla's words, and despite her past, Rosella believed that Lycilla could be speaking truth and wished to change herself.

"Thank you, Lycilla, truly. Give me a few days to think, and I'll come back to you," Rosella said to her, and Lycilla bowed her head once more. Rosella turned and walked away further into the dungeons, realizing Elaras still had a tight grip on her hand. She pulled him along with Varran and Joss following suit.

"That was brilliant and weird," Joss said, and everyone chuckled.

"Truly, though I have to admit I'm not looking forward to the next conversation," Varran said, rubbing his hands together and clearing his throat.

"I still believe Spinal Stone will be the best place for that asshole," Joss said, turning down the hallway with everyone else into a darker corridor.

"Spinal Stone? Is that a prison?" Rosella asked, aware that not knowing this simple piece of information made her feel ignorant.

"Yes, it's where the worst prisoners go, and they never leave the island. It's far off the coast of Trihale," Varran informed her in his patient manner.

"What is it with prisons for the worst criminals always in the ocean?" Rosella asked mainly to herself, and she felt Elaras' eyes fall on her in curious confusion. "I'll explain later," she said while shrugging and waving her hand in a dismissive way.

They all approached a line of guards that blocked a closed-off archway. Joss nodded at them, and they separated, one of them opening the door for the group to pass through.

Inside the door was a room that held four cells, and there were only four torches on the walls, making the room darker than the rest of the dungeon. The smell alone made Rosella want to leave as the vile stench of filth and decay was in every pore of the walls, dirt, and even metal. Varran sang a few words, and four balls of light hovered over his hand, and he moved three of them to hover over the left shoulders of Rosella, Elaras, and Joss.

With the added light, Rosella could see that this sectioned-off room was much more unkempt and dirtier compared to the rest of the dungeon. In the far left cell, a curled over figure could be seen, their back rising and falling with each strained breath. As Joss approached, the head lifted, and Kaine's menacing orange eyes landed right on Rosella.

"Come to kill me, *My Queen*? Wish to get payback for what I made your stupid little boyfriend do to you? You should, because I would happily do it again," hissed Kaine, tilting his head as he unraveled his body and stood up.

A deep growl came from Akuna's pouch, and Rosella could feel his anger build.

"Do you wish to be killed, Kaine?" Rosella said, clearly and authoritatively.

"Watching the life drain from you was *marvelous*, and watching my pitiful son dig his dagger into you on *my* command was so satisfying and delicious," Kaine said through gritted teeth, approaching the bars and pressing his face against the space between the metal bars. "To say that I'm disappointed to see you and that brat standing here, alive, would be an understatement. You ruined the sweet taste of victory for me, and you shall now shed my blood to satisfy your own tongue."

"I'm not here to kill you or to satisfy my own needs, Kaine. If you wish to be killed, then that can be arranged," Rosella said, straightening her back. She felt Elaras twitch beside her, and she took a tentative side step in front of him.

"That is your mistake, *Queen,* not having the desire to end my life. If you do not kill me, I'll just come back and kill you again. I will escape whatever place you put me in, and make sure you truly are the last Nightstone to ever live. You see, I will not stop until I get what I want, and I will kill whoever I have to, to do it. You cannot control me!" Kaine yelled, spittle flying. He grabbed the copper necklace and tried with all of his might to wrench it off his body, but the necklace itself did not budge and looked as if it had sewn itself into his skin. He screamed at the top of his lungs as he tried to dig his fingers under the chain but was only left with deep scratches.

"You've lost all of your control, Kaine. The last thing you can have control over is if you wish to die here, or not," Rosella said, growing tired of Kaine's painful words.

Kaine laughed so hard that it looked like the veins in his neck were going to burst. "Kill me, and I will haunt your dreams. Take me to prison, and you will fear for my return," Kaine hissed with such malice that he reminded Rosella of an angry viper.

Elaras bumped into her back, and she held an arm out.

At this, Kaine laughed even louder and directed his gaze toward his eldest son. "Oh, you imbecile child, you don't have the nerve to kill your own father! Your fear of me is what fueled me for years! You would piss your pants before you even drew your dagger at me again. The strength you had the other day was only in your veins because of the fucking dragon. Now? You're nothing and always will be *pathetic*."

"Elaras will be king consort of Arja. He has no reason to fear you now because he will have more power than you will ever see again. You, Kaine Moonshadow," Rosella said, sneering down at his filthy feet then back up to his face, "no longer have any power over anyone, and never will again. You are under *my* control and will be until your demise at Spinal Stone."

Kaine stared at Rosella, and for the first time since they entered this room, he was silent. She let her eyes linger on the now weak and fallen man as she pivoted toward the door and pulled Elaras behind her. Joss banged on the door, and it was promptly opened by a guard. Rosella pulled Elaras out of the room as quickly as possible and moved down the hall to separate themselves from the heaviness that still clung to the air.

Elaras was breathing heavily, downcast, gripping Rosella's hand tighter than ever, but she welcomed it. His body trembled slightly, and his breaths quaked, sweat trickling down his forehead in small beads.

After a few minutes of standing together alone, Elaras finally looked at her. His gray eyes were wide and panicked, lines in his face growing deep, and his eyebrows rose then furrowed. His lips quivered, and he let out small sounds that sounded like the beginnings of a sentence, but the words never formed.

Instead, he let go of her hand and wrapped his arms tightly around her, pulling her into a deep hug. She pushed her arms inside his jacket and stroked his back in soft movements, and she pressed her ear against his heart. She felt his chest quake once in a while with a sniffle between every few breaths, and she knew that he needed this hug more than she could ever fully understand. When Varran and Joss approached after talking to the guards, Rosella squeezed him tightly and took a deep breath.

"Are you going to be okay for now, or would you like time to process everything?" Rosella murmured to Elaras, not letting him go. He stood silent for a minute before loosening his grip and putting her in front of him, his hands in hers.

"We can process this together later?" Elaras asked with a somber smile, his eyes still welling up with tears.

Rosella nodded with a smile and wiped two falling tears off his face. With a thankful smile, he reached down and gave her a quick kiss, pressing his forehead against hers for a moment. Hand in hand, Rosella nodded to Varran, and the group walked out of the dungeon to see what preparations were being made for the coronation.

40

There is a Ghost in My Throne Room

Echoes of the previous day's events rang through her mind as Rosella walked the darkened halls of Nocturnal Manor. Akuna rested on top of her head as she traversed corridors lit with moonlight and torches, the sounds of distant voices and clambering objects bringing life to the air. Rosella and Akuna remained silent, passing guards and servants, all bowing and saluting as she rambled by. The paintings on the walls were filled with many things she had glanced at before, but this time she chose to focus on each and every one that portrayed a Nightstone. They all bore crowns of various sizes and styles, various colors of green skin adorned with a night stone somewhere: rings, bracelets, earrings, or necklaces. One member, a younger light green elf male, had a small stone set into a septum piercing.

Down a far hall on the second floor, a grand portrait with a dark green-skinned elf hung with two candles on each side of the frame. Rosella had not come across this portrait before as it was in a corner, so she stepped closer and examined it. However, within a few seconds of looking at this painting, a heavy weight of familiarity sunk into her stomach. The contentment she felt earlier changed to confusion and shock, forcing a quivering breath into her sore lungs.

Akuna, rumbled his chest as he moved to her shoulder. "Rosella...?" he asked audibly.

She let her mouth fall open in lieu of a response. Her eyes fell to the small plaque that sat below the portrait that read, *Princess Mystrias, eldest child of King Raynne and Queen Kayline.* She looked back up, and she choked on her words. This was impossible. The sight had to be a mistake. Surely there were similarities and not an exact resemblance, right?

"Rosella?" Akuna asked again, digging his claws gently into her shoulder.

"That," came a voice that she knew belonged to Varran, "is exactly who you think it is, Rosella."

She turned to him, watching him approach her quietly and slowly, as if quick movement would scare her off.

"But my mother's name was Olympe, not..." She trailed off, looking at the face of the portrait again.

"Olympe was Mystrias' nickname. I knew the moment you said her name that you were truly and undoubtedly a Nightstone. A princess, no less. The tattoo, the same one that matched our coat of arms, helped, of course, but your mother's name solidified my belief," Varran said, standing next to her and gazing up at the portrait.

"How? She was human—always a human," Rosella stammered.

"Mystrais, your mother, was a shiftling. She must have been in a human form to birth you, thus resulting in your human traits. We, Joss and I, knew a member of the family was missing that dreadful night. After some time, we learned it was Mystrias. Not long before the family was taken from us, they performed a teleportation ritual, and it seems they sent Mystrias to Earth to protect you both," Varran said as calmly as possible, and she was thankful for his soft demeanor. As his words sunk in, she realized what he had said was as if a brick struck her in the head.

"'Protect you both'... Was she pregnant that night?" Rosella asked, looking at him.

"Yes," Varran said. "She had just become pregnant after many years of trying with her husband, Asterion, and elves carry their babies for twenty months before they give birth. So, the timeline matches."

Rosella had to force herself to take a breath. She looked back to the painting, landing on the birthmark that matched those on her mother's face, the beauty marks that sat on her forehead and on her chin. The wavy black hair Rosella knew so well pinned to perfection, the poliosis that reflected Rosella's own fit neatly behind Mystrias'—her mother's—ear. The dark green skin and long, pointed ears were the only difference between Rosella's memory and this portrait of who her mother truly was.

"So, she got out, *shifted* herself into a human, lived for a few decades, only to die of some trivial disease on Earth," Rosella said, her voice wavering and soft.

"She lived to raise you into the woman you are today," Varran said, tentatively placing a hand on her arm.

"Why did it take so long to bring one of us here, then? Why not bring her back after everything happened? Why wait until she was dead, and I was by myself?" Rosella said, feeling a surge of heightened emotion. Rattling off questions in hopes of adequate answers would be the only thing that could help her now.

"Because sending someone somewhere is easier than bringing them back," Akuna said, staring up at Rosella, and she looked back down at him. "Locating you or your mother took years, and focusing on the stone was the only way to get you here.

I had expected your mother to come through when I performed the ritual, but I pulled you instead. I saw the world before I pulled you here to Dorthos and knew you would be worthy of the crown before you even set foot in this land."

"Does that make me a shiftling?" Rosella asked.

Varran squeezed her arm. "I do not believe so. Shiftlings start to show themselves when they are young, and you have yet to transform into anything else, correct? So the likelihood of the genes transferring to you is minimal."

"Thirty years..." Rosella whispered.

"Thirty years and two days from now will be a new beginning, a new era," Akuna said.

"A resurrection of a dynasty," Rosella said. Her hand went to her necklace and grasped it in her palm, hoping somehow to feel her mother's presence in this place. Rosella was the true heir of the throne, and not just by namesake, but by blood.

"Akuna, if you knew, why did you not tell me?" Rosella asked, her voice wavering.

The silence between them was thick, crackling with anticipation.

"Because the time was not right. I wanted to see how you would handle this world on your own, to see your full capabilities," Akuna finally said, and he had the grace to sound sheepish.

Varran grimaced slightly then nodded. He grabbed hold of Elyphr's symbol on his neck and breathed deeply.

"There is something else you should know, Rosella," Akuna said, and Rosella let her eyes drift to his once more. "The bow and quiver I gave you when you first came here belonged to Mystrias. Along with the cuirass, boots, and bracers you were given. I knew of the items well, and knew they were in the manor. So, I teleported them to you in hopes that her presence could be felt and be of comfort."

Rosella grasped the pendant tighter and smiled to herself. In the back of her mind, she *had* felt comfort in the items Akuna had given her. Confirming that those items belonged to her mother brought more comfort and reassurance that she was where she belonged.

"You're lying to me. Are you actually Mystrias' daughter?" Elaras asked, his face and voice not hiding the shock he just received.

"Yeah. I recognized her from her birthmarks," Rosella said, standing up straight and looking toward the grand front entry doors of the manor from a high second-floor landing. The morning air of the next day warmed the manor halls as gentle beams of light poured in from the windows. Two guards stood sentry at the front doors while many house servants were running around completing tasks.

"Your mother was extraordinary. It's no wonder you are too."

"Elaras..." Rosella whispered, her heart fluttering.

"So, you really are the heir to the throne?" Elaras said, gasping slightly.

"Yeah...."

"How does that make you feel?"

Rosella felt her tensed muscles soften when her eyes landed on his kind face. "Honestly? Relieving. Having a shiftling mother that got teleported to save the family line and then me, the daughter, being brought back to take up the throne makes way more sense than some weird multiverse thing."

"Yeah, that's on the list of things you still have to explain to me," Elaras said, pulling out a small notebook and flipping to a page within it, showing her a physical list he had written.

Rosella laughed, leaning into his space. In neat handwriting, the list contained:

- Skydiving
- Red Bull
- Star Wars/Trek/Gate
- The multiverse
- Bubble gum
- Treasure Planet
- Macaroni and cheese

Items that were crossed out were:

- Bombs
- Cars
- Electricity
- Music
- The Oxford comma
- Prisons on islands

"I already explained what mac and cheese was to you!" Rosella laughed, and Elaras gave an exaggerated shrug.

"Yes, but I need to actually try it! It'll be crossed off when it's in my mouth."

"Why are you keeping this list anyways?"

"I need to know *everything* about you, and in turn, you need to know everything about me," Elaras said, stuffing the list away and grabbing her waist to pull her close.

"Tell me something new about you, then," Rosella said softly, tilting her head and giving a shy smile.

Elaras gazed down and held her eyes, matching her smile. "All of my daggers were given to me by my mother, Evanora. She always had a grand taste when it came to weapons, and only chose the best blacksmiths to craft something she wanted. She would give me a new one every year for my birthday, and I've kept them all." He said before he knelt and pulled a sheathed dagger from his boot before saying, "This one is my favorite. See this small fluorite in the pommel? She said she bought it from an elder in the underworld who had mined it herself, though we both take that story with a grain of salt. My mother said that this dagger stabilizes emotions and mental states when wielded but doesn't give off a glow like Shadow Breaker does."

Rosella examined the sheathed dagger and watched as the light danced off the light green fluorite, symmetric layers cutting through the gem. Elaras pulled the dagger out of the sheath slightly, and she saw the blade was a dark matte gray that matched the handle and hilt. The entire dagger looked pristine; the thought of blood ever covering the blade seeming outrageous. There was no question why this was his favorite.

"It's beautiful," Rosella said, staring at the dagger before he put the blade back in his boot. A thought struck her. "Did your mother give you Shadow Breaker?"

"She did, actually, and I believe I'm thinking the same as you are. The emperor knew what Shadow Breaker was and was terrified of it, as he should be. That leaves the question, where did my mother get it?" Elaras pondered, taking some of her hair in his fingers and twirling it.

"Exactly what I was thinking," Rosella said. As she peered down at the front entry, she felt her lungs surge, and a coughing fit erupted from her.

"Rosella! I've got you," Elaras said, pulling her from the balcony's edge.

Within a moment, his blue silky smoke appeared in his hand, and he held it up to her face, the smoke drifting into her nose and down to her lungs. Rosella breathed in the magic like it was pure oxygen and felt her lungs begin to soothe. The pain seeped away, and her coughing ceased. After a minute of feeling normal, she nodded to Elaras. Elaras' healing magic had always been slow in nature, so this time she was surprised to see that the healing did not take as long as past attempts to heal her.

"Did you learn that from Akuna?" Rosella asked, rubbing her chest gently.

"Yes. Akuna said that you may have coughing fits for some time, as the damage was, well, extensive. He tried to tell me where to heal you, but I..." Elaras began to say, looking away as he trailed off.

Rosella placed her hands on his face to make him look at her. "Thank you, my love," Rosella whispered, and he smiled down at her before kissing her forehead.

"Oh, my father was transferred out last night. He's on his way to Spinal Stone as we speak," Elaras said.

Rosella's eyebrows shot up. "Really? That was quick. I thought we were waiting until after the coronation?"

"I thought so too, but I think Joss wanted him out as soon as possible. Tordias escorted him to the copper-lined carriage late last night."

"Were you there?" Rosella asked, grabbing his hand.

"Yeah. He wasn't even remorseful. It's nice to know that the last gift I got from him was his spit on my boots," Elaras said, grasping her hand. She felt his fingers trail to her wrist and push down gently.

"I truly am sorry, Cricket, for everything he has ever put you through," Rosella said.

Elaras simply nodded and gave a weak smile. Instead of speaking, he leaned down and gave her a warm kiss. When they broke apart, a thought came to mind, and it flooded everything in her to the point that she felt her body twitch, craving to move.

"I need to see the throne room," Rosella said abruptly.

Elaras looked down at her with furrowed eyes and a slight tilt of his head. "Are you sure?"

"Yes. I need to see the throne, I think. Something in me is pushing me to go," Rosella said, and she started pulling Elaras toward the far set of stairs that were closest to the throne room and chapel.

They flew down the hall and stairs, running the distance to the throne room. Once she stood in front of the grand and masterful double doors, she froze. The realization that no one had been in this room since the Nightstones—her family—were murdered hit her hard in the chest, and she felt her heart surge violently.

"Rosella, are you going to be okay?" Elaras asked, placing a hand on her hand and wrist.

As she felt him press down on her wrist, she felt her breath tremble slightly, and she struggled for a moment to find words. "What if...we find something from..." Rosella said, feeling the words escape roughly from her throat.

"To my understanding, they cleaned it up thoroughly before shutting the doors. There shouldn't be anything nefarious inside," Elaras reassured.

In a nearby hallway, soft footsteps could be heard before stopping around the corner. Rosella looked toward the noise and saw close to six house servants peering around the corner. When her eyes locked onto them, one of them stepped out and bowed, saluting proudly.

"I'm sorry, My Queen. High Cleric Varran told us to wait until you opened the doors for us but to not ask you so you could be ready on your own to see the room," the female hobdrig named Orra said calmly. "Whenever you're done, we will begin preparing and cleaning, but only when you're ready."

Rosella simply nodded, feeling a rush of gratitude toward Varran once again for his thoughtfulness. She turned back to the door and took a few deep calming breaths. The night stone buzzed as she picked it up and held it up parallel to the floor, copying Temel from weeks before. Before she could step forward to touch the stone to the wood, the locks thudded loudly and clicked open. When the necklace stopped buzzing and the doors quieted, she dropped the necklace and grabbed the handles. Slowly, she opened the doors wide, and stepped inside, Elaras taking them from her and closing them after her.

The walls were the similar dark brick that lined the rest of the Nocturnal Manor, but there were silver and white ornate details everywhere. Unlit chandeliers of silver with white metal stars hung from chains, a crescent moon as the centerpiece of the chandeliers. High arches of the room were painted in various night skies depicting moon phases and constellations. Massive pillars holding the highest ceiling she had ever seen were dull silver, and at the top of these pillars was a glass ceiling. During the day, the sun shone in streams of dust and stale air, but Rosella knew at night that this ceiling would beautifully show the night sky. Rows upon rows of dust-covered blue benches lined the walls for a nonexistent audience, and the long rug with moons and stars that began at the door led to the throne. The moment she set eyes on the massive rock, the name of the throne came to mind as she started walking towards it.

The Astral Throne, which stood shining and proud, looked to be made of the same snowflake obsidian rock as her necklace. The massive yet smooth night stone chair served as the centerpiece of this room, and the chair was double the size of her, tall and wide. Despite its near perfection, the only noticeable blemish she could see was a mysterious slash that was about two feet long and right at neck height. Everything in the room was covered in grime except for this chair, even though the throne itself was embedded to the floor.

As she slowly approached, she felt gravity bear down on her, becoming aware that for over two thousand years, this was the throne every Nightstone ruler sat on. She saw there were worn indents from past rulers, consistent movements and placements of limbs wearing down the stone over time. The arm rest had dents where elbows were placed, bottom and thigh divots after prolonged sitting, even small scuff marks from boots scraping down the front of the chair from standing or bouncing heels.

The necklace buzzed softly as she drew closer, and when she was right in front of the chair, it started to warm up. The feeling of wanting to touch the throne grew desperate, so she raised a single finger and gently touched the armrest. When her finger made contact, a humming could be heard as the chair itself began to vibrate with power. She turned her back to the throne, adjusted her robes, and eased down on the throne.

All at once, flashes of white light flooded her vision, and voices were echoing in her mind and her ears. Nothing said to her was distinguishable, but words were not needed as the emotions she was feeling began to overwhelm her. Sorrow, fury, elation, glee, terror, despair, merriment, and so much more flooded her veins and muscles as she felt each emotion enter then leave. Physical, emotional, and mental pain surged through her body as the voices grew louder and less distinguishable. Flashes of lives that were not her own overtook the white that blinded her vision moments ago, and she saw full lives begin and end, pain and elation, stress and happiness.

Hands reached and grabbed at her, but their touch was light and gentle, calming and reassuring in nature. One set of hands lingered longer than the others, and a feeling of two sets of lips on her forehead made her heart explode with a happy longing. More words were said in a familiar voice, and more from another that was deeper and calming. The throne under her grew warm under her fingers and legs, and the humming rang so loud that she felt like her own brain was vibrating. Everything she was experiencing all at once had an undeniable feeling behind it, and everything began to fall into their final resting place.

After what seemed like days, everything stopped, and Rosella was left gripping the armrests with a vise-like grip, gasping for breath.

"Rosella! Are you alright? What just happened?" Elaras said, rushing to her and crouching in front of her, his hands landing on her knees.

Rosella looked up at him, and after a few gasps of breath, she smiled. "They've accepted me," Rosella said without a second thought, and she felt tears rolling down her cheeks. "They've accepted me, the Nightstones. My father, he... He said he was so proud of me and who I had become."

Elaras clasped his hands on her cheeks, his thumbs wiping away her fresh tears. "That's amazing, Rosella."

She ripped her hands from the throne and placed them on top of his, moving one to kiss his palm. Her lips lingered on his hand and looked down at him, breathing in the scent of his skin and of her salty tears on his fingers. Nerves tingled throughout her body, and her leg began to bounce, her heel gently scraping against the throne.

"Being queen of Arja is my destiny," she said. "I've known that for some time now. Getting to that point was difficult because I felt like I did not belong. However, I'm ready to become queen now. This is my life and who I need to become."

Elaras locked eyes with her. His face broke out in a large smile, and his eyes shone so brightly that they could have been moons themselves.

"Then please, give me the honor of being the first to honor you properly," Elaras said, standing up and taking his hands out of hers. He backed up to about five feet away from her, then he did something that he had never done with her before: kneel. Placing a knee on the ground, he bowed his head and made the moon symbol with his hand and placed it to his chest. "I, Elaras Dekarios Moonshadow, promise to serve my new queen in whatever capacity she deems worthy. I promise to never betray my queen, and I promise to always be loyal to Her Royal Majesty. I, Elaras Dekarios Moonshadow, wish to always remain by my queen's side and to remain loyal to the Nightstone name for the rest of my lifetime."

He looked up, and the smile on his face was genuine and proud. He kept the moon symbol to his chest as he continued, "And I, Elaras Dekarios Moonshadow, wish it to be known that I love my queen with all of my heart, mind, body, and soul."

Rosella wanted to jump up and launch herself at him, hug him and kiss him, wrap him up in her arms and be whisked away to her chamber. However, she resisted as she let one of the biggest smiles spread across her face.

"Rise, my good sir," Rosella said, and he walked up to her and kneeled again, grabbing hold of her hands.

"How was that?" Elaras said in a cheeky tone.

"Perfect. Everyone after you could never compare. Also, thank you, my love," Rosella said, leaning forward so she was only inches from his face.

"What for?" he asked with a suave tone.

"For being my first and most meaningful. I love you so much, Elaras," Rosella said.

Elaras kissed her deeply. They broke apart for a moment, and he stared at her, his eyes full of thoughts.

"You were serious about making me your husband, then?" he asked.

She placed a thumb on the scar upon his lips. "I was. I'd make you my husband no matter the circumstances."

"Hmm. Well, in that case..." Elaras said as he dug into one of his jacket pockets. When his hand reappeared, there was a small dark box propped open in his fingers. "I know this is quick, and I know this may be too soon, but I know for a fact that I cannot live my life without you. My world is cold and empty when you are not next to me, and I feel lost if you are not there to remind me that we are alive and breathing. You are the air I breathe, and you are the blood in my veins. Please, Rosella Elinor Nightstone, marry me and make me all yours for the rest of our living and eternal lives."

Elaras took out a black metal ring. The black band was encrusted with small opal stars and glimmered in a kite-shaped sapphire. The entire ring sparkled brilliantly in the sunlight that poured in from the ceiling.

When she finally found her words, she wrapped her hands around Elaras' hand that held the ring.

"Please marry me and be mine. Please marry me so I can be yours. Please, be my husband, Elaras Dekarios Moonshadow," Rosella said.

They kissed, tears running from both of their faces and joining together on their cheeks. Elaras let go first and held the ring out to her, and she promptly held her hand out like she'd see countless people on Earth do. In his large fingers, the ring seemed dainty, but the ring itself fit her finger perfectly. She stared at it on her hand, and her chest swelled so large with happiness that she felt like she was going to explode.

"It's so perfect and beautiful, Elaras," she whispered before looking up at him.

"I'm glad you think so, though nothing compares to your beauty, my sweet," he murmured at her, and he kissed her once more, this time not letting her go any time soon.

41
Bring the Triumphs, Bring the Torment

Rosella and Elaras stayed out of sight and remained in her room after vacating the throne room the day before. They were brought their lunch and dinner by Rosella's lady's maids, as neither of them were needed by staff and they desired to be alone. In between their moments of heightened and long-awaited intimacy, Elaras taught Rosella the royals of Dorthos, and Rosella taught Elaras the differences between *Star Wars*, *Star Trek*, and *Stargate*.

As morning light poured into the room, Elaras kissed his fiancée and ripped himself away so he could venture to his room next door to get ready for the day. Rosella, ever since he left the room, was surrounded by bustling bodies as Lodmora, Mija, Qax, Nimue, Avy, and Bebbie worked on and around her. They dressed her, accessorized her, fed her, and even helped her to the restroom at one point. Hours later, she was left in a state of pure majesty.

Floor length and long-sleeved, the soft fabric of her coronation dress glided across her skin like velvet. Rainbow-colored galaxies covered every inch of the dark blue material. Cut below her collarbone on the front and back, the dress fit snug against her body, with the skirt flowing like water with every step. The radiant sunlight made the dress sparkle brilliantly with every movement made. The ten-foot-long train swept behind her with ease.

She had to admit that this was one of the most beautiful dresses she had ever seen, and it was *her* coronation dress.

Her engagement ring was still on her ring finger alongside other silver rings with various types of stones and designs. Her night stone necklace was the only one around her neck, and her bracelets were similar to tight bangles with a few chains, all showing moons and stars. Her earrings were the symbol of the Goddess Elyphr, and to her understanding it was requested by Varran for her to wear these. Rosella, having grown extremely fond of Varran, did not argue and even welcomed the choice with glee. Her shoes were small velvet black pumps with embroidered constellations. Her hair was braided into a crown that wrapped around her head, the white streak peeking out in the strands periodically. Two small pieces of hair hung on either side of her face, framing the simple eye and lip makeup that was applied.

As she examined each detail of her outfit in the mirror, a soft knock on the door echoed through the still room, and Mija opened it swiftly. Without looking, Rosella instantly knew who it was by the gasp they gave off upon entering the room.

"My gods, Rosella. Avy and Bebbie have done spectacularly on that dress! And your maids did exceptionally well with the everything else. You look simply magnificent" High Cleric Varran said, with Akuna resting on top of his shoulder.

She turned and smiled wide, feeling her face crack from keeping the stony appearance for so long. "I feel amazing! I've never looked this beautiful before," Rosella said, and she bowed her thanks to Avy, Bebbie and her lady's maids, who were all packing up their supplies.

"Are you ready?" Varran asked, stepping up and taking her hand.

"Yes, more than ever," Rosella said. Akuna flew up and rubbed his face against her cheek. Then he dove out of sight, and she felt movement in a pocket on her side. "Why am I not surprised by the pocket made just for you, Akuna?"

"I asked them to put a pocket in everything you would wear that was big enough for him to sit in," Varran said wisely. "If you don't wear a cloak or have a belt with a pouch, you need somewhere for him to go. You need to be protected now more than ever."

"Yes, because like I said, I'm not leaving your side outside of this castle," Akuna said out loud from inside the pocket.

She stuck a hand in her pocket to find his body, and she stroked a finger along his back once she made contact with his scales. "That's quite alright with me," Rosella said, grinning.

"Remember what we discussed? The order of events to happen?" Varran asked, and Rosella nodded.

Varran and Mellis had gone over the plans for the day during breakfast the day before. She understood that the coronation itself would not take long, as there were no other royals or family members there to bless the newly anointed queen. Due to the quickness of events, no other Dorthos royals could be invited to the coronation. To make up for this, Rosella would travel to every kingdom in Dorthos to introduce herself to the royal families. The only people outside of the Nocturnal Manor that would be in attendance would be Empress Loka and Prince Zaas, as Rosella wanted to keep the promise of inviting her and her son.

"Are they here yet?" Rosella asked.

"Yes, they teleported here this morning. They also brought their royal Scribe Keeper, Takara Sake. I'm not sure how long they plan to stay, but I do believe it was smart to invite them, nonetheless. Also, I would like to discuss hiring a Scribe Keeper of our own soon."

"What happened to the Nightstone Scribe Keeper before? I wasn't aware we even needed one. I guess they record history and events for Dorthos?"

"Yes. The one we had left about a week before the family passed, and the one we had for that week, well, left shortly after," Varran said, and his eyes wandered away from the conversation as he got lost in thought.

"Varran?" Rosella asked, concerned. A soft growl issued from her pocket, and her nerves began to tingle. However, Varran perked up and turned his attention back to Rosella.

"My apologies. Nothing to be concerned of at this moment," he said as he patted her hand. "We will focus on today and discuss other matters tomorrow. Congratulations on your engagement, by the way. Elaras has proved himself to be a worthy man, and he truly is quite fond of you."

"He's something I would have never expected to enter my life, along with everything else that has happened since I came to Dorthos," Rosella said, and Varran gave his sweet smile Rosella had grown immensely fond of.

"We have much to discuss after the coronation. Are you ready?" Varran asked.

"Absolutely," Rosella said, and Varran kissed her hand before leading her to the door. He opened it, and at the door frame stood Elaras in blinding glory.

His entire outfit was pitch black and darker than she'd ever seen. The robes he wore over his shirt and pants were long and had a high collar. Soft silver jewelry accented his fingers, ears, and even a bracelet hung from his wrist that depicted a moon and three stars. The moonstone necklace she had worn ever since meeting him was around his neck, and Rosella made him promise to give it back after the coronation. His hair was neat and slicked back, and the top layer was pulled into a ponytail. The blue in his hair was vibrant against the black of his clothes, and his icy purple skin was flawless. He was more handsome than she had ever seen him, and her heart fluttered at the sight.

"Gods, Rosella," Elaras breathed, breaking her fixation on his attire. He approached her and held her at arm's length, his eyes sweeping all over her in brilliant admiration. This man that Rosella had come to know, someone that killed without a second thought, someone that seemed to flaunt himself whenever he could when they first met, was now speechless. He tried to find words, but he simply opened and closed his mouth like a fish, and Rosella giggled slightly at the sight.

"I didn't know you cleaned up so well, Cricket. You're missing a bit of dirt on your nose," Rosella said smirking, and Elaras' focus shattered as he laughed with her.

Elaras held his right arm out like a gentleman, and Rosella promptly grabbed the crook of his elbow. Together with Varran ahead of them and Akuna in her pocket, they walked down the three flights of stairs. At one point, Rosella's lady's maids appeared and held up the train of the dress for her, checking her jewelry and makeup. In what seemed like a flash, they all stood in front of the double doors of the throne room.

"Stay here and walk in when the doors open. We'll head inside now. It shouldn't be long," Varran said before he slipped off to the side and went into the chapel, presumably to go through the door that led into the throne room.

Elaras bent down and kissed Rosella deeply, a hand squeezing hers and the other holding her face. Footsteps from her lady's maids issued from behind her, and she knew they were scurrying off to get into the throne room from the chapel as well. Rosella dipped her hands under the robes he was wearing so she could pull him close, wanting to be enveloped by him. Before long, Elaras broke them apart and kissed her forehead, grabbing her left hand and fiddling with her engagement ring.

"I'll see you inside, my sweet," Elaras whispered in her ear before releasing her from his grasp, and in turn making the air around Rosella cold and lonely. When he walked through the chapel door, she felt truly solitary in this section of the hall. Thoughts and memories began to swirl in her mind, and she felt like the hall was spinning around her.

"*Are you alright, Rosella?*" came Akuna's voice internally, and the spinning stopped.

"*I'm nervous, I think,*" Rosella replied. She felt Akuna move in her pocket and fly out to hover in front of her.

"*It's a normal speaking kind emotion, nervousness. I'd say get over it before the emotion eats you alive, but I know that isn't helpful in this situation.*"

"*Very insightful of you, Great Wrath of Dorthos.*"

"*I take it back. I hope you urinate yourself up there.*"

"*AKUNA!*"

"*Joking!*" Akuna said, laughing and bobbing in the air from his laughing fit.

Nonetheless, Rosella smiled at him and laughed along, appreciating the break. That tension returned to her veins when faint musical horns could be heard from inside. Akuna dove into her pocket as the double doors slowly opened in front of Rosella.

The throne room, which had been empty and dreary the day before, was now filled with blue and white flowers and decorations that dazzled, making the room look completely alive. Gold and silver streamers ornamented the ceilings, sparkling in the reflected sunlight from the glass ceiling above. The moon and stars chandeliers were lit and despite the time of day, their lights reflecting brilliantly onto the walls. The bleachers were occupied by staff of the Nocturnal Manor, and at the very front the interim leader of Arja, Ruler Beldris, sat next to the suave and elegant Empress Loka with her son Zaas next to her looking extremely regal. Without the emperor beside them, they seemed at peace. Elaras sat off to the left side of the throne against the wall with the remaining staff, and Joss stood sentry next to him. Varran, Rosella's beloved confidant, looked stunning in his religious garb that she seemed to finally notice. The bright blue and sparkling white of his robes and hat stood out against the Astral Throne.

She locked eyes with him, knowing that if her eyes left him that she would stumble from nerves. As she walked, soft gasps and whimpers filled her ears from the staff around her. This seemed to take hours, but within minutes she was in front of Varran and curtsied to him as he bowed to her. She then moved to stand before the throne and placed her clasped hands in front of her.

Various songs and hymns were sung as she stood, words Rosella did not know. By the looks of it, when Rosella took a glance at Elaras, he also did not know the words, and this made her feel better. After the singing was completed, the Nightstone Clerics walked up one by one and sprinkled a dust-like substance onto her now open hands. When these Clerics were done, Varran poured holy water that was blessed by the Goddess Elyphr on top of the dust.

At once, Rosella felt a pleasant warmth in her hands, and soft glittering stars soared up and through the ceiling above. When Rosella looked down, the dust and the liquid were gone. Nothing was left behind. The crowd let out noises of awe at the sight, but

Rosella remained silent and observant. Before she could put her hands down, the Clerics approached on both sides, and all began to kneel in unison.

Two Clerics on each side of her held items that Rosella had only seen in coronation ceremonies in television shows and movies: a scepter and an orb. The modest silver scepter was three feet long, the top ornamented with a sapphire-encrusted crescent moon. Three diamond stars lined the staff itself. The orb was a hollowed-out sapphire a foot tall and wide. An ornament of five diamond stars rested on top of the orb, opposite the scepter.

"This scepter is to show the power of the queen in her rule. Only those of royal blood shall wield the power of authority and nobility in Arja. Rosella Nightstone, do you promise to rule over Arja with a gentle hand and an authoritative mind? Protecting those of this land from those that wish to do them harm? To never betray the name of Nightstone and break the loyalty of those that have pledged allegiance to you?" High Cleric Varran asked as he reached for the scepter and turned to Rosella, extending it toward her.

"I promise to rule with a gentle hand, to rule with an authoritative mind, to protect the citizens of Arja, to never betray the name of Nightstone, and to remain loyal to those who have pledged allegiance to me," Rosella said in a few long breaths.

Varran gently placed the scepter in her outstretched right hand and took a step back. "This orb is to show that the power given to the queen is granted full heartedly by the Goddess Elyphr, the goddess of night, the moon, and the stars. Do you, Rosella Nightstone, promise to obey the gentle and well-mannered commands of the Goddess Elyphr? To respect the power given to you by the goddess and to never abuse said power? To wield authority in the name of the Goddess Elyphr if she wishes for you to intervene?" Varran asked, making the same movements as he did with the scepter. but moving slower and more carefully.

The promises she was supposed to make at this moment were odd to her, as she herself had never been religious. Possibly this was *another* thing she would have to get used to, having a goddess in her back pocket.

"I promise to obey the gentle and well-mannered commands of the Goddess Elyphr, to respect the power given to me and to never abuse said power, and to wield authority in the name of Goddess Elyphr if she wishes for me to do so," Rosella said boldly, trying her best to not sound speculative.

Varran reached up and gently placed the large sapphire orb into her left hand, and she was thankful she had strength to hold it upright. The scepter weighed nothing compared to the orb, which was easily about thirty pounds with the gemstone itself.

"May the Goddess Elyphr pass judgment onto Rosella Nightstone! Please, Your Majesty, if you may take a seat upon the throne," Varran said, and she did as he requested.

The moment she sat on the throne with the scepter and orb in hand, her vision turned black, and everything in front of her disappeared in a shadowy mist. Her thudding heartbeat filled her ears. The scepter and orb shook in her hands as she gazed around her, looking for anything or anyone. A soft white light shone and began to fill the room like smoky water. The black mist that enveloped the throne room was washed out by the white light, and after a few moments, Rosella heard a chorus fill her ears.

"Rosella Nightstone," an angelic voice said.

Rosella felt the courage to open her eyes despite the blinding light. A beautiful woman with flawless features and flowing white and blue hair stood before her in a long midnight-blue gown. Her arms were slightly aloft, and she was standing over Rosella's sitting body. The chorus behind her was singing something in another language, but the song reminded her of gospel groups back on Earth. Trying her best to take everything in and not drop the scepter or orb, Rosella risked a look up into the goddess' face.

Elyphr was smiling down at her like a proud mother would, just like how Rosella's mother would. A hand made of smoke and dust gently brushed against Rosella's cheek, and she felt a few tears drop onto her skin. She was unsure if they were her own or Elyphr's.

"Goddess Elyphr..." Rosella managed to choke out before being rendered completely speechless, and she heard her voice echo repeatedly as if she was in a valley. She pushed her feet into the ground but felt nothing under her toes, so she placed all her weight onto the throne to keep her body stable.

"You are Dorthos' savior, Rosella. You may not be of this world, but your blood is of Dorthos, of true Nightstone lineage. Now, go bring peace and happiness to all of Arja. They are waiting for you," Elyphr said in her angelic tone. She moved her hand from Rosella's cheek and placed it flat to Rosella's chest.

As soon as her hand made full contact, Rosella felt the skin where the goddess touched burn immensely, and she along with the throne plummeted through the air. Rosella shut her eyes tightly, clutching the scepter and orb to her chest to prevent them from flying out of her hands. Moments later, gasps rang out around her, and she felt the now familiar air of the throne room fill her lungs.

"Rosella Nightstone has been blessed by our goddess!" a Cleric said on her right.

Rosella took the opportunity to open her eyes. Brilliant light filled her vision and the room around her, and her eyes moved to the sapphire orb which was now emitting a blue glow. The place where Elyphr touched her chest still burned slightly, but when she looked down, her dress was unscathed. She straightened up and puffed her chest, ignoring the stinging in her heart and lungs. A Cleric appeared with a luxurious purple pillow, a black ring of sparkling metal and cloth resting on top.

The Crown of Night was made of iron, black diamonds rimming the band. Gothic-style spikes poked up from the band, and each spike was embedded with sapphires and diamonds in the shape of stars. There were thick flat metal bands that arched up from the front, sides, and back of the headband and met at the top. The ornament on top of the crown was in the shape of a crescent moon but was noticeably hollow. Royal blue velvet lined the inside of the bands that met at the top of the crown.

A second Cleric walked up with black silk gloves and placed them onto Varran's hands. Varran gently took the Crown of Night, hovering the crown just above her head. Sudden buzzing from the throne and her necklace issued, and Varran's arms closed together slightly. The cold of the metal and softness of the velvet hugged her head. The crown felt like it was giving her head a loving embrace and did not move, though she herself could easily remove it if she so wished.

Soft light emitted from the crown's ornament, and Rosella saw Varran's eyes shoot up. A wide smile spread across his face as the light dissipated from his face. Goddess Elyphr had given her another night stone, placed in the hollow crescent moon in the crown's ornament, just as Varran said the day before.

"May I present for the first time, Queen Rosella Nightstone of Arja, first of her name, Protector of Arja, Queen of Night, and Queen of the Seed! All hail Queen Rosella Nightstone!" High Cleric Varran announced.

Everyone in the room, including the Empress Loka, repeated after him. They repeated the phrase three times, and cheers rang throughout the room. The sounds echoed as her hearing became muffled. Her lungs ached as she released a deep exhale, and she began to cry, smiling as every single person in the room grinned back at her.

At this moment, everything clicked into place for her. She was queen, and she finally felt complete.

42
My World, My Life, My Destiny

As the coronation concluded and the scepter and orb were locked away in glass display cases, High Cleric Varran addressed the audience.

"Please convene to the ground level garden for the initiation ceremony," Varran said boisterously. "Empress Loka, Prince Zaas, and Royal Scribe Keeper Takara Sake, you may join us as we make our way to the fifth level. Queen Rosella, would you like a moment alone to gather your thoughts?" Varran said quietly, and she nodded in response.

At once, everyone in the audience stood up and started making their way through the doors. Empress Loka, Prince Zaas, their Scribe Keeper, and Mellis joined Varran, who ushered them to the side of the room. Elaras and Joss joined the small group shortly after. As feet shuffled and voices chatted, Rosella sat back in the throne and rested her head on the warm stone, causing the crown to clink against it. The cut that was in the back of the Astral Throne rested right where her crown sat, the curve of the crown's band settling nicely in the crevice.

"I'm a queen now," Rosella said telepathically to Akuna.

"Did you not believe this day would come?" he replied, snarkiness coming through like slick oil.

"It took a while for me, but now that we're here, it's overwhelming in the best way," Rosella replied. Her fingers glided along the armrests, and she felt grooves left by countless past Nightstones. The Astral Throne was smooth to the touch, small grooves left behind from clenched hands. She glided her fingers along the handmade concaves in the armrest, feeling her chest cease burning. As her fingers slid along a particularly deep groove on the right armrest mindlessly, she felt the throne vibrate softly.

"My darling Rose, you make the most beautiful queen," came a mysterious yet familiar feminine voice from inside her mind.

Rosella perked up but did not look around. She did not need to find the source of the voice. She had heard this voice her entire life up until three years ago, and her eyes welled up with tears.

"Mama?" Rosella called out in her mind.

She felt two invisible gentle hands place themselves on her cheeks. *"Yes, my sweet girl. I'm so sorry I did not prepare you for my world, and I am sorry I was not here in person to see you be crowned. Your father and I knew from the day we found out I was pregnant with you that you would be queen, and despite the circumstances, we are so proud to see you on the throne. After everything you have been through to get here, it is my only wish to see you succeed and to thrive."*

Rosella dared not move in case this somehow broke the connection. *"I love you, Mama, and I miss you,"* Rosella said, at a loss for words at hearing her mother's voice again.

A sensation of warmth brushed against her cheek, and the throne ceased vibrating. She took a deep breath as she felt her own soul heal itself. Her muscles relaxed, and her heartbeat finally eased to a normal pace. She did not realize how quickly it had been beating until she rested her head against the stone once more. Her eyes drifted to Joss, who was staring at her with something of despair and a bit of sadness.

"Are you ready, My Queen?" Varran's soft voice said, cutting across her thoughts, and she looked up at him. Varran had walked back over to Rosella, leaving the small group behind.

"Yes, but I have a question," Rosella said, and Varran nodded expectantly. "May I ask why Joss is looking at me like that?"

Varran put on a face that was strikingly similar. "Perhaps now is not the time. Just know that his sadness is not a reflection of you or your position. He is sad because of events that took place in the past."

"The...passings, I'm assuming?" Rosella said, trying her best to sound kind.

"Yes. We shall tell you later, unless the throne tells you itself," Varran said.

"The throne can tell me past events?"

"In great detail."

"I just thought it was a one or two-time thing."

"Oh, no, my dear Rosella. The throne is older than the Nightstone family itself, and upon request you can have it draw up anything from the past as long as it took place where it resided at the time. Along with those that ever sat on the throne, that being the entirety of the Nightstone family lineage at one time or another, they can also commune with you. As well, anywhere you go, you can commune with them using your pendant," Varran said, and he smiled at the shock upon Rosella's face. He chuckled and placed a calming hand onto her knee before saying, "You still have much to learn, and now that you are queen, you can do so much more than you ever expected."

"Consider me impressed, Varran," Rosella said.

Curiosity overtook her as she thought of Joss' sad face, and she rubbed the grooves in the right armrest. At once, her vision turned black, and sounds washed out of her ears and mind.

Gray smoke issued from all sides of her and formed three-dimensional figures, people made of ash standing before her. The smoke turned into the same throne she sat upon but was now facing her, and multiple smoky figures ran around her. Distant shouting and noises of fright filled her ears, scuffling feet and trembling heartbeats echoing in this new place.

One tall, strongly built figure walked calmly to the throne and sat upon it, their weight landing roughly, and heaved a sigh so large that the smoke swirled violently from his breath. The figure seemed to be saying something to the group before him, though she could not make out words.

From behind the throne came a parade of horned people, all wielding swords, mauls, and daggers, and they rushed and scattered across the room that laid behind her. Screams of terror resonated, and she felt herself grip the chair, afraid of turning around to see who or what was causing such noises. The figure on the throne remained frozen where he sat as slashes on skin and unnatural gargling came from behind Rosella. The figure simply placed his head in his hands, as if what he was seeing in front of him was too much for him to bear, and he knew he could do nothing.

Minutes passed, and the fear around her filled the air with such a palpable energy that Rosella felt her fingers dig into the stone under her hands. The figure Rosella was focused on did not move once from the throne. Overwhelming defeat filled her veins and chest as the sounds continued for so long—too long.

Soon enough, a large smoky horned figure wielding an ax

sauntered over the throne, and the figure in the throne merely looked up at the ax-wielder before them.

"Why?" said the male figure upon the throne, and the ax-wielder laughed.

"Because we simply don't like you or your family, King Raynne," the person said, twirling the staff of the ax in his hands.

"You're willing to end a dynasty because of your disdain for us? Do you know the implications of destroying us?" the figure she now knew as the king and grandfather before her said.

The person holding the ax began to rear back, holding the ax at the top of a massive swing. "We don't care. We just want *your* throne. It's on you for not stopping us," the person said, and they swung the ax.

A thundering *crack* echoed throughout the room as the ax met the stone and wedged itself into it, clean through King Raynne's neck. The person, a Rockshire, dislodged the ax as the king's head flew past Rosella's vision, her eyes remaining on the throne and the remainder of King Raynne's body. Laughs issued around her, and multiple figures strolled past her to the tunnel that was behind the throne.

"That was easier than I thought!" came a high-pitched voice, ringing with ecstasy and glee.

"Fuck the Nightstones!" one person called out, and they all joined in the chant.

As they were doing this, the throne itself burst into a bright light and issued white smoke that covered the entire room.

"What the Hells?" came one voice, panicked.

"Let's get out of here!" the ax wielder said, and they all clambered into the tunnel.

When the tunnel door slammed shut, the light dissipated, and the throne was no longer in front of her. All that remained was an outline of where it once stood and King Raynne's lifeless body slumped on the ground.

In a rush of air, she was pulled back to the throne room of the present, and she had to gasp for breath once she felt her body stabilize. Once she gained her bearings, her eyes scanned the room, and she found Joss and Varran standing close by, watching her.

"Rosella?" Elaras' voice rang in her ears, and she felt his presence next to her, but she rushed off the throne and headed straight to Joss and Varran.

Stopping short of the two of them, she reached her arms out and hugged Varran tightly in one arm and held out the other to Joss. Joss picked up Varran and Rosella in his massive arms and held them both to his chest, her head bumping into his chest plate. After a few long moments of hugging each other, Joss lowered Varran and Rosella to the ground gently and wiped a tear from his eyes.

"You saw, then," Varran said quietly, and she simply nodded.

She felt the air around them turn dreary as they gazed at each other, the weight of the past coming full force at them. Words could not express her emotions in this moment between them, and they seemed to not feel the need to say anything else. The only thing that could be expressed was unspoken understanding and mutual pain. Rosella grabbed both of their hands and gripped them tightly.

A knock came from the double doors, and a Queens Guard poked their head in, scanning the room.

"It's time, Your Majesty," the guard said, and they bowed and saluted before standing to one side of the door.

Rosella looked to the throne once more and heaved a sigh, trying her best to rid herself of the heavy emotions. Thumps came from her pocket, and she knew that was Akuna checking on her.

"You're okay, despite what you just witnessed," Akuna said wisely, and Rosella nodded, afraid to speak in case her voice cracked.

She turned back to Varran and leaned down to kiss him on the cheek, and when she turned to Joss to do the same, she saw that he had bent to one knee. A grin spread on her face as she kissed his large cheek, feeling immensely grateful for the both of them.

Elaras walked up and gently wrapped his arm around her waist, and while she knew he did not understand what she had seen, he must have been able to tell that it was something intense. Everyone except Rosella and Elaras left the room in sets of two, and Rosella, with her arm wrapped around Elaras', followed them closely after.

Everyone climbed the five flights of stairs to the grand balcony at the top of Nocturnal Manor. Once in front of the solid wooden and metal doors, Elaras gave Rosella a gentle kiss and strode through, leaving Rosella alone once again. She waited in silence, not speaking to herself or to Akuna, and she made sure the crown was straight on her head. Soon enough, Rosella heard Varran's magically amplified voice ring out from behind the balcony doors.

"Citizens and visitors of Arja, may I present for the first time, your new ruler, Queen Rosella Nightstone of Arja, first of her name, Protector of Arja, Queen of Night and Queen of the Seed! All hail Queen Rosella Nightstone!"

Both doors in front of her opened, and the highly charged air made her skin prickle as she walked onto the balcony. Below, people as far back as she could see gathered and cheered, chanting, "All hail Queen Rosella Nightstone!"

She smiled and waved, and the crowd grew louder and more amplified. Horns and drums were ringing in the air along with the crowd below as people moved around her on the balcony. Rosella finished greeting the crowd and took a few steps away from the railing.

Two Clerics now stood between her and a metal box that was hoisted onto an extravagant stand, now spiked into the stone of the balcony floor. Quickly, they unlatched hinges and panels to reveal a glowing orb that had white and blue smoke swirling around inside. Remembering Varran's instructions, Rosella stood before it, still facing the crowd while the sphere now sat between her and the people below. Her necklace began to buzz and heat on her chest as she hovered her hands over the sphere. There were several rings below the sphere that hummed.

"*Those rings, are they the conduits you made with King Purtdrell?*" Rosella asked Akuna.

"*Yes. Now, we only need your necklace and blood to restore the land. You've got this, human.*"

"*Thank you, Cheese Ears.*"

Closing her eyes as a soft rumble from Akuna filled her chest, she felt static energy pass between her and the sphere, the necklace vibrating more violently than ever.

"By the name of Nightstone, heal this land and its citizens. Make crops flourish, make animals thrive, mend and destroy the impurities of the earth upon which Arja stands. Clean the air and purify the water. Bring life back to Arja, by the name of Nightstone," she said to the sphere, and she felt her hands grow hot in tandem with the night stone necklace. The air around her grew quiet, and the silence rang louder than her own racing heart.

A gust of wind cut across her as the energy from the sphere burst through the air like a shockwave. She opened her eyes just in time to see a gigantic wave of blue and white smoke ripple through the crowd and into the distance. The crowd below grew louder than ever before as they cheered, calling her name and praising her.

As the wave of magic covered the land, the trees grew lively, and the grass turned purple. Frail flora that had been hanging on by a thread grew strong and fluttered in the wave as it blew by. Birdsong erupted from the surrounding trees, and bugs came to life to join in. The pink clouds Rosella loved appeared and pushed out the dark blue clouds, conquering the skies once again. The sun shone brightly on everything the rays touched, and Rosella had not noticed how dim the sun was before. A cascade of happiness flooded her body, a weight lifted at last. Applause erupted around her, and she turned to see everyone, including the empress and the prince, smiling and clapping.

Two months ago, she had been living a simple life during a time of war. If Akuna had not pulled her out, she would have met the same fate as many others on Earth. Now, not only was she the queen of a land in a world she never knew of, but she had also just become the savior of that land.

She turned back to the crowd, and for a moment, she expected to see a red sky filled with bombs, people running for safety within her walls. With a sigh of relief, the only thing she saw was the colorful world of Dorthos, surrounded by her new family.

That night, for the first time in thirty years, the night queen flowers around the manor and all of Arja bloomed, greeting the moon and welcoming Rosella home.

Epilogue

Rosella stood on the second-story landing and watched as servants scrambled around the halls of the Nocturnal Manor, gathering supplies and checking off lists of things needed for the several-month-long trip that awaited Rosella and Elaras. Guards did their best to avoid the running servants as Mellis called out orders, and Joss checked with each Queens Guard in turn for their status. Varran ambled through the halls with a Scribe Keeper, avoiding the hurried bodies as they rushed past. The Scribe Keeper, a young male berhog named Zevlor Nov with black and white fur and white robes, listened to every word Varran spoke, frantically scribbling notes in their notebook.

Five months had passed since Rosella was crowned queen, and the majority of those five months had been spent organizing the Nightstones estate and Arja itself. Now that hurried responsibilities and forgotten or unattended tasks had slowed tremendously or were completed, Rosella had to travel to every region of Dorthos to present herself to the royals and their citizens. Organizing such a trip was left to Mellis' most trusted assistants, and the trip itself would last close to three months if everything went according to plan. Rosella and Elaras agreed to wait to wed when they got back, so the staff could plan the wedding while they were away.

Joining them on this trip would be two of Varran's Clerics, as he himself needed to stay at the manor. Scribe Keeper Zevlor would also be joining the trip, sticking close to the Clerics. Joss ordered twenty trusted Queens Guards to escort Rosella for her trip, as he also needed to stay to protect the manor. Joss also ordered Tordias to join Rosella and Elaras on their trip, and Gerrart managed to persuade Joss to let him accompany the escort as part of his training for High Paladin status. Rosella convinced Mellis to let her lady's maids come along, and while Mellis gave a weak argument as to why they should stay, they easily folded and allowed the maids to go. Flitch, Paton, and Temel were planning to come as part of Temel's training regime, but they would stay at a distance as good spies did.

Lycilla, as part of her redemption, agreed to serve on Mellis' staff and willingly agreed to be closely watched at all times. Despite some tasks being difficult for her to do because of her hands, she quickly proved to Mellis that she had no ill intentions and simply wished for what she could do to be forgiven. While everyone around her still could not trust her, Rosella full heartedly believed that Lycilla did not want to cause any more harm to anyone. Whenever Rosella passed Lycilla in the halls, Lycilla always smiled with kindness, bowing and doing her best to salute with her mangled hands. One day, Rosella would like to think that they could even be friends. Today was not that day, though.

"It's almost time, sweet love. Have everything packed?" Elaras called out from above her on the third-story landing.

She gazed up and saw he was wearing the black leathers she

had met him in along with his black cloak. Feeling something stir in her body at the sight of him, she smiled and nodded.

"Yes, I'm just waiting on your slow ass!" she called out, and his hand flew to his chest in shock.

"From what I recall, it was me who had to wake you up this morning!" he called out hysterically, his hand landing on his hip and leaning forward.

"I still get ready faster than you!"

"You're a cheater. You have maids to help you!"

"When you're king consort, you'll get your own maids!"

"True! Which means we need to hurry and get this trip started so we can get married!" Elaras said in a goofy tone before walking toward their room.

She smiled and looked back down at the floor below, propping her arms against the railing.

An hour later, she was at the front entry and was bidding farewell to every member of staff, hugging each one and bidding them blessings, promising to be back soon. She had given heartfelt goodbyes to Varran, Joss, and Mellis earlier in the day, so they watched on as the staff received their own farewells. Rosella promised to have a sparrow sent every day to assure them they were alright, and she planned to keep that promise to them.

When she approached Lycilla, the devlair immediately bowed and gave her best salute. Rosella smiled and tilted her head, feeling the Tiara of Twilight—an all-black tiara with spikes topped by diamond stars and a hanging sapphire crescent moon that fell onto the center of her forehead—shift slightly. They stared at each other for a moment before Lycilla looked away, panic filling her eyes and taking a small step back.

"Take care of yourself, Lycilla," Rosella said, and when Lycilla did not respond, she moved onto the next servant.

After she said goodbye to everyone, she waved once more and walked out of the manor and onto the front steps. Tordias was waiting next to Elaras by the center carriage with four horses attached, and the other two larger carriages that were in front and in back had the maids, Queens Guards, the Scribe Keeper, and the Clerics waiting beside each of them. Gerrart, who was in the driver's seat of Rosella's carriage, waved excitedly as she approached, and she waved back with vigor. Rosella smiled at Elaras, and he returned the smile, but before she could approach him and Tordias, she felt the air around her shift.

She turned around and saw glowing gold smoke swirling in a cylinder. Two sets of hands grasped her arms and pulled her back. Tordias and four Queens Guards stood at the ready in front of her as Elaras had her hand in his, all waiting for the smoke to dissipate.

Within a few moments, a woman appeared where the smoke once was, and both Tordias and Elaras froze like statues after lowering their weapons. She had lavender skin and pinned-up deep blue hair, and her eyes were remarkably like Elaras'. The look on the strange woman's face was of relief and astonishment, somehow portraying both effortlessly.

She dusted off her robes and stepped forward, revealing a second woman, a female elf with light blue skin and white braided hair. This second woman had gray smoke and gold glitter wrapped around her body like the person in the Nocturnal Stalkers Guild. Before Rosella could ask who the strange women were, Elaras spoke up.

"Mother?" he gasped out. He let go of Rosella's hand and approached her.

"Evanora, my lady, we thought you were dead," Tordias said, and Rosella saw him halfheartedly bow to her. Possibly out of respect or of fear, Rosella could not be sure.

Evanora Moonshadow smiled at Elaras as he approached, cupping his cheeks, and shedding a tear. She glanced over at Tordias for a moment, still smiling, before turning back to Elaras and planting a motherly kiss on his cheek.

"I'm so sorry I made you think I was gone, my precious boy," Evanora said, pity filling her tone as she spoke.

Varran and Joss came out of the front doors and watched on as Evanora gave Elaras a tight hug.

"What are you doing here, and how did you know I was here, Mother?" Elaras said as he hugged his mother back.

"Well, I had sensed you were with Rosella, and I waited until you both left the manor. I did not realize that it would be some time before you *both* came out, rather than just you, Elaras. I apologize for my timing. I understand you have places to be," Evanora said, releasing the tight hug but still holding Elaras at arm's length.

While Elaras had made trips into Rion for supplies, Rosella had been unable to leave due to duties thirty years overdue. She had many citizens come and give grievances, and she helped where she could.

"I apologize as well, but may I ask how you're alive?" Rosella said unabashedly, but Elaras and Tordias faced Evanora, expecting an answer.

Evanora gave a deep sigh and looked between the three of them. "Simple: I can self-resurrect. Kaine did in fact kill me, but my maid and I knew what he was planning and used it as an opportunity to escape," Evanora said with a heavy tone, then gestured to the woman wrapped in smoke and glitter that was standing behind her silently.

The woman regarded Rosella with surprise, her eyes scanning Rosella's just as Rosella did to her moments before.

"I thought you couldn't use magic?" Elaras asked, and Evanora beheld him square in the eyes.

"Oh, you just never saw me use my magic. Your father was very restraining, so I pretended to be weak, so I would be unthreatening. That's why I eventually killed him myself, to show how strong I truly was," Evanora said, and the world grew silent as the weight of her words hit everyone present.

"You killed Kaine?" Tordias said, the first to break the shocked silence.

Evanora looked at him and gave an innocent smile. "Oh, yes, months ago. He was on his way to Spinal Stone, I believe, and I paid off the transport crew to keep silent. They were thankful, really. He was being unruly, and they feared what he might do if he somehow got that necklace off of him. Oh!" Evanora said before pulling something from a pouch on her waist. A chain of copper glinted in the sun as she pulled out the necklace that Kaine had worn months before. She turned to Varran and held out the necklace to him before saying, "I believe this is yours, High Cleric."

Varran took the necklace without looking at it, keeping his eyes on her.

Unfazed, Evanora stared back at Elaras, Rosella, and Tordias and took a step forward.

"Mother..." Elaras choked out, but Evanora moved her gaze to Rosella.

Rosella and Evanora locked eyes, and before Rosella could say anything, Evanora asked, "So, where are we going first? We have much to discuss."

END OF BOOK 1

Acknowledgments

Hello fellow reader or listener! My first acknowledgement goes to you, as you chose to pick up this book. Whether you liked it or not, I'm still appreciative of you taking the time to read Rosella's story! This is my first published novel, so any attention is good for me! Thank you so much for reading this and giving this self-publisher a chance, and I do hope you liked my book! (Though, it's okay if you didn't, thank you nonetheless <3)

I want to thank a few specific people that helped get this book become a reality, and without them my book would not be how it is today!

i. Cassandra my cartographer (@oakleaf.arrow.studios)! She was the first collaborator I reached out to for my book! Cassandra is a gem of a human being, and seeing her create an amazing piece of art from my scribbles of a "map" was literally breathtaking. She helped make my world into something real, skyrocketing my creative drive every time I looked at the map. Thank you, Cassandra!

ii. Kai my character artist! (@kaijuskies)! He created artwork of Rosella and Elaras (seen on my website) and brought them to life, making them real and not just imaginary people in my head! Thank you, Kai, for your beautiful art and for being a great long-time friend!

iii. Clara my editor! Every author needs their book edited, and I was NOT going to do that myself. Clara was the first editor I reached out to and when she took my book on, I knew my story was in good hands. She took my rambling words with the lack of commas, and the overuse of the word "and" manuscript, and helped me turn it into the book it is today. I have learned so much from her, and I cannot wait to learn more! Thank you, Sister Queen Clara!

iv. Joe Tricomi my cover designer (@jtricomi)! As Joe always does with any of his art, he put in so much work for this cover and it turned out beautiful! He is also a tattoo artist who has worked on both of my arm sleeves, so I knew I was in good hands when it came time to work on this cover! Thank you Joe (and Sara!) for your support and for this great cover!

v. Cody, my audiobook narrator! Cody is one of my best friends, and he so happens to be great at voices. Part of his personality influences Akuna's character, so having him narrate this book for me was fitting. Thank you for accepting the challenge of making the audiobook for this, so that those listening can enjoy this book!

Now, a grand thank you to my friends, family, and coworkers. From the moment I said, "I want to write a book," many of y'all flooded me with support and took a chance in me. That alone is wonderful and fueled my drive to finish my work. Everything from showing interest and having faith, to helping me with plot lines and encouraging me to never stop.

My husband has been one of the biggest supporters. You built my website and reminded me that my creative side is something to strive for. One of my best friends, Cody, has also been one of my biggest supporters. I was able to bounce ideas off you and get validation when I needed it most. My parents and siblings (birth and in-laws) have been wonderful in encouragement and showing faith in me in ways I never knew I needed.

Lastly, to my therapist, who helped me through so much in my life. Without your help, I'm not sure who I would be as a person. I do know one thing: this book would not be at all possible without you. So thank you for helping me find my lost self.

About the Author

Allie Dars is a Texas-based author with a passion for crafting intricate worlds and vivid narratives. With a background in journalism and history, she honed her writing skills through years of research and storytelling, developing a love for exploring both facts and fiction. As a child, Allie wrote short stories, but it wasn't until she dove into the dystopian genre that she truly embraced the creative freedom and in-depth research that comes with writing fiction. When she's not busy writing or world-building, Allie can be found enjoying life with her husband and their children— two beloved cats named Mango and Kiwi. A fan of Dungeons & Dragons and fantasy video games, Allie's love for adventure and complex characters seeps into her work (which might explain how she managed to write a fantasy novel in just two months).

instagram.com/allie_dars_author

tiktok.com/@alliedars

goodreads.com/alliedars

www.ingramcontent.com/pod-product-compliance
Lightning Source LLC
Chambersburg PA
CBHW020631020726
47494CB00001B/148